A Dark Devotion

CLARE FRANCIS

A Dark Devotion

First published in England by Macmillan in 1997

Copyright © by Clare Francis, 1997

First published in the United States in 2003 by
Soho Press, Inc.
853 Broadway
New York, NY 10003

Library of Congress Cataloging-in-Publication Data

Francis, Clare.
A dark devotion : [a novel] / Claire Francis.
p. cm.
ISBN 1-56947-325-0 (alk. paper)
1. Attorney and client—Fiction. 2. Norfolk (England)—Fiction.
3. London (England)—Fiction. 4. Missing persons—Fiction.
5. Women lawyers—Fiction. I. Title.

PR6056.R268D3 2003
823'.914—dc21

2002044651

10 9 8 7 6 5 4 3 2 1

For Tom

Chapter One

A FAMILIAR three-rap knock and the smooth untroubled face of Sturgess appeared around the door, bringing the drift of raucous voices in his wake. 'Champagne's flowing, Alex.'

I looked at my watch, though I knew what time it was. 'I'll be along in a moment, Gary.'

'Fantastic result, eh!'

I said, 'Fantastic is one word.'

Sturgess hovered in the doorway, unable to contain his jubilation. 'You should have seen the faces of the other side.' Sturgess was newly qualified and still young enough to be elated by the drama and ruthlessness of a court victory.

Giving up thoughts of more work, I capped my pen and sat back in my chair. 'Very lucky with the jury, from what I hear.'

'Lucky? Ah, but doesn't a good defence create its own luck?' he beamed, quoting one of my own maxims back at me.

'That's one view.'

'In the sense of forcing the best result.'

'Absolutely.'

'The hacks had us at two to one against.'

This was probably what I would have offered too, from what I had heard of the case. 'Yes, they usually get it wrong.'

'*Two to one*,' Sturgess laughed jauntily. 'Just goes to show how out of touch they are, the press. No allowances for the jury's sense of fair play.'

'No allowances, perhaps, for how little the jury knew of our client or his history.'

Sturgess hesitated, uncertain of the spirit in which I had

offered this remark. 'Well, that's only right and proper, isn't it?'

'It's the only system that protects the maximum number of people on the greatest number of occasions. There's a difference somewhere.' I gave a sudden grin. 'One day you must remind me what it is.'

Taking this as a joke, Sturgess laughed again before heading back towards the party. We had hired Sturgess not so much for his qualifications, which were distinctly average, but for his keen ambition and South London background, which had taught him lessons impossible to glean from any textbook. He understood instinctively that in criminal practice victory counts for everything and justice for little. Whatever reservations I might try to plant in his mind, he would never lose sight of his main function as a solicitor, which was to promote and defend his client's interests with single-minded determination.

I reviewed my notes for Monday and, gathering the files I would need for the weekend, squeezed them into my briefcase. Rising stiffly, I went to the mirror that hung inside the tall document-cabinet by the door. On the shelf below the mirror were laid out, in precise arrangement, my comb, clothes brush, powder and lipstick. I couldn't remember when the order of these objects had taken on such permanence, it must have been a year or two ago, but the sight dismayed me suddenly and, finishing my hair, I jumbled everything up.

The lipstick seemed garish on my lips, or maybe my skin was particularly pale. The result appeared too harsh, at any rate. I looked tired, and the lines at the corners of my eyes seemed more conspicuous. For no apparent reason I thought: In just over five years I'll be forty. Following fast on this came other more unwelcome thoughts to do with biological clocks and babies and the family it seemed Paul and I would never have.

At that moment I would have given a great deal to go home to a hot bath and some reading unconnected with the law. It had been a very long week, full of small frustrations and nagging anxieties. But my absence would be noticed, not least by Paul, who would want to know if I were ill, or what else was troubling me, and who would find tiredness an odd excuse.

Our office manager Corinthia was still at her desk in the next room, leafing through a thick wedge of documents while she relayed details into a phone jammed against her shoulder. As I looked in she picked up a message slip and waved it at me.

Please call your brother, it said, and gave Edward's number in Norfolk. I mimed a query. Corinthia shook her head: no more information. We exchanged a look that contained both history and understanding. Corinthia had two brothers who were also quite a bit younger than she was, who'd also had a shaky youth. In the past both of us had known what it was like to receive phone calls asking for money or help, and, though Edward had been settled, not to mention prosperous, for three years now, I couldn't quite shake off the suspicion that he must be calling because he needed something.

I went back to my room and dialled Wickham Lodge. I still thought of the house as Aunt Nella's, I still pictured it as it had been during her long and idiosyncratic occupation, with its dark cluttered spaces, its worn mahogany floors and musty guest rooms that saw no guests, its ancient kitchen with cracked quarry tiles, large stone sink and baskets of wet spaniels.

Edward answered at last. 'Wickham.'

'The way you say that, it sounds like your name.'

'Well, why would I give my name? Either they're calling here or they're not. And if they *are* calling here, they'll get me, won't they?'

I didn't suggest that they might also get Edward's long-standing girlfriend Jilly, since their relationship followed a mysterious cycle of abrupt estrangements and unannounced reconciliations, so that no one ever knew whether Jilly was in a state of grace or banishment, or being tolerated in small doses.

'How are you?' I enquired, knowing the sort of reply I was likely to get.

'Oh, bloody roof's leaking. The next job, I suppose. This place sucks up money like a sponge.'

Since inheriting Aunt Nella's estate, Edward had been well-off, by some standards rich. A new roof was hardly going to break him. 'But otherwise?'

'Oh, okay, I suppose,' he growled. 'Listen, umm . . .' His tone was grudging, as though he blamed me for forcing the subject on him. 'I finally got those papers from that dozy solicitor in Falmouth. The statements from Pa's bank. It's just as I thought. Well, no, *worse*, actually. *Far* worse.'

I perched on the edge of the desk, reconciled to a trying conversation. 'In what way?'

'In the amount missing, of course. It's *thousands* more than I thought. In fact, the total is over a *hundred* thousand. Over a *hundred*, Lex.'

'Look, Ed, if Pa wanted to spend that money then he must have had his reasons. I really don't think it's any business of ours.'

'But it was our inheritance!' he declared stiffly, and his anger was directed as much at me for failing to grasp the magnitude of the offence as at our father for failing to deliver everything he felt he was entitled to.

I said, 'If he'd wanted us to have it then he would have left it to us in his will.'

'But supposing he meant to. Supposing that money's just lying around in an account somewhere. It could lie there for ever.'

'I doubt that very much. People come forward. There are always records somewhere.'

But Edward was too firmly determined on his course to take notice of rational argument. 'I need your signature,' he announced uncompromisingly.

'What for?'

'A request for full disclosure from the Falmouth solicitors.

They have to give it to us under some law of probate. I checked.'

I thought: Yes, I'm sure you did. 'But they don't have to disclose anything that doesn't directly relate to Pa's estate,' I pointed out, drawing on my limited memory of probate.

'Well, if *this* doesn't relate, then what the hell does?' His impatience was petulant and fiery, like a clever child despairing of dim adults. For Edward, this wasn't about cash, this was about reparation, about the unyielding sense of aggrievement he felt against Father, with whom he'd had a brittle and uneasy relationship, and I backed down, as I usually did, partly through a lingering guilt at having failed Edward in some obscure way, partly because it was simply much easier to give in to him. 'Okay, send it on to me.'

He rang off with a grunt, and I reflected that my brother managed to work on my emotions more surely than anyone I knew.

A bellicose guffaw greeted me as I slipped into the party. Our victorious client, Mr Ronnie Buck, was standing beside Paul, laughing expansively. He was an ox of a man, broad-boned and squat, with a plump face, pasty skin and small yellowing teeth. Laughter made his cheeks bulge and his eyes crease up, though not so completely that he didn't register my arrival as I walked in.

Accepting a glass of champagne that I didn't really want, I looked up to see Paul waving me over. 'You've met my wife, haven't you, Ronnie?'

'I have indeed had that pleasure.' Buck inclined his head and thrust out a hand which was thick and square yet smooth as a woman's. 'Mrs O'Neill. Your husband has done me proud today. And the rest of the team, of course.'

'It was a good win.'

'It was a *great* win,' Buck corrected me, so firmly that it was almost a rebuke. 'Though it has to be said that we had the occasional moment, didn't we?' He raised a lazy eyebrow at Paul.

Playing the game, Paul blew out his cheeks in a theatrical display of relief. 'We did indeed, Ronnie. I won't pretend we didn't. There's no such thing as certainty in this business.'

'Well, if you were worried you put a good face on it, Paul. A bloody good face.'

Paul gave a delighted chuckle. His glass was empty, I noticed, and, though the champagne couldn't have been open for more than fifteen minutes, I found myself wondering how many glasses he'd managed to consume in that time.

Buck turned back to me with a smile that was both facile and guarded. 'I was just saying to Paul, the two of you must come and join us in Spain. We're near Marbella. Guest suite, pool, girl who cooks proper nosh – the lot. You'll love it.' I imagined that this was Buck at his most personable, the man of property and largesse..

For form's sake I glanced towards Paul, although there was never any question of what our answer would be. 'Thanks,' I said, 'but we're overwhelmed with work at the moment.'

'Just a weekend!' he urged. 'Out on the Friday, back on the Sunday. My office will organize it all. Tickets, cars – you won't have to worry about a thing.'

Seeing that Buck was someone who liked to get his way, I left Paul to answer this.

'Bit tricky at the moment, Ronnie. A lot of work. But we'll keep it in mind.' He signalled across the room to Sturgess to refill our glasses, though his was the only one empty. 'If things ease up . . .'

'*Make* time! That's the secret of life, believe me!' And now there was an edge of insistence to Buck's good humour. 'Come on. You deserve a break.'

Paul hesitated and caught my eye. Following his gaze, Buck looked at me to see if I was creating difficulties.

'Maybe at Easter,' I heard Paul say, and it was all I could do to keep the astonishment out of my face.

'Easter, then! Excellent.' Congenial again, Buck said to me, 'I'll be taking the family straight out there tomorrow morning.

We can't wait – you can imagine. It'll be the first time in a year that we'll have been able to sleep soundly in our beds.'

'Oh?' I queried with a show of innocence. 'Why is that?'

'The police harassment,' Paul interjected quickly, with a small admonishing smile which told me I was at risk of sounding gravely ill-informed.

'Ah,' I murmured. 'I had no idea they'd given you such a hard time. I thought—'

Catching the dangerous note in my voice, Paul interrupted brightly, 'Somehow I don't imagine they'll be in a hurry to bother you again, Ronnie.'

'They'd better bloody not, eh?' Ronnie Buck lifted his glass in an ironic toast, and I thought of the young policeman who'd been attacked so mercilessly and left brain-damaged, and the bitterness and betrayal his colleagues must be feeling after what, for them, must have been an incomprehensible verdict.

Sturgess arrived with a fresh bottle and began to refill our glasses.

'You weren't in court to see our great moment?' Buck asked me.

'No. Paul and I work separately. We don't get involved in each other's cases.'

'Really? Not even when it's a big one?'

Taking a long gulp from his recharged glass, Paul turned away to speak to someone else, but not before casting me a look that contained a glint of warning.

'Not even then,' I replied. 'It's a matter of time and efficiency as much as anything else.'

Buck's steady eyes regarded me unblinkingly. 'You do the same sort of work, though?' I wasn't sure if he was trying to get my measure or to establish my status in the firm's hierarchy or both.

'I take on quite a bit of family work,' I explained. 'Child custody cases and so on. But I do pure crime, too.'

'Pure crime. I like that.' He creased his face to show he

could appreciate even the subtlest humour. 'But family work? Won't be bothering you on that score, glad to say.' More relaxed now, confident of my relative insignificance, he glanced across the room to a tall tightly dressed blonde dragging on a cigarette, and joked heavily, 'Tracy and I have been married twenty years and every time I try to trade her in for a younger model she gets herself all tarted up and sees them off.'

I didn't smile, although I knew it would count against me. 'Goodbye, Mr Buck. Congratulations again.'

His face took on a surly look as though I had just confirmed his most uncharitable suspicions of me. ''Bye then, Mrs O'Neill.'

I would have turned away then but he put out his hand once more. Shaking it, I wondered if it was the hand that had held the baseball bat used to bludgeon the young officer, or whether Buck had delegated the task to the man described as his driver.

Moving off rapidly, I decided that Buck was probably the type to keep his distance, that he would regard punishment and retribution as an administrative matter, to be enforced by the most proficient person who, with his soft beer belly and smooth hands, was unlikely to be Buck himself. A Herod rather than a Genghis.

Ronnie Buck had begun his career as a security-van robber, for which he had served five years, and quickly progressed to drug wholesaling with a sideline in pornography, for which he had served no time at all to date. This career move had earned him what the press described as a 'spacious home set amid fortified grounds' in a green suburb of south-east London. It was into these grounds, according to the evidence Paul had submitted in Buck's defence, that the young officer, DC Tony James, had climbed uninvited one dark night the previous October, thereby committing trespass and opening the way to Buck's plea of self-defence. Mrs Tracy Buck had given evidence for her husband, describing her terror at the sight of this prowler, and how as a result of her screams Buck and his 'driver' had grabbed a baseball bat and rushed out to investigate. On entering a dark shrubbery the two men had been alarmed by a menacing figure who appeared to be on the point of attacking them, and felt they had no choice but to defend themselves. Both had stated in evidence that they were 'absolutely horrified' to discover they had struck a police officer. Buck himself had called the ambulance and, according to Mrs Buck, had been reduced to tears by the incident. The thought of Ronnie Buck producing tears stretched everyone's imagination to breaking point, certainly mine.

Draining the champagne, I picked up another glass and joined a circle of younger staff. The banter was witty and elaborate: at any other time I would have entered the fray, but in my preoccupied mood their jokes were too quick for me and I soon lost track. The champagne tasted metallic and sour in my mouth, several of the juniors were smoking heavily, and without warning my nerves tautened, it became an effort to breathe and I made for the door. Corinthia touched my elbow. 'You all right, Alex?'

'I'm just slipping away.' I remembered that I had come in to work with Paul that day and had no car. 'Tell Paul I've made my own way home, would you?'

'Shall I get you a cab?'

'No, I'll walk. I need the air.'

'Walk?' She gave a giggle of disbelief. 'Are you sure?'

'Absolutely.' I was longing for the sharpness of the night air.

'Shall I tell Paul which way you're going?'

'No. I haven't decided.'

'You certain you're all right? You've been looking a bit tired.'

I managed a smile. 'Nothing the weekend won't cure.'

I was almost out of the building when Sturgess's voice called from the top of the stairs. 'Your briefcase, Alex. Did you want it?'

I was tempted to leave it behind. 'Give it to Paul, would you, Gary? Ask him to bring it home in the car.'

'Anything I can do for you? Find a cab?' He was half-way down the stairs.

'No, thanks.'

'Walking companion?' He was like a young lion, cocky and eager to please.

'It's Friday, Gary. You'll have better things to do.'

'She can wait a while.'

I wagged a finger at him and laughed. 'Don't be so sure. Goodnight, Gary.'

When I had arrived that morning a thin sun had bathed the February dawn in misty yellows and the sky had been clear. Now a cold drizzle hung over the dark streets, and the lamps were large hazy globes. I set off in the direction of home, heading north-west towards King's Cross, but after a few minutes I left the barren façades of the Farringdon Road and entered the dark side-streets of Clerkenwell and St Pancras. Without my briefcase I walked quickly and freely, and did not pause until I'd crossed into Somers Town. Here, among the council blocks which had replaced some of the most notorious slums to survive the First World War, I found a bench and sat for a while, listening to the shrieks of the children, the tuneless beat of amplified music and the angry revving of an unhealthy car engine.

Quite a few of my clients came from Somers Town. Usually I saw them in police cells or magistrates' courts, but occasionally I came here on child custody cases and went inside the flats. It was a district of harassed lone mothers and frail pensioners, of unruly kids, addicts of every known substance, and recidivist rogues; but also a community of buoyant families, devoted couples, hard workers and gentle no-hopers. For the most part the criminals were feckless small-timers, for whom self-improvement was something to do with body-building or winning the lottery.

Sitting there, listening to the cacophony of their lives, I felt a sudden burst of affection for all the joy-riders and drunken brawlers of my acquaintance for whom consequences were rarely a consideration and detection a constant surprise. Unlike Mr Ronnie Buck, they didn't plan or scheme, there was rarely any malice in their actions, just stupidity and impulse and false bravado. Most were feckless, not wicked. They didn't have the brains, ruthlessness or brutality to acquire a villa in Marbella. None of them, in the event of half killing a policeman, could have pulled off a plea of self-defence. Quite apart from having no spacious grounds into which a policeman might trespass unrecognized, they would have been sure to sabotage their own defence in some way. They usually did.

When my feet grew cold, I walked on towards Primrose Hill. By the time I reached Regent's Park Road the drizzle had thickened, the air had a harsh bite to it and angry flurries of wind blew against my face. In the steady flow of Friday-evening traffic a car slowed and drew up a short way ahead. The passenger door of the Mercedes swung open and Paul's greying head appeared.

He gave me a look of injury and faint exasperation as I climbed in. 'Where on earth have you been? I've been driving around for hours.' Abandoning this approach with a lift of one hand, he pulled out into the traffic and said in a conciliatory tone, 'I was worried. You all right?'

I said, 'I'm okay. Just a bit tired.'

'Why on earth didn't you take a cab, then? Walking in this weather. And in that coat. And through King's Cross. You might have been mugged.' He chuckled drily. 'And by one of our own customers.'

'I wanted to walk. I needed to clear my head.'

'Something happened?' He kept glancing across at me, searching for messages in my face. He seemed sober but then he rarely showed his drink at this stage of the evening. 'Something you haven't told me about?'

'No. Nothing.'

'A bad outcome?'

'No, a good week mostly.'

'That's what I thought!' he asserted instantly. 'A not guilty on that assault. And those children out of care and back with the mother in Shoreditch. Mrs Singh, wasn't it?' Paul had a faultless memory for such things. Though we rarely discussed each other's cases in anything more than outline, he never forgot a name or a significant detail. 'All highly satisfactory,' he reminded me.

'Yes.'

'So . . . Are you unwell, darling girl?' He put anxiety into his voice and followed it with a quick squeeze of my hand.

'No, like I said, just tired.'

'Ahh. You and me both. We're behind with our holidays, aren't we, Lexxy? Should never have cancelled that West Country weekend. My fault. Entirely my fault.' He blinked at me contritely. 'When's the next one? What have we got in the diary? I *promise* not to screw it up this time.'

'Crete, in about five weeks.'

'Crete? What, for a weekend?'

'A long weekend. Four days.'

'Oh,' he murmured doubtfully, sounding the holiday's death knell as surely as if he had torn up the air tickets. 'At any rate, we'll do *something* in March. Definitely.'

We had left Primrose Hill behind and were entering the white-stuccoed terraces of Belsize Park. Almost home.

Paul's mobile rang and he pulled over to speak to Ray Dodworth, the former police officer we used as an investigator. Someone had been found, an important witness in an assault case. Elated, Paul punched the heel of his hand against the steering wheel and made a delighted face at me. He rang off with: 'Ray, you were wasted in your previous life!'

Driving on, he outlined the case to me, talking rapidly and exuberantly, and it occurred to me not for the first time that he felt truly alive only when he was winning a case.

He laughed, 'Cheer up, Lexxy. You'll be all right after the weekend. After a bit of sleep.'

'I wish we weren't doing quite so much.' I said it lightly, so he wouldn't take offence.

'We aren't, are we? No, we *aren't*. Just out tonight. And the Johnsons' tomorrow. And a meeting on Sunday. Not so much. You'll be fine after a bit of sleep. Just fine.' He flung me a rousing smile and kept glancing across at me. 'You sure you're not unwell?'

The single wiper raced frantically across the windscreen, the lights of the houses blurred. 'No, I'm just . . .' I cast around for the right word. '. . . A bit concerned, I suppose.'

'*Concerned?*' He manoeuvred the car into a parking space opposite the house. Switching off the engine, he waited expectantly but I didn't want to talk about it here and, gesturing postponement, I got out and led the way in through the front gate and up the steps.

The phone was ringing as I opened the door but by the time I reached it the machine in the study had picked up the call.

Wordlessly Paul and I went about the tasks of homecoming, a ritual honed over the ten years of our marriage. Mail briefly glanced over and placed on the hall table. Lights switched on in the kitchen and living room. Curtains drawn. Two long-stemmed glasses taken down from the cupboard, Chablis from the fridge. All the time I could hear the indistinct tones of a male voice being relayed through the tinny speaker of the answering machine. Passing the study door I made out the words: '. . . *could call me back as soon as possible. As you can imagine we're fairly desperate.*'

I stopped abruptly. The voice had jogged my memory in a place that belonged to a time long ago. Images from childhood washed through my mind, old ties and affections stirred a corner of my heart. For an instant I felt disorientated, displaced.

Then the machine reset itself with a loud click, the memories fell away and I realized that, by some mysterious association, the voice had reminded me of a childhood friend named Will Dearden. I hadn't seen him in twelve years, not since my parents had moved from Norfolk to the opposite corner of

England. I had no idea why my memory should have played such a trick, but trick it surely had to be. He wouldn't know my number; he would have no reason to call.

Fairly desperate . . . I was going into the study to play back the message when Paul called me from the kitchen. 'Smooth and crisp and beautifully chilled and waiting for your custom!' This was another ritual: the taking of the first glass together. We tried not to let telephones or mobiles or faxes get in the way, though in the last year or so this resolution had increasingly gone by the board.

Paul had filled both glasses.

I said, 'I think I'll have water.'

'Water! Oh, come on, just half a glass.' Paul always hated to drink alone.

'No. That champagne . . . I couldn't drink any more.'

'*Half a glass.*'

'No, really.'

Shrugging, he tipped my wine into his glass in such a rush that it overflowed. He swore under his breath and fetched some kitchen paper to mop up the spill. Skirting round him, I helped myself to mineral water from the fridge. Finally we sat down and faced each other across the kitchen table.

'What's this big concern, then?' Paul asked breezily. 'If it's about that holiday in Marbella, don't give it another thought. I just said it to make him happy. Of course we won't go.' He gave me his most reassuring smile, boyish and candid, though behind it I noticed that his eyes were ringed with tiredness and his mood wary. 'Well?' he said. 'Was that it?'

'It's going to be hard to turn Buck down now that we've more or less said we'll go. He's not someone to take no for an answer.'

'Nonsense. It'll just be a question of finding the right excuse.'

I couldn't help thinking it would have been simpler to refuse straight away, but there was no point in saying so now. Putting off the moment of truth a little longer, not wanting to detract too heavily from Paul's achievement, I said warmly, 'It really was a fine win. Well done.'

He waved this aside with a small movement of his glass, but he was pleased all the same. 'Well, it was Jenkins mainly.' This was the bumptious but painstaking QC.

'But it was you who produced that witness.'

'Oh, lucky!' He cast his eyes heavenward and chuckled. 'Dead lucky!'

'And she was a good witness?'

'Brilliant. A gift. Karen Grainey. Clear, confident, credible. No form in the family, not so much as a parking ticket. Quietly dressed, well-spoken. Didn't pretend she'd seen DC James's face, nothing that might have got her into trouble under cross-examination. Just what he was wearing. Just the fact that she saw him climb the wall and disappear into Buck's garden.'

'And she was at the window looking out for her daughter?'

'Waiting for her to come back from a disco, yes.'

'No difficulties with that?'

'No,' he said, a little touchy all of a sudden. 'Why should there be?'

'I mean, the prosecution didn't question it?'

'No.'

'And what about the trespass story?'

Paul made a wide gesture. 'He trespassed, that's all there was to it.'

'Didn't the prosecution point out that he would never have gone over the wall without radioing his partner?'

'They wouldn't have dared try that one! He was disobeying orders, wasn't he? He wasn't likely to announce it to anyone, was he?'

Yet I would have thought that was exactly what he would have done, especially when his partner was the one person who could watch over him, especially when the garden belonged to Ronnie Buck. But I could see that more questions wouldn't go down too well and, nodding in vague agreement, I let the subject drop.

Paul took a gulp of his drink and said expansively, 'So . . . what is it, Lexxy? Out with it!'

It was hard to begin; harder still to hit the right note. 'I know it's difficult to get these things right,' I said carefully. 'But the party this evening. I feel it was . . . well, a bad idea.'

'A bad idea?' He was immediately defensive. 'Why, for heaven's sake?'

'Having all the staff there. And most of Buck's family. And holding it in the office.'

'Well, we couldn't very well have gone to the pub, not with all the press around!'

'No, but . . . I think a quick drink with just you and him might have been more suitable.'

Paul spread his hands in a show of bewilderment. 'He's a client. I don't see the problem. We've had a few drinks after big cases in the past.'

'He's a villain, Paul. I think it's unnecessary to extend the relationship beyond the professional.'

'But it hasn't gone beyond the professional!' he retorted, looking offended. 'I told you, there's no question of our going to Spain. And a party, for God's sake. What's a party?'

'We didn't have to do it, though, give the party. It was inappropriate.'

'Nonsense! How can it be inappropriate? Dozens of our clients are villains, Alex. That's our business. Defending villains.'

'Not like Buck. None of them are like Buck.'

He shook his head slowly and deliberately, as if I had taken leave of my senses. 'But the whole basis of our job is that we don't make judgements. How can we? How can we draw the line between a mugger and a murderer? They're all in deep trouble when they come to us. They all have a right to a defence. For God's sake, Lexxy, don't get on your high horse all of a sudden. *Someone* had to defend Buck. If it hadn't been us, it would have been another firm. And at least he pays good money, on time. For heaven's sake . . .' He took another gulp of wine, a large one. His drinking was another subject which, going by past attempts, we also found impossible to discuss. Paul rarely drank more than a pint or so during the day – not openly at any rate – but he had taken to drinking in the evenings with regularity and determination. Except at the occasional wedding or wake, he rarely showed his drink and most people would never realize he'd had more than two or three, but I realized all right. I saw the change in him, the steady descent into stubborn argument and futile confrontations with traffic wardens and waiters, the unresolved anger which was a legacy of a childhood scarred by alcohol and deprivation, and the self-denigration which was the other side of his insecure nature. I watched him drink with apprehension, but most of all with helplessness.

'It's our *job* to defend people,' he stated doggedly.

'But Ronnie Buck's in a totally different league, isn't he? A drug dealer on a large scale, the worst sort. A leech living off the misery of kids. And sheltering behind his money, doing his best to put himself beyond the law. He's got absolutely nothing to recommend him.'

Paul scooped up his glass and drained it. 'Are you saying we should never have taken him on?'

'I would have been happier if we hadn't, yes.'

'You would have been happier,' he echoed, pouring himself some more wine. 'Well, you should have come out and said so at the time, shouldn't you!'

'But . . .' I softened my voice. 'I did, darling. I did say so.'

'What do you mean?'

'I said . . .' I tried to recall my exact words. 'I think I said the case was likely to be a can of worms. That Buck wouldn't make a very pleasant client.'

'I don't remember that.' His mood was unyielding. 'You never said that. No, Alex, I'm *sure* you never said that.'

'Well . . . if not that, something very like it.'

'No,' he said with finality. 'I would have remembered.'

There are small moments that eat into your trust for ever,

small moments that undermine your love and, try as you might to erase them, stick hard in your memory.

Catching my expression, Paul said in a tone of good-natured injury, 'Honestly, Lexxy, I would have remembered. *Honestly*. Something of that sort!'

I let it pass. 'Well, it's history now.'

'Anyway, since when could we afford to be choosy about our clients? Since when could we afford to turn business *away*, for God's sake?'

'This isn't about money,' I argued with sudden heat. 'It's about doing the sort of work we *want* to do.' I sighed, and added in a calmer voice, 'Besides, we're doing fine, aren't we? Financially. Well up on last year.'

'But higher costs, too. Don't forget the salary rises. And the legal aid budget's going to be slashed for sure. A swingeing reduction. We could be in real trouble.' For Paul, no amount of success could ever banish his sense of financial insecurity, no amount of money convince him that it couldn't at any moment be snatched away from him. Born into poverty in Liverpool, to an impecunious Irish father who drank himself to a quick death and a mother who succumbed to apathy and despair, the uncertainties were too deep. Nothing I said ever lifted his anxiety on this score, but it didn't stop me from trying.

'Darling, even allowing for the salaries, we're well into profit for the year.'

His mobile began to ring in his jacket, which was hanging over a nearby chair. 'Yes, but next year's another year, isn't it?' He was about to take the call when he glanced at my face and, thinking better of it, turned the mobile off.

'But we've never had a bad year yet, have we? Each year's been better than the last.'

Unable to deny this, Paul frowned at his glass and twisted the stem back and forth. 'So what are you saying, then – that we should pick and choose our clients in future?'

'I think we should, yes.'

Hardly meeting my gaze, looking indignant, he continued to rotate the glass stem. 'But what happens when Buck offers us more business?'

I understood then: it had already happened.

'He's likely to, is he?'

'Well, the family is. His brother's being investigated for VAT fraud.'

'We could tell them we don't do fraud.'

'Come on! Every criminal firm does fraud. Besides, fraud's hardly a heinous crime.'

'But the family business is heinous!' I said hotly. 'Crushing a young officer's head is heinous! VAT fraud is just the tip of a large and unpleasant muck heap.'

He paused as if to consider this, but the wine had already darkened his mood and I could see that he didn't want to face this kind of argument after a day that should have earned him nothing but celebration and praise. 'It's a job,' he repeated truculently. 'And we're just jobbing lawyers. It's not for us to reason why, not for us to look down from some great moral height. Really, Alex, I think you've lost sight of what it's all about. I think you've got too high an opinion of yourself.'

The words were out, there was no taking them back. For a moment he looked as though he might try, then he shook the thought away and stared crossly into his drink.

I could see that it'd be best to leave things alone before further damage was done. We were both tired, we had a dinner party ahead of us, the evening had to be weathered before we could fall exhausted into bed.

'Okay,' I said, signalling my retreat with a thin smile. 'Let's leave it there.'

'I don't see that there's anywhere else *to* leave it, Lexxy. Honestly.' And he gave a baffled gesture that contained a measure of reproach.

I stood up and said, 'Perhaps you're right.' On my way past him I leant down and lightly kissed his forehead.

'Honestly, Lexxy,' he repeated softly, but not so softly that I couldn't make out what he'd said. As I left the kitchen I heard the clink of the wine bottle as it met the rim of his glass.

I was half-way upstairs before I remembered the phone message. *As you can imagine we're fairly desperate.* I hesitated – there was precious little time for a bath as it was – but duty got the better of me, as it usually did, and I went down to the study. The display on the machine registered three messages. The first was the window cleaner, the second a tennis-playing friend of Paul's, wanting to fix a game for Sunday morning.

And then the voice which took me helplessly back to my past.

'This is a message for Alex O'Neill . . .'

I reached for the chair and began to pull it out from the desk.

'This is Will Dearden, Alex, from Deepwell. It's been a long time . . . Can't think how long. Though I thought I saw you in the village not so long ago. With your brother, was it? Anyway . . . Look, this is a bit out of the blue, you may not be interested, but something's happened and I thought you might be able to help. The thing is—' A pause and he exhaled, as if suddenly disheartened at having to speak to an answering machine. I sat down on the chair and reached for pen and paper. *'The thing is, Grace is missing. She, er . . .'* A sigh now, or a gasp of suppressed emotion. *'She, er, disappeared over a week ago. They're looking, but – well, she might have gone to London. I mean, she was due to go to London that morning, and . . . well, we're not satisfied that they've covered that end of things. They say they have, but it seems to me that they've been . . .'* An exclamation of open impatience. *'But look, it's no good on the phone. If you could call . . .'* There was haste in his voice now, as if he suspected the whole conversation would prove to be a complete waste of time. He rattled off his number so quickly that I had to replay the tape to make sure I had it down correctly. *'So, er . . . if you could call me back as soon as possible. As you can imagine we're fairly desperate.'*

As the machine bleeped and rewound, a vivid image flashed into my mind, of Will and Grace in the garden at Wickham Lodge. It was just before their wedding, in that last brief summer before my parents moved to the West Country. It was the day of the fête, there was quite a throng, and it was a while before I glimpsed them in the distance, standing by the home-made jam stall: Grace, in a pale peach dress and large cream hat, looking as if she had floated out of a Beaton photograph, Will wearing a cream linen jacket, pale slacks and white collarless shirt, an outfit so urbane, so artfully put together that I couldn't imagine he had chosen it himself. It suited him, though. It emphasized his height and dark looks. It made him a perfect adjunct to Grace, with her pale ethereal beauty.

There is a fascination in seeing two such people together, a strikingly good-looking couple on the brink of marriage. You feel curiosity, and something like awe, but also a sense of exclusion, of looking through glass at a miraculous aspect of life which, in your youth and uncertainty, you fear may be for ever out of your reach.

I couldn't get to the wedding, and in the years that followed I didn't see them again. In the beginning I stayed away more or less deliberately: the idea of seeing Will was simply too painful. Later I was bound up in work, married to a man who didn't like country weekends.

Dialling Will Dearden's number now, my stomach tightened with half-forgotten memories. As the number began to ring, I saw the pink-washed house above the creek and the wide sweep of the marshes and the distant line of the sea.

The number went on ringing for a long time before it finally answered.

A woman's voice said a composed, 'Hello.'

'Maggie?' I had always called Will's mother by her first name, even when I was a small child, the only adult for whom it had seemed perfectly natural.

She barely hesitated. 'Alex.'

My throat constricted suddenly. 'Yes,' I said, with a rush of emotion. 'Yes, it's me.'

'*Alex*.' And there was pleasure in her voice. 'How are you, dear Alex? It has been so, so long.' The exotic accent was still there, the long Rs, the elongated vowels, the upturn in mid-sentence that betrayed her first language.

'Oh, I'm fine, Maggie. But I got a message from Will, about Grace.'

'Yes.' Her voice seemed to fade a little. 'Yes, he told me he had called you.'

'He said she was *missing*. Is that right?'

'Yes.'

'God, Maggie, I'm so terribly sorry. You've no idea what might have happened?'

'None.'

'But when was she last seen?'

'Wednesday, last week.'

This was nine days ago. 'I see. What are the police doing? Have they mounted a proper search?'

'Oh, they have searched. But they seem to have stopped now.' Her voice was steady, without discernible emotion.

'Who's the officer in charge?'

'I may have been told but . . . No, you must ask Will about that.'

'Is he there? Can I speak to him?' My nerves tautened at the thought.

'He's just gone out. To the police in King's Lynn.'

The professional in me had to ask, 'Any particular reason?'

'He went with photographs, I think. And to ask if there's any news.'

'And are there no clues at all as to what might have happened, Maggie? Is anything missing? Clothes? Money? Passport?'

'No, nothing.'

'What about credit cards? Bank accounts? Have they been used?'

'No.'

'I see.' This didn't bode well. 'Maggie, there's not a lot I can do tonight, not if Will's not there, so I'll come down first thing in the morning, if that's all right. I'll be with you by ten, earlier if I can.'

'I'll tell Will.' And then, with echoes of her old warmth, 'I look forward to seeing you so much, Alex.'

'Me too, Maggie.'

For several minutes after we had said goodbye I sat in the silence, trying to absorb this news with some semblance of calm, but the force of the past was very strong. Memories kept crowding in at random, sudden visions and abrupt emotions which overturned my thoughts and got in the way. It was only with an effort that I imposed some sort of order.

Grace Dearden was missing. Suicide, abduction, intentional disappearance . . . Even with such sparse information I found myself starting to sift through the possibilities. Part of me thrilled to the challenge; I knew I could do this task well. I was thorough, I rarely missed a detail: that was my strength. With some of the more tragic cases I had also been known to get emotionally involved; Paul would say that this was my weakness, and he would probably be right.

Thoroughness and detail. Normally, I would start by ringing the police and trying to establish what they were doing, what their thoughts were – if any – and how they intended to proceed. However, if Will was there at the station it wouldn't be appropriate to interrupt, and it struck me that I had no mandate to do so anyway. Will might not wish me to act for him in any official capacity at all. For me, used to clients who were in deep and unequivocal trouble, this was altogether more delicate territory.

This did not stop me from taking a sheet of paper and making detailed notes of the areas to be investigated if I were instructed.

A sound at the door and Paul put his head round. 'Don't forget we're going out.'

I looked at my watch and stood up hastily. 'On my way.'

'We're meant to be there in ten minutes.' He said it without any sense of urgency; we were often late.

'I won't be long.' Climbing the stairs ahead of him, I said, 'I have to go to Norfolk tomorrow.'

'*Norfolk*. Why, for heaven's sake?'

'An old friend.' It was strange to describe Will this way. 'His wife's missing. He's not entirely happy with the police response. He's asked me to help.'

'Wouldn't he do better with someone local, someone who's on the spot?'

'But he's asked *me*.' Saying this, I felt a burst of feeling, a jumble of pride and rekindled emotion that seemed to fill my chest. 'I can't say no.'

'But you could point out that you're not well placed to help. Can't you deal with it on the phone?'

I paused in the bathroom doorway. 'Not really. It sounds serious.'

'You complain about work spilling over into the weekends, about us never having time off, and you're the worst offender.'

'This is an old friend.'

Paul blinked at me through a haze of wine and rueful affection. 'Ah, and you're a loyal friend, that's for sure. That's one reason I fell for you, if I remember.'

A moment of regret passed between us. I put my arms around him and, though we embraced with tenderness, it seemed to me that our difficulties and tensions had the tighter grasp, that our years of happiness already belonged to another more distant time.

I showered first, then Paul. Meeting again in front of the bathroom mirror he said, 'So who's this friend?'

'Someone I grew up with.'

'Called?'

'Will Dearden.'

He wove his tie through the last loop and pulled it into shape. 'Have you ever told me about him?'

In answering I realized I'd rarely spoken of him to anyone, and that it was an effort to do so now, even after all these years. 'I'm not sure.'

'Friend of Edward's?'

'No.' I knew very little of my brother's life since he'd moved back to Deepwell, but of one thing I could be sure, he wouldn't be a friend of Will's.

'Wait . . .' Paul frowned as he searched his memory. 'Dearden. Didn't your pa tell me about him? Yes, yes, wasn't he the fella who saved the girl from the flood, saved her life, only to go and sweep her off her feet himself?'

'It wasn't a flood, it was a ditch.'

'Well . . . ditch, flood. A lovely romantic story all the same.' He made another search of his memory. 'She was trapped in a car?'

'Yes.'

'On the point of drowning? Yes, I remember your pa telling me.' He flattened his hair with alternate passes of the comb and the palm of his hand.

'It wasn't that dramatic. She wasn't in any danger.'

'No? But the drowning makes for a better story, doesn't it?'

The village had thought so. I remembered the way the tale had grown more sensational with each telling.

'She hasn't just waltzed off with another fella?'

'Unlikely.'

'Well, don't be so sure. There's usually a fella somewhere. Was she pretty?'

I saw her at the fête again, under the cream-coloured hat. 'Beautiful.'

Something in the way I said this made Paul cast me a curious glance in the mirror. 'Ah, then money might be a factor too.'

'I don't think it's going to be anything like that. These are country people. Money isn't that important to them.'

Leaning towards my reflection as though to impart a great

confidence, he gave me a sardonic smile. 'Money's always important!'

I said sharply, 'You don't understand – the police are searching for her. She might be dead.'

He looked unimpressed.

Pulling on my dress, abandoning earrings and lipstick, I went down to the study and took out my old photograph album.

I flipped past snaps of my parents when they were first married, of my mother holding me as a baby, of the family on holiday in Cornwall when Edward was a podgy toddler and I, at ten, was hardly less plump. Then came the pictures where my mother was always sitting in a chair or on a garden seat because she hated to be photographed in her wheelchair. The two pictures in the garden at Deepwell were my favourites from this era. Mother was still relatively free of pain then, she was smiling in both pictures, while Father was wearing that rather mischievous grin of his. Apart from Edward, who had always pulled a grumpy face at the sight of a camera, we all looked relatively happy and, despite Mother's illness, we had been for much of the time.

I paused two pages on, at a picture of Maggie standing in the shaded kitchen doorway of Marsh House on a summer afternoon – in these pictures it was always summer. She wore a pale cotton dress in fresh mint green, her dark hair haphazardly pulled back to the nape of her neck. In the reflected light, with her smooth Mediterranean skin, her large expressive eyes, she looked no more than thirty, still young, but middle-aged to me then. Her kitchen, visible over her shoulder, was an exotic place to an untravelled child like me, with its jars of rices, pastas and wild mushrooms, its pervasive scent of garlic and herbs, and, tacked to the walls, the posters of misty landscapes and hill villages in Lombardy and Piedmont.

While my mother lay at home for long hours, losing the slow battle with her illness, Maggie had become my surrogate mother, the mother of my happiest sunlit days. The photograph captured all that drew me to her, the generosity of her affections, the vitality of her mind, the enthusiasm she used to find for the simplest things.

On the opposite page was a picture from another summer, taken against the same doorway but from a little further away: Maggie and Will together, two handsome people with the same dark eyes, thick lustrous hair and wide expressive mouths, a testament to the power of genes; mother and son in the flesh, and in the spirit too, though in those days Will's eyes did not meet the lens with quite his mother's gaiety and overt confidence.

I was looking for a photograph Maggie had sent me some years ago with her regular Christmas card, a picture of Grace and Will and their child, but if it was here I couldn't seem to find it.

Leafing back through the album I came across a shot of Will, aged about sixteen, sitting against the side of his dinghy. The boat, a small green pram called *Pod*, was pulled up on the edge of a salt-marsh, next to dense reeds lit a brilliant gold by the afternoon sun. The oars weren't shipped properly: they sat in the rowlocks with the blades angled up like small wings. Will was reclining lazily, with an arm hanging over his raised knee, looking away towards some distant horizon. I was planning to become a famous photographer then: I'd thought the composition very artistic.

A last search through the bundle of loose snapshots tucked inside the album's back cover, but I couldn't find a picture of Grace from this or any other Christmas.

Hearing Paul on the stairs, I shut the album and slipped it back into the cupboard.

We were the last to arrive at the dinner party but our hosts seemed in no hurry to get the food onto the table. I watched with creeping anxiety as Paul drank steadily on an empty stomach. When we finally sat down to dinner just before ten, he had no appetite and hardly touched his plate. After the main course he started arguing with a girl in magazine publishing about the pernicious influence of anorexic models on the impressionable young. His eyes were like slits, his voice took on a heavy hectoring note, he repeated himself continuously. For once there was no question of the drink not showing, and I couldn't help wondering if this was the beginning of another stage, where the last bastion of restraint was going to be thrown away. When he gestured clumsily and knocked a glass of wine over, I said, rather too quickly, 'Paul had a great win today,' and everyone cheered, except Paul who glared at me resentfully across the table.

At midnight I pleaded a headache and managed to get us away half an hour later, though not before Paul had downed another glass of wine and a large brandy. He slept most of the way home and I had to shake him hard before he would get out of the car. He went unsteadily upstairs, humming what might have been an Irish ballad, and undressed with heavy dignity before keeling over on top of the duvet, his feet on the floor. Filling a glass with water, I took it to the bedside and shook him again. When I had persuaded him to sit up, I placed his hand around the glass and helped him raise it to his mouth. Suddenly, with an angry gesture that almost caught me round the face, he sent glass and water onto the carpet. 'Muck! Filthy muck!'

'Oh, sure,' I breathed, brushing the water off my dress.
'Poison.'

'Oh, Lexxy,' he moaned.

'Come on,' I said. 'Sleep time.'

As I helped him into bed he muttered thickly, 'The hell with it.'

I lay awake for a long time, listening to his breathing, looking into the darkness and seeing a path of unhappiness that seemed to stretch out before us without end. I felt our relationship was slipping further and further beyond our grasp and, in my present mood, it seemed to me that neither of us was capable of stopping it. Our periodic attempts at shoring it up, our brief moments of tenderness and communication, seemed to get swept away with each tide.

It would have been easy to blame Paul's drinking or the pressures of our work, or myself for not having given up more time to our marriage, but blame was an empty road and I didn't want to go that way. All I knew was that both of us had changed. At some point Paul's aims and mine, our priorities and ambitions, had diverged, and each small crisis, far from pulling us together, only seemed to emphasize the growing divide.

Then I thought of Will Dearden, and my worries seemed a small thing by comparison. I tried to imagine what it must be like to love someone and to have no idea what had happened to them, to live in a state of agonizing uncertainty, caught between dread and hope, and it seemed to me that it must be unendurable.

I slept restlessly until four. At four thirty I gave up hope of getting back to sleep and, pulling on some thick country clothes, left a note for Paul and made my way out into the night.

Chapter Two

THE RAIN had vanished with the wind and the night was sharp
with sudden cold. There was little traffic and, encircled by
sparkling hoarfrost and a canopy of country-bright stars, I felt
as though I were in some sort of time machine, flying through
a silvery firmament towards the kingdom of my childhood. For
the last ten miles I took the back lanes because I had time to
spare and it was completely deserted that way. I paused on the
crown of the last hill to look for the view, but it was too early,
the dawn was still some way off, and beyond the beads of light
that marked the coast road the marshes and the sea were just
another stretch of blackness in the night.

Descending the winding hill to a junction lit by a single
sodium light, I turned east along the coast road and after half
a mile slowly entered Deepwell. It was nearly seven but few
people were about. Passing almost the whole length of the
village, reaching the shadowy walls of the ancient round-
towered church and, beyond it, the dark windows of the village
school, I saw just two cars.

The Deepwell Arms had been painted in garish new colours
and sported a large sign that promised hot food all day. Pausing
beside it, I considered taking the lane to Wickham Lodge, but
Edward had never been an early riser, even as a small boy, and
I had spent too many mornings trying unsuccessfully to drag
him out of bed to risk disturbing him now. I decided to pass by
later, though my chances of catching him were probably slim.
On winter weekends, if he wasn't organizing his own shoot,
complete with armies of beaters and vast picnics, he seemed to

be invited to another estate, to pick off someone else's birds. For a person who had been anti-social to the point of solitude as a child, my brother had become astonishingly gregarious in his new life.

I wondered why he hadn't told me about Grace Dearden's disappearance on the phone yesterday. He must have known: this was a small place, news travelled fast. Not least of all, Will Dearden was a tenant of the Wickham Estate, which Edward had inherited from Aunt Nella. It was inconceivable that Edward hadn't known but not, perhaps, inconceivable that he hadn't bothered to tell me.

I carried on along the main road to Deepwell Staithe and turned down towards the quay. With an emotional heart, I paused by Sedgecomb House where I had grown up. An eighteenth-century merchant's house with mellow bricks and white-framed bays topped by arched windows, like eyes, it stood a narrow and incongruous three storeys tall behind high ornamental railings and a rose-edged lawn. The house was in darkness apart from a porch light, but I caught the glint of a brass plate on the gatepost. My father had run the practice on his own, with the help of an occasional locum, but now there were two or more partners, working from a new and much enlarged surgery in the stables. I'd heard that the main house, occupied by the senior partner, had also been renovated. According to Edward, one wall of the sitting room had been knocked down and the panelling ripped out to create a giant kitchen. With its morning light and view of the garden, the sitting room had been my mother's favourite room while she could still move about the house. It was disturbing to imagine it entirely gone.

I drove slowly down towards the water, following the lane as it curved to the right along the edge of the hard-standing that flanked the creek, an area known as the quay, though the stonework, such as it might have been, had crumbled long before anyone could remember. At the far end, on a slope overlooking the salt-marshes, I came to a large pink-washed farmhouse set at the end of a stone-walled garden: Marsh House, the home of Will and Grace Dearden. A battered Range Rover was parked in front of the gate behind a small Citroën, while a Volvo estate stood in the drive, which led up the right side of the house to a garage hidden among the outbuildings at the rear. For all these cars, the house itself might have been deserted. A single lamp shone in the porch but the windows were dark, and, to the left side of the house, the garden wall reflected no light from the kitchen. As a kid I had always run straight up to the side door and into the kitchen unannounced. But that was long before Will and Grace took the place over, in the days when this had been Maggie's house and her kitchen my second home.

I parked behind the Range Rover, walked down to the water and sat huddled in my coat on the bank of the creek. The smell of salt and mud was pungent, like the sea and the earth rolled into one. At my feet, the stillness was alive with soft plops and faint murmurings as the water stole gently between the mud banks; ebbing or flooding, I couldn't tell. As the grey dawn seeped slowly over the landscape, I could make out the smudge of the horizon and a trickle of reflected light on the distant dunes, and felt a tremor of excitement at the view to come. When I was young I had thought this the most beautiful place on earth, I had been sure I would live all my life here. I had believed nothing could ever take me away.

I heard a tractor somewhere up in the village and the first muted calls of the brent geese far out on the salt-marsh, and climbed stiffly to my feet. A light had appeared in a lower window of the Deardens' house. I took my bag from the car and ran a comb through my hair before climbing the path to the front door.

My knock brought the sound of an inner door and light footsteps on flagstones. A bolt slid back, the door swung open and Maggie stood before me in the unlit hall, a shadowy figure in a pale wrap. 'I knew it would be you,' she said, and held her arms out to me.

Embracing her, I found myself grasping a woman smaller and slighter than the Maggie of my memory. There was no flesh on her, no weight or substance.

'Alex,' she murmured in her low throaty voice. She gestured me into the house and down the dark passageway to the kitchen. 'Will is not here,' she offered. 'I'm not sure where he is gone.'

'Is there any news?'

'No,' she said flatly. 'Nothing.'

In the kitchen I took a proper look at her and it was an effort to keep the surprise out of my face. Maggie, who had always appeared so vigorous, so invincible, so incapable of change, had become thinner, with a complexion the colour of grey stone, a web of harsh lines around her eyes and skin that seemed to have been sucked against her cheekbones. Before I could stop myself, I gasped, 'Have you been all right, Maggie?'

'Me?' She gave a wry smile. 'Oh, Alex, I'm just *older*. We all get older. It comes as a surprise, but there is no escape. Arthritis, gallstones . . . such very dull things. Sit down, my darling girl, sit down.'

She turned away to fill a kettle. Her black hair was dry and wiry and peppered with grey, while her wrap did nothing to disguise the gauntness of her body. She looked as if she'd been neglecting her health for some time, not eating properly or smoking too much.

I sat down at the table and glanced at a room I barely recognized. Gone were the rough walls, the stand-up furniture and posters of Italy, gone the old pine table burnished with splashes of olive oil, gone the rickety chairs and the tall dresser with the delphinium-blue china. The kitchen had been stripped out and refitted with lime-washed units by Smallbone, a shiny new Aga in racing green, a slate floor and a blaze of low-voltage star-lights across the ceiling. Everything was pale polished wood and green chintz and immaculate taste; nothing was remotely cheap. It was as if every trace of Maggie's occupation had been erased in favour of a complete package from *House & Garden,* and, though I had no claims on the place, I felt a pinch of indignation and loss, as though I had been denied a small segment of my past.

'I was sorry about your father,' Maggie said, pausing behind a chair. 'He was a good man.' I couldn't help noticing her hands as they rested on the chair-back: bony, almost clawed, with prominent bumpy veins. I looked back to her face and met a gaze that was both fierce and exhausted. 'The end – it wasn't too bad for him?'

'Well, it was quick,' I told her.

'He was at peace?'

'Oh, I think so. In so far as anyone's at peace when they're stuffed full of morphine. The only thing that really got him down was the local consultant, who never stopped smiling and telling him he'd be fine.'

I didn't have to explain the irony of this to Maggie, who'd always understood people's contradictions. 'Yes,' she said, 'that would have annoyed him, being the same sort of doctor himself, always so bright and full of hope.' Her voice was still beautiful, with its lilting accent, its deep melodious tones. 'And his last years, Alex, the time after your mother died – were they happy?'

'I think so. Though it was hard to be sure, living so far away.'

'Cornwall,' Maggie murmured, with one of those eloquent shrugs I had always admired so much, somewhere between a question mark and an expression of surprise.

'It was Mum who wanted to live there. I always thought it was mad myself, going so far from their roots and all their friends. Especially when she was so ill.'

'Yes . . . to leave so much.' With a single shake of her head, Maggie went to make tea, moving across the kitchen with echoes of her old feline grace, all flow and continuity. 'It's been so long, Alex. So long. I meant to ask you to come and visit us – and your husband, of course. So *many* times I meant to ask you, Alex, but somehow . . .' She made a pure Maggie gesture,

a long Italian lift of one hand, palm upturned, as if to indicate
fate and its inexplicable mastery of events. 'And then, with
your brother so close, I thought you would be visiting him, I
thought you would drop by when you were near us. I looked
for you at the fête.'

'I've had no time, Maggie. Not recently. Too much work. I
don't seem to get anywhere or do anything very much. And
Edward – well, he's so busy with his country pursuits. Somehow we don't get to see each other.'

'Ah, yes,' she nodded. 'Yes . . . So *different*, you two.'

Inadequate though my explanation had been, she let it pass.
She didn't ask about the early years, why on my six-monthly
visits to Aunt Nella I'd never dropped in on her, why our
meetings had been restricted to occasional lunches in London,
lunches that had finally petered out when Maggie had stopped
going to town. If she'd guessed the reason I had avoided coming
to see her here, if she'd realized how difficult I had found the
idea of seeing Will again, then she'd never mentioned it.

Placing the tea on the table, Maggie went on purposefully,
as if to postpone discussion of Grace for a little longer, 'But tell
me, Alex, are you well? Are you happy? I want to know all
about your life. You look so fine, so . . .' Sitting down, she
made a show of considering me afresh. 'Yes . . . you look as I
always knew you would look when you became a little older –
yes, *serene*. And *lovely*. And *elegant*.'

'Maggie.' I smiled a denial, though the plump unlovely
adolescent that I had been for much of my teens was quietly
pleased at everything she had said. 'I don't know about the
serenity – you should see me in the office sometimes.'

She reached out a hand and grasped mine briefly. 'But you
are happy?'

'Oh, yes.' I said it too quickly, smiling and blinking at the
same time, and compounded the mixed message by reaching
too hastily for my tea.

A small silence, a slight shift in the atmosphere as we came
to the matter in hand.

I said, 'So tell me, has no one any idea what might have happened to Grace?'

'No.' A pause and she added, 'But I think it is not good.'

The apparent indifference with which she said this took me by surprise. Always a passionate person, full of feeling, Maggie seemed to have suppressed all emotion.

I asked, 'Why do you say that?'

'Many things. Small things. Things that I feel.' And she touched her fingertips against her stomach. 'Of course, I can say such a thing to you, Alex. To no one else. You understand this? William . . . well, he still hopes. He thinks somehow that she will come back.'

'But she won't?'

She lifted a dismissive shoulder, she stirred her tea. 'Grace was not a person to go away into the blue, to say nothing about where she was going.'

'And there was no reason for her to leave?'

'No.'

'There weren't any problems, Maggie?'

She gave me a close look to be sure she had understood my meaning. 'No,' she stated. 'Grace did not have problems. Grace had her life as she wished it. Grace was not a person to . . .' She took a moment to find the expression. '. . . to be defeated in any way.'

It was a strange choice of words. 'So she was happy?'

'Grace was always . . . How can I say it? Grace did not find it possible to be unhappy.'

How rare, how lucky. How awe-inspiring. 'Why does Will think she might be in London?'

'He has to believe something.'

'Did any of the neighbours see anything on the day she disappeared? Anything out of the ordinary?'

'No.'

'There was no sign of forced entry to the house, or violence of any sort—'

'Nothing like that.'

'And her car?'

'Still here.' She tilted her head towards the side of the house, and I remembered the Volvo estate.

'When was she missed, Maggie?'

'On the Thursday morning, when Will got back. He had been up most of the night. He . . .' She faltered and stared at the teapot in an intense unfocused way. This was a Maggie I did not know, a Maggie absorbed and troubled and uncertain of how to proceed. She looked up suddenly, establishing contact again, a flicker of recognition and affection in her gaze. 'He was mending a sluice. He didn't get back until the next morning,' she resumed. 'When Grace was not here and there was no note – well, he was too tired to think. You understand this? He just thought she had gone to London as she planned. It wasn't until the evening that he realized . . . When she did not come back, when she did not phone.'

'I see. So – have I got it right? – Will was out all night?'

'Most of the night, yes. He came and made himself some coffee, he slept an hour on the sofa—'

'On the sofa?'

She frowned momentarily. 'At Reed Cottage, with me. He had coffee and a short sleep at my house. He had to wait for the tide, you understand. To close the sluice again.'

I didn't understand entirely; in fact, I was baffled as to why a sluice should need so much attention, but I didn't feel I could press her for complicated explanations.

'Tell me about the police, Maggie. What have they done so far?'

'Ha!' Showing signs of her old fire, she blew out her lips. 'They came, they asked questions. They came *often* to begin with. All day, then twice a day. But now, not so much.' She looked away towards the window, and her mouth was tight, her eyes dark with harsh emotion.

'But they did mount a search?'

'A search? I *suppose*.' A lift of both shoulders. 'They sent a helicopter' – she swept a hand through the air – 'something

that can see things with heat, something which finds people.
Then they looked around here, in all the gardens' – she
described another circle – 'and in the meadows – *our* meadows
– and the creek. And the salt-marsh – well, *some* of it, but . . .'
She indicated the impossibility of searching the entire marsh,
then, tightening her lips, got up suddenly and went to the
worktop where she picked up a packet of cigarettes and tapped
one out. She had given up smoking when I had last seen her.

I felt my way cautiously forward. 'They're not mounting
any more searches?'

Lighting her cigarette, Maggie came back to the table. 'It
appears not,' she said, and her hands were trembling. 'They
think they will do better by talking to Will.' She drew hard on
her cigarette and sat down again.

'What do you mean?'

'I mean,' she said angrily, 'they think Grace met a violent
end and that Will can tell them about it.'

Many thoughts went through my mind, most of them
alarming, before I asked calmly, 'Are you saying they're
treating Will as a suspect in some crime? Is that what they've
told him?'

'No,' she admitted reluctantly. 'But that is what they *think*.'
She cut the air with the edge of her hand. 'That is what they
think.'

'Why do you say that, Maggie?'

She took a long pull on her cigarette and inhaled deeply.
'There's this policeman, an inspector or whatever,' she said
through a wall of smoke. 'I can see it in his mind. Look to the
husband! Look to the marriage! He comes back every day, he
has these cold eyes, Alex, and he looks at Will and I can see
what he is thinking. He wants to know if Will is really upset or
if he is secretly happy. He is looking to blame Will. Oh, Alex,'
she said with despair, 'I see it all!'

'But the police *always* seem like that, Maggie. They always
look suspicious about absolutely everything. It's just their way.
It doesn't necessarily mean very much.'

'You say that, but I know, I *know*. And,' she added in a tone that would have been frivolous if it weren't so full of indignation, 'I have no doubt that they have asked around to find out if there is another woman!'

'But no one's said they have? You don't know for sure?'

She shrugged.

I put on my most reassuring voice. 'Maggie, I honestly wouldn't fret too much about the police at this stage.'

'But I am full of bad feelings on this, Alex. I am—' Something distracted her, she raised her head and listened, as still as a painting, and in that moment, with the light full on her upturned face, she was almost the Maggie of old, sleek-haired and smooth-skinned, dark and vivid, a lustrous sun-warmed creature from another land.

Hearing nothing, she turned her ravaged face back to mine and sucked in another lungful of smoke. I must have let the concern show in my face because, catching my eye, her expression flickered with understanding, she turned the cigarette round and regarded the end with mild curiosity before reaching for an ashtray and stubbing it out.

I asked, 'And Grace reported nothing unusual in the days before she disappeared? She didn't see anything, or hear anything out of the ordinary?'

Losing heart or energy, Maggie gave a weary shake of her head.

'And she didn't seem – I don't know – *different* in any way?'

A silence while Maggie appeared to gather her thoughts with difficulty. Finally she said, 'She was very busy with the festival.'

'The festival?'

'The music festival.'

'Oh. What's that? A local event?'

'Yes. Grace, she started it, with Anne Hampton. She had—' She broke off as a floorboard creaked above our heads. 'Charlie,' she whispered with pride.

I followed her glance upwards and when I looked back
Maggie's face was transformed by the same magical collusive
smile that she had kept for me and Will when we were children.
'I was about to wake him anyway,' she declared happily. 'I
won't be long.'

I tried to think how old the boy must be. Ten. No, more
like eleven. I wondered how much he'd been told about his
mother's disappearance.

On her way out, Maggie paused at the door. 'There is a
diary for you to look at.'

'A diary?'

'William left it out for you. On the desk in the drawing
room. The trip to London.'

The drawing room. It had been called the living room when
I'd first known it, but I could see how it had earned itself the
more exalted title. Magnificently decorated in lemon yellow
and pale blues, the walls were lined in what looked like silk
and hung with portraits and landscapes which I had never seen
before. The curtains – definitely silk – were looped open with
tasselled tie-backs and fell in heavy folds onto a pristine carpet.
The chintz sofas had puffy seats and a scattering of cushions,
while the side tables were sprinkled with sporting magazines
and a variety of small *objets d'art*. It was the sort of room
where you always feel that however clean your shoes might be
they are soiling the carpet.

There were a number of silver-framed photographs
arranged on a circular table, and two or three more on a
bookcase. I recognized the one of Will's father that had always
stood in this room, showing a smiling man with a flop of dark
hair over his forehead, pictured on a day so bright that his eyes
were largely in shadow. He had been killed in a car accident
when Will was four. I also recognized the picture of a young
Maggie, taken in the Italian garden of her youth. Next to it
was a studio portrait of an elegant fine-boned woman I took to
be Grace's mother, then a picture of Grace and Will sitting
rather formally in a window, on their engagement perhaps,

then a wedding picture in front of the church, Grace in a slim white dress, Will looking tall and rather tense in a morning suit. Then Will and Grace with Charlie as a baby. Then Charlie at five or six. Then Grace alone, a studio portrait.

I picked up this last picture. The portrait showed a flawless Grace at nineteen or twenty, smiling wistfully, a gentle lost expression in her eyes, stating herself meekly to the world. This was the Grace I remembered from twelve years ago. I had met her only twice, but both times I had been struck by the delicacy of her beauty, the fragility of her tiny almost childlike body, and the way she had smiled, with great sweetness, the corners of her mouth curved shyly upwards. My parents had been equally struck. I remembered my father describing her as 'an exquisite creature', while my mother had used the word 'glorious'. I hadn't known what word to use; Grace had fallen outside my experience. I had never come into contact with anyone who dressed so perfectly, whose hair, immaculate and shining, radiated such colour and light, who moved with such effortless poise. Grace in name, grace in spirit and movement, someone who made the whole business of being feminine seem like a rare foreign language whose grammar and vocabulary was beyond my grasp. I had just sat my finals then and was preparing to leave on a Zoological Society field trip to Belize. I had an ugly short haircut and practical clothes and a scrubbed face and, after three years on a student diet of pasta and curries, was still eight pounds over my target weight. Grace made me feel as though I had come from an alien planet.

Grace's diary was lying on the flap of an antique bureau in the corner of the room. I approached it with mixed feelings. During my years as a lawyer I had seen into many people's lives, had heard many of their most intimate and harrowing secrets, but until now it had been strictly professional. This was different, this was almost family, and it was hard to approach the examination of Grace's life without a sense of intrusion.

The diary was a large desk journal with two pages to a

week. It had been left open at the week of Grace's disappearance. Before examining this, I went back through the diary to its earliest pages at the beginning of December, to get some feel for the pattern of Grace's life. Each day had three or four neat entries, with times and either initials or surnames, often with descriptions like 'electrician', 'Aga man'. The telephone numbers of the tradespeople were entered next to their names in a meticulous hand. The people shown only by their initials were those she seemed to meet regularly. Many of these entries were carefully annotated with reminders such as 'Take printer's estimate' or 'NB: *Times* article'. On most days she had also listed the people she needed to phone, usually five or six. The overall impression was one of great neatness and efficiency.

Many of the appointments were with AH, whom I took to be Anne Hampton, the joint organizer of the music festival, but there were at least two other people Grace met regularly, marked only by the initials BG and SM, and I noted these down. In late December Grace had had a meeting with someone whose initials leapt out at me because they matched my brother's: EW. Yet I couldn't imagine what festival business Grace would have had to discuss with Edward, a confirmed philistine and proud of it. The initials could have been a coincidence.

On one or two evenings a week Grace and Will dined out, and on at least two occasions in January they'd held dinner parties for eight or ten people. Grace had recorded the guests' names and what she had given them to eat – meals which I, as a culinary dimwit, would only have attempted in a fit of insanity. One was a four-course dinner with wild mushroom salad, beef *en croûte*, cheese and two complicated puddings. Weekends were even more social, it seemed, with drinks parties at midday or six thirty, and regular Sunday lunches.

I recognized quite a few of the names in Will and Grace's circle: members of families I had known as a child, local notables and former patients of my father. There was a sprinkling of professionals, including a doctor from the neighbouring practice, plus an occasional local artist and writer. I noticed that Will and Grace had taken drinks before Christmas with a prominent landowner, and then, just after New Year, with the local earl at his Palladian mansion a few miles along the coast. These were people who were notoriously reluctant to move outside their own exalted circles, and I could only think that Grace had lured them over to talk about the festival.

Between the start of the diary at the beginning of December and her disappearance, Grace had made six visits to London, three in December, two in January, and one in early February. On the first five occasions she had taken a train from King's Lynn at eight thirty-five in the morning and arrived at King's Cross at ten sixteen in time for an eleven o'clock appointment with her dentist in Wimpole Street. The first December visit showed no other entries for the day, and gave no indication of the train she had taken back. On four subsequent dates, however, she had gone from the dentist's to a restaurant called La Brasserie, but the companion or companions she had met there at twelve thirty were not identified either by name or initials. Later in the afternoon she had gone shopping – the shops were carefully listed, places like Harvey Nichols and Peter Jones – before catching the four forty-five train home.

On 5 February she'd taken a later train and gone straight to 'lunch' – the restaurant unidentified. The afternoon had no entries except 'Hat'.

I moved on ten days to the beginning of the week when Grace had disappeared. There was nothing unusual in her entries. She had gone to a supermarket on the Monday and intended to make eight telephone calls to firms and trades-people, as well as to AH and BG. On Tuesday she had met AH and BG, simultaneously this time, and two tradespeople had been due to call: someone to mend the gutter, and an oil delivery. On the Wednesday at two in the afternoon there had been a meeting with – the initials jumped out at me again – EW. I couldn't imagine why Grace should have needed to meet my brother, but if this EW was indeed Edward then it occurred

to me that he might have been one of the last people to see her
– I caught myself thinking *alive* and amended it to: before she
disappeared.

Grace had planned to go to London on the Thursday,
taking the usual eight thirty-five train from King's Lynn for yet
another appointment with her Wimpole Street dentist at eleven.
At twelve thirty she'd had another lunch appointment at the
Brasserie, again with person or persons unnamed. After that
was written: *5.00 Mother*, and below that an entry which had
been crossed through with a single line: *6.30 AWP*, with an
address near Regent's Park. There was no indication of which
train she had intended to take home.

I copied these details, such as they were, into my notebook,
before going back through the diary to see if I had missed an
earlier reference to the 'AWP' in the cancelled six thirty
appointment, but there was nothing. A search through the
weeks ahead was equally unproductive, though I saw that the
music festival was due to start on 2 June and last three days,
and that the preceding weeks were packed with appointments
and memos regarding marquees, caterers, flowers and sponsors.

I closed the diary with the feeling that whatever else may
have happened to Grace it was unlikely to be suicide. Her life
was too full, too wrapped up in events of her own creation to
allow time for introspection. The unremitting neatness of her
handwriting suggested confidence and optimism, while her
impeccable planning was the work of someone in effortless
control of her life.

Her bureau was a fine antique, Georgian or Queen Anne,
with two ranks of pigeonholes, filled with the stuff of her
existence: papers, letters, cheque books, leaflets, brochures,
notebooks. I would have liked to go through the correspondence and maybe some of the cheque books too, but didn't feel
I could do so without permission. An address book was
different, however; an address book was no more private than
a diary. I glanced into a small notebook – it contained a
collection of proverbs and sayings, copied out in Grace's hand

– and had moved on to a small leather-bound book – this had a list of birthdays – when I was distracted by footsteps on the stairs and a child's piping voice answered by Maggie's low murmur. Then Maggie called, 'Would you like some breakfast, Alex?'

When I went into the kitchen the boy was already eating. To my inexperienced eye he appeared older than eleven, more like twelve or thirteen, certainly closer to adolescence than childhood. In looks he was all Grace, so blond as to be almost white-haired, with the same finely drawn features. Only his eyes were different, paler or clearer, more grey than blue. He gave me a surreptitious glance before returning to his cereal, which he spooned into his mouth with concentration.

Maggie said, 'Charlie, this is Alex.' When he didn't respond, she touched his hand, 'Charlie – say hello.'

He looked at his grandmother, as though for a reprieve, before offering a brief glance in my direction. 'Hello.'

Maggie grinned at me. 'Always hungry at breakfast time.' And she gave a rather forced laugh, as if to remind me of the need for a light-hearted mood.

Taking my cue, I smiled, 'It's been a long time since I sat down to breakfast in this house, Maggie.'

'Ha!' she declared. 'I used to make good big breakfasts in those days, didn't I?' She had dressed in a long sweater and trousers, in matching dark burgundy, and pulled her hair into a coil at the back of her head. There was a trace of lipstick on her mouth, but far from lifting her colour it only seemed to accentuate the dullness of her skin. 'I used to fry ham and eggs in those days, ha? Before we stopped eating these bad things that we liked so much. And me, who loves to eat what I want!' This last remark was made as much to Charlie as to me, and, flashing a glance in my direction to signal what was clearly a set-piece, Maggie prompted the child, 'Ha, Charlie? Granny likes her food, doesn't she? Ha? Doesn't she?'

Charlie's spoon paused, he glanced at Maggie in cold dread, willing her not to go ahead.

'Hey, Charlie,' Maggie urged in a softer voice, 'what do I like? Ha?'

The boy looked for escape and, finding none, recounted unhappily, 'Pasta.'

Maggie pressed her hands together with delight. 'And why do I like pasta?'

He stared at the table. He counted himself too grown up for this childish game.

'Why does Granny like pasta?' Maggie repeated even more brightly than before.

'Get more on your plate.'

Maggie threw back her head and laughed. 'We have competitions to see who can get most pasta on their plate, don't we, Charlie? And Charlie wins *always*. He builds *castles*!' She made a show of clapping her hands high in front of her, as an Italian opera-goer might applaud a brilliant aria. 'Bravo!' she cried. 'Bravo, *caro mio*!'

Charlie's mouth twitched slightly. Taking it as a smile, Maggie gave an exclamation of affection and, bending over the table, took his face in her hands and kissed him repeatedly on the forehead. When she pulled back, Charlie's face had taken on a weary, troubled expression.

Maggie began to chatter about the art class that Charlie was going to in a few minutes. As she talked Charlie finished his cereal, put his spoon down and stared out of the window.

I asked, 'You enjoy art, then, Charlie?'

He gave what was probably a nod.

'What sort of things do you do there? Painting? Drawing?'

His eyes fixed determinedly on the table.

'I always liked clay modelling the best.'

A small spark of interest.

'Making shapes. Getting mucky.'

Unexpectedly he volunteered, 'We make pots.'

'Ah!' I found myself sounding a little too bright, like Maggie. 'Do you make them with a wheel or by hand?'

He dropped his eyes. 'Both.'

'More skill by hand. And wheels can be tricky. The first time I tried a wheel, I made a mess of it. Got out of control. Lumps and bumps all over the place. And then the top of the pot flew off. Landed on someone's foot.'

He examined my face to see if I was serious.

'It only does that if you squeeze it really *really* hard.'

He thought about this. 'Are you meant to squeeze it?'

'No! It's strictly forbidden!'

I was rewarded with a faint smile, and for a brief instant he became a child again, living in the moment.

'Have you got a pot I can see?'

Maggie said, 'Where's that lovely green one?' Turning to look along the shelves, she missed the sudden tension that shot through Charlie's body. 'Where is it, Charlie?' She glanced back and caught his expression. 'Gone?' she said hastily, then with realization: 'Oh . . . broken?'

Charlie's lips tightened.

'Oh, Charlie, you can make another. I insist you make another! Just for *me*. Yes?'

Charlie's face cleared, and the tension passed.

'Time to go!' Maggie cried, clapping her hands like a schoolmarm. 'Come on, young man!' She shooed him towards the door with sweeping movements of both hands. 'Coats! Hats!' As Charlie climbed dutifully to his feet and left the room, Maggie explained, 'I drive him to a neighbour who will take him to the class.' Taking a last gulp of coffee, she said in a voice that had lost all its false cheer, 'If you feel like walking, you might find Will. I can't tell you where he is. But on the marshes somewhere, or the meadows. He walks a different place every day, you understand. He covers each part, to make sure . . .' She threw up a hand that was suddenly full of anger.

'I'll go and look for him.'

Pausing on her way to the door, she said with agitation, 'I wish they would get on and find her, Alex. I wish it was over. You understand this? I wish they would find whatever there is to find and be finished with it. This waiting, this hoping – it is killing Will, *killing* him. He is like some creature that has been run down and hurt, he must be put out of his agony. I wish . . .' But dissatisfied with this thought, she abandoned it. 'And Charlie.' Drawing closer again, she lowered her voice. 'It is terrible for him, Alex. He thinks somehow he is responsible for his mama going away. You understand – *this* is how children think. When something goes wrong, they think somehow that they could have stopped it.'

'He's been told she's missing?'

'He knows she's gone away. *Gone away* – what does this mean to a child? It means that she has left him. Nothing else! Nothing, Alex! Children, they only understand that they have been *abandoned*. And he thinks, somehow it is his fault.' She made a fierce exclamation of despair. 'No, no! Better they find her soon. Even if it is bad.' She gave me a look of sudden doubt, as if this had sounded harsher than she had intended. 'You understand this, Alex?'

'I understand that not knowing is almost the worst thing of all. But don't give up hope, Maggie. She could be alive.'

Maggie's face emptied, her expression told me that I had understood nothing of the importance of instinct in these matters.

As soon as Maggie had driven Charlie away I took some walking shoes from the car, wrapped a woollen scarf around my head and went down to the water. No sight of Will, though this didn't prevent my heart beating high in my chest, my nerves tautening.

The morning was the colour of pewter. The marshes seemed very wide, almost as broad as the sky itself, which stretched in bands of light to the edges of the visible world. A wind had sprung up from the sea, an ice-wind that promised colder things to come. The tide was trickling in and the creeks and riverlets that criss-crossed the salt-marshes in silvery cords glimmered with chill light. To a stranger the marsh might seem bleak, a sombre expanse of flatland, but to me it contained all the life and colour of my childhood. I saw the myriad migrant birds which took refuge there each winter, and the skylarks which camouflaged their nests in spring, and the carpets of sea-lavender and sea-campion waiting for summer, and the canny uncatchable fish which flitted through the dark creeks.

Striking out eastward along the bank that followed the edge of the salt-marshes, I made for the wide embankment that stretched out towards the dunes, marking the start of the fresh-water lands. I met two sturdy ramblers with rucksacks and steaming breath, then no one. The bank snaked around a bend until, set back from the path on low-lying land, five cottages came into view, a huddle of four known as the Salterns, then, some thirty yards on, another called Reed Cottage, where Maggie had lived since leaving Marsh House.

In 1953 there had been a terrible disaster, when a northerly storm of previously unimaginable force, well past the hurricane mark, had funnelled the waves into this corner of the North Sea on top of a high tide, creating a massive surge which had inundated miles of coast and cost hundreds of lives. At the height of the flood it was said that there had been nothing to see of these cottages but their roofs.

This disaster had happened some ten years before I was born, but it had reverberated through my childhood, a brutal and revered thread to our history, a constant reminder to us of the power of the sea and the possibilities for luck and misfortune.

There was another flood when I was sixteen. The storm wasn't as bad as the one in '53, but it was bad enough to seek out two weak spots in the dunes off Deepwell, to punch holes in them in the night and send a wall of water across the marshes. The sea had poured over the grass-covered bank I was walking along now and sought out the five cottages once more, flooding them to a height of three feet. I knew it was three feet because Will and I had helped to carry the cottagers' possessions to the upper rooms, and the two of us had measured the tidemark on the wall when the last of the mud and silt had dribbled away.

After these catastrophes, the most important sea-defences –
those protecting homes and villages – had been raised and fortified, but wide tracts of reclaimed land and fresh-water marsh
had been abandoned to the tide and the wildlife organizations
for ever. The first storm had deprived Will's grandfather of a
quarter of his marshland grazing, while the second flood had
reduced the size of the tenancy held in trust for Will by almost
a fifth again. The landowner had looked into the possibility of
saving the land but the cost was prohibitive. It wasn't just the
expense of rebuilding the defences and the redraining of the
meadows, it was the lack of yield for up to three years while
the rain cleansed the earth of the corrosive brine. I knew this
because the landowner had been my aunt Nella, who, vague
though she was in many ways, had always been fiercely
protective of the land and felt its loss keenly.

Some hundred yards beyond Reed Cottage was a major
sea-defence built by indomitable optimists two centuries earlier
to protect a large swathe of drained meadowland, an embankment which had proved high and wide enough to withstand
the worst of both floods. The path divided here: one path
followed the ridge of the embankment as it ran in a straight
line towards the dunes and the sea half a mile away, while the
other continued along the bank at the edge of the land that
rose towards the coast road. I could see no one on either path,
nor on the further reaches of the flatlands, though without
binoculars it was hard to be sure.

I decided to take the embankment path because it was
higher and I would be able to see further from there. Setting
off, the reclaimed land lay to my right: first an area of brackish
marsh then an expanse of fresh-water reed-beds, and beyond
that, land that was farmed by Will, most of it used for grazing,
with one distant rectangle ploughed for spring planting.

After fifty yards I came to a sluice, and wondered if this
was the one that had needed so much of Will's attention.
Resembling a squat guillotine, it sat above a brick-walled canal,
its heavy wooden frame supporting a metal gate raised and

lowered by means of a vertical screw-threaded shaft and worm gear. There was no sign of any damage. Rather the opposite: the mechanism was well greased, the metal of the gate, what I could see of it, good and solid. The gate was fully lowered, the operating handle removed, as was the custom.

I walked on, though not without the growing feeling that I had made a mistake in coming this way. At one point a match-like figure appeared on the switchback of dunes far away to the east, only to be joined by three more hikers, backs ridged by rucksacks. After another ten minutes without another soul in sight I was almost ready to give up. The salt-creeks to my left were cut deeply into the mud and scoured regularly by the tides and I caught myself thinking: No possibility of a body there. The meadowland to my right was flat and open, the rather muddy grassland broken only by an occasional stand of reeds or a line of taller vegetation which marked a drainage ditch or fresh-water brook.

I paused regularly to make a complete sweep of the horizon but saw only redshank and a delta of pink-foot geese flying inland to raid the winter wheat. After half a mile I reached the second and last sluice, as well greased and sturdy as the first. With only the dunes and sea ahead, I finally made the decision to turn back. I retraced my steps for a short distance then, changing course, scrambled down the bank and set off across the meadows at an angle that would take me back to the coastal path a mile or so from the village.

The ground was soft and wet underfoot, as though there had been persistent and heavy rain, and at one point I had to make a wide detour to avoid a particularly boggy patch. Reaching a drainage ditch, I found my way to a crossing point – two planks of wood retained by stakes – but at the next ditch either I had forgotten where to find the planks or they had been moved, and I was reduced to leaping the water at a narrow point and landing in a squelch of heavy mud.

Water seeped into my shoes, I could see more boggy ground ahead and, cutting my losses, abandoning the diagonal route, I headed straight for higher ground. I was negotiating another mire when I became aware of a figure standing on the far edge of the meadows. My heart leapt painfully. He was a long way off but I could see the height of him, and the pale disc of his face as he looked towards me, and the frame of his dark hair. He was motionless for a while, then he began to lope slowly along the path as if to cut me off. Picking up speed, he ran raggedly, stumbling a little as he kept looking my way, before veering down onto the meadow and heading towards me.

I stopped and waved, trying to suppress the memory of the last time Will had run towards me like this, when I had been sixteen and light-headed with love.

He was quite close before he recognized me. Then, with a cry of realization, he came to an abrupt halt and threw his head back, as if in disbelief.

I continued uncertainly towards him.

'God,' he panted as I got closer, 'I thought for a moment . . . God.' His face contorted into a harsh grimace. 'I thought . . .' But he was beyond words and, while he regained his breath and some measure of self-control, he turned away from me and shook his head.

When he finally turned back, he was still white-faced. 'God, Alex, you looked just like – just like Grace, for heaven's sake.'

I stammered, 'Grace?'

'God,' he muttered again, running a savage hand over the top of his head and down his face. 'God.'

'I'm sorry. I'm really sorry.' I couldn't imagine how he could have mistaken me for Grace, we looked so utterly different.

We stood silently for a moment before Will, with a last shake of his head, faced me properly. 'It's good of you to come,' he said.

'I'm glad to help in any way I can.' The well-used expression sounded trite in my ears.

He smiled suddenly and, reaching out, pulled me into an all-enveloping hug. The gesture was so intense, so spontaneous that the emotion surged into my throat, I couldn't breathe and for a moment I clung to him, overcome by a rush of compassion and feeling, not only for him and everything he was going through, but also, in another part of my heart, for myself.

He pulled back and kissed me firmly on both cheeks, Italian style. Holding me at arm's length, he said, 'You look well, Alex.'

Somehow I managed a wide smile, a short laugh. 'Oh, I'm okay.'

He dropped his hands. 'How long is it?'

'Twelve years, I think.'

'*Twelve*,' he murmured. 'God.'

The time had been good to him, better than to me. There were lines around his eyes and beside his mouth and between his eyebrows where he had frowned against the light, but he still had the vivid dark eyes, the thick unruly hair of the corsair. Only his skin, denied the southern sun, seemed too white, so that it accentuated the dark stubble on his cheeks and the strain in his eyes.

We began to walk slowly in the direction of the village.

'You've seen Maggie?' he said.

'She told me that the police didn't seem to be making much progress.'

'I'd say that about sums it up at the moment!' he declared with a trace of bitterness.

'What are they doing exactly, Will? What lines are they following?'

'You may well ask! That's the one thing they don't seem to tell me.'

'But why on earth not? What reason?'

'Oh, they don't give reasons.'

'But that's ridiculous!' I exclaimed. My vehemence surprised him, and he shot me a quick glance.

We reached a patch of mire. Negotiating my way across the more solid tussocks, I said, 'They should always tell you. That's one of their main duties, to keep the family informed. I can get

on to them for you, get them to tell us what they're doing, find
out if they've covered everything.'

He looked doubtful. 'Well . . .'

'Believe me, in cases like this it pays to put steady pressure
on the police, it keeps them on the ball. But I can take care of
that for you, give you one less thing to worry about.'

He had begun to shake his head long before I'd finished.
'No. You see, I'm *glad* to speak to the police. At least I feel I'm
doing something that way. No – it's just the London end of
things . . . if you would. I thought you might be able to help
with that.'

Evidently I had sold myself badly, or too hard. 'If that's
what you want. Of course. I'll get someone on to it straight
away.'

He stopped and turned his gaze on to me. His eyes were
achingly familiar and I felt a fresh lurch of emotion.

'You can do that?'

'We have an ex-inspector who does our inquiry work. He's
very thorough, very professional.'

Accepting this, relaxing a little, Will immediately grew tense
again, as if poised on the edge of some question too difficult to
ask.

I said, 'I looked through Grace's diary.'

'You did? You can see, then,' he argued with sudden vigour,
'that she could easily have gone to London that day.'

I saw only that I would have to go cautiously if I wasn't to
destroy his hopes too unkindly. I asked, in a neutral tone, 'Do
the police know if she got as far as London?'

'No.' He plunged into a momentary gloom. Watching this
rapid transformation, I remembered the way his face had
always done this, reflected each passing thought like a mirror
to his mind.

'But, then, they haven't looked properly,' he retorted,
regaining his fire, 'so it's not surprising, is it? They haven't
checked some of the most obvious places.'

'Such as?'

'Well—' He struggled with this. 'I don't know – shops, hairdressers.'

I went more carefully still. 'What about getting to the station? Her car's still at the house, I gather.'

'She could have got a lift.'

'A lift. You mean, with a friend?'

'It's possible! She might have got a lift all the way to London.'

'Has anyone come forward to say they drove her?'

'No. But, then, why should they?' Turning on his heel, he started off again at a brisker pace.

I tried to work out what, if anything, I was meant to glean from this remark. Sometimes anxiety made people angry, and anger made them irrational, and it wasn't always possible to know how much weight to give to their wilder statements.

Marching briskly to keep up, I said, 'Do you have any thoughts on what might – or could – have happened to Grace?'

He threw me a desperate look. 'Thoughts? I have no *thoughts*! None!'

'But what makes you think someone might have given Grace a lift without coming forward? Have you a particular reason to think that?'

'No! No reason.' He stopped once more. I noticed his eyes again, I saw the frustration in them, and the pain. 'But every possibility should be looked *into*, surely. *Investigated*. Otherwise . . .' He threw up an outspread palm in a gesture that was almost pure Maggie. 'What I can't stand is all this waiting around doing nothing. This waiting for . . . *what*? Tell me – *what*?' He thrust his hand in his pocket. 'The London thing . . . She was planning to go there, that's all. It doesn't seem unreasonable to suppose she might have arrived. That's all!' He glared at me, daring me to disagree, yet at the same time half expecting me to.

'She didn't turn up to any of her appointments?'

'But something might have happened as soon as she got there. She might have changed her mind and gone somewhere else.' His voice cracked. 'I don't know!'

'Well,' I offered calmly, 'it seems to me that, first and foremost, you need to find out what the police have done so far, then take it on from there.'

The exasperation fell away, his expression softened a little. We trudged on at a companionable pace.

I said, 'Maggie told me you had trouble with the sluices on the Wednesday night.'

He didn't answer immediately, and when he did his tone was vague. 'Trouble? One of the gates was leaking, yes.'

'And you had to stay up all night, she said?'

'Well . . . Some of it.'

'And you didn't get home at all that night?'

'It was easier to grab some sleep on Maggie's sofa. I didn't get back till breakfast time.'

'Would Grace—' I stopped abruptly, aware that I was ploughing on relentlessly, as though Will were one of my regular clients born and raised on police interviews. 'I'm sorry – you don't mind my asking all this?'

'No. Go ahead.'

'It'll help me to get the full picture—'

'I understand.'

'It's essential with disappearances—'

He gave me a curious look. 'It's all right, Alex. Ask whatever you like!'

Feeling I had let myself down in some way, I nodded rapidly and glanced away. 'Okay . . .' I put on my professional voice, quiet and low and detached, the one I had acquired in the early days to impress people who had thought I was too young and inexperienced. 'Would Grace have locked the house while you were out that night?'

'I always told her to. But she might have left the kitchen door open. We often did.'

'Was it open when you got back in the morning?'

A slight hesitation. 'Yes.'

'But you're saying there wasn't anything unusual in that?'

'No.'

'And Grace wasn't there?'

'I thought she'd gone to catch her train.'

'And Charlie? He was on his own, was he, when you got back?'

'No, no. He was with Mum. He was always going to be with Maggie that night.'

'Any particular reason?'

'Because Grace was leaving so early in the morning. And because Charlie always goes to stay with Mum at least once a week.'

'I see. So once you'd gone out to mend the sluice that evening, Grace was alone in the house?'

'No.' He cancelled this with a gesture. 'What I mean is, I don't know. I don't know if she was there. You see, I didn't get back to the house at all that day,' he explained in the tone of someone going over a much-repeated story. 'I went into Norwich in the morning to do some business. I was there all day. I was on my way back home when Mum called me in the car and told me about the sluice. I drove straight there. I never went home at all.'

'What time did you get there, to the sluice?'

He searched a rapidly tiring brain. 'About six thirty, I suppose.'

'Dark, then?' I murmured.

He shrugged, 'Yes.'

'So who was the last person to see Grace before she disappeared?'

'We don't know.' His voice rose again in agitation. 'Well, the police aren't *sure*, which amounts to the same thing. After Charlie got back from school Grace took him over to Mum's—'

'She drove?'

'Yes. She stayed for a while, then drove back home.'

'At what time?'

'About four, I think.'

'So after Maggie, no one else seems to have seen her?'

'Well, no one so *far*. But someone might well have seen her driving back or parking the car or going into the house. Or . . .'

I thought he was being rather optimistic. Marsh House stood alone at the end of the quay some distance from the nearest house. It was perfectly possible that she had returned home – or travelled elsewhere – unseen.

We reached the edge of the meadows and the promise of drier ground.

'Well, it seems to me that there are at least three areas worth looking into,' I announced, following close behind Will as he advanced up the slope in long strides. 'The first is to check out the London end, which I'll arrange. The second is to make sure that no local information has been missed – make sure the police have made sufficient house-to-house enquiries, asked the neighbours if they saw anything odd, that sort of thing. Sometimes neighbours don't realize the value of what they've seen, don't think of telling anyone about it until they're actually asked. The third . . .' Will, listening hard, slowed down and I almost bumped into him. '. . . is to decide if the police search was adequate, to make sure they haven't missed any obvious places that Grace might have gone to or' – it had to be said – 'been taken to. I would add a fourth area – forensic testing, fingerprints and so on – but if it wasn't done almost immediately . . .'

'It wasn't,' he reported darkly.

'And you didn't notice anything when you got back that morning – or since? Tyre marks, smears of dirt, footprints, things like that?'

'No!'

The agitation had come back into his face and I added hastily, 'It was only a thought. It's very rare to find anything like that.'

Reaching the path, Will paused. 'Look . . . perhaps it might be best if you did go and talk to the police,' he said awkwardly. 'You know which questions to ask.'

I said, in a rush, 'Of course.'

'I always get so angry when I see them! I feel they're being so bloody *useless*! And the way they look at me, Alex! I know what they're thinking – they make it so bloody obvious!' He gave a short bitter laugh before shooting me a quick glance to see if I could guess what was coming. 'They think I'm responsible! They think I must have done away with her.'

'They're bound to think that.'

He wasn't quite sure how to take this remark.

'The great majority of disappearances are linked to family situations,' I explained. 'To stress or money worries. Or violence within the family. It's a statistic that gets drummed into the police, I'm afraid. They're apt to get tunnel vision.'

He gave a long ragged sigh which was almost a laugh. 'So I shouldn't take it personally?'

'Absolutely not.'

'You're sure about that?'

But he wasn't really expecting an answer and, walking on, we fell into step. Aware of his eyes on me, I looked across at him.

He said, in a rough voice, 'Glad you're here, Alex.'

'Me too.' And I reached for his hand and squeezed it.

Chapter Three

'THE FESTIVAL – all to do with the music festival.' Will turned a page of the diary and waved a hand at various entries. 'Anne Hampton, the doctor's wife – she was running the thing with Grace. And BG is Beth Gregson. She does the secretarial work, types the letters.'

'And SM?' I asked, wishing that Will hadn't insisted on my taking Grace's chair at the bureau, hadn't perched himself on the arm of a nearby sofa so that he was forced to lean awkwardly across the flap of the desk.

'That's the accounts man, umm . . . Stephen . . .' He pressed his fingertips against his eyelids in an effort of memory. 'For heaven's sake . . . Stephen . . . Stephen . . . *Makim*. That's it – *Makim*.'

I wrote the name down. 'All these people are local?'

His doubt finally erupted in a violent shrug. 'Yes. But they're friends, Alex. *Friends*.'

'Of course. I was only trying to establish if Grace had met anyone recently she *didn't* know well.'

He was persuaded, but only just. 'There's nobody here she wouldn't have known, except for a few suppliers and tradesmen.' Seeing from my expression that I was ruling nothing out, he looked incredulous, then thoughtful, until, reluctantly coming round to the idea at last, he leafed back through the pages. 'Okay,' he said, settling down to the task. 'Goddards . . . they're the marquee people. I think so, anyway. And . . .' He went to the next entry. 'These are the caterers. And Lamb, he's the plumber . . .'

I was listening and making notes, but also watching him quietly. On the marsh he had seemed almost like another person, the anxiety in him and the frustration, the way his emotions had flown across his face. I had been thrown, too, by the inadequacies of my memory, the way it had managed to leave out whole aspects of him, had lost the subtleties and idiosyncrasies of his character, the details of his face. Yet gradually the person sitting beside me began to blend into my recollections of him. The gestures, the expressive hands, the long fingers that drew sudden patterns in the air. The line of his eyebrows, the wide well-shaped mouth, the distinctive voice; and the dark hair – always the hair – thick and wavy and rather wild. Recognizing these things, he seemed both familiar and extraordinarily new to me, a faded memory repainted in bright colours.

In the diary he had reached the Wednesday before Grace disappeared and a service call from the oil delivery man. 'That's it,' he said and glanced up so quickly that he caught me staring at him.

'Well, I'll check them all out, just to be sure,' I said, looking down at my notes.

'Even virtual strangers?'

'*Especially* virtual strangers, perhaps.'

His mouth tightened.

I referred back to the diary. 'There's an EW mentioned somewhere. At two p.m. Who's that?'

He raised an eyebrow, faintly surprised and decidedly cool. 'Your brother.'

'Oh.' I turned this into a question with a lift of my hand.

'You didn't know? He's lending Wickham Lodge for the festival.'

'Good God.'

'Grace felt it was the ideal place for it.' Something in Will's tone suggested that he himself hadn't been quite so enthusiastic about the idea. 'Not too grand,' he recounted as if quoting from a brochure, 'not bound up in National Trust regulations like the stately homes, but big enough for a decent marquee and a field for car parking.'

'I had no idea. Edward never tells me anything.'

'It was settled months ago.' He returned to the diary. 'That's it. I don't think there's anybody else in here.'

We moved on to Grace's planned trip to London, and Will became animated again.

'The dentist's called Bennett. I've got his number in the kitchen. Hang on.' He padded across the pristine expanse of carpet in thick socks – he had left his boots at the back door – and returned a few moments later with a wide green leather-bound book with alphabet indentations cut into the pages. 'Bennett.' Settling on the sofa arm once more, he thumbed open a page and ran his eye down the list. 'Here.' He passed the book to me so that I could copy the number. 'I called him, of course, first thing on Friday.'

'And Grace hadn't turned up for her appointment?'

'No.'

'You tried the restaurant as well? The Brasserie?'

'Yes, but there was no reservation in Grace's name.'

'You don't know who she was having lunch with?'

He lifted a casual shoulder. 'A friend ... A potential sponsor. She still had seven thousand pounds to raise. It was hard work.'

The telephone rang. Scooping up the receiver, Will listened for a brief moment before informing the enquirer that there was no news and briskly ringing off. 'I wouldn't bother to answer the damn thing at all,' he said, banging the phone back on the hook, 'except I don't want to miss the police.'

'How often do they call?'

'Oh, twice a day. But it's usually this DC Barbara Smith. She's pleasant enough, but *junior*.'

'And the officer in charge?'

'Ramsey? He just turns up now and again. Though not for a while now. A day or so.'

I wondered if Ramsey, far from treating the disappearance

as a possible fatality, had relegated it to a non-vulnerable missing person (matrimonial). It was a sub-category of missing person which never appeared on any official form but which guaranteed a case low priority. Yet, even as I considered this, I dismissed it again. The police could hardly ignore the fact that Grace had taken no clothes or money. Was Ramsey just being secretive, then? Or busy following leads elsewhere?

I said, 'What about friends in London? You checked with them?'

'Yup.'

'None of them was due to lunch with Grace on Thursday?'

'Seems not.'

'And had any of them lunched with her in recent months?'

He looked at me with sudden intensity. 'Didn't ask that.'

'When you spoke to the Brasserie did you happen to ask them if anyone had failed to show up for lunch that day? Anyone with a reservation?'

He grimaced at missing such an obvious question. 'Didn't ask that either.'

'We can find out easily enough.' I looked at the five o'clock entry. 'Now, Grace's mother . . .'

'Veronica.' His eyes flashed.

'Did she hear from Grace that day?'

'No.'

'Has she got any idea what might have happened?'

'None. But then she . . .' For no obvious reason he lost momentum and frowned into the distance.

I left it a moment before asking, 'Was there any particular reason that Grace was going to see her, do you know?'

'Sorry?' He tore himself away from whatever was absorbing him. 'Reason? Umm . . . No . . . Nothing special. She hadn't seen Veronica for some time, that was all. And she felt she should.'

'You wouldn't mind if I went and talked to Veronica?'

He stared at me intensely again, and his eyes were very dark. 'I don't know. I'd have to speak to her first.'

'Of course.'

'She can be' – he cast around for a diplomatic word – '*difficult*. She's apt to harp on about things which don't have a great deal to do with whatever you're talking about. She has her favourite bugbears. One of which' – his abrupt smile was ironic and devoid of humour – 'is *me*. She thinks that Grace married beneath her.'

'Ah,' I murmured sympathetically. 'But of course she wouldn't be the first parent to think that.'

'But most parents wouldn't take every opportunity to say so! She's even trying to blame me for what's happened. You know – why wasn't I here for Grace, why did I leave her alone in the house, all that sort of stuff.'

'People do that when they're frightened – look for someone to blame.'

'Oh, she's not just *looking*.' And he rolled his eyes expressively, though more in weary disbelief than rancour.

I took us back to the diary, to the crossed-out entry with the address near Regent's Park. 'And this cancelled appointment? Who's AWP?'

The tension came back into his face. 'Don't know. The police say they've checked it out and are satisfied that this person can't help them with their enquiries.' He repeated dangerously, '*Can't help them with their enquiries*. What does that mean?' he added caustically. 'The person doesn't exist? Wasn't there? Went up in smoke?'

'They haven't told you the person's name?'

'Nope.'

'Well, we have the address, it shouldn't be difficult to find out. It would help to have a photograph, though, if you can spare one.'

He looked at me blankly.

'A photograph of Grace.'

'Of course. The police took . . . I'm not sure if . . .' Losing the thread, he put his hands over his face and dragged them down his cheeks, momentarily distorting his features. I wondered if he was getting any sleep, and whether he'd asked his doctor for anything in the way of a tranquillizer.

'No, I remember now . . .' He clasped a hand to his forehead, as though to clear his thoughts. 'They returned it. It's in the office. I'll get it out for you.'

'And may I take this?' I indicated the green leather address book.

'I'd like to say yes, but it's all I have.'

There was a moment of complete misunderstanding between us.

I placed my hand lightly on his arm and said with compassion, 'I'll return it safe and sound in a couple of days, I promise. I know how precious these things can be.'

Looking puzzled, he said, 'But I need it. I use it all the time.'

I withdrew my hand. 'It's not Grace's?'

'No, it belongs to the house. Grace had her own address book. Well, a sort of miniature Filofax.'

'I *see*. I thought . . .' I smiled briefly and awkwardly. 'May I have a look at Grace's book, then?'

He seemed puzzled again. 'But it's missing. With her handbag.'

I absorbed this slowly. 'I hadn't realized. I thought there was nothing missing.'

The bafflement lingered in his expression. 'I thought I'd told you about the handbag.'

'It doesn't matter. I know now.'

He pulled a face, as if this lapse of memory was both inexplicable and faintly alarming.

'She would have had a bit of money with her, then,' I murmured.

He nodded inattentively.

I picked up the large green address book. 'I'll copy what I need from this, if I may. It won't take long.'

Still looking rather dazed, he said, 'Would you like some coffee?' He attempted a smile, which only succeeded in tipping his mouth askew and making him look rather cross.

I smiled. 'I'm fine, thanks.'

He stood up and, thrusting his hands into his pockets, looked away towards the window. 'The worst thing is deciding what to tell Charlie.'

'I'm sure.'

'Maggie keeps telling him that his mother's just gone away for a while but I don't think he believes that for a minute. He's not stupid.'

'And you? What have you told him?'

A pause, or a hesitation. 'Nothing.'

'He hasn't asked?'

It was another moment before he answered. 'No.'

'Perhaps it'd be best to leave it there, then.'

He stared intently at the window. 'I don't know what to do, Alex. I don't know what to . . . *understand*.' It wasn't the word he wanted or intended, but I knew what he meant.

'The important thing is to make sure that everything possible is being done.'

'Yes.' He turned back. 'Yes.' His smile worked a little better this time, and it was difficult to meet his gaze without remembering the humour and ebullience that had always lain behind it in the past and the powerful affection he had stirred in me.

'One thing,' I said as he moved off. 'Was Grace planning to come back from London on that Thursday night?'

He paused at the door, his back to the window, his face in shadow. 'She wasn't absolutely sure.' His voice had deepened. 'If she missed the last train she was going to stay with her mother.'

When he'd gone I thought how simple it was to re-establish the basics of friendship, the easy communication, the sense of shared experience, but how difficult to take such a relationship into the realms of disclosure. To ask Will if Grace could have had friends he didn't know about, if he was aware of what she did when she was away from him – even to ask if she were happy – was to imply a measure of evasion, even deceit, in their relationship, and draw him into a defensive position where he might be tempted to offer less than the truth.

Before starting on the address book, I lifted the phone to try DI Ramsey. Sitting there at Grace's desk, her phone pressed to my ear, her diary in front of me, her presence suddenly seemed very strong. I remembered Will introducing me to her all those years ago. It was in the garden here at Marsh House, only yards from this room. We hadn't spoken for long, just a minute or two, but I could still see her with absolute clarity as she stood in front of me, a slender figure in a long summer dress, offering her thin white hand to me. She had listened to Will's introduction with a slightly quizzical expression, she had murmured some greeting. I knew she hadn't caught my name, I knew she had no idea who I was, but she smiled her famous smile anyway, lifting her mouth sweetly at the corners while dipping her head, so that she looked at you upwards, from under her brows, and you couldn't help noticing the blueness of her eyes. A moment later she turned to smile at the person next to me, it might even have been my father, and I noticed the way her eyes widened and sparkled with sudden laughter as if the two of them were enjoying some enormous private joke. I had stood there watching her, listening to her, not joining in, yet at the same time quite incapable of moving away. Then all other perceptions had been swept aside by the mention of a birthday. Someone was going to be twenty-one. I understood with a shock: *Grace* was going to be twenty-one. Even twelve years later I could remember the astonishment I had felt, and the stab of mortification. When Will had hit the age of pubs and parties and student holidays, I had suddenly become too young for him. The three years between us had become an apparently unbridgeable chasm. We had still gone for walks on the marshes, we had still talked, we had still been close – or so it had seemed to me – yet increasingly I had become the one to search him out. He had other friends for the evenings, for trips to the cinema, for skiing holidays in Austria.

Then just as the age gap had begun to narrow again, I had gone away to university and discovered junk food and insecurities and clothes that did me no favours. At twenty-two, finals over, confidence blooming, I had been packing up to come home when the news of Grace and Will's engagement had broken. Meeting Grace that day, finding her two years younger than me and infinitely more lovely, had proved altogether too much for my raw and tender heart, and I had slipped quickly away.

I closed the diary and put it on one side. I dialled Norwich CID. When I had first tried them on our return to the house I had been lobbed into the telephonic black hole peculiar to police stations everywhere, in which you are left connected to a ringing extension which neither answers nor returns your call to the switchboard. This time, however, I was put through to an extension that answered immediately. A chirpy female voice announced herself as DC Smith and confirmed that she was assigned to the Grace Dearden case.

I explained who I was and that I wanted to come in and talk to DI Ramsey that afternoon.

'I'm not sure anyone will be available,' she said.

Were they so busy? I wondered. Was the inquiry so far-reaching? I said, 'What, no one at all?'

'I'll have to check,' she said. 'Can I come back to you?'

I was getting a feeling here, and the feeling wasn't good. I gave her my mobile number and said I'd like to come in between two and four that afternoon, if that was at all possible.

Ringing off, the feeling intensified. After ten years as a crime solicitor I'd developed an instinct for the sort of regime under which a divisional CID operated. Within the Met there were happy stations and miserable ones, squads where you couldn't help suspecting that some of its officers were less than scrupulous and others where such a thought would never enter your head; CIDs where almost everyone seemed to have lost heart and to drift through the motions, and CIDs where they all drove themselves into the ground, trying to do their best under crime statistics and paperwork that rose at an equally depressing rate. It seemed to me that a CID where a detective sergeant couldn't invite me round without permission was not likely to be a very efficient or happy division.

I opened Grace's diary in mid-December and, with the help of the address book, started to make a list of the names, addresses and numbers of every person Grace had met by appointment over the intervening two months. Half-way through the January entries I was distracted by the sound of a knock at the front door and voices, Will's first, then a female's, which was high and rather piercing. The voices faded down the corridor towards the kitchen.

Finishing my notes, I closed the diary and took the address book back to the kitchen. The female voice reached me well before I saw its owner, a slender woman in a cream roll-neck sweater and jeans sitting at the kitchen table. Under the star-lights her heavy shoulder-length hair seemed startlingly yellow and her skin rather too pink, giving the effect of a doll. Maggie, sitting opposite this vivid creature, wearing one of her more unreadable expressions, appeared yet more grey. Will, if he had been there at all, had disappeared, and there was no sign of Charlie.

Maggie introduced Anne Hampton.

'Hello,' she cried, swivelling in her seat to offer me a firm hand and a wide smile topped by an exaggerated expression of sympathy and concern. 'Gather you're going to get things going. Thank *goodness*. High time.' She spoke in the spirited tones of the hockey field, with a little too much volume and reach. 'It's so awful, this lack of action. *Awful*.' She was about thirty-five with clear brown eyes and fine arched brows. Close up, the extraordinary yellowness of her hair looked entirely natural, and the overall effect would have been of prettiness if it hadn't been for the pink blotches that dappled her cheeks, as though from an allergy.

Maggie pushed a mug of coffee towards me as I sat down.

'I gather you're organizing the music festival with Grace,' I said to Anne Hampton.

'Oh, just helping, really. It's Grace's thing, you know. She's the brains. I'm just the brawn. Chasing up promises, pinning people down. The *dragon*.' She raised an eyebrow, not at all displeased with the epithet.

'It sounds quite an event.'

'Oh, *yes*. Grace had got—' She paused as Maggie pushed her chair back with a loud scrape.

'I have to do things,' Maggie announced, standing up. 'Thank you for coming, Anne.' And she fluttered the fingers of one hand as she passed by.

''Bye, Mrs Dearden.'

The term of address was strangely formal for such an informal person as Maggie, and I couldn't help thinking that Maggie must have wanted it to stay that way.

Anne continued to smile at the door for a moment after Maggie had closed it behind her. 'Honestly, what an *awful* thing this is,' she cried, turning her smile into a grimace of fellow feeling. 'I can't *bear* to think of poor Grace, of where she could be! Of what might have happened! And *Will*. It must be just *appalling* for him, don't you think? Just *dreadful*. So happy together. Such a fabulous couple. Honestly, life's ghastly sometimes, isn't it?'

'Sometimes.'

'I mean, she wouldn't have just *gone*. Not Grace. It's inconceivable. Something must have happened. I hate to say it, but something *awful*.'

'Well . . . Let's hope not,' I murmured, more for something to say than anything else.

'You're right,' she declared instantly, with sudden fervour, 'we must hope for the *best*, mustn't we? Yes, you're right! Yes!'

Maggie's coffee was delicious, and I drank it avidly. 'Presumably you've seen quite a bit of Grace in recent weeks. Did she seem ... different in any way? Did you notice anything unusual?'

'*Unusual?*' An expression of puzzlement came over her face while she tried to work out what I could mean by this. '*Unusual?* No. No ... Grace was the same as always. You know, calm and together. Organized. Always on time. Always prepared. Always *immaculate*. Never looking anything but absolutely *perfect*,' she cried, with open admiration. 'Don't know how she did it! Hard work, I suppose. And planning. Never managed it myself, not the meals *and* the shopping *and* getting the children in the right place at the right time. My children are always the ones to lose their shoes and start screaming just when they're late for school.' She rounded her eyes in mock exasperation. 'But Grace – she always had the whole thing organized. Never a moment's panic. I mean, *never*. But *unusual?*' she echoed, considering the idea once more. 'No, can't think of a thing. I mean, she didn't *say* anything. She certainly didn't *look* any different. She was terribly busy, of course. A little more *rushed* than usual, perhaps. I mean, not so much time to talk on the phone, and out a lot. But that was the festival. Trying to raise the sponsorship money. It was a bit of a slog.'

'She seemed happy?'

'Happy?' Anne Hampton's brows twitched with faint disapproval, as though in asking the question I had made a vaguely dishonourable suggestion. 'Absolutely. *Very* happy. She was the same as she always was, sweet and lovely and ...' She jigged her head from side to side as she searched the limits of her vocabulary. '... well, *divine*. I mean, just divine. Always a total sweetheart. Honestly, everyone loved her. *Everyone*. In the village, in the neighbourhood. Everyone she met, really.' She blinked back a gleam of tears. 'Actually—' She pushed her elbows further onto the table and, leaning her pink face towards me, said in a low confiding voice, 'Actually, I have wondered if ... well, *because* she was so gorgeous and lovely,

and everyone adoring her and all that . . . well, I do wonder if
some nutter mightn't have got a *thing* about her . . . Mightn't
have – you know.' Her look conveyed unmentionable
possibilities.

'A local person, you mean?'

'Well, a farm worker, a tramp, someone like that. You just
never know nowadays, do you? All these batty people watching
horrible videos.'

I made no comment on this. 'Apart from the festival, Grace
wasn't involved in anything that might have put her in the
public arena? I don't know – local politics, committees?'

'No. Nothing like that. No . . . Though we did get our
picture in the local rag last summer, when we announced the
festival. But *everyone* gets their picture in the local paper at
some time or another. It's not like making the pages of *Tatler*.'
And she gave a bark of a laugh before rearranging her
expression into something more serious. 'Why?'

I shrugged. 'No particular reason.'

'Ahh,' she cried, raising an index finger as if to admonish
me, 'what you mean is, was she anywhere where she might
have got noticed by a nutter? Was that it?' She examined my
face before rushing on to the next idea. 'Or doing something
that might have made her enemies? Well, I can tell you,' she
continued without drawing breath, 'that Grace had no enemies.
She *couldn't* make enemies. Just couldn't. She was always so
lovely to everyone, *whoever* they were. Dustmen to dukes – not
that we've got any dukes around here – but she could talk to
anyone, charm them completely. Oh, I don't mean charm them
in a *horrid* way, like *some* people one knows! No, she only had
to be herself, no more than that. Only had to be *divine*.' There
was admiration in her tone, and something like awe, as though
Grace had been as much an icon to Anne Hampton as a friend.

I drained my coffee. 'Well, thank you—'

But Anne Hampton touched a staying hand to my arm and
said with the urgency of someone who still has important
truths to impart, 'No, really, we went to see this rather

terrifying car dealer. Trying to get some money out of him. It must have been October or November – no, October. He was really very offhand when we walked in, almost rude in fact, and then he took one look at Grace and sort of began to melt, and went on melting until he was just a lovely money-producing person. That's what Grace called him!' She chuckled delightedly. 'A *lovely money-producing person*. By the end, he couldn't do enough for the festival. Thought it was the best thing that had ever happened to north Norfolk. Gave us a thousand pounds – well, it *was* only a Volvo dealership, but it was quite a lot to us, more than we'd hoped for anyway. And he promised us two cars for the week of the festival, to shepherd the musicians around. And it was all due to Grace. I'm just hopeless at the common touch – always have been – but Grace . . .' She paused, her eyes grew sharp with new insights. 'Grace had no side to her, you see. She was open and sweet and lovely, and I think men just wanted to *help* her. Yes,' she said, with the satisfaction of someone who is making a good point, 'I think they felt they *had* to help her. They felt *protective*. She had that effect. And it wasn't just men – we all felt we wanted to help her.' The veneration was back in her voice, the sense of wonder. 'I can't explain it, really, I—' She winced suddenly and pressed her fingers against her lips. 'Oh, how *awful*!' she whispered. 'I'm talking about her in the past tense, as though . . . *Really*. How awful . . .'

The phone began to ring. Anne Hampton spread her hand against her chest and continued to sigh at her lapse. 'Really,' she repeated twice. Then, when the ringing continued unabated, she said, 'Do you think I should answer it? They usually put the machine on, if they're out.'

'I'll do it.'

The phone sat on a worktop by the door, beside an answering machine.

'Hello,' I said into the phone. 'The Dearden house.'

Silence.

I said hello again and recited the phone number off the base

of the phone for good measure, to be met by another silence
made still deeper by the strong feeling that someone was there.

Abruptly the line went dead.

I replaced the receiver.

'Who was it?' Anne asked.

'Just missed them,' I said. I dialled 1471, and was given a
local number which I jotted down on the phone pad and folded
into my pocket.

Above the phone was a glass-fronted cabinet containing a
neat row of cookery books, with, at the far end, two bound
notebooks with handwritten labels on their spines: *Dinner
Parties I*, *Dinner Parties II*.

'Grace is quite a cook, I gather.'

'Oh, yes,' affirmed Anne Hampton. '*Terrific*.'

I wondered if there was anything that Grace didn't do
terrifically well, or whether Anne Hampton was just easily
impressed.

'Very French,' she said.

'I'm sorry?'

'Her cooking. Bit rich for me, to tell the truth. Oh, it's
always delicious, but too creamy for my taste. I'm a simple
cook myself, roasts and chops. Grace did a proper diploma,
you know, with Prue Leith or someone like that, just before
she met Will.'

I put my coffee mug on a draining board whose surface was
like a mirror, and glanced at my watch. 'Well, I'd better get
back to—'

'You know how they met, of course?' Anne Hampton
continued, undaunted.

'Yes.'

'*Well!* It had to be destiny, didn't it? *Fate*. I got her to tell
me the story once. Normally she didn't like to talk about it.
Felt that people made far too much of it. But what a story! She
would have drowned, no doubt about it. Just a *whisker* away.'
She held up a finger and thumb that were almost touching and

gave a shudder. 'Will got her breathing again, you know. Saved her life! I mean, there's something sort of wonderful in it, isn't there? Restores your faith. The power of love and all that.' She sighed sadly. 'And now this! It all seems so . . . *tragic*.'

I went to the door. 'I've got to go and talk to the family now. I'll probably see you again.'

'Oh, yes! I'll be around. I'm only up the road.' She added brightly, 'In your old house! Did you realize?'

I stared at her.

'We took it over five years ago. We absolutely *love* the place. You must come and see all the things we've done to it.'

'So your husband is . . .?'

'Senior partner now. Oh, you mean, his *name*? Julian.'

She marched past me into the passage and, in her most penetrating voice, sent a series of goodbyes reverberating through the house, as if this might spirit up some occupants. Only when her fourth call received no answer did she put on her coat. 'Wonder where they've got to.' She pulled open the front door and, peering out, exclaimed, 'Oh, *there*.'

I looked past her and saw a gathering of fifteen or twenty people on the edge of the marsh. At first I couldn't make out what they were doing and then I saw three men detach themselves from the main group and set off purposefully along the path to the east. By the time I had gone back through the kitchen to grab my coat and made my way down to the water the next search party had set off, also heading east.

My eyes looked for Will and found him standing to one side of the group, peering at a partially folded map in someone's hand. His shoulders were hunched high as if against the cold, and he was frowning deeply.

Maggie was standing on her own, wrapped in a scarf and ankle-length coat. 'They are searching the Gun Marsh,' she announced in a flat voice.

I recognized a few people, a farmer called Yates, a man called Simons, who had been leader of the Fishermen's

Association in my father's day, the bibulous publican from the Deepwell Arms, the woman who ran the fish shop. 'Who's organizing all this, Maggie?'

'Frank Yates, I think,' she replied vaguely. Then, with something like contempt, 'They've already searched the Gun Marsh. They found nothing. Why search it again?' And she clicked her tongue.

'They've done this before? Gone searching like this?'

Maggie stared into the distance. 'Twice . . . three times. They find nothing.'

More cars drew up, people grouped and departed. I became aware of two arrivals who did not join the others but stood a few yards away from us, watching silently. It wasn't just the older man's raincoat and neat haircut and city shoes which identified his occupation as surely as if he had worn his warrant card on his lapel, it was the way he stood, weight balanced equally on both feet, shoulders back, with the impassive expression police officers acquire with the job. The other officer, round-faced, overweight and a decade or more younger, wore jeans on his plump legs, and chunky trainers, and a quilted bomber jacket.

'Which is the investigating officer?' I whispered to Maggie.

Following my gaze, noticing the men for the first time, her eyes flashed with indignation, her lips trembled and she scoffed hoarsely, 'Why do they come and stare like this? Why don't they search too?'

'They've probably searched the area already.'

She was breathing in ragged snatches, her eyelids fluttering with anger.

'Maggie, it's all right.' I hadn't realized how close to the edge she was.

Eventually she began to breathe more easily. 'He thinks bad things, that man,' she said finally, with a desolation so deep that it might have marked the end of the world.

'Go back to the house, Maggie. Go back and get warm.'

Dropping her head, she nodded soundlessly before drawing her scarf closer round her face and walking away.

I had it wrong. It was the overweight jeans-clad man who was Ramsey, while the older straight-backed figure in the raincoat introduced himself as Detective Superintendent Agnew, commander of Norfolk CID.

I told them I was the Deardens' solicitor. If this implied that I was a family lawyer more used to conveyancing and wills than crime, then for the moment that suited me very well.

Agnew appeared to offer the name of the firm against some list in his head. 'Not a local outfit?' he asked, in the tone of someone wishing to be put right.

'No.' I gave him my card.

He examined it and raised a slight eyebrow. 'Ah.'

I didn't need to be told that London was going to count against me.

Meeting Ramsey's moon-faced gaze, I asked him for an update on his investigation.

'We have made extensive enquiries.' His voice was so flat that he might have been giving evidence. 'But as yet have no indication as to what might have happened to Mrs Dearden. We have made extensive searches of the immediate area. We have circulated a recent photograph of Mrs Dearden and put her on the missing persons' register. Local television and local press have carried items and shown photographs. We have checked the usual places, the hospitals and emergency departments.' He added, 'All to no avail.'

'House-to-house enquiries?'

'Indeed.'

'The village?'

'The immediate neighbours. The adjacent lanes.' He spoke stiffly, his small eyes seemed to recede into the plumpness of his face, and I guessed he had inferred some sort of criticism from my question.

Having no wish to rub him up the wrong way, I nodded

lavishly to show that I found his answer entirely satisfactory. 'And I understand you've followed up the possibility of her having gone to London on the Thursday, as she'd planned.'

'That's correct.'

I waited for him to expand on this. For a while we held each other's gaze, I expectantly, he with wariness or resistance.

'There is no indication that she went to London,' he announced finally.

'No obvious means of transport.'

'That's right. Nothing with the local taxi firms. Checked the station and rail staff – nobody saw her. And she didn't turn up to any of her engagements.'

Again, I made a show of agreeing with him because a little deference never did any harm when you were tarred with the London brush. 'And the Brasserie restaurant, they hadn't seen her either?'

He gave me a wary look, as though, with all this information at my disposal, I must be trying to catch him out. 'No.'

'Did they know her from previous visits?'

A slight pause which told me the question probably hadn't been asked, at least not in that form. 'Apparently not.'

'And the last appointment at six thirty, the one that was cancelled?'

Again, the slight defensiveness. 'Checked out.'

Agnew had remained studiously aloof from this exchange, keeping his gaze on the activities by the marsh. Now he said to me in his quiet voice, 'You specialize in crime, I take it, Mrs O'Neill?'

I had rather given myself away. 'With family law too.'

'Go together in London, I suppose, family and crime, as often as not?' His mouth twitched amiably, to show that I shouldn't take offence from any of this.

'Not as often as one might think,' I said, just as mildly.

'I was with the Met for five years,' he said, coming clean. 'Then Manchester, then Devon. When I came here they told me Norfolk didn't see much serious crime. But nowadays there's not a lot of difference wherever you go. Cars, drugs, TV violence. It's all universal.' He was in his mid-fifties, I judged; a wiry man with a bony face, a narrow head and steady eyes that gave the impression of judgement and compassion. His thin mousy hair was cut like a soldier's, very short at the sides, and his collar was a little too big for his birdlike neck. 'This is a difficult business, Mrs O'Neill,' he said as though he had made up his mind to be frank with me. 'I wish we could say we had something to go on. There's no suggestion of foul play. There's no suggestion of mental distress or domestic upset. It would appear that Mrs Dearden has vanished into thin air.'

'So what next?'

With a movement of his head, Agnew deferred to Ramsey, who said blandly, 'We'll keep monitoring the case.'

I went through my nodding routine again. 'Had you thought about a national TV appeal, on one of the crime programmes?'

Ramsey's fat jaw tightened, he pushed out his thin mouth. 'A decision will be taken in due course.'

And something told me it would be Agnew, and not Ramsey, who took it. I was tempted to press Agnew straight away, but I sensed it would be a mistake. 'Anything on forensics?' I asked.

Adopting the patient tone of a hard-pressed divisional commander, Agnew answered, 'Mrs O'Neill, we have expended a great number of man-hours on this incident already, an incident, I don't need to remind you, where we have no indication that any crime has been committed, nor indeed that any sort of mishap of any description has occurred. I can't justify putting any more resources into the matter at the present time.'

'No mishap, Superintendent? Surely it's abundantly clear that a mishap *has* occurred. She took no clothes, has spent no money. No one has seen her, no one has heard from her. She has a child and husband she loves. I think that at the very least there must have been a *mishap*.'

Taking his time, or choosing not to reply, Agnew kept his impenetrable gaze on the dwindling knot of searchers. Finally he tipped his head towards them. 'Certainly *they* don't seem to be in any doubt that a mishap has occurred.' There was no obvious irony in his tone. 'And the marshes. They seem to think it's the place to look, don't they?' Before I could work out what, if anything, he meant by this, he added, 'Let's hope they're wrong.' Turning his gaze back to me, he seemed to make up his mind about something, and with a glance at Ramsey, said, 'I would have thought we could look into this TV appeal as a matter of priority, Mrs O'Neill. I would have thought that would be entirely possible.'

'Excellent, Superintendent.' Pushing my luck, I added, 'And the forensics, you wouldn't think—'

But Ramsey had subtly directed Agnew's attention over my head towards Will, who was approaching fast.

He came to a halt close by my shoulder, frowning deeply, and said to Ramsey, 'No news?'

'Afraid not, sir.'

It was clear he'd expected little else. I told him about the possibility of a national TV appeal, but either it didn't register or he didn't hold out much hope for it because he nodded without enthusiasm.

He said rather briskly to Ramsey, 'Well, unless there's anything in particular, I'm going to go and join the search.'

'Just one small point, sir,' Ramsey said in his oddly toneless voice. 'I was wondering if you'd had a moment to go through your wife's papers. Any bank accounts that might have been missed. Building society passbooks, that sort of thing.'

'I've looked, yes, but it's like I told you – there's only the one account.'

Ramsey's eyes did not leave Will's face. I saw curiosity there, and keen appraisal, but little of the distrust that had so alarmed Maggie. 'No savings accounts?' he asked.

'One.'

'You'd know if there were withdrawals?'

'I'd know.'

Agnew slid Ramsey a meaningful glance, clearly intended as a reminder.

With a small confirmatory nod, Ramsey turned his moon-face back to Will. 'Any place that might have sentimental associations?'

Still frowning, Will searched his memory. 'I really can't think of anywhere, no.'

'Any place that might have childhood memories for her?'

'Not particularly. She was brought up in London.'

A moment in which the mood seemed to tauten, then Ramsey said, 'We'll let you get on, then, sir. Needless to say, we'll keep you in touch with any developments.'

As Agnew and Ramsey walked towards their car, looking for all the world like a couple from a before-and-after ad for Weight Watchers, Will said, 'What do you think, then, Alex? Have they got the faintest idea what they're doing?'

'Hard to tell,' I began cautiously, as I watched Ramsey manoeuvre his considerable bulk into the driving seat. 'They *seem* competent. Reasonably thorough. Though we'll know just how thorough when we've checked on the London end.'

He gave a sharp rather desperate nod, and glanced restlessly over his shoulder at the search parties on the marsh.

I said, 'I'll need Grace's photograph before I go.'

'Go? Do you have to go? Yes, of course you must go.' He touched a hand to his head, as if he wasn't thinking straight. 'They're on the desk in my office, a pile of photographs. Take what you need. Must you go? *Must* you?' But now it was a routine lament for a departing friend.

I said, 'I'll call as soon as I have anything from our investigator. Hopefully some time tomorrow, but Monday at the latest.'

'Monday.' He made it sound an impossibly long way off.

He leant forward and embraced me as suddenly and completely as he had done on the meadows, an impulsive all-enveloping hug that pressed my face hard against his shoulder, before turning away and setting off at a steady hike, head lowered against the bite of the wind.

The police car had stopped some way along the quay, beside the metalled surface of the lane. In the side window Ramsey's face was twisted back to stare in our direction, his fat cheek almost touching the glass, as if he had seen something that needed a second or third look. Watching one of the search parties perhaps? Wanting another glance at Will? Or – I couldn't believe it, but then again perhaps I could – agog at our embrace. Doubtless Ramsey was one of those all too predictable types for whom a hug between a man and a woman had only one meaning.

When I got back to the house there was no sign of Maggie in the kitchen, nor any reply to my calls. Searching for Will's office, I put my head into the room opposite the drawing room which I had remembered as a musty place full of old books and frayed Persian rugs and a battered upright piano. Now, brighter books stood in orderly file along Palladian-style shelving with fluted mouldings and cornices, a shiny baby grand stood in one corner, the rugs were new, the carpet too, while to one side of the fireplace stood the latest-fangled wide-screen television.

The transformation of the dining room was equally dramatic. Where I had a memory of painted furniture against white walls, of a scrubbed-pine refectory table with high-backed chairs and bright curtains, there was now a rosewood reproduction antique table with a glassy surface, matching chairs, dark green silk wall hangings, brocade curtains and pastoral oil paintings lit by low-voltage spots. Again, I thought: Money. Perhaps five or six thousand for this room alone, if you counted the oils, perhaps double or triple that if you counted the furniture. I wondered where it had all come from. I hadn't remembered Grace having money, but then in the old days I wouldn't have been curious about that.

Passing through the kitchen I put my nose into various pantries and larders, all in immaculate order. In the back yard there was none of the clutter of the old days, no stacks of logs or kindling, no machinery or old tractors. Instead the outhouses were freshly whitewashed, the window frames gleaming with new paint.

A smaller outhouse had been converted into Will's office. The blinking fluorescent light revealed a square room with three filing cabinets, copier, fax, and a metal desk strewn with papers. Posters and charts were fixed to the walls. Next to a chart of what looked like farm yields but could have been anything that fluctuated was a poster of a misty Tuscan landscape not unlike the one that had always hung in Maggie's kitchen. Immediately above the desk was a cluster of photographs stuck haphazardly to the wall, most of Charlie: Charlie riding a bike, Charlie kicking a football, and – a moment of recognition and pleasure – Charlie in *Pod*, the pram dinghy which had carried Will and me on so many of our childhood expeditions. In some pictures Charlie was smiling, in others he was engrossed, but always there was an underlying sense of amiability, of an open undemanding nature.

The desk was untidy, with disorderly heaps of invoices and forms, letters and farming publications. The pictures of Grace lay in a scattered pile in the centre. I took the one I guessed to be the most recent, an outdoor shot that looked natural and unposed, as if she had been captured on the instant of turning towards the camera. The harsh light exposed no blemishes on her skin, and her mildly enquiring expression revealed only the faintest trace of a line on her forehead. The overall impression was of freshness and beauty, of a person who would never show her age. Only her eyes had some other, more knowing light.

I found a blank piece of paper – not an easy task – and left a note for Will, describing the photograph I had removed and promising to return it shortly.

Seeing the phone, I sat down quickly and, finding the number I had noted from the 1471 call, dialled it.

A female answered with a jolly hello.

I said, in my secretary's voice, 'I'm calling from the Dearden household. Someone phoned earlier—'

'Oh, it must have been Charlie! Do you want to speak to him? He's covered in glue at the moment, but I can wrap something round the phone—'

'No, no. I wouldn't want to bother him. No – I was just checking. Because of the call.'

'Oh, he's fine, just fine. We're doing a montage, a forest scene. Charlie's looks *amazing*. Very colourful.'

'How lovely. Thank you.'

Ringing off, I sat back for a moment and imagined Charlie calling home and hearing my voice. With the scene on the marsh fresh in my mind, the vision of Will's shocked face burnt on my memory, I wondered if by some awful chance I had sounded like Grace.

Straightening up, my eye was caught by a letter protruding from a particularly precarious heap of papers. The letterhead, graphic-designed and conspicuous, announced: Wickham Estates. I couldn't help noticing that the letter began *Dear Mr Dearden, Reference: Gun Marsh Tenancy.*

In the house there was still no sign of Maggie and, leaving a further note on the kitchen table, I let myself out.

It was strange to think of Wickham Lodge without Aunt Nella. Born in the house shortly after it was built in 1908, she had lived in it continuously until her death eighty-five years later. Driving in through the gates, passing between the dark laurels and onto the gravel sweep, a part of me still expected to see her battered estate car standing there like a tank from a forgotten war, still looked for the yellowing holland blinds in the tall windows, hanging like ancient banners, still got out of the car bracing myself for the onslaught of the five hysterical spaniels, their muddy paws clawing at my legs, their coats reeking of long walks and damp bedding.

Instead, there was a fresh layer of gravel on the drive, no blinds at the windows, new paint on the frames, and, parked casually in the middle of the semi-circular sweep, a shiny red Mercedes coupé. This, I guessed, was Edward's – he'd always liked sporty cars – while the pale blue Golf tucked unobtrusively into a corner next to a flowerbed was almost certainly Jilly's. I didn't pretend to understand how she stayed with my brother, though I admired her for persevering with him, in much the same way that one admires a faithful animal for refusing to abandon a bad master.

I rang the front doorbell, like the visitor I was, and heard the deep bark of Edward's Labrador. A minute later Edward swung the door open, wearing an irritated expression that did not improve on seeing me.

'I would have called,' I said, 'but I didn't know I was coming until late last night.'

'I'm just going out,' he said, as if I and the rest of the world should have been aware of this fact.

'Oh, well. It was just on the off-chance.'

As so often with Edward, his brusqueness was followed by a grudging retreat. 'There's still some coffee in the pot, if you're not going to be too long.' Without waiting for a response he strode back into the house.

'I thought you'd be out shooting,' I said, closing the door and following him across the hall.

'*Shooting?*' He flung an incredulous look over his shoulder. '*Shooting?*' he repeated on reaching the kitchen, and rolled his eyes as if I were quite mad.

'I thought you went every weekend.'

'Alexandra, where *do* you come from? What *planet* do you inhabit? The season ended three weeks ago. I'd be arrested!'

'Oops.' I put on a stupid face. 'Forgot.'

He sighed heavily, 'What *planet?*' before filling a mug from a cafetière and pushing it across the table towards me. He slid sugar and milk after it, then perched himself on a high stool, lit a cigarette, and crossed his arms, as if to hear what I had to say. He had put on a bit of weight, I noticed, which was no bad thing for someone who had always been on the skinny side, but his eyes were puffy and his skin sallow, and I wondered if he wasn't overdoing the smoking or the drinking or both. 'Well?' he demanded.

'Will Dearden asked me to come down.'

He made an exaggerated show of amazement. 'Good God, why?'

'Well, Grace Dearden has disappeared—'

'Yes, yes, I know *that*! But why involve *you*?'

'Because he wants me to make some enquiries for him. And to liaise with the police.'

'But why *you*?'

'Well, this is my field, Ed,' I said. 'This is what I do, among other things.'

He was shaking his head, oddly furious. 'Seems nuts to me. I mean, what good are you going to be from London?'

'Hopefully, as good as I'd be anywhere else.'

'Jesus, Lex, what the hell are you thinking of? You should have kept well clear.'

'I don't see why.'

'Well, it's obvious, isn't it? This guy's our tenant.'

'*Your* tenant, Ed. This estate's nothing to do with me. Anyway, why should—'

'Okay, okay,' he interrupted aggressively, 'your *brother's* tenant. I mean, close enough. Family, for heaven's sake.'

'So?'

'Well . . .' He gestured impatiently. 'We're in dispute, aren't we?'

'In dispute?' I stared at him. 'I knew nothing about this, Ed.'

He was going to challenge me on that but quickly thought better of it. If I knew nothing about the dispute, it could only be because he hadn't told me. 'Oh, he's been haggling over a price for the Gun Marsh,' he said dismissively.

'What do you mean?'

'The Gun Marsh,' he repeated heavily, as if I were being particularly dim. 'Tried to sub-let the tenancy, if you please. Well, I soon put a stop to that! He had no right, no right at all. Could have taken him to court for deception.' Taking my bewilderment for doubt, he insisted crossly, 'I *tell* you, I could have taken him to court!' When I nodded my understanding he continued in a tone that was hardly less aggrieved, 'And *then* he wanted a ridiculous price to let me have my own land back! It almost went to arbitration. We've only just settled. Took months. And the concessions I've made – bloody generous. And the thanks I get? He's mucking about, not returning documents on time, not signing things. Just to cause the maximum bloody inconvenience and disruption. I ask you! These people.'

I still couldn't get over it. 'Will's giving up the marshes?'

'Just the Gun, not Thorp.' He snorted, 'He needs the money.'

But at that moment no explanation, however logical, made any sense to me. The Gun Marsh had been farmed by the Deardens for four, maybe five generations. I couldn't imagine Will giving it up except as a last and desperate resort. Money seemed a paltry reason, avoidable somehow, or at least capable of postponement. I took a long and troubled breath. 'Well, I'm sorry you've been in dispute, very sorry indeed, but it's not going to affect my being able to act for them.'

'But the *Deardens*, for heaven's sake,' Edward muttered reprovingly. 'You should have kept clear.'

'I think that's for me to judge, Ed,' I said, in a neutral tone.

He shrugged in the way he had shrugged as a child, with a flash of anger quickly succeeded by an expression of superiority, as though the whole matter were really beneath him.

'Anyway,' I said, 'I thought you were lending the garden to Grace Dearden for her festival.'

'That was different.'

I raised my eyebrows. 'Oh.'

'I agreed to it before all this bloody nonsense came up.'

I remembered the diary. 'You had a meeting with Grace on that Wednesday, I gather.'

'Not a *meeting*.' He gave me an irritated look, as though I had got this wrong on purpose. 'She wanted to come up here and look at something – I've forgotten what it was, the size of the lawn, the access to the field, something like that – and I told her to make herself at home, walk around all she wanted, I wouldn't be here, couldn't be here, but just to go ahead and make herself at home. No, no – not a *meeting*.'

'Ah. She'd put your initials in her diary, that was all.'

Rapidly losing interest, he dismissed this with a flip of his fingers. 'Oh, yes, while you're here . . .' he said, in an affectedly offhand way. Without further explanation he swung off his stool and went out of the room, leaving me to wish that time had done more to smooth his feathers. They say that the wounds of childhood never heal, that in adulthood such hurts can be rationalized but rarely forgotten, and Edward certainly seemed to prove the point. It would have been easy to put all his pain down to Mother's death when he was sixteen, almost as tempting to blame Pa for uprooting him from school and friends two years earlier and taking him to a remote corner of Cornwall. But I knew it went beyond that, that Edward's relationship with Pa had broken down in some irrevocable way when he was ten or eleven, that nothing had ever been right for Edward after that, and this was why I felt bound to stick by him, why I let him push me further and harder than anyone else. I did it because there was no one else for him apart from Jilly, no one else who understood his history.

He returned with a typed letter which he slapped down in front of me. 'Just needs your signature.'

The letter was written in the names of Edward and myself, and addressed to the Falmouth solicitors Pa had appointed as executors of his estate. It made a formal application for a full disclosure of Pa's assets. According to the letter, Edward and I believed that a substantial sum might have been overlooked in the calculation of Pa's assets. It referred to two bank withdrawals by date and amount, and requested all relevant information.

I said, 'I'm not sure we have the right to ask for information about transactions made during Pa's lifetime.'

'Oh, for heaven's sake!' Edward exploded. 'I told you, it could be *our* money, it could be rotting away in an account somewhere, totally forgotten. You may be doing fine with all your fat legal fees, but I'm very far from flush, I can tell you, not with this damn roof to replace and all the modernizing of the estate. Aunt Nella did nothing, absolutely *nothing*, in the way of maintenance, not for *years*. There are three cottages to repair, and a drainage problem over on Mill Farm, and God knows what. I tell you, it's going to cost a fortune.'

I ignored the comment about my fees. Whatever the size of Edward's income – and it must have been comfortable by any standards – he couldn't be accused of spending a lot on himself. He preferred sweaters and tweeds to anything which, for him, smacked of style or affectation. He hadn't been abroad for some time, he rarely came to London, I had the impression he didn't eat in restaurants very much. Wickham Lodge may have been large – counting the attic rooms, there were something like ten bedrooms – but apart from painting the woodwork against rot and a slap of blazing white emulsion on the kitchen walls, the place was largely as Aunt Nella had left it. There was the Mercedes in the drive, but, in our family, the men had never counted cars as an extravagance.

'Okay,' I agreed, preparing to sign the letter. 'But don't bank on this producing anything.'

But he didn't want to hear any of that. He was consumed by the suspicion that Pa had deprived him of this money on purpose, as a final reproof.

He hung over me while I scribbled my signature, then swept the letter out of sight like a conjuror.

'Christ,' he said, thrusting his watch up to his nose, 'we're going to be late.' He strode into the hall and yelled Jilly's name.

It was typical of Edward not to have told me she was in the house. I waited by the front door while he lifted a jacket off a hook and pulled it on, alternately commanding the wildly excited dog to calm down and shouting to Jilly.

Eventually light steps sounded on the landing and Jilly came running down the wide staircase, trailing a handbag and sweater. 'Hello!' she exclaimed in surprise, and still at a run came and kissed me on the cheek. She appeared in energetic spirits, a great deal more lively than when I had last seen her. Sometimes when she despaired of her relationship with Edward she fell into a bleak and impenetrable mood; at other times she managed a more philosophical front. Rarely had I seen her confident or lighthearted. She was twenty-nine and desperate for marriage and children. After four years with Edward and no sign of a marriage proposal, she was tormented by the thought that she had invested all her time and effort in a relationship which would fail to deliver.

'I didn't know you were coming,' she said in her little-girl voice.

I explained what had brought me.

All expression faded from her face. 'She was organizing the music festival, you know.'

'So I gather.'

Edward strode up to the front door and flung it open. Jilly and I moved obediently outside.

'Perhaps she was depressed,' Jilly said, speaking as someone who knew all about the subject.

'Apparently not.'

'People don't always talk about it,' she said gravely. 'Sometimes they hold it in.'

'But there are usually signs, I believe. Most people give some hint, so the experts say.'

She considered this as if it were a new and rather curious idea. 'Well . . . perhaps.'

Jilly had grown her hair and had had it streaked a rather startling blonde colour. She wore no lipstick but, as always, her eyes were heavily rimmed with mascara. With her finely pencilled eyebrows and newly bleached hair, the effect was of someone wearing rather more makeup than was necessary or flattering. Her clothes were determinedly tweedy, as though she had gone to Aquascutum and asked for a female version of Edward's wardrobe, yet the country look only succeeded in emphasizing the incongruity of her makeup. I suspected that Edward was secretly ashamed of her, that in the sporting circles in which he now mixed he felt she didn't quite pass muster, and but for the fact he'd got used to having her around he would have called a halt to the relationship some time ago.

Edward, having slammed the front door and locked it, swore suddenly. 'The *camera*, Jilly! The bloody *camera*!'

Jilly moved as though jerked by hidden wires. 'Oh, sorry, *sorry*.' She rushed back towards the house. 'Let me get it.'

'No,' Edward sighed, reopening the door. '*I'll* get it.'

For some moments after he had disappeared Jilly hovered on the threshold in case she might yet be called upon to help. Turning back finally, she muttered in self-reproach, 'Forgot the camera. We're going to look at a horse . . .'

I nodded mutely. There was nothing one could say to ameliorate Jilly's misery when things went wrong. 'Did you see a lot of Grace?' I asked.

'Oh, no.' In her agitation her voice was even wispier than usual. 'I mean, we didn't see them socially, except at other people's parties. And then when this tenancy thing came up—' She pressed a hand to her mouth, frightened that she might have spoken out of turn.

'The dispute.'

'The *dispute*,' she affirmed with a small wince of relief. 'Well, it all got a bit awkward after that.'

'Edward couldn't very well withdraw his offer to host the festival, I suppose.'

'Oh, but he didn't want to! No, he rather liked the idea of—' She withdrew awkwardly, as if she had been on the point of saying something disloyal. 'I think,' she said, with a glance towards the house, 'that he liked the idea of hosting such an important event for the neighbourhood, the idea of having everyone here. He had plans to replant the garden.'

Quite the country squire. The image pleased me. 'And Grace?' I asked. 'She wasn't bothered by the dispute?'

'Oh, no. She just pretended it wasn't happening. Behaved as if we were all the closest of friends – which we weren't, never had been. But that was her way, of course.'

'Her way?'

'Always smiling. Always full of sweetness and light.' And to show she hadn't meant this unkindly, she gave one of her apologetic laughs, one shoulder raised, head tilted. Her gestures, like her voice, were excessively feminine, as though such mannerisms might make her more desirable. She added confidingly, 'Rather too grand. I always thought, anyway . . .'

'Grand?' The word surprised me.

Jilly, who reacted to any challenge, however slight, by distrusting her own judgement, backed down immediately. 'Well . . . gracious, perhaps.'

I still wasn't absolutely sure I understood her and the doubt must have shown in my face because Jilly said, 'What I mean is, to meet her you'd think she was out of the top drawer, born with a silver spoon in her mouth. You'd never think she was just an ordinary person. The way she talked, you know. And her clothes, her whole manner – like a duchess.'

I hadn't thought of Grace in quite this way, but now that Jilly mentioned it I recognized the seeds of this grandness in my memory of her.

Edward reappeared at the door and began the process of locking up again.

Jilly, on duty once more, hurried off towards the Mercedes. 'Lovely to see you, Alex,' she called with a wave.

Edward strode up and planted both feet heavily on the gravel. 'Sorry we couldn't have more time.' Then, making a visible effort to be brotherly, offering something that resembled a smile: 'Why don't you come and stay one weekend? You and Paul?'

I made my usual excuses for Paul, how his workload kept him in London at weekends. 'But if this business brings me to Norfolk again I might need to beg a bed off you.' I tilted a mocking smile at him. 'If that's okay.'

'I think we could manage that.' His pretended indifference could not conceal the gleam of satisfaction in his eyes, and something else I couldn't quite identify, like sorrow. Seeing this, I felt a lurch of guilt for not having made more of an effort to come and stay before. Edward's invitations had always been so equivocal, his manner so perfunctory, that even I, the one person who should have seen through this subterfuge, had fallen into the trap of believing he didn't really want to see me. I should have remembered that Edward's greatest talent had been for alienating those closest to him. On the emotional front, he was an expert at own-goals.

'Maybe even next week,' I said.

Recoiling from the dangers of such intimacy and affection, the demon in Edward shot back to the surface. 'So soon?' he said acerbicly. 'But then, you always had a soft spot for Will Dearden, didn't you?'

I said coldly, 'Don't be ridiculous.'

'Oops, hit a nerve, did I?'

'Don't be pathetic with me.'

'Was I?' He paused and took stock. 'Oh, Lally,' he moaned placatingly, choosing the name he had used as a child, 'don't take any notice of me.'

'You should take more notice of yourself, Ed. You should be more careful of what you say.'

He gave an exaggerated nod. 'You're right,' he said ruefully. 'Always were.'

Chapter Four

BARE CONCRETE and gunmetal, sudden cacophonous clangs and long echoes: the cold world of the cells behind Clerkenwell Magistrates Court. I passed through the familiar succession of security doors and windowless passageways, and approached the desk sergeant, a stony-faced man with a well-honed brusqueness.

I wished him good morning and informed him that I was Duty Solicitor for the day. 'How many do you have for me?'

Taking his time, leaning an elbow wearily on the desk, he referred to the list on his clipboard. 'Ten, eleven. Could be more,' he murmured lugubriously. 'There's two still winging their way from Islington.'

As Duty Solicitor there were very few certainties about the day ahead, except that Mondays were never quiet. Not only did a Monday bring two days' arrests into the courts, but they were the two days of the week on which people thieved and fought and misbehaved with far greater energy than usual.

I noted the names and charges. Hearing the name Hedley, I asked the warder to start there first.

The warder lowered the wicket and called into the cell. The face that appeared in the slot could have been sixteen instead of twenty-two. Large troubled eyes and deathly white skin under a fiery scattering of acne.

'Jason, Jason,' I said in mild despair. 'Short time no see.'

'Hi, Mrs O'Neill. What you doing 'ere?'

'I'm Duty Solicitor today, so you get me on tap, lucky thing.'

He smiled at me.

'Jason, the charge is theft from Sainsbury's.'

'Yeah.'

'What was it?'

'A chicken. Four quid's worth.'

I felt like asking him why he hadn't gone for a steak, which would have been far easier to conceal, but I wasn't supposed to say things like that.

'Guilty, then?'

'Yeah.' He knew the form. He had been committing petty misdemeanours since he was twelve. He was already on bail for stealing whisky from a rival supermarket.

'What about your family history? Do you want me to refer to that in court?'

'Sure.'

'Just to make certain I have it right – your father was killed when you were three? And your mother died a year ago, wasn't it?' The mother, who had also been a client of mine, had died from injecting contaminated drugs into her veins, but I wouldn't be mentioning that.

We were both momentarily distracted by loud shouting from an adjacent cell, a stream of obscenities culminating in, 'It's a frame! They fuckin' framed me!'

'Where are you living, Jason?'

He made a rueful face.

'Rough?'

'Mostly, yeah.'

'What happened to the hostel?'

'There was this guy there. Gave me a bad time.'

'And your probation officer couldn't find you anywhere else?'

He dropped his eyes.

I sighed. 'Do I take it you haven't been reporting to your probation officer?'

His expression said no, and, like a mother admonishing a hopeless child, I gently shook my head at him. It was no good getting angry or fierce. Quite enough people in Jason's life had done that already. If he was going to be one of the sixty per cent of young offenders who made up their minds to stop offending in their mid-twenties he needed unbiased advice, not censure.

Footsteps sounded at the end of the passage. Out of the corner of my eye I saw a figure approaching. Something about the jaunty walk was familiar, and I took a proper look. It was Sturgess, who fanned out a hand of greeting. I could only imagine something important had come up at the office and he'd rushed over to tell me about it. Gesturing that I'd be with him shortly, I turned back to the face in the open wicket. 'Look, Jason, I'll try for bail, but the magistrate is going to lose patience with you if you don't promise to meet the terms of the existing order. You understand? I'll tell the court that you were bullied at the hostel and you've been sleeping rough ever since, that you stole this chicken because you hadn't had a proper meal for days. But it might not wash, you realize that?'

'There's a place in Islington I wouldn't mind.'

'A hostel? You've got mates there?'

He nodded.

'But good mates, Jason? Not people who are going to get you into trouble?'

He couldn't answer that. All of them were in some sort of trouble, trouble with drink or stealing or drugs, trouble with not having homes or families or education or prospects.

'Okay, I'll have a word with the probation people. But I can't promise anything, Jason.'

'Yeah. Thanks, Mrs O'Neill.' He pulled away from the door.

I put my face back to the slot and said in a low voice, 'Why a chicken, Jason? They're so damned *bulky*.'

'Thought there weren't no one watchin' the chickens.'

I made a face at him before raising the wicket.

Sturgess was nowhere near. Looking back along the line of

cells, I was surprised to see him leaning against a cell door at the far end, conferring with the occupant.

I asked the warder which detainee he was talking to.

'Munro. GBH. Remand at Brixton.'

It made no sense. If this was one of Paul's clients and it was simply a remand, I couldn't imagine why Paul hadn't asked me to stand in for him. Sending Sturgess was both inefficient and unnecessary.

With barely half an hour before court began I still had to receive instructions from the nine other people who might be in need of representation. The first was the gentleman who had been making the noise, a shimmering vision in a vermilion-and-silver disco suit so tight that it appeared to be painted onto his lanky body. He was charged with possession of a quarter gram of heroin and a stolen and doctored road-tax disc.

'Hello, I'm the Duty Solicitor. My name is Mrs O'Neill. I'm here—'

'It's a frame-up, man.'

'Would you like me to represent you, then, Mr Finn? My function is to represent you if you would like me to . . .'

As I was talking, Sturgess passed soundlessly behind me. I kept an eye on him in case he should turn and make some signal to me, but he rounded the corner and disappeared in the direction of the duty desk without a backward glance.

A joy-rider, an actual bodily harm, an offensive weapon and a possession of drugs completed my tally for the morning, which, typically, was fewer than the desk sergeant had predicted since many detainees had managed to locate their regular solicitors. I hurried into court as everyone was upstanding for the arrival of the magistrate, a stipendiary named Alice Knapp who had served her time as a criminal defence solicitor in Isleworth. She had a reputation for toughness. Famously, she had once told a knife-wielding yob that if it had been in her power to have him whipped, she would have done so publicly. This, with her exuberant fluffy hairdo not entirely unlike a soft Italian ice cream, had earned her the nickname Miss Whippy.

Sliding onto the bench next to Sturgess, I whispered, 'Who's the client, then, Gary?'

'One of Paul's. GBH, a remand. Paul's on his way, but he wanted me to confirm the client's instructions.'

'But why didn't he—' But whatever Paul should have done was no concern of Sturgess's, and I cut myself short with a wave of one hand.

The first two cases did not find Ms Knapp in benevolent mood and I began to worry about Jason, but swayed by the bullying he had suffered at the hostel she allowed him bail on the condition he found another place to live and reported twice a week to his probation officer.

Three more cases, both adjournments, and Paul's grievous bodily harm was coming up the list fast. Sturgess, increasingly fidgety, finally slipped out of his seat and held a whispered conversation with the clerk. My irritation with Paul was rekindled by the knowledge that all this duplication and bother could have been avoided if he'd taken the simple step of briefing me.

The vermilion-and-silver disco suit entered court muttering hotly, twitching his shoulders and generally exhibiting the body language of a storming bull. Despite my attempts to restrain him, he sealed his fate by directing a stream of four-letter abuse at Ms Knapp and earning himself two weeks inside for contempt.

As the fracas died down and he was led away, I sank back onto my seat, to be met by Paul's breezy smile from the far end of the lawyers' pew. I sent him a questioning look which he chose to misunderstand or to ignore.

My joy-rider, already on bail for two similar offences, got bail again, which was more than he deserved. Then Paul's GBH. I listened in expectation of something unusual or difficult, but it was a simple remand for a further two weeks, no request for bail, nothing complex, nothing mysterious, the whole thing completed in three minutes. The moment it was over Paul bowed hastily to the bench, threw me a quick nod and flew out of the court with Sturgess close on his heels, the very image of the busy lawyer. Or, bringing it closer to home, the image of Paul in one of his increasingly evasive moods, anxious to avoid explanations.

When court rose for lunch, I came into the crowded hall and saw Ray Dodworth at the far end. He was unmistakable at any distance both because of his height, which was several inches over six foot, and because of his fondness for slick Italian-style suits and spivvy haircuts. A peacock among sparrows, he looked like a successful crook or a policeman on the take, neither of which seemed to prevent people from giving him information.

We went to the pub round the corner, newly renovated with replica Victorian windows and replica Victorian furniture, bought in at vast expense to emulate the genuine Victorian furnishings that had been torn out during a previous refit. The ersatz effect was reinforced by canned music, ham-filled baguettes, and ten different kinds of lager. I knew the pub well: in less pressurized times it had been one of Paul's regular watering holes.

'Bennett, the dentist,' Ray began as soon as we had found a gloomy table. 'Very helpful. Told me he'd made two crowns and four veneers for Grace Dearden. That Thursday was due to be her last session with him, to have any problems sorted. Rough spots, fit not quite right, whatever. Until that day she'd always turned up for her appointments regular as clockwork. Always seemed very charming, Bennett said. And very pleased with the work.' He gave a dry smile. 'Well, he would say that, wouldn't he? Norfolk CID called him just a few days ago to confirm that she hadn't shown for that last appointment.' He looked over his notes. 'That's it on the dentist.' Still a policeman at heart, he examined the next page of notes before proceeding.

Ray was over fifty but could have passed for less. His hair was short and thick and swept back, and if the uniformity of its blackness owed something to the regular use of a bottle, it didn't seem to do him any harm with the numerous women who came and went in his busy life. Wives, long-term girl-friends, ladies of shorter acquaintance: he seemed to keep them in separate orbits. His companionable easy-going manner belied a firm determination to order his life precisely as he liked it.

'Right . . . the restaurant,' he began again. 'La Brasserie in Knightsbridge. There are two other restaurants of the same name in London, but this is the fashionable one. Big clientele, something like a hundred-and-twenty seater. Different waiters on different days, though. Some work a six-day week, some three, some only do days, others do evenings, and sometimes they swap around. There's quite a turnover in staff too. Won't or don't keep them long. One waiter did think he remembered seeing Grace Dearden, but he couldn't remember who she was with – man, woman, one person, three – so not a lot of help there. They did let me have a glance at their old bookings ledgers, though.' I had never worked out how Ray persuaded people to do him such favours. A quiet authoritative manner, perhaps, or the gift of the gab, though what line he strung them I couldn't guess. Going by his invoices he didn't use bribes regularly, not unless he'd found a foolproof tech-nique for hiding them in his expenses. Either way, I never enquired too closely.

'The bookings weren't made in her name, as we know,' Ray went on in his soft voice. 'Now, I couldn't find a name that booked for lunch on all five dates you gave me, but I did find one that booked for four of them. The name of Gordon.' He turned it into a question with a lift of his eyebrows.

I searched my memory, knowing there was no Gordon there.

'This Gordon was booked for two December dates and two January. Table for two. They don't keep a record of genders. No Mr or Mrs.'

'What about a telephone number, in case of a no-show?'

He gave me a look of mock reproof for robbing him of his

small moment of surprise. 'Normally they don't bother for lunch bookings. Never that busy. But near Christmas they got much busier, and then they *did* take numbers.' He swivelled the notebook round and showed me a central London number.

'Got an address for it?'

'There's no Gordon in the book with that number. Checked with my BT contact – no go there, either. It's ex-directory. Tried calling it. No reply, no answering machine. It's a Knightsbridge exchange, so can't be too far from the restaurant. That's all I can tell you for the moment.'

There was a small silence that was entirely familiar to us. It was the silence in which I judged how badly I needed the information and Ray worked out which of his police contacts he could go to if I really pressed him.

But Ray pre-empted me. 'My other source, the one I can usually rely on – it'll be no go.'

'Oh? Any particular reason?'

'How shall I put it? Our name is mud at the moment.'

'The Ronnie Buck case?' I knew it could be nothing else.

'Quite a lot of people are feeling a bit upset about it.'

Something about his tone made me ask, 'What's the word on it, Ray?'

He hesitated for a moment. 'The word is that the witness was bought.'

I knew it was possible, I knew it would be Buck's style. 'The neighbour?'

'The neighbour who just happened to be standing at her window at dead of night and supposedly saw the officer climb the wall,' he said, showing nothing in his face.

For argument's sake, I said, 'But it's always meant to be a set-up, isn't it?'

'The officer was a good bloke, Alex. Tony James. Much liked. But even allowing for that, the word is very strong.'

He was telling me that it was almost certainly true. In which case a lot of people had been misled: Paul, Ray, the firm, not to mention the jury.

'You had no doubts about her at the time, this Karen Grainey?' I asked.

Ray gave me a startled gaze, followed by a look of dawning comprehension. 'I never worked on the case, Alex. Never met the woman.'

'Who did Paul use, then?'

He looked slightly embarrassed. 'I believe he used someone in Chislehurst, someone who knew the patch.'

All my half-acknowledged fears about the Buck trial leapt to the fore. I'd assumed that Paul had used Ray because that was what he always did. Now I saw powerful reasons for Paul to avoid using Ray, powerful reasons to let himself be talked into using another investigator. I saw, too, why he should have failed to mention any of this to me, and unease crept into my stomach, a sliver of ice.

'Oh well,' I said to break what had become a long silence. 'The Bucks of this world always get their comeuppance in the end, don't they?'

Diplomatically Ray made no reply to this, and after a last moment of awkwardness we turned back to Grace Dearden's planned trip to London.

'The cancelled six-thirty appointment . . .' I said, with a sigh that belonged to the last subject.

Ray went back to his notes. 'Avon Court is a block of flats. Expensive, uniformed porters, car park at the rear, views of Regent's Park out front. The penthouse went for a million not long ago. Arabs and foreigners mainly, by the look of the Rollers and stretch Mercedes and the people using the lobby. Problem is, the porter won't give out on who lives at number twenty-five. Muttered about terrorism. That's the trouble with having Arabs about. Everyone gets paranoid. Though he did swear blind that it wasn't anyone with the initials AWP. Couldn't get any more out of him. I tried him with AW, AP, you name it. No go. I'll keep trying, but no promises. Could the flat belong to a third party? Could she have been using it to meet this AWP?'

'Impossible to say. But there's no mention of any AWP before.'

'Likely to be having an affair?'

I was on the point of dismissing this when I forced myself to consider this possibility with more care. Accustomed to the tumultuous world of my regular clients, whose lives were a wide-open book of adultery, broken homes and abandoned children, it was all too easy to associate the quiet ordered existence of Grace in her beautiful home at Deepwell with contentment and marital fidelity. Yet if experience had taught me anything it was to distrust assumptions. 'Unlikely,' I said, thinking aloud. 'She lived in the country, she seemed very happy in her marriage, she was very involved in her local community. She came to London once a week or once every two weeks. Shopping mainly, and lunches. If she was seeing anyone in London, it must have been a very part-time relationship.' Voicing this, the possibility seemed to grow more unlikely. 'I'd say not. No – too happy, too busy.'

Accepting this, Ray said, 'I'll give the Regent's Park flat another try later. Night shift, different porter. Might have a more positive attitude.' For Ray, half the fun was the challenge of obtaining the unobtainable. 'I'll keep trying this Gordon person in Knightsbridge as well.' He took a bite of his baguette and frowned as the ham and shredded lettuce filling spilled out over the table. 'What about where she lived?' he asked, salvaging what he could of his lunch. 'Do you want me to do anything there?'

I gave him the list of the suppliers and tradespeople from her diary. 'That's it for the moment.'

'No indications of what might have happened to her?'

'No.'

'The suicide type?'

'Very unlikely.'

'Victim of a stalker?'

'Only if he had an exceptionally low profile. No suspicious people lurking in the area.'

'Husband, then?' Seeing my reaction, Ray added quickly, 'Just asking. A friend?'

'Yes.'

He nodded, eyeing me thoughtfully. 'There was a missing person once. Years ago, when I was young and green, first CID job, with the Surrey Force. Looked for this woman everywhere. Allotment, shed, common, lovers' lane. Kept passing this rough ground near her house, covered in big clumps of gorse and bramble. I thought, that's a place to look. But I thought, well, they're bound to have given that a good going over, aren't they? Didn't dare open my mouth. Didn't want to make a fool of myself. Finally, two days on, took a look in my own time. Just shone a torch into all these clumps.'

'And she was there.'

'She was there.' He gave up on the baguette with a grimace and washed the taste away with a long swig of beer. 'I'm only saying it's always worth checking the obvious.'

With five minutes until court resumed, I slipped into the lawyers' room and called Corinthia for my messages. The Norfolk Police had just phoned, she told me, wanting to know if Mr Dearden would be free to take part in a national TV appeal on his wife's disappearance tomorrow at four p.m. in Norwich.

Moving closer to the window to get the best of the mobile air waves, rehearsing what I would say, I called Will at Marsh House. I had tried him last night but the line had been permanently engaged, or he had taken the phone off the hook. Now the number rang without reply and the answering machine didn't pick up. I tried his mobile, but a robotic voice informed me that the phone was switched off and invited me to try again later. To be certain I hadn't misdialled, I called the house again. Listening to the distant ring, I pictured the shiny kitchen, the photographs in their silver frames, the undented cushions and pristine carpet, I heard the hush and stillness of the empty rooms. My mind carried me outside, beyond the garden to the marshes, but they too were empty.

Abandoning the call, the tension escaped me in a rush, and I hurried into court, reflecting on the power of emotional memory.

My last case came up at two thirty, the possession of drugs, who turned out to have a previous for drug-dealing which, all too predictably, he had omitted to mention to me. He seemed an unpleasant piece of work and I wasn't too upset when he failed to get bail.

I came out into a hall that was almost empty. Making for the stairs, I recognized a familiar figure going through the double doors ahead of me and called out to him. Dave Adamson was one of the few policemen with whom I was on reasonable terms. For most police officers, defence lawyers were the enemy, almost as contemptible as the offenders themselves, amoral touts who sold their souls for devil's gold and used trickery to undo all the police's painstaking work. But Dave Adamson was made of more pragmatic stuff. We went back five years or so, to a missing-child case. He had done me a favour then, and I'd been glad to defend his brother-in-law on a drink-driving charge a couple of years later. Now and again he slipped me information though, typically, nothing that would get either of us into trouble.

Normally the first to say hello, Dave greeted me with something like coolness.

'What a day!' I exclaimed, while I tried to work out what might be wrong. 'I was Duty. Got everything under the sun. How about you, Dave? How're things?'

We went through the pleasantries, but all the time there was awkwardness in his manner.

I dropped the pretence of jollity. 'I do something, Dave?'

'Nothing personal.'

I knew then that the new reputation of the firm had gone before me. 'Ah. The Buck case?'

'Tony James was a friend of mine.'

'I hadn't realized. I'm really very sorry.'

Accepting this, he nodded solemnly and we started down the stairs.

'You know how it is,' I said. 'Someone has to take these cases on.' The old argument, old as the law. I was sounding like Paul.

'Sure, I know that,' he said. 'Sure, but . . .'

I glanced at his steadfast face. 'But?'

He halted at the bottom of the stairs. 'There's talk,' he said uncomfortably.

'Yes, I know.'

He looked at me curiously, though whether it was the fact that I'd heard the talk which surprised him or my offhand reaction to it, I couldn't tell.

'Dave, I can only say that no defence team would ever go ahead with a case if they thought anyone was perjuring themselves.'

He gave me another odd look. 'Maybe not,' he said without conviction. 'But this one really cut deep. This one really . . .' But whatever he was about to say, he thought better of it. 'I see Tony every week. Can't speak, can't feed himself.' He tapped a forefinger to his temple. 'Everything scrambled inside. Won't ever get better. I see his family struggling to give him some sort of a life. And now they're going to have a battle to get the full compensation because the records have it that he was disobeying orders, climbing walls and trespassing. That makes him partly responsible. That's how they see it anyway, that's how they measure it up. Not entitled to the full whack. Not entitled to everything he'd have got if it had been attempted murder during the course of duty, pure and simple.'

'I'm sorry.'

'Sometimes the system does not serve,' he declared, with rare passion.

I couldn't argue about that, and we stood for a moment in silent agreement before making for the revolving doors.

I said, 'I hope he gets the full award.'

'Nice to think so.' He paused with a hand on the door. 'But he could win the lottery, couldn't he, and it still wouldn't buy him his brain back.'

I got away from the office in good time and drove towards Kensington, taking the Embankment and cutting up past the Palace to Hyde Park. The twilight had the clarity that comes with prolonged cold and absolute stillness. The sky was deep blue and transparent as glass, while the taller buildings were tipped with a vivid and dashing pink.

I thought of Norfolk, and knew that such windless conditions would bring a fierce overnight frost. I remembered the winter mornings of my childhood, the way the marshes would be covered in a thick crust of rime and the smaller creeks in sheets of star-crazed ice, how the cold would settle low in a thin white mist. On the Gun one harsh January, Will and I had slithered along the frozen ditches, and dared each other to slide across the wider stretches of fresh-water ice. On the half tide we had taken *Pod* to a broad expanse of salt-marsh that for most of the winter was too boggy for walking and found the frozen mud hard and crunchy beneath our feet.

Picturing the ice, another image flew into my mind without warning, an image so vivid, so startling that I gripped the wheel involuntarily. I saw a transparent sheet of ice and beneath it, trapped, Grace's body, frozen in all its beauty, arms outstretched, hair spread in a golden fan around her head, like the Gaia symbol. Her skin was still perfect, full of colour and light, her features serene, and it was the incongruity of this that made the image evaporate as rapidly as it had come. I had seen dead people, young and old: they did not look beautiful or frozen or pink, they looked grey, diminished, void. I loosened my grip on the wheel and, breathing deeply, drove on.

The road was in a smart residential area behind Kensington High Street, in a devious one-way system designed to deter through traffic. Parking amid Mercs and BMWs, I tried calling

Marsh House again, but there was no reply and no answering machine. Will's mobile didn't answer either, while Maggie's number seemed to be permanently engaged.

In the streetlights I double-checked the address. Grace's mother lived in a flat on an upper floor of a grand white-stuccoed house, next to an embassy whose mother country one would be hard-pressed to locate with any precision. At the top of a short flight of marble steps there were smart shrubs in china pots and large mirrored half-lanterns on either side of a glossy black front door. The five bells were marked with numbers, no names. A notice warned: STRICTLY NO HAWKERS, NO SALESMEN, NO CIRCULARS.

I pressed the bell of Flat 3 twice before the intercom crackled into life. I gave my name.

'*Who?*' the voice cried.

I reminded her that we had spoken on the telephone that morning.

'But the *name*.'

I repeated it.

'I thought it was *Wood*-something. William said you were called *Wood*-something.'

'Woodford was my maiden name,' I explained. 'My married name is O'Neill.'

'Well, *really*,' she complained, with a sharp sigh. The intercom went dead and the electronic door-release gave a fierce buzz. Flat 3 was on the first floor. It was a while before the door was unbolted and opened. Veronica Bailey was a tall woman with a long gaunt face, a slash of scarlet lipstick and the sort of upswept hairstyle that can only be maintained by frequent trips to the hairdresser. Her hair was an indeterminate shade, somewhere between mouse and blonde, and her skin seemed to blend into the pallor of her rheumy eyes.

She murmured ungraciously, 'You'd better come in.'

Shutting the door behind me with a resounding thud, she marched past and led the way across a narrow hall into a room decorated in a style reminiscent of Grace's drawing room at

Marsh House, pale carpets, overstuffed chintz furniture, heavy silk curtains, gloomy oil paintings, fine antique furniture and horizontal surfaces covered in knick-knacks and framed photographs. The effect would have been one of comfortable opulence if the carpet hadn't been threadbare around the door, the curtains faded at the edges, the chair arms shiny and bleached, and the skirt of the wine-coloured sofa blackened by the scuffs of men's heels. It was the sort of wear that comes with long residence and the indifference of familiarity.

She indicated a chair beyond a low gilt table piled high with glossy magazines. She sat on the sofa opposite me, on the far side of a fireplace containing a mock coal fire, unlit. In the glow of the pink-shaded table lamps it was hard to tell her age. Her face and hands suggested sixty, while her clothes, which were formal and curiously old-fashioned, seemed to fix her in another generation altogether.

'Well,' she said, in a commanding voice, 'I can't imagine why you should be here. I can't imagine why you should be involved in this matter.'

'I'm a solicitor, Mrs Bailey.' Putting a slight slant on my qualifications, I added, 'With experience in missing persons. I'm checking on your daughter's appointments in London, both on the day after she disappeared and on previous visits.'

'Why?'

'Well . . . To see if we can find anything which might shed light on her disappearance.'

'Shed light?' she scoffed. 'There's only one way to do *that*.' Her eyes flashed with sudden fury. 'I must say, he's got a nerve. Sending you to ask questions. Really!' Her agitation sent her forward in an abrupt movement to scoop up a packet of cigarettes from the low table.

'It's a matter of assembling all the available information, Mrs Bailey, so that every possibility can be covered.'

'Every possibility,' she repeated, with a furious laugh. She leant forward again and scrabbled around the piles of magazines. 'There's only one possibility as far as I'm concerned.' She scooped up a gold lighter and lit a cigarette. 'He was always out of his depth,' she declared, launching into what was clearly a favourite grievance. 'Never up to her standards. Always dragging her down!'

Ignoring these remarks, I asked, 'I was wondering if you might be aware of who she was going to see later that Thursday, after she was due to see you, a meeting she might have cancelled. Someone with the initials AWP who lived in a block of flats on Regent's Park.'

'No idea. I've already told *him* that. Really, this is such a farce!' She smoked in the grand manner, supported her elbow in the cup of one hand, sweeping the cigarette from her mouth to some point in space in a wide flamboyant arc accompanied by an elegant rotation of the wrist. She talked with the cigarette too, swaying it back and forth, bringing it up short, weaving it through the air to make her point. 'It doesn't matter who this A— A-whoever person is. This whole thing's a complete waste of time.'

'I appreciate that these questions might seem irrelevant at this stage, but without much to go on, we have to consider—'

'Nothing to go on? Rubbish! He's just playing innocent. Trying to make you think he doesn't know anything about what's happened to Grace! Trying to make the *world* think he doesn't know!'

Nothing Will had said had prepared me for the strength of Veronica Bailey's prejudices, nor the malevolence of her delivery. She was burning with contempt and unshakeable righteousness. Even allowing for her anxiety over her daughter, her animosity was without the slightest moderation or self-restraint.

'You're making some extremely serious allegations,' I said.

'Indeed I am!' she retorted. 'It's been deceit all the way along the line, so why should he change now? He tricked her into marrying him, he—' Watching my face, her eyes lit up avidly. 'You didn't know that? Oh, *yes*, totally tricked her. Pretended he owned all that land, pretended he was the lord of the manor,' she recounted with bitter relish. 'So grand, so full of himself. And all the time he hadn't got a penny, not a penny! He was a cheat! Leading her on! Never saying a word until after the wedding. Just wanted her money, you see! Just waiting to get his hands on it!'

This picture of Will was so grotesque that for a moment I couldn't think of anything to say. Recovering a little, I asked tentatively, 'And did he? Get her money?'

She drew on her cigarette and glared at me through the spiralling smoke, suddenly wary. 'Some.'

'Was it a great deal of money?'

'I don't think that's any of your business,' she stated royally.

Letting this pass, I referred to my notebook. 'So . . . What about the people she lunched with when she was in London. Could you tell me anything about them?'

'Oh, she had lots of friends. *Old* friends,' she emphasized in case I hadn't appreciated the superiority of Grace's former life. 'She lunched with them all the time.'

'Could you give me a few names?'

The cigarette waved this aside. 'I'm no good at names.'

'Anyone who lived in Knightsbridge?'

'Thousands of people live in Knightsbridge. I mean, among one's friends.'

'What about her close friends?'

'There were lots,' she said curtly, and I began to wonder just how much Veronica Bailey really knew about her daughter's life.

'Old friends, then? From school days. Family friends.'

She stubbed out her cigarette with enough vigour to crush a dangerous insect. 'I *suppose* I could give you one or two, but I assure you it'll be a complete waste of time.'

'Thank you anyway,' I said politely.

She gave a heavy sigh and, getting up, swiftly left the room, chin high, shoulders back as if making a stage exit, and I wondered if she had been an actress at one time. The framed photographs scattered about the room showed groups in Ascot clothes, groups in evening dress, a young man in regimental dress uniform taken some years ago – husband, perhaps, or brother – and two pictures of Grace. No clues as to Veronica's past. On the mantelpiece was an impressive line of invitations, though on closer examination I saw that every one was for a charity event, the type organized by professional fund-raisers armed with long lists of ladies who lunch.

Veronica marched back in and handed me a piece of paper with three names and addresses on it. She leant over and stabbed a finger against one name. 'You probably won't be able to get hold of *her*, though. They travel.'

'Thank you.'

As Veronica had pointed out the name I'd caught a whiff of something on her breath. Now as she moved back to her seat I caught it again, and this time there was no mistaking the scent of the distillery, something malty from north of the border. The smell was too strong to be anything but fresh. Since it was five thirty I was left to wonder if Veronica was fond of late lunches or early cocktails or regular nips from a supply in the kitchen.

As she lit another cigarette and planted it in her mouth her hands were perfectly steady, and her eyes also when she caught my gaze. 'He's very clever, you know,' she said, and I didn't need to ask who she was talking about. 'Fools people with that smooth manner of his, that charming smile. Thinks he can get round anyone. Well, he did, of course,' she said with sudden feeling, staring fiercely at the unlit fire. 'He got round Grace. That's the pity. That's the absolute tragedy.' For an instant I thought she was close to tears, but it wasn't sorrow that was stirring her, it was the old fury again. 'Did you know Grace wanted to leave him?' she demanded.

'No.'

'Soon after they were married. When she discovered the truth about the farm. Rented. *Rented.*' For all the disgust in her face she might have been talking about a hanging offence. 'She felt totally betrayed – and who could blame her? I encouraged her to leave. God only knows, she had reason to, if anyone did! But she was too good, of course. Too *forgiving*, too *generous*. That was Grace – *generous* and *loving*. She felt she should stick it out. Ha!' And now her eyes contained the glitter of old disappointments, the shine of bitter tears. Collecting herself again, returning to the fray, she added, 'And he was cruel, you know. *Cruel*.'

I couldn't hide my incredulity any longer. 'Cruel?'

'Oh, yes! He would deny her things all the time. Belittle her. He seemed to have this . . .' She flicked her hand repeatedly, indicating matters too unpleasant to mention. 'To have this ghastly sick *hold* over her. You know – some dreadful *power*.' It was such a curious phrase, so histrionic, that I was reminded of the theatre again.

'Power?'

'*Power*,' she insisted impatiently, as if I were being extraordinarily slow. 'He *frightened* her in some awful way. These people always do that, don't they, when they get hold of someone like Grace. Men who've landed someone out of their league, someone who shows them up for what they are – they hate it, don't they? They get to be bullies, they get their own back in horrid *nasty* little ways!'

I could only stare at her. The scene was painted so thickly and so garishly that I could only wonder how much of it was imagination, how much vindictiveness, and how much stemmed from her own experiences with men. 'Out of his league. In what way?' I prompted, trying to gauge the extent of Veronica's grasp on reality.

'Well, a tiny farm in a corner of Norfolk – I mean, he's a country boy, isn't he? No idea about music or travel or life in the real world. Just mud and animals!' She made a face before pushing herself abruptly to her feet. For a moment I thought she was going to ask me to leave, but she merely said, 'I need some water. Do you . . .?' She was on her way even as I shook my head.

When she returned she had a full glass in her hand, and if

it contained water it was no more than a dash. 'Almost six.
Needed something stronger,' she said, raising the amber liquid
to her lips and taking a long gulp. 'I'm meant to be at some
party or another...' She indicated the invitations on the
mantelpiece.

'I'm sorry. I won't keep you—'

'No, no. They can wait. I'm out every night, you know.
Every night.' There was a desperate pride in her boast, the
lament of a woman facing age and time alone. 'It gets too
much sometimes, all these parties.' She waved her glass, as
she had waved her cigarette, with flamboyance, so that the
whisky almost slopped over the rim, and I realized that, in a
remarkably short space of time, she had crossed her alcoholic
threshold and become indubitably tight.

'She wasted her life when she married that man,' she sighed,
alighting on what was clearly another cherished refrain. 'She
had everything, *everything*. The world at her feet. Men falling
in love with her. Dan Elliott was crazy about her, you know,
just crazy about her.'

'Dan Elliott?'

She pulled an expression of amazement at my ignorance.
'Daniel Elliott. You *must* have heard of him. The actor.
Terribly famous. Oscar nominations.'

I placed him then. 'Of course.'

'She could have had him just like that.' She snapped her
fingers. 'But no, she was worried about all the separations you
get in the film business, wanted a normal family life. I told her,
I warned her she was wasting herself on Will Dearden. What
else could I do?'

'But she had Charlie,' I said.

'Oh, the *child*.' She cast her eyes heavenward. 'That was all
she needed!'

I wasn't sure what she meant. 'Oh?'

'Well, he's *slow*, isn't he? What do they call it nowadays?'
She fluttered her fingers at me as if I should be able to produce
the expression she was looking for. 'What *do* they call it?' she

repeated with a sigh of impatience. Finally it came to her. *'Dyslexic.* I ask you! Well, they can call it anything they like, but it's *slow* to anyone who can still speak English.'

'I don't think dyslexia is related to intelligence.'

'Of course it is! He's *slow,* I tell you. Born that way. Genetic. Defective genes. Well, there you are!' And she left me to conclude that the blame for this was also to be laid at Will's door.

'He seems a sweet child.'

'Sweet?' She lunged for a cigarette and this time the lighting did not go quite so smoothly. 'Sweet?' she repeated, dropping the lighter onto the table with a clatter. 'Well, if you like children who're half wild and totally uneducated.' She shuddered visibly before catching my gaze and amending her expression to something more compassionate. 'I could never understand why he couldn't go to a special school. After all, they have *wonderful* places for these children nowadays, don't they? *Wonderful.* All those games and – well, things they *like.* I don't know – *activities.* He'd have been much happier there. *Much* happier. But' – her eyes narrowed, her chin came forward – 'of course *he* wouldn't have it. Oh, *no.'* The hand with the cigarette made a stabbing motion at me, and a pillar of ash dropped onto the floor. 'Oh, he *said* it was because he wanted to keep the child at home. But no, it was the money! That's all – the money! He always used that as an excuse for getting his way. Always said they were short, just so he could stop her doing the things she wanted to do, stop her getting out and about. She had no freedom, you know. None at all! Oh, it was so *heartbreaking* after everything she should have been, should have had. Heartbreaking.'

Her diction was beginning to go, the words skidding ever closer to a collision. She was holding her head high, with a kind of shaky defiance, but I sensed the rapid approach of tears or rage. I knew it wasn't the moment to point out that Grace had enjoyed the freedom of trips to London, of giving and going to plenty of parties, of organizing a music festival.

I folded the list of names and put it in my bag. 'Thank you for seeing me.' I shifted to the edge of the seat, preparing to leave.

'Is that all?' she cried.

'You've been most helpful.'

She eyed me with sudden suspicion. 'What did you want anyway? Why did you come?'

'The names,' I reminded her. 'Grace's friends. I'll be contacting them as soon as I can.' I stood up.

'But they won't know anything, I'm telling you! There's only one person who knows anything!'

When she saw that I was fixed on going, she slid her drink onto the table and rose carefully to her feet, straightening up with exaggerated dignity, the grand lady at full height. 'He'll say anything,' she declared. 'Anything to make it look like Grace's fault.'

Now she had confused me, or possibly she had confused herself. 'Grace's fault?' I asked.

She frowned as she realized what she had just said. 'I meant . . . whatever it is, whatever the situation, it's never *his* fault. Never. He tries to blame her! Always has.'

'He hasn't mentioned blame to me.'

'No, well . . . He's probably got you just where he wants you, hasn't he? Yes . . .' The idea seemed to take root in her mind. 'Worked his charm on you, like he works his charm on everyone who doesn't know what he's really like!'

'I'm just doing my job, Mrs Bailey.' I made a move towards the door and waited.

She dropped her cigarette into an ashtray and progressed in stately fashion across the room as though to lead the way out. Seized by a last bout of suspicion, she halted abruptly a few inches away from me and gave me an unfocused glare. 'Why did he hire you, anyway?' she demanded. 'Why did he choose you?'

'Our families knew each other years ago.'

'Knew each other?'

'We used to live in Deepwell.'

She considered this information with distrust before slow realization spread over her face, a dawning so conspicuous as to be almost comical. '*Woodford*. I thought I knew the name.' She loomed closer to me and I caught the whisky again. 'Isn't that . . . *Edward*? Is he . . .?'

'My brother.'

'Your *brother*!' she cried. '*Edward*! Well, well . . .' And her eyes took on an admiring light. '*Well! Such* a nice chap! And that lovely house of his – lending it for Grace's festival! Well, well – you should have said! Why didn't you say?'

'I didn't know you'd met.'

'But of course!' she sang, in a voice heavy with approval. 'Grace took me to see the house. We had tea. *So* nice! You should have told me!'

Making the most of my newly enhanced status, I asked, 'May I phone you if I have any queries?'

'Of course!' she cried, the vision of cordiality and co-operation. 'Of course!'

We reached the door and I asked, 'Was Grace planning to stay with you that Thursday night?'

'She hardly ever stayed in town. Not allowed to.' She added darkly, '*He* hated town. Never wanted to come.'

'But that night?'

She dismissed the question briskly. 'No, no.'

'Might she have been planning to stay with anyone else?'

'I really wouldn't know. Goodbye, Mrs O'Neill.' And with a stately inclination of the head, a gracious smile and eyes grown suddenly bleak, she showed me out and closed the door.

The house was dark when I let myself in at eight, the mail littered across the mat, the stale scent of last night's cigarettes in the air. Mechanically I shuffled through the buff envelopes and circulars before going to check the answering machine. There were two messages: the cleaning lady to say she was down with the flu, and Paul informing me that he was tied up and wouldn't be back until late. I recognized his tone. It was the chirpy voice he used to signify that all was well with the world, and that Paul O'Neill was a fine trustworthy fellow, the tone he adopted after the first three or four drinks. He made no mention of what was keeping him late and in my present state of pessimism I didn't imagine he was poring over case files in the office. I also noted that he had not called me on my mobile because then he would have run the risk of speaking to me in person.

I went and splashed my face with cold water before sitting at my desk and trying Marsh House for the fourth or fifth time that day. There was still no reply, but this time the answering machine was on and Will's calm voice invited messages. I outlined the Norfolk Police's plan for a TV appeal and briefly summarized Ray Dodworth's findings. I mentioned that I had been to see Veronica, but gave no details.

Putting the phone down, I faced my empty home.

I went through the rooms, clearing the last of the debris from the evening's party. Paul's lunchtime business meeting – 'just a short half-hour, Lexxy, and, *honestly*, it had to be Sunday, no other day they could do' – had turned into an afternoon marathon, fuelled by beer, sandwiches and coffee. No sooner had the clients left, no sooner had I started to look forward to a quiet evening, than a couple of Paul's tennis buddies had arrived, invited – so I gathered – for a quick drink. This session had also turned into something of a marathon, an altogether noisier affair, fuelled by three bottles of wine and a scrappy meal I had produced from the freezer.

I went about the clearing up with a mindless energy, collecting ashtrays, unloading the dishwasher, putting out the empty bottles in one continuous seam of action, for fear of losing heart half-way through. It hadn't been so long ago that Paul and I had made the chores into an opportunity for talk and jokes.

I straightened the last cushion, wiped the last surface of its glass mark. My home was immaculate once more, and I could hardly bear to look at it.

I ate a little and did two hours on the paperwork I'd collected from the office. When my mind began to wander I read a few pages of a crime novel in which two policemen crack a murder alone, without a back-up team or any obvious contact with their headquarters. When I had started the same page three times, I took a sleeping pill. After a hot bath, a glass of lemon and honey, a warm dressing gown – the comforters of my youth – I went to bed, trying to believe that I would sleep.

I must have dozed off quite quickly because before I knew it the telephone was trawling me from the depths of a dark and distant dream.

'I'm sorry, did I wake you?'

Will's voice.

'No, no.' I fumbled for the light and sat up.

'This TV appeal, why do they want *me* there?' Will's tone was light, but not so light that I couldn't detect the tension in his voice.

'It's the coverage . . .' My brain was still steeped in darkness, it was an effort to think. 'There'll be much wider coverage if you can take part.'

'But it's so . . .' He wrestled with the thought. 'So . . . *public.*'

'But very effective. Your being there will make all the difference. I do urge you to agree, Will.'

I heard him exhale sharply. 'I hate the thought, Alex. *Hate* it.' Then: 'Well, I can't do it tomorrow anyway.' There was finality in his voice.

'Not at all?'

'I'm taking Maggie to the hospital.'

'Oh. Nothing serious?'

'Her gallstones. They're trying to persuade her to have an operation.'

'Wednesday, then? You could do it on Wednesday?'

'I suppose so, yes.'

'I'll call them first thing in the morning.'

'Must I do it?' But there was capitulation in his voice; he was almost reconciled to it.

'Yes.'

A pause and he said, 'Veronica didn't eat you, then?'

'It was a close-run thing.'

He gave an arid laugh. 'She doesn't mince her words, does she? I suppose my name was mud. It usually is.'

'Fairly murky, yes.'

'I'm responsible for everything, I suppose? What about Grace's disappearance? That too?'

'I didn't take anything she said too seriously.'

'But she said it?' There was an edge to his tone.

'Yes.'

He sighed heavily. 'God.'

I pushed the pillow up behind my head and lay back. The bedside clock read past midnight. 'Tell me . . .' I framed the question, only to glimpse pitfalls ahead. 'No . . .' I amended quickly. 'No, it's all right. Nothing.'

'Say it, Alex.'

I cursed the sleeping pill. I had forgotten what the stuff did to your brain: the slowness and the fog. 'It was only that the police have been to see Veronica, haven't they?'

'I think so, yes.'

'And do we know what she told them?'

'No,' he exclaimed wryly, 'but with Veronica it's fairly safe to assume that she didn't hold back.'

'In which case the police will have got a' – I struggled to find the right word – 'a fairly *biased* view of things.'

'You mean, it'll give them all the more reason to think I've done something terrible to Grace?' he said tightly, sounding trapped.

I wished I could see his face, I wished I was with him. I sat forward again and dug my fingers hard into my temple. 'I think perhaps I should have a word in Ramsey's ear, suggest that anything coming from Veronica should be treated with the utmost caution.'

'If you think so.'

'We don't want any untruths floating about, Will.'

He made a nervous sound, half gasp, half laugh. 'Bit late for that probably.'

'Not at all. But I'll need to go through it with you first, to get the facts right.'

'If you say so.' He was sounding distracted now.

Trying not to picture the pile of work on my desk, I heard myself say, 'I'll come up tomorrow afternoon if I can, Wednesday morning at the latest.'

'You'll stay around for the TV thing, though, won't you?' he asked anxiously.

'Of course.'

A long silence, which we broke at the same moment. I began, 'I'll phone you—' as he said, 'Sometimes I can't help—' Another pause. When he finally spoke again his voice was very taut. 'I can't help thinking that she's somewhere close by.'

I waited.

'Sometimes I have this nightmare,' he went on. 'I see her ... in this place ...' A long pause. 'Trapped in some way. With water around her.'

I closed my eyes, I was very still. The picture danced grotesquely before me, an unnerving echo of my own brief vision, and for an instant my memory played wild tricks, mixing up time and place, reality and imagination. For a crazy moment I thought I might have told him of my own vision of Grace, might in some bizarre way have planted it in his mind.

He went on in a rough whisper, 'Sometimes it's all happening years ago, when Grace and I first met. You know – when I helped her out of that ditch. But then it's not like that after all.' He made a sound that was both a gasp and a shudder. 'There's water . . . And it's awful. *Awful*.'

'Doesn't the mind do that, though?' I ventured to fill the silence. 'Doesn't it try to make sense of disturbing things by

linking the past with the present? Equating the first incident
with danger, any danger, and then updating it. I'm sure you'll
find that's all it is.'

Another silence before he said, 'You're probably right.'
Then, in an attempt to convince himself: 'Yes, you must be
right!' It was another moment before he shook himself free and
said in a more conversational tone, 'I was on the salt-marsh
today. By Thorp Creek, near that rotting boat – do you
remember?'

'Of course. Is it still there?'

'Well, just the ribs. But, tell me, we took *Pod* there once,
didn't we?'

'More than once, I think.'

'And was that where we cooked the sausages? I was trying
to remember.'

I couldn't suppress a small leap of pleasure. 'Yes.'

'That's what I thought.' And he spoke like someone trying
to slot the various aspects of his life into some sort of order.
'We didn't eat them, though, did we?'

'Not enough dry wood for the fire. They were still raw.'

'That's right. I *knew* there was something. Yes . . .'

A pause in which he appeared to forget I was there.

'Goodnight, Will. We'll speak tomorrow.'

'Goodnight. And, Ali?'

Ali. No one else had ever called me this. 'Yes?'

'Thanks for everything.'

I lay awake for a long while. Just as I was sliding towards a
troubled sleep, I was woken by the click of Paul's key in the
front door. In recent months when Paul had come in late I had
taken to feigning sleep rather than endure a rambling inarticu-
late conversation. Tonight, however, I switched the light on
again and, propping myself up, pretended to read a book.
There were brief clatterings from the kitchen, then Paul's heavy
tread on the stairs.

His head appeared round the door sideways, like a co-
median at a theatre curtain, getting a feel for the audience.

'Hi!' I said with false cheer.

'Still up?' he said amiably, testing the water further.

'Couldn't sleep.'

Squinting at me from under drooping lids, trying to determine if it was really a smile on offer or something less welcoming, he finally wandered into the room. I could see the sweat glistening on his forehead, the blood pressure in his cheeks. He halted suddenly and, tapping a finger to his forehead in a gesture of memory, turned unsteadily and went out to the bathroom.

The disappointment never lessened, the pain never became any less sharp. However hard I tried to suppress my hopes they always bobbed foolishly back to the surface: the belief that he might change, that somehow or another he would rediscover his self-respect, that against the odds the next evening would be different.

When he reappeared I produced another smile. 'Ships that pass in the night. I wasn't expecting to see you in court this morning.'

Amid heavy breathing he stepped out of his trousers and draped them over a chair. 'Oh, goodness . . . it was just a remand, you know. Just a remand.'

'That's why I couldn't work out why you didn't ask me to do it for you.' I kept my voice light, and my smile too.

He began to unbutton his shirt with studied concentration. 'No, no . . . had to do it myself. The client . . . wasn't sure what he wanted, you know.'

'Was there a question of a bail application, then?'

'Possibly. Yes, that was it – bail.'

'But you sent Sturgess to get the instructions. I could have done that.'

The shirt was proving a nuisance and he tugged impatiently at the top buttons. 'It's a tricky case. Tricky.'

'Then why Sturgess? He's junior, after all.'

The buttons finally succumbed and Paul threw the shirt in the approximate direction of the laundry basket. 'Lexxy,

Lexxy, I just felt I should be there. Nothing more to it. Don't give me a hard time, *please*.' He sank ponderously onto the edge of the bed.

But I had to go on, I couldn't stop myself. 'It just seemed rather a duplication of effort, that's all. I can't understand why the office didn't tell you I was there. If the system's failing somewhere along the line, then we should make sure it doesn't happen again.'

'It's late, Lexxy.' He gestured weariness, his voice rose peevishly. 'Can't it wait, for God's sake? Tomorrow's another day!'

'I wasn't suggesting we go into it now. It was just on my mind, that's all.'

'It was just a titchy little thing, a titchy little case, for heaven's sake!'

'Was it?' And asking this, I was finally voicing my real concern. 'Who's Munro anyway? Is he an old client?'

'New.'

'What's his history?'

'Nothing much at all.'

'So it wasn't a case for special treatment, then?'

'*Lord give me peace!*' Paul cried, with a great shudder of exasperation. 'It was just one of those things, for God's sake. Just – just . . .' He splayed out a furious hand, the veins on his neck and temple stood out, and for an instant I thought he might burst a blood vessel. He let his anger go in a rush, with a long sigh, then hunched forward and clutched a hand to his forehead. 'Oh, Lexxy, Lexxy . . . I was going to tell you tomorrow. Honest to God, I was.' He twisted round to cast me a sheepish look. 'To tell you the honest truth, Lexxy, I *forgot*.'

I waited.

'I forgot the case was coming up today and by the time I realized . . .' He put on a mortified expression, the errant child who had meant no harm. 'I sent Gary because I couldn't get away in time.'

'If that was all, why didn't you say so?' And I forced a smile.

'Oh, Lexxy . . . I felt so damned stupid, didn't I?' And he gave me the Irishman, all charm and penitence.

There was something about this story that still worried me, though I couldn't put my finger on it. 'Corinthia should have known. She should have reminded you.'

'No, no. Nothing to do with Corinthia. Entirely *me*.' He clapped a hand to his chest like an actor of the old school. 'Foolish Paul! Forgetful Paul! Feather-brained Paul!'

This was a cue we both knew well, the cue for me to reach out to him, to ask for and receive forgiveness, to offer the phrases of affection and understanding we had honed over the years. Yet for once something stopped me. My throat was tight, the words stalled on my tongue, I couldn't bring myself to make the first move. Finally I said matter-of-factly, 'Next time we'll be sure to compare notes then, shall we?'

He did not miss the significance of my tone. When he climbed into bed I could feel his reproach. 'I simply forgot, Lexxy. That's all. Forgot.'

I grunted noncommittally.

'Anyone would think . . .'

'I'll have a word with Corinthia in the morning.'

He rolled away from me, onto his side.

Reaching for the light switch, I said, 'By the way, I've been hearing things on the grapevine. About the Buck case.' I snapped the light off and lay back. When he didn't reply, I continued, 'They're saying Karen Grainey was a bought witness.'

There was still no response.

'Did you hear anything?' I persisted.

'Well, what kind of a question is that?' And his voice was thick with drink and irritation. 'Not our job to hear things like that, is it?' And with a throaty cough, he dug his head into the pillow and was soon asleep.

Chapter Five

I MEANT to get away by noon, but the day started badly with a series of crises and continued as it had begun, a day in which everyone in the firm seemed to be running madly just to stand still. I didn't need a time-and-motion expert to tell me that, for perhaps the third time in six months, the firm had taken on too much work. At the last partners' meeting I'd brought up the thorny old subject of a fifth partner, but, to no one's great surprise, and certainly not to mine, Paul had squashed the idea yet again. I'd argued harder than ever, but there was no budging Paul when he was in a state of financial insecurity, and so we continued to hit these mountains of work, the staff struggling to get briefs ready on time, racing across London from case conferences to courts, from police cells to prisons, giving up more and more of their own time. Everyone was beginning to look haunted. Even Corinthia had lost her smile. Only Sturgess seemed to thrive on the pace, but then the whole business was still a game to him.

I finally set out for Norfolk at seven that evening. Even then, like some brash whizzkid living on the hoof, I used the mobile to dictate a couple of urgent letters into Corinthia's answering machine. Clear of the worst jams by eight thirty, following the stream of commuters through Essex towards the greater darkness of Cambridgeshire, I had a sense of leaving the worst tensions behind.

I reached Wickham Lodge at ten thirty and stepped into a silence broken only by the ticking of dripping leaves and the distant call of a night bird. A thaw had left the air damp and heavy with the scent of soil and mouldering grass: a sweet poignant smell that took me back to the past.

Edward opened the front door in old clothes and slippers and waved me in with a glass of whisky. 'There you are. I was just having a nightcap. Like one?' He lifted his eyebrows in enquiry.

'A sandwich and a cup of tea would be great.'

He made a doubtful face. 'Ham? On second thoughts it might have to be cheese.'

The bread was white and steam-baked, the butter salty and hard from the fridge, the cheese a deep yellow mousetrap. I hadn't expected much else. Edward took a perverse pride in shunning fine foods and sticking to what he called perfectly good English nosh. He was a roast beef, shepherd's pie and whisky enthusiast, who stretched to pheasant and claret on high days. His taste had been fixed at an early age by the hearty Mrs Hill who had cooked for us after Mother had become too ill to manage the kitchen. Mrs Hill had been a follower of the old English school of cookery, a dedicated exponent of over-cooked vegetables, viscous gravy and dense apple pie. Within a year of her arrival I'd put on almost a stone and discovered teenage misery. Father had muttered about finding another housekeeper but he'd never quite mustered the courage to fire her, and in the end she'd stayed four years.

'Jilly here?' I asked.

'God, no. She's in Cambridge, working.' He lobbed a teabag into a mug.

I smelt traces of frying in the air and saw two sausages sitting in a blackened pan on the Aga. 'Who cooks for you?'

'*I* do,' he exclaimed, feigning offence. 'Sausages, chops, porridge. I'm perfectly capable, you know. Why do women always assume men are so helpless?'

'We like to think you need us.'

'Jilly buys a bit of stuff at weekends. Rabbit food, most of it.' He pulled a face of mock revulsion. 'Salads, fruit – women's fodder. But she tops up the freezer with pies and meaty things

as well, thank God.' Picking up the mug of tea, he led the way
into the hall. 'And then, of course, I'm out quite a bit. In fact,
it gets ridiculous sometimes, the social life in this place.' His
pretended irritation couldn't disguise his considerable satisfaction. Edward liked being in demand.

Nudging open the sitting-room door, he put the drinks on
a low table. I saw with surprise that, unlike the rest of the
house, this room had been done up, though in deference to
Edward's rather Spartan philosophy the effect had been kept
simple. The walls had been painted off-white, there were plain
cinnamon curtains at the windows, while the sofas were draped
with Indian cotton throws and scattered with bright floral
cushions. Someone had tried to achieve the maximum impact
on a limited budget, and I immediately thought of Jilly. A
blazing fire and the glow of table lamps added to the sense of
snugness you get from small rooms in large draughty houses.

Avoiding Edward's chair, clearly marked by the piles of
newspapers and remote controls, I took my plate to the
opposite side of the hearth. 'Grace Dearden was a leading light
on the social scene, I gather.'

'Well, most of the women *are* around here. Sometimes life
seems like one long drinks party.' He dropped into his chair
and lounged back, whisky clutched loosely in one hand.

'But Grace gave dinners, I gather. Impressive ones.'

'I believe so. I wasn't asked, of course.'

I chewed a dense mouthful of cheese and bread. 'What,
never?'

'Oh, once. No – *twice*. Ages ago, when I first moved in. But
Will made it fairly plain that he'd rather entertain Hitler.'

'Oh, come on.'

'I'm *telling* you,' he maintained with a fierce glare. 'Bloody
unfriendly. Sulked at the far end of the table. Threw dark looks
in my direction. That sort of thing.'

I took this with a pinch of salt: Edward had always been
prone to exaggeration. I suspected that in this case he'd let his
insecurities get the better of him. He had never been at ease

with men who didn't share his own rather blunt approach to life.

'Grace was in her element, though?'

'What? Oh, definitely. Brilliant cook.'

'Wasn't her food rather rich for you?'

'I *beg* your pardon.'

'I've seen some of her menus.'

'Not *too rich*, actually, *thank* you very much,' he protested. 'I'm not a total Philistine when it comes to food, you know.'

I put the wedge of waxy cheese and dry bread back on the plate. 'How would you describe Grace?' I asked. 'What's she like?'

He pulled his head back in mock recoil. 'Don't ask me. I'm the last person to ask. I'm hopeless on people. I mean, I take them as they come. I like them or I don't, but don't ask me to say *why*.'

'Okay then – did you *like* her?'

Exhaling slowly through pursed lips, he considered this. 'Yup,' he said reflectively, then with more decision: 'Yes, I did. She was always very charming. Very nice. Funny, too.'

'Funny?' I paused with my tea half-way to my mouth. 'Funny? In what way?'

'There you go again. Don't ask *me*. She just made me laugh, that's all.'

'What was she funny about?'

'Oh, for heaven's sake.' He gestured irritably. 'Umm . . . the neighbourhood, I suppose. People. The gossip – you know.'

I absorbed this slowly, and asked the question I'd already asked Maggie and Anne Hampton. 'Did she appear happy to you?'

'Happy?' His expression suggested that the very concept was an enigma to him, and I saw him as a kid again, hurt and permanently angry. 'God,' he sighed, looking into the fire, 'you do ask some questions. *Happy?* Well . . . she seemed *cheerful* enough. Always bubbly and sort of . . . positive. But the rest? I just wouldn't know. I didn't see that much of her.'

'Could she have had a lover somewhere, do you think?'

His head did a slow revolve towards me, his stare hardened, he searched my face to see if I were joking. 'A lover?' he repeated incredulously. 'You're asking *me*?' And now he gave a short laugh. 'Lex, I'd be the last person in the world to know something like that.' The dry laugh again. 'If there's any gossip doing the rounds I'm *always* the last to hear.' He scrabbled in his pocket and pulled out some cigarettes. 'Why? Is she meant to have had someone tucked away?'

'Not at all, no. But you were the one person I could ask without creating a rumour.'

'I think you just *did*. Create a rumour.' He rolled his eyes.

'You know what I mean! I was simply considering it as a possibility, that's all.'

'So there's no suggestion of a lover?'

'Well, no. But you never know.'

He lit his cigarette. 'Suspicious little mind, Lex.'

'Too much time in crime and family law.'

'You said it.' He shook his head with an exaggerated show of pity. He had always made a point of finding my devotion to the criminal classes totally incomprehensible.

I picked up the sandwich again, without enthusiasm. 'I went to see Grace's mother, Veronica Bailey. She says she's met you.'

He looked blank for a moment. 'Oh, yes – once.'

'She thinks you're wonderful.'

'Some people do, you know.'

'I wouldn't doubt it,' I smiled. 'What did you think of her?'

'*God*. Can't remember.' I waited but he made no effort to nudge his memory. 'Have a whisky!' he urged, sitting up as if to get one. 'Come on.'

'No thanks.'

'Abstemious Alex.'

'Not always.'

'Iron discipline.'

'I wish.'

He threw me a look of blatant scepticism before saying casually, 'So, what's the thinking on Grace's vanishing act?'

I abandoned the leaden sandwich for good. 'Complete blank. No ideas at all.'

'But the police must be thinking *something*.'

'I'm pretty sure they think she's dead.'

'And you?'

I took a moment to answer. 'I do too.'

'*So?* How do they think she died?'

'Murder must be a possibility.'

'A possibility,' he mimicked savagely. 'Really – you and your lawyer's talk, Lex.' For some reason he was getting angry with me. 'What else could it be?'

'Suicide. Mental breakdown.'

He waved this aside with a movement of his glass. 'No one believes that!'

'What *do* they believe, then?'

His eyes darkened, as though I had caught him out in some way. 'I told you, *I* don't know! I don't listen to gossip. But it seems strange that she disappeared on the very night someone tried to flood the Gun Marsh.'

Now it was he who'd caught me by surprise and I didn't attempt to conceal the fact. 'Someone tried to flood the marsh? Deliberately, you mean?'

'You didn't know?' And he took pleasure in being able to tell me. 'Sure. Someone opened the sluices.'

'I thought—' But I kept the rest of this to myself. 'Who would want to do that?'

'Who indeed?' he said with heavy emphasis. 'Someone who wanted to make the land worthless, perhaps? Someone who wanted to get at *me*?'

'*You?*'

'Sure! The tenancy reversion was almost agreed, they thought it'd be a good way of getting at *me*, didn't they?'

It was late, I was tired; I wasn't in the mood for games where everything was implied and nothing spoken. 'What are you trying to suggest exactly?'

'Nothing,' he argued unconvincingly. 'Just seems mighty *odd* that she should disappear on the very same night, that's all.'

'How do you know, anyway? That the flood was deliberate, I mean.'

'Those sluices don't open themselves.'

'But they could have been damaged.'

'Is that what *he* told you?' When I didn't reply, he nodded with irritating superiority, as though I had just confirmed my own gullibility. 'They weren't *damaged*, Alex.'

'But how do you *know*?'

He whistled softly to the dog and, gesturing for me to pass my plate over, picked up the remains of the sandwich and dropped it neatly into the dog's mouth. 'I was around the next morning,' he said, watching the dog snatch the food deeper into its gullet. 'I saw how much water there was on the marsh.'

'So?'

He gave me a pitying look. 'So *both* sluices had been opened. *Wide*. For a *long* time.'

'But . . .' I groped for my point. 'Why would Will try to drain the marsh if he'd only just flooded it?'

He shrugged. 'Make himself look good.'

'That's ridiculous, Ed.'

'It's *not* ridiculous!' he insisted, with a flash of his old vehemence. 'He's a tricky sod. Take my word for it! He behaved bloody badly over the Gun Marsh, tried to go behind my back. *Devious*, I tell you.' Perhaps I didn't look too convinced because he added hotly, 'And that's not even the half of it, believe me!'

I gave up then. There was no discussing things with Edward in this mood. When he felt himself to be aggrieved he was like a blunt instrument, beating away at the same argument until he battered his opponent into submission.

I said, 'I think I'll go straight to bed, if that's all right.'

Cheated of his argument, he sneered, 'No time for the truth, eh?'

'I haven't been sleeping, that's all.'

'Tossing and turning over our Will?'

I stood up. 'Sometimes you're so juvenile, Ed.'

He made a wide gesture of innocence. 'Just asking.'

'You're not just asking, you're stirring. It's a habit of yours, you know.'

'So touchy, Lex.'

'I'm tired. That's probably why.'

He twisted his mouth into a semblance of a smile: the retreat after the skirmish. 'I've put a hot-water bottle in your bed.'

'Thank you.'

We exchanged a look that contained the possibility of a truce.

'I'll show you up.' As he led the way across the hall he said in the tone of someone alighting on a safer subject, 'I sent that letter off to Pa's solicitor, by the way.'

'Oh, yes,' I said, only half listening.

He mounted the stairs at a slow trudge. 'I'll phone them tomorrow, just to make it clear we're not prepared to hang about too long.'

Still preoccupied, I picked a question out of the air. 'How did you know it was missing, this money?'

'Arithmetic.'

'Oh?'

He turned onto the last flight. 'The proceeds of the Falmouth house plus the value of his savings, less the nursing-home fees.' He spoke in the cool emotionless voice he kept for anything to do with Pa.

'And there was a hundred thousand missing?'

'It was hard to tell precisely, but I knew it must be well over seventy.' He paused at the door of a guest bedroom.

'And you have some idea of where it's got to?'

He glared at me. 'Did I say that?'

'No. I just thought . . .' I made a gesture of forgetfulness. 'I don't know.'

'I have no idea at all of where it might be. Which is the whole point of finding out.'

'It may be very hard to track down after all this time,' I suggested.

'It's only a *year* ago.'

'Well, don't get too upset if it can't be found.'

'Too upset?' He made a brittle exclamation. 'Of course I'll be bloody upset. It belongs to us.'

'Maybe Pa gave it away to a good cause.'

'I'm not interested in any of that,' he retorted.

There was no soothing such relentlessness and, letting the subject pass, I leant forward to kiss him.

Responding to some childhood reflex, he stiffened slightly as my lips met his cheek. 'Goodnight, Lex,' he said. 'Sleep well.'

'Goodnight, Ed. Thanks for having me.' And I smiled to show that I meant it.

'Make the most of it,' he remarked, in his most flippant tone. 'I may not ask you again.'

The dawn was soft with rain as I walked quickly up the side path to Marsh House and tapped on the kitchen door. A shadow moved across the lighted window, the door opened swiftly and Will stood silhouetted against the starry interior. He stepped back and beckoned me in.

'Breakfast?' he asked, and his eyes were dull and distant, like someone who has neither slept nor woken properly.

'Some toast would be lovely.'

While he cut some bread, I poured myself a cup of coffee from the jug on the table. 'Charlie not up?'

'He's at Mum's.'

In the silence that followed I was struck by a sudden

awkwardness. 'I told Ramsey we'd be in Norwich by three,' I said as Will put the bread into the toaster. 'I said I'd like to have a quiet talk before the news conference. I told him it was to do with Veronica. Never does any harm to give them an idea of what you're going to say.'

Will nodded vaguely as he moved to the Aga and stirred something in a pan.

'I thought I'd go and see Maggie later,' I hurried on. 'Is she all right? You said you were taking her to the hospital.'

'What? Oh, yes, she's fine. Fine. It was just a routine thing.'

I chattered on. 'Is there anyone else I should talk to? Like friends of Grace's? Or her doctor? Had she seen him recently, do you know?'

Will tipped scrambled eggs out of the pan onto some toast. He took his time to answer. 'I don't think so. Her doctor's Julian Hampton, up the road in—' He shook his head abruptly in disbelief. 'For heaven's sake, in your *father*'s old practice.' His lapse of memory seemed to cast him into a deeper gloom.

He brought the plate of scrambled eggs to the table and stood in front of it, staring in an unfocused way at a point somewhere on a far wall. His hair was wild and uncombed, his chin unshaven, his shirt wrongly buttoned so that one collar stood too high. He looked like a gypsy just in from the marsh.

'Did Ramsey call you yesterday?'

The toaster popped and he came to with a jolt. 'Er, no . . . Just the woman, Barbara Smith.' He brought me the toast then butter and marmalade. When he finally sat down he fell back into a trance.

I got up and searched a couple of drawers until I found a knife and fork which I put beside his plate.

'Oh.' He looked surprised. 'Thanks.'

I found myself another knife and sat down again. 'Are you taking anything to help you sleep?'

'What? Oh . . . just valerian, if you count that.'

'Does it work?'

'Apparently not,' he said with a faint stab at humour.

'Perhaps you should consider something stronger.'

'Trouble is, I always forget to take pills. Even the valerian – it's sometimes two in the morning before I remember.'

'Well, try eating some breakfast. Might make you feel better.'

He looked down at the fast-cooling eggs as if seeing them for the first time, then cast me a look which was suddenly very focused.

'Always so practical, Alex. Always so sensible.'

For some reason this pricked my vanity. 'Not a failing, I hope.'

'God, no. No – I always thought it was a wonderful thing to be. When we were kids . . . well, you weren't like other girls.'

'Oh?'

'More like a boy.' Appreciating his gaffe, he laughed. 'In the nicest possible way.'

I smiled back, but faintly.

Focusing on the meal at last, Will began to eat half-heartedly. 'So . . . Veronica . . . What heinous crimes am I meant to have committed?' he asked without rancour. 'I lose track.'

'Well . . . there were quite a few.'

'There always are.'

I began at the milder end of the spectrum. 'She suggested that Grace was unhappy.'

He shook his head with something like pity. 'That's what Veronica wanted to believe, of course. Always did. *Desperate* for it to be true. But what Veronica wants in life and what she gets are two very different things, and that's what she's never been able to accept.'

'So Grace was happy?'

He looked towards the window, his expression taut. 'Grace wasn't capable of unhappiness.'

Maggie had said almost the same thing. Anne Hampton,

too. I wondered again now, as I had wondered then, at the sort of person who was immune to unhappiness.

Will began to eat again, with more enthusiasm, as though he had suddenly developed a hunger. 'What else did she say, the witch?'

'She said there was a time when you and Grace almost split up. Soon after you were married. When Grace discovered she had been – I think Veronica used the word – *tricked*.'

'Ha!' The insinuation had touched a nerve; his face came alive, his voice too. 'Yes, yes. I failed to inform Grace that I was a man of straw. I *lied* to her! I was a devious trickster who'd deprived Grace of her one great chance of marrying money. Ha!'

'There was no question of splitting up, then?'

'After this great betrayal came to light, you mean? After I'd ruined Grace's life?' He gave a contemptuous scoff and attacked his toast with a sawing motion. 'Though Veronica would have loved it. Would have loved Grace to cut her losses and find someone better.'

'Even with Charlie . . .'

'Oh, children aren't a consideration for Veronica. They barely enter into her reckoning at all.'

'Though she obviously felt so passionately about Grace.'

He acknowledged the point with a lift of his fork. 'But only in a vicarious way. Only when she saw that Grace was going to attract notice. When she realized that Grace might achieve the sort of life she'd always hankered after. The life that she herself had been' – he gave the words a mocking emphasis – 'cruelly denied.'

'How was it denied her?'

'Oh, by Grace's father. A great disappointment to her. A nice man, from what I hear, but no ball of fire. Quiet and long-suffering. Never made it beyond major in the Guards, then had some poorly paid job as a club secretary. Generally useless with money. Veronica never forgave the poor bloke. He died young. Most men would have done the same in his position.'

'But Veronica's got a bit of money?'

'Very little.'

'But that flat?'

'Only three years left on the lease.'

'Ah.' I saw Veronica's despair in a new light. 'And Grace? She has some money?'

He gave me a look of mild reproach. 'Ah,' he said coolly. 'Are we on to another allegation?'

I said hastily, 'I should have spelt it out. I'm sorry. Yes . . .' Slowing down again, getting it right, I recounted carefully, 'Veronica said that you had married Grace with an eye to her money and had then gone and spent most of it.'

Abandoning his food, Will put down his fork and pushed the plate away. 'What was I meant to have spent it on?'

'She didn't say.'

'No, I didn't think she would,' he said scathingly. 'She'd have difficulty in listing my extravagances.' He sat back in his chair and fixed me with an open gaze. 'Grace had something like a hundred thousand pounds when we married. It came from an aunt, I believe. She spent some of it on the house, on the redecorations and so on. I don't know how much. She didn't want to tell me.' His mouth twitched slightly at the memory. 'We agreed a budget and she overspent it. She wouldn't say how far over she'd gone, but she used her own money to pay the difference. It was her idea. I mean, I didn't ask her to.' Another memory caught him and sent his gaze to the window. 'What was left after that – well, I assume it's still invested. But I really don't know. It's her money.'

'Did the police ask you about your financial situation?'

'Yup. Asked if we had money worries.'

'And what did you tell them?'

'I said we were managing.' He grinned bleakly, without humour. 'Which wasn't strictly true.'

'I should have said straight away that I know about the Gun Marsh, and I'm very sorry. More sorry than I can say.'

He gave a slow shrug, he dropped his eyes. 'These things have to be done sometimes.'

I searched his face, but if he felt bitter at losing the Gun he was hiding it well. Only a flickering muscle in his cheek betrayed the slightest tension.

He glanced inside the coffee pot and, pushing back his chair, took it to the counter.

I said, 'There was no way to avoid selling the marsh?'

He plopped the kettle onto the Aga. 'Apparently not.' And something in his tone told me he didn't want to discuss it.

I took the breakfast plates to the sink. It was impossible not to think of Grace standing where I was standing, talking to Will on a thousand sunnier days. In my imagination she looked immaculate even first thing in the morning.

'So,' Will declared with brittle amusement, 'what other crimes am I supposed to have committed? I'm sure Veronica wouldn't let me stop at lies and making Grace unhappy and running through her money. Hardly a *start*, really.'

But he didn't want to hear any more, he was tired of it all, I could see it in his face. I remembered Veronica's final salvoes, the sinister hold Will was meant to have had over Grace, the freedom he was meant to have denied her, and as I put the plates in the dishwasher I said, 'There was nothing else.'

'Well, I suppose I should count myself lucky.' He measured coffee into the pot, then, spoon in mid-air, halted suddenly. '*No*. Let's go out.'

'Sorry?'

'Out.' He chucked the spoon back into the coffee tin, jammed the lid on, and, already on the move, tipped his head towards the door. 'Come on.'

Caught up by his sense of urgency I didn't ask where we were going, or why, but pulled on my jacket and followed him outside into the freshness of the morning. Pausing only to take some boots from the car, I fell into step beside him as he strode towards the marshes.

The boat trickled across the creek towards me, gliding over a perfect unbroken mirror, carried forward by its own mysterious momentum. Will, standing in the stern, rotated the scull a degree and the nose swung gently round to bring the boat neatly alongside the two planks forming the narrow jetty on which I stood. Will grasped one of the piles to halt the last of the boat's progress and, lowering the scull, reached his other hand to me. Taking it, I stepped down into the boat. I aimed for the centre line but my foot landed a few inches short. The boat lurched, and I with it.

'Oops.' I reached for the far gunwale.

Will laughed, 'Forgotten it all, Ali?'

Ali.

'Looks like it.'

I settled myself on the thwart, facing forward, and this time I made sure I was dead on the centre line so that I didn't unbalance the boat. The boat was longer than *Pod* and broader, a flat-bottomed oyster boat.

Will pushed off and the boat began to sway gently to the rhythmic motion of his scull. Neither of us spoke. The only sounds were the chuckling of the water under the bow and the whisperings of the wake and the occasional creak of the oar in the rowlock. The rain had stopped, leaving a mist that hung on the air in a heavy curtain, blotting out the horizon so that the greyness of the marsh merged imperceptibly with the greyness of the sky. As we travelled through this silent world, enclosed in a soft globe of land and water, I felt the extraordinary sense of space and distance that I had felt in this place as a child. It was as though we were sliding through a vast and mysterious universe which had no end.

Reaching a bend, the surface of the water was corrugated

by ripples, marking a stronger current, and Will had to work the scull a little harder. The gentle roll of the boat, the murmurings of the water, were like a lullaby, and I let them carry me forward in a kind of dream.

A bank rose darkly out of the mist to our right: the embankment marking the edge of the Gun Marsh. We weren't far from the sluice I had passed the other day, and I wondered if it was the sluice which had been damaged, or – Edward's emphatic voice reverberated in my mind – opened deliberately.

I saw the break in the bank first, then the curving brickwork marking the tunnel, and above it the sturdy wooden frame with the slots that housed the guillotine-like gate. As we drew level I looked into the tunnel arch and saw the top of the gate with the tall threaded shaft above. I kept looking until we were past and the sluice was hidden again by the bank and the mist. Swinging my legs over the thwart to face Will, I found him staring back over his shoulder, the oar motionless in his hand. When he turned round again I asked lightly, 'Was that the one which was damaged?'

He nodded.

'It's all right now?'

He nodded again and as he looked into the distance his eyes were unreadable. He began to scull again, moving his weight slightly from foot to foot as he wove the oar blade through the water in a flowing figure-of-eight motion.

'How was it damaged exactly?' In the silence my voice seemed too loud.

'Oh, one of the slots gave way,' he replied abstractedly.

I absorbed this slowly. 'There was no question of intentional damage?'

Suddenly I had his full attention. 'What do you mean?'

'I don't know. Vandalism?'

'No.'

'And it couldn't have been opened deliberately?'

The muscles in his cheeks began to work furiously, he threw

me a violent stare. 'Where did you get that idea from?' When I didn't reply he said just as forcefully, 'Is that what people are saying?'

'No. Not at all. No, just . . .' Having got this far, I told him the rest. 'It was Edward's idea.'

'*Edward.*'

I was regretting having raised the subject. 'He seemed to think – I'm not sure why exactly – that both gates had been opened deliberately.'

'How could he say that?' Will exclaimed, looking terribly upset. 'How could he possibly have any idea of what really happened?'

'I don't know.'

'Well, it's rubbish! He's talking rubbish! It all happened at night. By morning I'd repaired the blasted thing. Of course he didn't see the damage to the gate! No one saw the damage! He's just making trouble, for God's sake. *Deliberate* . . . ?' Words failed him.

'I'm sorry. I should never have mentioned it. I'm sorry.' And saying this, I was apologizing as much for Edward as myself.

Will lowered the oar and, letting the boat drift, sank onto the aft thwart, his knees almost touching mine, and gave a sharp sigh.

'Don't take any notice of Edward. You know how he is.'

'But people believe these things, don't they? It only takes a rumour or two. Has he been telling people this stuff? Has he been spreading it around?'

'I don't know. I can ask him.'

'You can tell him from me that he's talking absolute rubbish,' he declared solemnly. '*Rubbish.*'

'I'll tell him.' For the little good it was likely to do, though I didn't say that.

The boat drifted into the marsh with an imperceptible bump and stuck there. Still agitated, Will jammed his arms onto his knees. 'Sometimes I think it's all a bad dream, Ali.

That I'll wake up and she'll be back. Other times . . .' He fixed me with his dark passionate eyes. 'Other times I think she'll never be found.'

'If it counts for anything, the majority of people missing in these sort of circumstances get found before too long.'

He grasped doubtfully at this. 'They do?'

'Found,' I repeated, meaning: one way or the other.

He understood me and looked quickly away.

'The people who aren't found are generally the ones who don't want to be found.'

He gave a curious half-formed smile. 'Not Grace. She'd never choose to be out of circulation for long.'

A bird began to call, a wild goose. It couldn't have been far away, but although the sky was brightening and the mist gradually dissolving I couldn't see it. Another call came from further away, echoing eerily across the watery landscape, and then a great cacophony of screeches rose up, as though the entire flock were squabbling.

'I'd forgotten what a noise they make.'

The boat rocked slightly as Will stood up. 'Thousands of brent this year. Most farmers would say far too many. They're all over the wheat. Some people are running their own private pest-control programmes.' He raised his eyebrows conspiratorially. 'During the shooting season, of course.' He picked up the oar and offered it to me. 'Want a go?'

I laughed, 'I think I've forgotten how.'

He shook his head in mock disapproval, his eyes sparkled briefly. 'City life. No good for you, Ali.'

'No good for anyone.'

He pushed the boat away from the bank and began to scull us further along the creek. After some time we passed the second sluice, lower built than the first, with a smaller frame and less brickwork. This gate also appeared sturdy.

I wondered if Will was making for anywhere in particular, if this trip was part of a pre-planned search pattern. Whatever reason we were here, I was happy to drift, remembering a time

when we had come this way in *Pod*, on the lookout for feathers
and driftwood in the high summer heat of a scorching July. I
must have been thirteen then, Will sixteen. It had been our last
summer of unconditional contentment, the last summer I had
lived under the illusion that such simple joys went on for ever.
I had missed most of the following summer with glandular
fever, and the beginning of the next too, when I was sent to
France on a miserable exchange visit. Returning, I had found
Will working his college vacation on the farm and spending his
evenings in the pubs with people of his own age. When we
walked the marshes we no longer talked about oyster-catchers
and *Pod*, but the arms race and the economic benefits of
vegetarianism. There had been moments of happiness then too,
if one is ever really happy in the full nervousness of adolescence.

The storm came the following winter: the relentless northerly wind and spring tide that inundated the four cottages at
the edge of the marsh. After that, nothing was the same again,
because it was then that I first dared to hope that I might not
be too young for Will after all.

The geese, having quietened down, put up one last noisy
protest. Now I could see three or four heads above the reeds,
swimming along a parallel but invisible stretch of water.

'This place hasn't changed a bit,' I breathed aloud. 'Do you
bring *Pod* here still?'

'In the summer. With Charlie.'

I remembered the photograph in Will's office, the little
green boat, the child's face. 'And in winter?'

'We walk. When we can.'

'The winds,' I murmured.

'The wilder the better.'

He laughed a little, and I laughed with him.

'Charlie loves it too, when it's wild?'

'Oh, yes,' he said with pride. Then, as if to answer my
unasked question, he added in a lower voice: 'Grace isn't so
keen, of course.'

'A summer person?'

'An indoor person. Never liked the marshes.' A pause. 'You've never thought of living in the country?' And he was changing the subject.

'Not possible with my job.'

'Don't know how you can stand it in London.'

'Oh, it's not so bad. There are compensations.'

He grunted doubtfully.

I asked, 'You never go there?'

'Not if I can possibly avoid it. All that noise. All those people. And the begging, and the young people living rough, and the old people standing in bus queues in midwinter. Not a place where I can ever feel that we're making a good job of the world.'

'But some people are stuck with it. They can't escape.'

'So you represent them, Ali. You try to get them off.'

'Ah . . . I may try to get them off – and sometimes, of course, I do – but most of the time I don't change anything, really. Just postpone it. Stop them from making things worse for themselves. They're very good at that, being their own worst enemies.'

He was quiet for a moment. 'In what way?'

'Oh, saying they know nothing about a fight when they're covered in someone else's blood. That's a favourite, despite a zero success rate. One guy even tried to argue that his victim's broken cheekbone was self-inflicted.'

Will made a sound of disbelief. 'All a long way from here.'

Looking up at him, I smiled. 'A long way.' After a moment I asked, 'But Grace . . . she enjoys London?' I was careful to use the present tense.

His mood shifted, the life went out of his face. 'She likes shopping, seeing people. But she hardly ever persuades me to go. I'm not a one for events and rushing about.'

'But you have a busy social life here?'

Will's eyes flashed. 'Well, I'd avoid that too, given half a chance. Same people, same gossip, only the houses alternate a bit. Left to my own devices I'd probably be a recluse. So it's good for me, really, to get dragged out now and then.'

The creek had divided. We were heading away from the Gun embankment, along a narrower tributary which led into the wilderness of the salt-marshes. The mist had almost vanished, carried away on a gathering breeze, and now the horizon was somewhere on the edge of the world, beyond the dunes.

Suddenly there was a splash and we were turning rapidly; Will was paddling the boat round in a tight circle. 'Stupid to come. I don't know why I thought—' He was in a hurry, almost a panic. 'Look, I've got to get back. I don't know why I thought—' Again he didn't finish but began to scull vigorously back the way we had come, the boat surging forward until it seemed to skid across the surface of the water. After a while Will muttered, 'I'd forgotten. It's coming up to high springs. The tide's falling fast.'

The water was still high and showing no sign of falling, but I said, 'Of course,' and was careful not to interrupt his thoughts until we had reached the rickety jetty once more.

Maggie had a visitor. A smart black four-wheel drive with high sides and fat corrugated wheels was parked beside her green Citroën in front of Reed Cottage. Ringing lightly on the bell, I heard voices stop abruptly. When Maggie appeared in the doorway she seemed startled, almost dazed.

'Bad moment?' I asked.

'No. No, come in, Alex.' She accepted my kiss impassively then stood back to let me in with the same slightly bemused expression on her face.

I had never been inside the cottage before, but the combination of plain walls and old scrubbed furniture and bright ceramics made it instantly identifiable as Maggie's: the Marsh House of old transcribed onto a minor scale. To the left was a low-ceilinged dining room, the table cluttered with papers and plants and a grooming cat, while straight ahead at the end of a short passage was a glimpse of Maggie's bright blue hand-painted china arranged over kitchen shelves, and to the right a sitting room containing the familiar blend of faded rugs and wine-coloured sofas. Maggie stepped towards the sitting room and said vaguely, 'I wonder if you remember . . .'

Maggie's visitor was standing by the hearth. A well-built man in his thirties with a round face and confident eyes, wearing a beige cashmere sweater and matching trousers, he had the look of a successful businessman on his day off. I had no sense of recognition.

He reached out a hand. 'Barry Holland.'

My memory did strange tricks, trying to marry this affluent well-fed figure with the scrawny teenager who used to hang around the village in tatty ill-fitting clothes.

'Good Lord,' I said.

He smiled easily. 'Bit of a transformation.'

I could only smile in agreement. 'Life has treated you well, then?'

'Oh, can't complain. Got into trouble when I was twenty. Did twelve months inside,' he announced, with the air of someone who liked to get this in the open right from the outset. 'But then I got started in the promotion business – bands, groups, gigs of all sorts. And since then – yes – life has been good to me.' He said it with consideration and thankfulness, and I found myself warming to him. 'Always travelling, that's the only problem. But I try to get back when I can. I've just bought a place up Salterns Lane here.'

The more I recalled of Barry Holland, the more extraordinary his metamorphosis became. He had been what my mother called an unprepossessing youth, watchful and sullen, with nothing to say for himself and what was generally acknowledged to be a large chip on his shoulder. I seemed to remember that his father had been unemployed for many years while his mother had been a barmaid at the Deepwell Arms. Something had happened, a separation, a divorce, something that had

taken Barry's father away. Recalling this, more fragments
surfaced, of Barry's lanky figure hanging around the edges of
the marshes, of people branding him a truant and no-good,
of early brushes with the law. And now, twenty years later, he
stood before me, a great rock of a man, assured, well groomed,
shining with the vigour that money can bring.

His mention of musical events prompted me to ask if he
was involved in the music festival.

He was briefly amused. 'No. Wouldn't know what to do
with classical stuff. I'm strictly mass-market – anything that
fills a big space. No, in fact I didn't hear about the festival until
a couple of months ago, not until Grace nobbled me for some
sponsorship.' He tempered this immediately with a lift of one
hand. 'Don't misunderstand me, I went willingly. More than
glad to help.'

'She came to see you?'

'Yes.' He was suitably sombre. 'Very impressive she was,
too.'

He signalled the end of the conversation with a dip of
his head, like a small bow, and I was struck once again by his
composure and the old-fashioned, almost formal, courtesy.

'Well, Maggie,' he called softly. He went over to where she
was sitting on the arm of a sofa, and, taking her hand, held it
gently between his own, with the paternalistic solicitude of a
priest comforting a parishioner. 'I'm sorry.'

Maggie threw him a glare which took me by surprise, it
was so full of antagonism.

He said to me, 'Goodbye, Alex.' And his still, calm eyes
were very self-possessed.

As soon as he had gone, I said to Maggie, 'Is anything the
matter?'

'No.' She turned her head away, but not before I had seen
the tightness of her lips, the fierce glint in her eyes.

'But he upset you?'

'No. It's nothing. No . . .'

'Can I get you anything? A drink?'

She shook her head. 'I'm all right, really. Just – *tired* of it all. *Tired*.'

But even as she said this I sensed she was keeping something back, and it struck me that, for all her openness and warmth, she had always kept a part of herself concealed from us. Looking back, I realized that in all the years I had known her she had rarely referred to Will's father or her feelings about his death, she had never talked about the difficulties of life as a widow. She must have been lonely, I saw now, and, since she was forced to sublet the farm for some years, probably under financial strain too. Yet she had never given any sign of this, had never mentioned anything that might have been remotely unsettling to us as children, electing instead to create a world of unremitting confidence and happiness. I had barely understood the nature of this achievement when I was young, yet instinctively I had loved her for it.

I put a hand on her shoulder. 'Will said you'd been to the hospital.'

She appeared to recall this with effort. 'Oh . . . yes, these gallstones.' Seeing that I expected more detail, she added, 'They take a look to see if they are still there. They want to cut them out – you know how they are. Always—'

A car sounded outside and she murmured, 'Charlie.' This time the prospect of seeing him did not succeed in lightening her mood.

Following her to the door, I saw Will getting out of the Range Rover, while Charlie, his head just visible in the passenger seat, appeared to be struggling unsuccessfully with his seatbelt. Will went round to the passenger door and, flinging it open, leant inside to deal with the recalcitrant belt. He stood back to let Charlie out, yet for some reason Charlie still didn't emerge, and Will was forced to lean into the car again. Then – a moment which sent shock surging into my throat – Will grabbed him by the arm and hauled him out. There was a shout, my stomach seized; fearing the witnessing of something deeply disturbing, I almost looked away.

More sounds, wildly incongruous. It was an instant before I understood: they were shrieking with laughter. I stared with relief and a sense of foolishness. So delighted were the two of them with whatever had just happened that they were clutching each other in glee, the boy reaching his arms around his father's waist and pressing his head against his chest, Will bending down to rest his cheek briefly against the pale hair.

They walked happily towards us and at that moment they mightn't have had a care in the world.

I said, 'Hello, Charlie.'

He looked up with the incurious glance of a child and it was impossible to tell if he remembered me or not.

Handing him over to his grandmother, Will stood in the doorway and wagged his finger at him. 'Remember what I said.'

Charlie giggled. Will narrowed his eyes in mock reproof and turned away, only to change his mind and turn back in the same movement. Throwing his arms around Charlie, he embraced him with such feeling that he might have been going away for days not hours. 'Take care of Granny,' he said.

Waving to Maggie, I followed Will outside. As soon as Maggie had closed the door, Will's smile was overtaken by a frown. 'Do we really have to go through with this? National TV's so *public*.'

'It has a way of getting people's attention.'

'Why can't we just do local TV?'

'Because Grace's photograph has already been shown on local TV.'

He stopped by the car and, like a man press-ganged into donning some sort of fancy dress, pulled open both flaps of his quilted jacket and demanded crossly, 'Too formal? Too dark? Wrong *image*?'

He was wearing a beautifully tailored grey suit, pale blue shirt and dark tie.

'No, you look just right,' I lied. In fact, even allowing for the wildness of his hair, he looked far too good, far too neat, the suit too classy. I guessed immediately that these clothes had been bought for him by Grace. When we reached Norwich I would have to find a tactful way of toning down his appearance: husbands of missing women were meant to look harassed and unkempt or people's minds began to turn in the wrong direction.

He made no argument when I suggested we use my car and, absorbed as he was, did not notice when, halting at the junction with the main road, I stared after Jilly's Golf as it swept past us on its way to Burnham.

'My *jacket*?'

I thought he was going to refuse outright, but then, giving in abruptly with a short sigh, he removed it and abandoned it to a chair. A moment later, as we prepared to go into the conference room, I touched his tie as if to straighten it and managed both to loosen it slightly and to push the knot a little off-centre. With his wind-blown hair and dark frowning eyes, his image was now a little closer to the agonized husband who'd been far too preoccupied to dress with any attention.

Agnew and Ramsey, wearing nondescript blue suits and blank expressions, led the way into a room that blazed with artificial lights targeted on a long green-baize table at the near end, with four chairs arranged behind it. Two clusters of microphones had accumulated on the green baize; Will sat before one, with me at his elbow, Ramsey before the other, with Agnew on his flank.

There was a good turnout. All the major TV channels seemed to be there, and I counted more than ten reporters, some of whom would be stringers for the nationals, as well as six photographers. All eyes were fastened on Will. I had no illusions about what they were looking for. The great majority of public appeals by relatives were completely genuine, but in a couple of famous cases in the recent past the police had asked husbands of murdered wives to make TV appeals purely as a means of gaining time and evidence against them. The press, who always reckoned on being sharper than most, liked to think they could suss out these situations at fifty yards. They would be looking for the smallest slip from Will, the slightest display of over-confidence or over-played grief. They would be looking to Ramsey, too, for coded signals, for signs of a double game. I had known there was a risk in setting this up; meeting the cold appraising eyes of the men and women before me, I began to wonder if I hadn't misjudged it.

Ramsey introduced himself in his monotonous voice and outlined the case and the problems his team were up against. The fact that, despite an extensive search, Grace Dearden seemed to have vanished into thin air, the police's concern for her safety, the lack of sightings, the need for help from the public, his promise that all information would be treated in the strictest confidence. He referred the audience to the ten-by-eight photograph of Grace in their information packs, and reminded them that she had last been seen two weeks back, at four thirty p.m. on 18 February, on her way home from her mother-in-law's in Deepwell, the village in which she, Grace, also lived.

Then it was Will's turn. I had prepared simple notes for him, but either he'd forgotten about them or preferred to do without. To the whir of camera shutters, he looked out at the audience and spoke directly, from the heart. He said he was desperately worried for Grace, that she would never have left of her own accord, he begged anyone with any information at all to come forward. He stammered once or twice, he stalled near the end and bit hard on his lip, he appeared deeply upset. My concerns rapidly evaporated: his sincerity made him utterly believable.

One reporter put a number of questions to Ramsey, run-of-the-mill stuff about search procedures, about the possibilities which could be excluded at this stage – 'None,' Ramsey announced crisply – then a young woman asked Will how he would describe Grace as a person.

Looking down at the table, clasping his hands tightly in front of him, Will took his time to respond. Once started, he seemed to force the words out, as though he were finding it painful to talk about Grace. 'I would describe her as outgoing. And . . .' He stalled awkwardly. 'Umm . . . generous. Positive.'

'What were her interests?'

Another pause, another battle to speak. 'She was very involved in the local community. She was . . . organizing a small music festival.'

'And how would you describe her as a wife?'

He stared into the sea of faces for several seconds, he opened his mouth to speak, only to look down abruptly. Eventually, he said, 'She was, umm . . . the perfect wife.' An instant later he half glanced at me, as though in panic, before adding, 'Well – that's the way it seemed to me.' Making a gesture as if to withdraw this, realizing that further comment would probably be a mistake, he clamped his mouth shut and stared at his hands.

I sat forward and tried to catch Ramsey's eye but he was looking out into the room. I whispered to Will, 'Shall we call it a day?' Before he could reply, the young woman was putting another question. 'And how would you describe her as a mother?'

The pause that followed was unlike anything that had gone before. There was a new tension about Will, a dark hesitation, and I had a sudden foreboding.

'She was . . . umm . . .' He appeared to hold his breath, sweat glistened at his temple. 'Umm . . .' He moved his mouth but no words came.

I leant over and whispered, 'Are you unwell? We can stop this now if you like.'

The sweat had erupted in beads over his forehead, his hands were clenched so tightly that the veins stood proud of the skin, and still he couldn't speak.

I grasped his arm and whispered, 'I'll stop it.'

When he didn't reply I said to Ramsey, but mainly to the

room, 'We're going to have to call a halt at this point. Mr
Dearden's not feeling well. As you can imagine he's been under
great strain over the past two weeks.'

I stood up. There was a respectful closing of notebooks, a
lowering of cameras. Grasping Will's shoulder, I said, 'Let's
go.' Still caught up in his strange panic, it was a moment before
he got clumsily to his feet and allowed me to shepherd him out
of the room.

I found a chair for him in a quiet corner and a moment
later Ramsey appeared with a glass of water.

'You all right, Mr Dearden?'

Will leant forward in his seat and buried his head in his
hands.

Ramsey waited a moment, then retreated.

I put the water into Will's hand.

'I knew it was a mistake!' he hissed.

'But it went well.'

Still hunched over, he shook his head inconsolably.

'Really,' I insisted. 'I wouldn't say so if it wasn't true.'

He kept shaking his head and I kept offering reassurances
until, lifting his head at last, he murmured, 'Just give me a
minute or two, will you, Alex?'

The urge to comfort him was very strong. Confining myself
to a touch of his shoulder, I walked away.

Ramsey was waiting at a distance.

'All right?' he asked, without any visible show of concern.

'The stress . . .'

Ramsey gazed at Will's slumped figure and narrowed his
little lips. 'The first broadcast goes out at five. We've got four
extra phone lines set up in the incident room, but I have to say
I'm not holding out a great deal of hope.'

'Oh? Any particular reason?'

Above the fat cheeks his small eyes regarded me steadily. 'It
was dusk running into night, the area is thinly populated. Not
likely to have been many witnesses about.'

'Assuming she wasn't abducted. Assuming she wasn't put

into a car and taken to the other side of the country. Assuming she didn't go to London the next morning.' I would have stopped there but his attitude annoyed me. '*Assuming* she didn't go to the airport and take a plane to the other side of the world.' Gesturing an end to this game, I said placatingly, 'I take your point, but don't let's give up before we've even started.'

'A good start would be a little more truth from your client.'

I kept the curiosity out of my face. 'Meaning?'

'I mean that when we next talk, you might persuade Mr Dearden that it would be in his interest to be a little more frank with us.'

'Is this to do with Grace Dearden's mother, Inspector? Because if it is, I can tell you that it would be wise to treat everything she says with extreme caution. Mrs Bailey has what is politely known as an alcohol problem. She also has a totally unreasonable grievance against her son-in-law, which has coloured her judgement – and that's putting it mildly. According to her highly biased viewpoint, Grace's hopes of fame and fortune were dashed when she married Will Dearden. She's never got over the fact that Grace ended up as a normal housewife and mother, and not some famous society figure in London. She blames Will, but I can assure you that none of her comments can be substantiated in any respect. In fact, quite the reverse.'

Ramsey straightened his plump shoulders. 'We are aware of what Mrs Bailey had to say.'

Reading all too slowly between the lines, I asked, 'This isn't about Mrs Bailey, then?'

His silence, the droop of his eyelids, were an affirmation.

'Well, I'm sure that my client can offer a perfectly good explanation for anything else you might wish to put to him, Inspector.'

'He agrees to an interview, then?'

'Well . . . If absolutely necessary.'

'Tomorrow? Here at nine?'

'Not here. Mr Dearden's exhausted. And he has a farm to run.'

We settled on Marsh House at ten.

A fierce wind had sprung up, buffeting the car whenever it emerged onto exposed ground. In the headlights the branches looked as though they would tear themselves from the trees, and the surface of the road danced with skittering twigs and dried leaves.

'This gale's very sudden,' I said.

'It was forecast,' Will murmured, and it was the first comment he had volunteered since leaving Norwich. 'Worse tomorrow.'

'How much worse?'

'A storm.' His head was pressed back against the seat-rest, his profile unreadable in the darkness. 'Northerly,' he continued dully. 'And it's coming up to extra-high spring tides.'

'Is that going to be a worry?'

'Doubt it.'

As if to contradict him, the wind slammed into the side of the car and I had to correct the veer of the steering. 'You're sure you're okay to see Ramsey at ten? You're not too busy on the farm?'

'Busy?' He was still very preoccupied. 'No.'

'He's got something he wants to talk to you about. I'm not sure what it is.' I glanced across at him. 'You wouldn't have any ideas?'

It seemed to me that there was a tension in his stillness.

'There isn't anything that Ramsey might have got hold of – I don't know, an area that might have been overlooked?'

Again, the stillness, as though something were weighing heavily with him. 'No . . . I don't think so. Unless . . .' I caught the glint of his eye as he glanced towards me. 'Lawyers have to keep things confidential, don't they?'

'Absolutely. Anything you say to me as a client will always remain absolutely confidential.'

'No, I meant . . . another lawyer. Another matter.'

My mind raced over the possibilities. The Gun Marsh sale? The fact that he might be broke? Something else? Something about Grace? I said, 'Any lawyer, any matter. It's a fundamental principle.'

'In that case, no idea then.'

'You're absolutely sure?'

Maybe I imagined a tiny hesitation before he said, 'Sure.'

Suppressing a slight unease, I negotiated a wide roundabout and took the road to the north.

As we left the sodium lights behind and entered the dark country lanes, Will muttered again, 'I knew it'd be a mistake.'

'But Will . . .' I had run out of reassurances. 'What do you feel went so wrong about it?'

'Those questions about Grace . . . I *knew* I'd foul up. I knew I wouldn't be able to answer them.'

'That didn't matter. In fact, it made it more *natural*. More – well, I hate to say it – more *moving*. That may sound cynical – *sorry* – but I'm afraid that's what the media go for. Visible emotion. Sincerity.'

'Sincerity.' He gave an ugly chuckle. 'Is that what it looked like?'

'Oh, yes.'

Another harsh sound. '*God* . . .'

I caught it then, the underlying irony and self-disgust. I looked across at him, I slowed the car.

He cried, 'Sometimes I don't know how much longer I can go on with it, Ali! Sometimes I feel like shouting at them!'

'It must be hard, I know . . .'

'Hard!' He gave a caustic laugh. 'Yes – *hard*. To go on saying the right things, to go along with the myth.'

I kept my eyes on the road. 'The myth?'

'The myth of *Grace*. The absolute bloody myth!'

I glanced across at him again, trying to read his expression in the reflection of the lights. I said softly, 'What sort of myth?'

'Oh, the idea people have about her! The image of her, the one she always *wants* them to have!'

One word came instantly to mind. '*Perfect.*'

'Perfect – *yes*! And *generous*! And *warm*!' He didn't attempt to hide the bitterness in his voice. 'It's her great talent, you see. Playing *Grace*, the Grace that she wants the world to admire, the great, beautiful, generous Grace!'

I gripped the wheel, a quiet dread knocking at my heart. 'And she's . . . something else?' I breathed.

'Something else? That's one way of putting it! She's—' He struggled for the words in a kind of fury. Then, calming himself, said flatly, 'She's *cold*, Ali. The coldest, most determined person I've ever known.'

I drove on until I found a gateway. Pulling in, I switched off the engine. The silence closed in around us until there was only the rushing of the wind.

'She's incapable of love or tenderness,' Will went on in the same bleak voice. 'Incapable of real generosity or warmth. She's without any feeling at all. She's never loved anyone in her life. Except herself, of course. She's very good at that.'

Absorbing this, I felt no shock, not even surprise, just an odd sense of affirmation, as if a part of me had known this all along. 'But she loved you?'

'Me? Oh, she never loved *me*! Not even at the beginning. Wasn't capable of it. I couldn't see it, of course, not for a year or so. Thought she was just . . . just *deep*. I was in love with the *idea* of her, you see. The mystery, the sweetness. I fell for the myth, just like everyone else.' The wind roared against the car, he inhaled sharply, and the two sounds merged. 'And when I realized . . . Well, I closed my mind to it, thought we'd muddle through somehow, thought she'd change, thought I'd change . . . But Grace didn't want to change – didn't see the need! She was quite happy in her own bizarre way. She had what she wanted – or at least enough to keep her going – the house, the dinner parties, the big social life. Quite a *simple* person in many ways, you see.' He gave a sardonic laugh.

I watched his face in the glow of the dashboard, I tried to read the darkness in it, whether it was the darkness of pain or of guilt.

'Am I sounding bitter, Ali?' he asked harshly. 'Am I sounding angry? The thing is, she killed everything in me! She killed any love.' His voice had risen, his words almost choked him. 'In the end I hated her for it, Ali. Hated her for making *me* like her, so cold and unfeeling.'

Hate was a strong word, I wished he hadn't used it.

'Hated *myself* for hating her. Hated *everything*. God . . .'

To stop him, I said: 'You didn't think of separating?'

'*Separating?* If only it had been that simple!'

'What was the problem?'

'The problem!' he exclaimed, as though this should have been obvious. 'The problem was that she would have gone for half the house and the farm and Charlie! She told me so. She was perfectly blunt about it. I might have survived losing the farm – just. I might have survived going and doing something else. But giving up Charlie – never that! *Never.* I couldn't have borne that!' The emotion broke in his voice, he twisted his head sharply away, only to rush on again, as if, now that he had voiced the worst, he wanted to air every last grievance. 'I might have stood it for longer,' he said in a steadier voice, 'might have put up with the endless little humiliations and the vast extravagances and the continual hunting around, but she started to make Charlie unhappy as well. *Charlie.*' He clenched his jaw, and his fist. 'She couldn't resist, you see. Just couldn't resist! She was used to Charlie fitting in around *her* because that was the way he'd always been. When Charlie was little he was lovely . . . You know, quiet and easy, always smiling. He was just the most undemanding kid you can imagine. But when he began to get a mind of his own, started to answer back, to have the normal sort of moods, then she couldn't stand it. Couldn't take it, because she couldn't control him any more.

Always on about his dyslexia, nagging him to do well at school, making him feel bad about himself – it never stopped. She couldn't leave him alone, just *couldn't leave him in peace*! I couldn't *stand* it! Couldn't forgive her for what she was doing to Charlie.' He pushed his head back against the seat for a moment. His voice dropped abruptly. 'That was the last bloody straw. That was why it had to end. I didn't care any more after that.'

I felt the cold calm of profound alarm. I didn't want to imagine where this was leading, I certainly didn't want to ask. While there was the smallest risk of a charge and a trial, the last thing I wanted was a private confession that contradicted what we were going to say in the witness box. Ethically, it would put me in a difficult situation; personally, it would tear me apart. Wanting to deflect him, needing to prevent him from saying anything irretrievable, I said hastily, 'Couldn't *you* have kept Charlie? Wouldn't Grace have given him up?'

'What, and look bad? Oh, *no*! Not good for the image. Proper mothers don't give up their children. Looks bad.' He gave a ragged sigh, a further descent into misery. 'No, she wouldn't consider leaving without Charlie. Although . . .' He lost momentum suddenly. 'Perhaps if the deal had been sufficiently tempting . . . If there'd been a man with enough money to whisk her away to an earthly paradise full of credit cards and grand parties. I was sort of hoping, actually,' he said with an attempt at flippancy. 'But she never seemed to find anyone rich enough.'

'There were lovers?'

He lifted his shoulders. 'No idea.' His tone was studiously offhand. 'I didn't want to know, frankly. Never looked too closely. But she was hunting, I could see that. On the look-out. Not for passion – she wasn't interested in anything as dull, as unrewarding as that – no, it was *things* she wanted, things that I couldn't give her.'

'Did she talk of leaving?'

'No. But, then, I'd be the last to know! You have to

understand that Grace was a *planner*. She made plans for everything, most of all her own life. She was obsessive, thorough, secretive. No . . . she would never tell *me*.'

In the pause that followed, I realized that the information I had gathered on Grace had been drawn from selected sources, a diary and address book that everyone at Marsh House had been free to read, that I had seen no more of Grace than the side she had chosen to show to the local community. Housewife, organizer, social star. There was little to suggest a secret life; or little to betray it.

'So!' Will gave a raw laugh, he spread an upturned palm. 'There we are, Ali! The real Grace! The *amazing* Grace!'

'I'm so sorry,' I said.

He bit hard on his lip, not comfortable with sympathy. 'And now they're going to think I've done something terrible to her.' He turned to me and said with attempted lightness, 'Well, they are, aren't they?'

I was careful to show nothing in my face. I said, 'It very much depends on what you tell them.'

'So what *do* I tell them, Ali?'

'I would suggest, as much as they ask for but no more. A little economy never did any harm, especially with the truth.'

He almost laughed. 'The truth . . . Yes, the truth is the last thing we need!'

I felt the cold creep of dread again. 'You must be careful. You must think about everything you say.'

Sounding flippant again, he said, 'Tell them I loved her, you mean? Tell them I cared?' He gave a sharp sigh.

As I restarted the engine, he reached across suddenly and, taking my hand, clasped it emotionally in both of his in a gesture of gratitude or solidarity.

Chapter Six

I HAD forgotten my sleeping pills, but for once it didn't matter.
I slept for six hours without waking. Perhaps it was being
under Maggie's roof, perhaps it was the battering of the wind
against the dormer window, but I felt oddly safe, like a
passenger in a warm train, insulated from the realities of the
landscape beyond the glass.

I woke as Maggie put a mug of tea on the table beside me.
A reluctant grey light glimmered in the dormer, more dusk
than dawn, and the two of us could have been ghosts.

'Still blowing?' I asked.

Maggie turned her eyes towards the window, and the
drumming panes, the roaring wind gave their answer. 'This
country . . . This climate . . .' She lifted her shoulders stoically,
an exile who had been away too long ever to consider returning. 'They have a warning out for tonight,' she said.

'They think it'll get worse?' I propped myself up on one
elbow.

'It's the tide. It will be very high tonight . . .'

'What about the furniture? Will it need to be moved?'

'Moved?' She seemed surprised at the idea. 'No, no. They
have warnings every year . . . it means nothing. They do it just
so we cannot say they didn't tell us. No, no – we will wait. If
the water gets too high, then . . .' She vaguely indicated some
sort of action.

The wind boomed against the cottage, something loose
tapped against metal or glass, and we were once again en-

veloped in sound. I had stayed the night partly to keep Maggie company, partly because I didn't want to go to Wickham Lodge and get a rerun of Edward's grievances.

'I never wanted this house,' Maggie announced now with sudden feeling. 'I hate being so close to the water, Alex. I hate being so low down. I feel I am *under* the sea here.'

'There wasn't anywhere else?'

She sat down slowly on the edge of the bed. 'Not at the price.' I didn't remember her mentioning money in this way before; she had always seemed unconcerned.

'Not even in the village?'

'That would have been too far away.'

I assumed she meant from Will and Charlie.

'Something couldn't have been converted for you at Marsh House? Some of the outbuildings?'

She turned to me and shook her head. 'Too close, Alex. That would have been too close.'

'But a separate entrance. Separate phone. Separate life?'

'For a mother-in-law, I was already too close.' The feeble light sculpted the side of her face in shades of grey, her eyes were shrouded and I couldn't read her expression. 'Oh, it was nothing anyone *said*, Alex,' she added crisply. 'But I felt it, you know.'

'I'm sorry.'

A slight shrug, a movement of her fingers. 'People have their reasons.' And her tone contained a significance I could only guess at. Before I could ask more, she was saying with old affection, 'I always wanted it to be you, Alex.'

I gave a short awkward laugh. 'Me?'

'With Will. I always thought it would be you.'

'Me? No! I was too young.'

'Three years? It's nothing.'

'But I was too young *then*.'

She gestured mystification. 'But, then, these things never happen as we think, do they? People don't love the people you want for them.'

I reached for the mug of tea and, sipping too hastily, burnt my mouth.

Maggie turned her face back to the window and murmured reflectively, 'Nor even the people they want for themselves . . . It's chance. You love someone and you cannot have them. You are loved by someone else and you don't know what is really being offered to you. The *true* nature of their offering, Alex. What is *really* there.'

It seemed to me she was talking about her own past. 'Were you happy, Maggie? You always seemed happy to us.'

Above the boom of the wind, rain rat-tatted against the windows, and the sound seemed to detain her. 'Me?' She smiled faintly. 'Oh, I was happy. Yes, yes, don't you worry, Alex – I was happy.'

'Your marriage . . .?'

'John? Oh, he was a good man. Not someone to set the world on fire, you understand. But good. Kind.'

'But afterwards . . . you were alone for so long.'

'Alone, but not lonely, Alex. No . . . I had many happy things in my life. Many, *many*. Ah!' Her eyes fired with a brief and brilliant light. 'But now . . .' The light left her face as rapidly as it had come. '*Now* I am lonely.'

Before I could speak, she had waved this aside.

'Not a reason for sorrow. It is a fact of age. You think about dying. You cannot help it.' She stood up slowly. 'You think of getting the whole business over and done with.'

'Maggie . . . you're not even – what? – sixty-five. You make it all sound so . . . *hopeless*.'

'Not hopeless. Practical.' She went to the window to check the latch before starting for the door.

'Maggie?'

She paused in the doorway.

'The other day you said that Grace had her life as she wished it.'

'Did I?'

'You said she wasn't a person to be defeated in any way.'

Maggie shrugged.

'I was wondering what you meant exactly.'

She turned away slightly, her profile in darkness. Twice she began to speak, twice she hesitated. 'I meant she was very . . . sure. Very determined when she set her mind to something.' She glanced over her shoulder at me, and her eyes were unreadable. 'That is all.' She went out swiftly then reappeared in the shadows beyond the door. 'Oh, your husband phoned for you. He said your mobile phone is turned off, and could you please put it on again.' She raised her eyebrows, an affectionate comment on the demands of my life.

My phone was recharging on a small table, next to a battered television set rigged to a computer-game console. The walls, too, had been appropriated by Charlie, with Batman posters and pictures of football teams and a scarf pinned above the door.

I lay in bed a moment longer, enjoying the strange tranquillity of the storm before getting up and switching on the phone. There were several messages waiting: from Paul, Corinthia, Ray.

'I can barely hear you,' Ray complained when I called. 'You sound as though you're in a hailstorm.'

I raised my voice. 'I am, sort of.' I moved to the window and, shivering, looked out at a cold luminous maelstrom in which all perspective and distance were lost. 'Is that better?'

'A bit. More like a rainstorm now.' His own voice was broken up and shot through with crackles. 'Listen, I finally managed to trace that Knightsbridge number, the one used for the restaurant booking. It's a flat in Hans Place, behind Harrods . . .'

I missed the next bit, but ventured, 'Well done.'

'What? No . . . what I'm saying is that I can't get a name for it. Checked the electoral roll and no one's registered as a voting resident at that address, certainly no one named Gordon.' His voice cut out for an instant, then broke up. '. . . the planning department had an application six years ago for some alterations ... seems the flat was owned by a family trust, based in Guernsey ... details untraceable. I took some neighbours' names off the electoral roll. One's in the book ... I'll keep trying him in case he knows who uses the place. But I wouldn't rate the chances. People with money are usually too ...' His voice faded completely for a moment. 'Hello? Did you get that?'

'Just missed the end.' I was transfixed by the glimmering white aurora which hovered above the marshes like some ghostly radiance – spray or reflected light, it was hard to tell – and the way the wind chased across the grass in ripples, making it quiver and shift. 'People with money ...?'

'Are usually too busy to get nosy.'

'Ah.'

'Checked those schoolfriends of Grace Dearden,' Ray continued faintly. 'One hasn't been in touch with Grace since they were twenty, another is in Africa somewhere, the third said ...' I lost him again. '... and they'd never been terribly close anyway. So not much there, I'm afraid. And nothing on the suppliers and tradespeople up there. Most done long service ... no form ... no one new or unreliable. Clean as a whistle.'

'Oh, well.'

'You're breaking up.'

'What about the flat in Regent's Park?' He asked me to repeat the question, and then I missed his reply except for the end, something about trying a porter again tonight.

Abandoning the call, I stepped closer to the window. The cold seemed to leap through the glass, while an icy draught crept around my feet.

When I was a child my father had talked about the harshness of the north wind. He used to say it came direct from Siberia. But it was Will who made me understand its nature. He taught me that a northerly wind has its own cadence, its own signature; that it's nothing like the westerlies, which are wet and sinuous, or the southerlies, which are light and fickle. The northerly, he used to explain, is a far steadier wind,

unbroken by the turbulence of weather fronts, a wind that
absorbs the air from the frozen Arctic and bowls it untempered
across the North Sea.

It was Will who explained the disaster of '53 to me. Local
wisdom had always maintained that the greatest risk of flooding came in spring and autumn, at the equinoxes, when the
winds were fierce and the tides frequently at their highest.
Then, so it was said, the sea was most likely to breach the
defences or even – the thought used to bring terror to my
childish heart – to pour straight over the top.

But theory isn't everything, Will had explained. Theory
tends to get ignored by nature and the law of averages, which
allows for the greatest of extremes on either side of the mean.
At twelve I was no mathematician, but I grasped the concept, I
took care to memorize the expression: *allows for the greatest
of extremes on either side of the mean.*

Most of all, Will told me, the theory didn't allow for the
sheer persistence of the north wind, didn't allow for the fact
that, when two weather systems collide and interlock, the north
wind can blow for days on end at storm force, funnelling water
down the North Sea, preventing the ebb tide from making its
retreat, piling the sea higher and higher until the force of the
waves seeks out the smallest weakness in the sea-defences.

Looking out into the gale, I remembered him explaining all
this to me. It had been summer, an afternoon of shimmering
heat, we were sitting among tall reeds, the only sound the
plopping of the mud and his voice as he said, *allows for the
greatest of extremes.*

The disaster of '53 had woven itself through my childhood
landscape for as long as I could remember. People would refer
to The Storm, as if there had never been anything even close to
it in the intervening twenty years. But it was Will who could
point out where the defences had been breached, just as he
could show you where the avocets were nesting, or tell you
how the old dredger had got to be wrecked on the sand bar at
the mouth of the estuary. He knew which homes had been

flooded and which had escaped, which fields were slowly being
cleansed of the brine, and which had been abandoned to the
salt for ever.

The north wind. One winter – it must have been years later
– we had walked out to the dunes in the teeth of a northerly
gale. The further we tramped along the embankment path and
the closer we got to the sea, the louder the thunder had grown,
a dull rumble that rose over the dunes like a warning. Climbing
to the top of the dunes, bracing ourselves against the onslaught
of the wind, it was like reaching the very edge of the world: the
spume and spray, the eerie haze, the crashing of the waves that
seemed to make the sand tremble beneath our feet. We laughed
as we leaned into the wind, we shouted with excitement as
wind-tears were torn from our eyes, we spread our arms like
gliders and felt the lift. And when the euphoria had passed we
just stood and stared, stilled by the spread and sound of the
sea.

Looking at the haze now, hearing the wind, I knew the
scene beyond the dunes would be the same, I knew the sea
would be a wall of thunder.

I found reasons to put off my call to Paul – the bad
reception, the need to get some clothes on before I froze, the
breakfast Maggie would be preparing downstairs – but the
truth was that I preferred to wait until he got to the office,
where we could stick to business.

Maggie had made strong Italian coffee and toast, and
prepared two halves of an Ogen melon. As soon as I was sitting
down, she stated with an element of rehearsal, 'What I said
before, Alex . . . don't misunderstand me. I meant that happiness is something very . . . *individual*. Yes? Sometimes it is
impossible to understand what makes someone else happy. Or
unhappy. You know what I am saying?'

I nodded tentatively.

'Grace, she may have had moments when she was not so
happy, but she never showed it. Nothing more.'

I nodded again, more definitely.

She watched me a little longer, to be sure I'd understood what she was saying, before sitting back in her seat with a small sigh. She turned her ear to the storm and murmured, 'What a climate, Alex.' Spreading her clawlike hands against her chest, lifting her bony shoulders, she gave a small defiant smile.

I drank a second cup of coffee and we talked about Charlie and art classes and schools. When I kissed her goodbye, her cheek was dry and papery against my lips.

Outside, the wind came sweeping around the corner of the cottage and blew my hair into my eyes. The car was covered in a soft white film of salt. Pursued by needles of rain and rushing leaves, I drove slowly up Salterns Lane towards the main road. After a hundred yards or so I came to a pair of cottages huddled behind a tangled hedge, and twenty yards further on I saw Barry Holland's smart four-wheel drive beside a house I barely recognized. A run-down cottage when I had last seen it, the place had been renovated and extended to at least double the size, with new pointing and clean brickwork and a conservatory at the far corner. Paving had been laid around the house, and on the walls young climbers, their labels fluttering in panic, clung desperately to their restraining wires. Festoon curtains hung in the upstairs windows and a chimney released a stream of wood smoke which was instantly shredded and dispersed by the wind. The place stood on rising ground; on a clear day it would have wide uninterrupted views of the marshes and, at that height, probably the sea as well. It was a solid house, well renovated, though I wondered why Barry Holland should have wanted to come back to a place that must have held mixed memories for him. A need to prove that he had overcome his past perhaps, or a simple nostalgia that managed to outweigh the negative associations of his youth; or a wish to stay in touch with friends and family, though I seemed to remember that his family, such as it was, had drifted away from the neighbourhood.

Once out of Salterns Lane and onto the main coastal road

there was barely time to get up speed before slowing down for the turning to Marsh House. Taking this route, along the eastern loop of Quay Lane, one did not pass Sedgecomb House and my father's old surgery but descended a single-track lane with the occasional cottage hidden behind dense trees and tall hedges. The vegetal screen was so effective that the occupants must have had a poor view of passing traffic. It was no wonder that Grace had driven by unnoticed on her return from Maggie's that last evening, no wonder that she had reached Marsh House unseen.

Nearing the quay, the sky became increasingly blurred, the wind more belligerent until, reaching the open expanse of the hard, the car trembled in the full force of the gale. Before turning along the track to Marsh House, I glanced to the left, down the length of the quay.

I stared, I braked, a dull dread rose in my stomach. At the far end of the quay some vehicles were gathered, and one was an emergency vehicle with a flashing blue light and fluorescent red panels on the sides.

A single thought filled my brain: they had found Grace.

Preparing for the worst, rehearsing the moves ahead, I drove towards the flashing light. Eventually I made out the shape of an ambulance, its back doors open, its interior brightly lit. Close by were two cars, one of them occupied by a driver who turned his face towards me as I drew up. When I walked across and bent down to speak to him, he wound the window down a couple of inches.

'What's happened?' I had to raise my voice.

'It's old Mrs Betteney. Being evacuated.'

It was a moment before it sank in. 'The flood warning?'

He nodded. 'They're taking her to the old people's home for a couple of days.'

The relief must have done something strange to my face because he gave me an odd look and abruptly raised the window again. Driving back along the quay, I realized that, relieved or not, I was resigned to the fact that Grace wasn't going to be found alive.

I had another surprise, almost as unpleasant, when I saw Ramsey's car parked in front of Marsh House. I swore loudly.

I gave the front bell a long impatient ring, and even as Will opened the door I was asking, 'Has something happened? Is there news? Why's he here?'

'I don't know why he's here!' He looked terrible this morning, ashen-skinned with bleak eyes.

'But what's he up to?' I demanded. 'Has he been asking you questions?'

Catching my anxiety, Will threw out his hands. 'Not so far.'

'Where is he?'

He tipped his head towards the sitting room. 'But cool down, for heaven's sake. What's the problem?'

'The *problem* is that he's not playing by the rules. We were due to meet at ten. It's barely nine.'

Will gave a loud sigh, as though he could have done without these machinations, and followed me into the room.

Ramsey was standing by the fireplace in a suit that was too tight for him, one plump hand splayed out towards the grate, as if to draw warmth from last night's ashes, while a sturdy woman with cropped hair whom I took to be DC Smith was sitting on a high-backed chair against a wall. A third officer, young and fresh faced, was settled in a corner of the sofa, looking very much at home, one hand dangling over the side of the arm, legs crossed. Seeing me, he pulled himself languidly to his feet.

I went up to Ramsey. 'I was under the impression we had arranged to meet at ten o'clock.'

'We thought Mr Dearden would be glad of an early update on the television appeal.'

I contained my indignation with difficulty. 'Surely a phone call wouldn't have been too much to ask? As a matter of basic courtesy? Either to Mr Dearden or to myself. Quite apart from the inconvenience to Mr Dearden of your arriving unannounced on his doorstep, and the considerable alarm it must have caused.'

Ramsey put on a show of bafflement. 'Alarm? I don't think Mr Dearden was alarmed at seeing us.' He glanced enquiringly at Will and back at me without waiting for an answer. 'He certainly hasn't been alarmed by any of our previous visits.'

'*Anyone* in this situation would be alarmed at an unannounced visit,' I insisted coldly. 'And there's the child to consider.'

'The child has left for school, Mrs O'Neill, a fact we were well aware of.'

Retrieving my dignity, I stated, 'Nevertheless, may I ask that you phone and let us know another time?'

'As I'm sure you'll appreciate, Mrs O'Neill, it's not always possible to call. But . . .' He made a show of considering the idea. 'We'll do what we can.'

I hadn't expected much more, but at least I'd made my point. As my Somers Town clients would have it, I was not to be messed about.

For a moment everyone was still, held in an uncertain tableau. Offering a less fearsome face, I asked, 'So, what have you had from the appeal?'

'Not too encouraging, I'm afraid,' Ramsey said, without surprise. 'Excluding obvious cranks and non-starters, just twelve calls as of this morning, and none too promising.'

'Anything local?'

'Possibly. *Possibly.*' He turned to Will, who was standing with his arms crossed, frowning deeply. 'In fact, there's one matter which has been brought to our notice which we would like to discuss with you, Mr Dearden.'

'Go ahead,' Will agreed immediately. As an afterthought he looked to me for approval, and I nodded because there wasn't much else I could do.

I suggested we move into the dining room, where the formality would be more likely to keep Will on his guard.

The five of us sat in a semicircle around one end of the table, beneath the murky gaze of the landscapes. I took a chair beside Will, with Ramsey and Barbara Smith opposite, while the young officer whose name appeared to be Wilson lounged in the carver at the end. Both the junior officers took out notebooks and pens. It was much quieter at the side of the house; but for the occasional rattle of the sash window and the whisper of the wind in the chimney the storm might have belonged to another day.

'Mr Dearden,' Ramsey said, settling his forearms on the table, 'could you possibly take us through your movements on Wednesday the eighteenth of February once again?'

Will's eyes darkened, he made a gesture of incredulity. 'What – everything?'

'If you wouldn't mind.'

'From when I got up?'

'Please.'

Will exhaled loudly. 'Okay . . . I got up at the usual time, at six. At about six fifteen I went to help Ken with the cattle —'

'Ken who?'

'Ken Wicks.'

'Your farmhand?'

'I share him. With my neighbour.'

'And the cattle, they're at your other farm, is that right?'

'It's not another farm,' Will explained patiently. 'It's only called Upper Farm because it's on higher land, on the other side of the coast road. It's all one farm.'

'Right. Do go on.'

'Yes . . .' Will tried to pick up his thread again. 'I was back by seven fifteen, when I took a shower and changed. I woke my son at seven thirty then went down to cook him breakfast. At quarter past eight I drove my son up to the main road to meet the parent doing the school run. Then at about nine I left for Norwich —'

'And your wife . . .?' Ramsey interrupted, like a prompter returning Will to the script.

'My wife got up at about quarter to eight. When I left she was having a cup of coffee.'

'When you left for Norwich, that is?'

'Yes.'

'And was that the last time you saw her?'

Will dropped his eyes and tightened his mouth. 'Yes.'

'So, how did you pass your time in Norwich, Mr Dearden?'

Will eyed Ramsey speculatively. 'I rather assumed you'd checked all this out.'

With exemplary politeness, Ramsey asked, 'If you wouldn't mind going through it once more, Mr Dearden.'

Will glanced at me, and raised a brief eyebrow that only I could see. 'I got to the Fergusson dealers some time after ten,' he recounted to Ramsey, 'and stayed an hour or so. Then at about twelve I went to Allen's the seed merchants and stayed there for half an hour. Then I went into the middle of town and did some shopping. At two thirty I went to a meeting with my bank manager . . .'

Watching Will, I had the strange sense of watching two different people. I saw the person who was my client, doing well under difficult circumstances; and I saw the person whom I knew from another life, someone who, in revealing himself to Ramsey, was also revealing himself to me, familiar yet increasingly elusive.

'. . . I dropped in at a computer shop to look at some software,' Will continued. 'Then at four – no, it was after four, at about four fifteen, four twenty, I suppose – I went and visited a friend in hospital, in the Royal Norfolk.'

'And that was Mr Jim McDonald?'

'Yes.'

'How long did you stay?'

'I'm not absolutely sure. Until five fifteen? Something like that. He'd probably have a better idea. Did you ask him?'

Dead-eyed, Ramsey conceded, 'We have been in contact with Mr McDonald, yes.'

'Well, he'll tell you. I think I left at five fifteen, but it may have been later.'

'And then?'

'I started for home. But then my mother called me on my mobile to say there was trouble with a sluice. So—'

'What time was it when she called you?'

'Well . . . I'd just left the hospital so it must have been half past five, something like that.'

Ramsey absorbed this slowly, with concentration. Wilson sat with his elbows on the table, watching Will from above an arch of clasped fingers, while Barbara Smith was taking assiduous notes.

'And what did you do then?' Ramsey prompted.

'I drove to the marshes to deal with the sluice.'

'When you say you drove to the marshes, where exactly are we talking about?'

'The Gun Marsh. The western side.'

'And which route did you take to get there?'

'There's only one route. Down Salterns Lane, past my mother's place.'

'Your mother lives close to the marsh?'

'Yes,' Will said in the tone of someone going over old ground. 'A few yards away. Her cottage is the closest you can get to it by road.'

'So just to get it straight, once you knew there was a problem with the sluice, you went directly to the Gun Marsh to deal with it?'

'Yes.'

'You didn't go home first?'

Will gave Ramsey a curious look, as though the question were new to the itinerary and he couldn't see the point of it. 'It would only have wasted time. From what my mother had said, water was pouring onto the meadows. I had to get there quickly.'

'But you phoned home to Marsh House?'

'Yes.'

'And?'

'I told you – the machine was on.'

'Didn't you think that was strange?'

'No. Grace could have been in the bath . . . anything. Just because someone leaves the machine on . . .'

'You didn't worry?'

'No. There was absolutely no reason to. Besides, all I was thinking about at the time was the broken sluice and what it was doing to my land.'

'You didn't try to call again?'

'I'd left a message, there was no point.' He looked mildly baffled at having to explain such an obvious matter.

'What did you say in your message?'

'God . . .' He had to think. 'Umm, that I was going to the Gun to sort out a sluice, going straight there. Something like that.'

Ramsey's small eyes did not leave Will's face. 'Go on, Mr Dearden.'

Will rubbed his forehead. 'Yes, so . . . I got to the marsh and—'

'What time was this?'

'Six thirty, I suppose. But I wasn't really looking at the time . . . it could have been ten minutes either way.'

'Could it have been more than ten minutes either way?'

Will had to put his mind to this. 'No, no . . . It was no earlier than six twenty, at the very most. And later? No, I don't think so. No, ten minutes either way, no more.'

Ramsey waited for him to go on.

'So . . . then I went to look at the sluice.'

'Could you describe the exact location of the sluice for us?'

'It's on the western embankment of the Gun Marsh,' he replied slowly. 'The first sluice.'

'And to reach it?'

'I explained . . .'

'Just so we get it clear.'

Will's mouth twitched slightly, a first show of nerves. 'You drive past my mother's place and over some grass till you reach the embankment. Then you have to walk. Unless you're on a tractor . . . which I wasn't.'

'Did you see anyone on the way?'

'What? No.'

'Not your mother?'

'Not until she came out later. No, I drove straight past the cottage. I tooted the horn and went straight on.'

'What about the handle? Isn't there a handle you need to operate the sluice?'

'It was already out there. They'd already tried to close the sluice —'

'They?'

An infinitesimal pause, no longer than a heartbeat. 'I meant, my mother had already tried to close the sluice.'

Ramsey creased up his podgy cheeks in a show of surprise. 'Your *mother* had tried to close the sluice? Would she have been able to do that? She doesn't seem a very strong lady.'

'Well, she's managed it before. Mainly when she was younger, of course. But . . . In fact, it's not that difficult so long as the sluice is properly maintained.'

'And was it properly maintained?'

Looking wary now, Will gave a small nod.

Ramsey assumed his puzzled expression again. 'But in this instance it was in fact broken, so she couldn't shift it. Is that what you're saying?'

'Yes.'

'And she told you this when she phoned you on your mobile telephone?'

'That's right.'

Ramsey pursed his narrow lower lip. 'I see. Normally, though, the handle was kept at your mother's?'

'Yes. In the outhouse.'

Ramsey's frown deepened. 'No one thought of calling a neighbour?'

'My mother had tried Frank Yates and got no reply. Another neighbour was away on holiday.'

Ramsey dropped in casually, 'Your wife didn't come and help?'

Will stared at him. 'I beg your pardon?'

'Your wife? She didn't arrive to help?'

'No,' Will said in a deliberate voice. 'Otherwise I would have told you.'

'You're sure about that, Mr Dearden? About her not arriving?'

'Of course I'm sure.'

'What if I tell you she was seen arriving?'

The room was charged with sudden tension.

'That can't be right,' Will protested, with a short involuntary sound, half exclamation, half bark.

'She was seen driving down Salterns Lane towards Reed Cottage and the Gun Marsh.'

'But she dropped Charlie off at my mother's, we've told you—'

'That was at four, Mr Dearden. I'm talking about an hour and a half later. At about five forty.'

Will shook his head, and kept shaking it. 'No ... She couldn't have been there then.' He was making the effort to sound reasonable. 'My mother would have seen her. Or I would. No, it sounds like a mistake.'

'There's no mistake,' Ramsey answered with quiet satisfaction. 'She was seen driving down the lane towards your mother's cottage at around five forty.'

'But she had no reason to go back. Why should she want to go back?' Will argued, sounding rattled.

'The sluice? Perhaps she wanted to help?'

'No, no. She never got involved in any of that. No – she wouldn't ...'

'Perhaps she was bringing something over that you might need for your repair work?'

'No, *no*.'

Ramsey leant forward a little. 'Perhaps you met up and had an argument, Mr Dearden. Matters got out of hand and you killed her. An accident perhaps.'

Will swallowed, he looked Ramsey steadily in the eye. 'No.'

A short silence, which contained both tension and relief now that Ramsey had finally come out with it.

'Perhaps you found her waiting for you and she wanted to talk about something else and you pushed her out of the way and she fell.'

Will's eyes glinted dangerously, and a very Italian anger rose into his face, fiery and immediate, yet when he spoke his voice was very controlled. 'Nothing like that. You're completely on the wrong track.'

'You and she didn't have an argument?'

'I told you, she wasn't even there.'

'Did you have an argument at any time that day?'

Will said with quiet emphasis, 'No.'

'The fact remains, Mr Dearden, that your wife came back to Salterns Lane, was identified driving down towards the marshes, and was never seen again.'

'But it was dark by five forty,' Will argued tightly. 'I don't understand how anyone could have seen anything in those conditions. It must have been a mistake.'

'The sighting was very definite.'

Will turned to me, as though for help, but I could only signal retreat. Challenging the veracity of an absent witness was never a productive route.

Ramsey said, 'So there was no disagreement between you and your wife that day, Mr Dearden?'

'No.'

'You were getting on all right?' Ramsey persisted.

Will appeared not to have heard. He said in bewilderment,

'I simply don't understand how – why – she would have gone back to my mother's . . .'

Ramsey eyed him for a while, as if to assess the sincerity of this remark, before saying, 'I must ask again, were you getting on all right, you and your wife?'

The muscles in Will's cheeks worked furiously. 'What? Yes. Everything was normal.'

'Normal . . . That doesn't quite answer my question, Mr Dearden. What I asked was, were you and your wife getting on all right?'

A pause in which Will was very still. 'We were getting on fine,' he replied softly.

'No problems at all?'

'Nothing out of the ordinary.'

'You're sure about that?'

'Inspector Ramsey,' I interrupted, 'you've asked the same question several times, you've had your reply. Could we possibly move on?'

Ramsey swivelled his raisin eyes briefly onto me and hissed, with unexpected rancour, 'Why, is this a problem area?' Then, to Will: 'Nothing out of the ordinary, you say?' And his tone left no doubt that he was about to produce evidence to the contrary. 'Suppose I told you that Mrs Dearden visited a solicitor on the thirteenth of February?'

Will waited, showing nothing.

'Suppose I told you she went to discuss a separation.'

Will stared at Ramsey and the life seemed to fade from his face. The silence stretched out until there was nothing but the soughing of the wind and the ticking of a clock in the hall. Only Barbara Smith moved, pressing her fingertips to her chin. Finally Will lifted a slow shoulder. 'I would say you were totally mistaken,' he said in a voice so low it was almost a murmur.

'You can't explain it, then?'

Will seemed to shiver, a small spasm that passed quickly up

his body. 'No, I can't.' His mouth opened, for a moment no words came, then he murmured, 'Whoever said this . . . they're wrong.'

'So you're saying that, so far as you were concerned, there was no question of a separation?'

'That's right.' His voice, which had picked up a little, was steady. Only the beat of a vein at his temple hinted at the tension beneath.

'No question of your wife being unhappy?'

'No. In fact . . . quite the opposite.'

'You mean, she was happy?'

'Yes. Very.'

Ramsey raised his eyebrows. 'Happy about your marriage?'

'*I* thought so.'

'So you never had arguments?'

'Well . . . everyone has arguments.'

'All right – *serious* arguments then.'

Will exhaled slowly. 'No. Absolutely not.'

'So if your marriage was in such good shape, Mr Dearden, how do you account for your wife going to a solicitor to talk about a separation?'

'I can only think it was about money. My wife had got into a state about money and Charlie's schooling and . . . well, all sorts of things like that. I can only think she wanted to discuss money with this person.'

'With a *lawyer*?'

Will said restlessly, 'Why not?'

'An accountant, a bank manager would have been more likely, surely.'

Will seemed to reach some threshold. His expression darkened, he began to breathe rapidly, he threw me a look of desperation.

I said briskly, 'Could we finish now, Inspector? Mr Dearden's answered your questions.'

'Has he?' said Ramsey ingenuously. 'If you say so, Mrs

O'Neill.' He made as if to shift his chair only to pause and lean forward again. 'Before we finish, you couldn't just recap on the rest of that evening, could you, Mr Dearden?'

'Can't it wait?' I asked.

'It won't take a minute,' Ramsey said, keeping his eyes on Will.

Before I could argue any more, Will was saying at breakneck speed, 'I went and looked at the sluice. It was broken, I tried to fix it there and then, but I couldn't. So I drove to the barn—'

'Where's the barn exactly?'

'At Upper Farm,' he continued even faster. 'I picked up the tools I needed and a generator and a pump, and went back to the sluice and cobbled a temporary repair together, and then I went to my mother's to wait for the tide, until it was low enough to let the water out and have another go at the repair, do a more permanent job on it.'

'And that took you all night?'

'Till half past nine, something like that. But then I had to drain the marsh. That took another few hours.'

'You didn't find time to go home at all?'

'No.'

'Not even for half an hour?'

Will slowed down at last. 'It didn't seem worth it. Not when I was going back and forth all the time, and waiting for the tide. It was more convenient to snatch a bit of sleep at my mother's.'

Ramsey pondered this quietly. 'So, what time did you finally get home?'

'Six thirty . . . something like that.'

'And your wife wasn't there?'

'No.'

'Where did you think she was?'

'I thought she'd left for the station.'

'Though her car was still in the drive?'

Will sat back wearily. 'It was still dark, I was very tired . . . her car was at the side of the house. Here.' He indicated the window. 'It was easy to miss it.'

Ramsey appeared to come to a rapid decision. Pushing his chair back, he poised himself to stand. 'Thank you,' he said brightly, as though we had just concluded a successful business meeting. 'When the weather improves – hopefully tomorrow morning – you may wish to know that we'll be launching another extensive search, Mr Dearden.'

Will looked startled but said nothing.

'We thought we'd focus on the marshes, unless there's any other area you can suggest. Any area which might have been overlooked.' Ramsey waited, his round head cocked to one side, eyebrows raised expectantly until, getting no reaction, he stood up and said to me, 'I take it Mr Dearden will be available to come in to the station over the next few days?'

'For . . .?'

'We'll need a statement.'

'Can we make a time now?' I was thinking of the office and the extra work my absence would be inflicting on everyone.

'If you like,' he said. 'Though, as I'm sure you'll appreciate, circumstances may alter. I trust this won't be a problem?' There was no obvious irony in his tone, but I caught it all the same, loud and clear.

We settled on five the next evening.

'And will you be wanting to speak to Maggie Dearden again?' I asked.

From the flicker of irritation in Ramsey's eyes I guessed he had been hoping to drop in on Maggie unannounced. 'At some point,' he said, attempting a casual tone he didn't quite bring off.

'Can't she be left alone?' Will said, coming back to life. He beckoned me closer and whispered, 'She's not been well. The *stress* – it'll only make her ill again.'

I said to Ramsey, 'There's a flood warning out. Mrs

Dearden's cottage is at high risk. She may have to be evacuated and her possessions moved out. Also, she's in poor health. Perhaps we can talk about it again in a few days?'

Ramsey smiled the thin smile of someone who knows he has been outmanoeuvred, and that, whatever happened now, I would get to Maggie first and prepare the ground.

When the police car had finally driven away, I went back to Will, who was still at the dining table, staring blankly at its gleaming surface.

'At least they've come out and said it now,' I commented. 'What they think, I mean.'

But he wasn't listening, he was miles away. 'I simply don't understand . . .' he murmured.

'What?'

'If she was there then . . . how could I have missed her?'

I could offer no suggestions. All I could think was: He isn't making this up. He can't be making this up. He really didn't see her. And I felt both relief and shame.

He clutched his head with both hands as if his brain was running riot and he couldn't keep a hold on it. 'It doesn't make sense . . . It just doesn't . . .' He exhaled suddenly, he turned his head sharply towards the window, he fell into an abrupt silence.

'Can I get you anything?' I asked.

'No,' he whispered finally.

As I left him, he slid his elbows further onto the table and covered his face with his hands.

I made my calls from the kitchen. The room had a chill about it, as though the Aga had gone out, there were dirty plates on the table and a stack of pans on the draining board.

I tried Maggie first, but there was no reply.

My office answered at the second ring.

'We're coping,' Corinthia told me, after we had been

through the most urgent messages. 'There was a time this morning when I thought we'd have to do a quick cloning job because almost everyone was due to be in two places at once, but somehow we managed to spread ourselves around a bit. Sturgess took three of your bail applications at Clerkenwell, and got to Thames in time to do an assault, all before lunch.'

'Give him an extra pat from me.'

'Oh, and that Jason Hedley of yours has been in trouble again.'

'You're joking,' I sighed.

'Pinched a rump steak from Safeway. Bail refused, of course. Remanded at Brixton. Paul reckoned something bad had happened to him and that he was desperate to get inside.'

'Paul handled it? Is he there?'

'He's been wanting to speak to you,' she said diplomatically, and put me through.

'Thank you for looking after Jason Hedley,' I said as soon as he answered.

'He was in a bit of a state,' Paul reported. 'Mixing in fast company, from what I could gather. Got himself nicked just to get a safe bed for the night.'

'It'll be more than the one night this time. You explained why I wasn't there?'

'I explained. How're things going?'

Involuntarily, I glanced around Grace's kitchen. 'No sign of her, no information, and the police are getting the wrong ideas.'

'Ah. Know when you'll be back?' His voice held a note of light concern, and I felt guilty for having postponed the call for so long.

'I expect it'll be the weekend now. I'm sorry.'

'Ah, well.'

There was something in his voice, a wistfulness, an anxiety, that made me ask, 'Everything okay?'

'Sure. Fine. Well, we're managing, you know. Just about.'

'Another partner would help, Paul.'

He gave a faint chuckle at my persistence, and I could almost see him shaking his head. 'Soon, Lexxy, I promise.'

'You eating all right?'

'Listen to you.' But he liked my asking, I could tell by his voice. 'I stayed home last night and made myself scrambled eggs. Quite good, they were, though I say so myself.'

As always, I wondered how much he had drunk, and what sort of a state he'd been in when he got to bed. 'I'll see if I can get back before the weekend,' I said.

'That would be nice.' A pause, he seemed on the point of saying more, but someone interrupted him, people were arriving for a meeting, and he had to go.

The moment I put the phone down it began to ring again. I thought of picking it up but, seeing the red light on the answering machine, I left it to take a message. As I reached the door the machine relayed a woman's voice. The voice was hushed and hasty and low. 'It's only me,' it began. I took a step back into the room to hear better. 'Just need to talk. I know it's difficult, but can you call me later?'

The machine clicked off.

A worm of doubt slid into my stomach. And – I couldn't deny it – a dart of something that may have been jealousy. The tone, the note of intimacy, the absence of names. More disconcerting still, playing the message back in my mind, it seemed to me that I had heard the voice before, that, softly as the words had been spoken, it resembled that of Anne Hampton.

When I got back to the dining room, Will had disappeared. There was no note, no indication of where he had gone. Looking out of the window, I saw that the Range Rover was missing.

I waited a while. When he still hadn't returned after an hour, I pulled on my coat and went out. The storm hadn't abated. If anything, the sky seemed more opaque, the wind denser.

I drove along the quay and up the lane to Sedgecomb
House. Morning surgery was still in progress. There were two
cars parked alongside the front railings and five more in marked
bays in the courtyard. Ignoring the reserved sign, I took the last
available place in a corner of the courtyard. The outbuildings
had been transformed since my childhood. The front wall of
the stables had been given large arched windows, while the
lofty coach house had been converted into a two-storey building with glossy town-house doors and signs marked 'surgery'
and 'dispensary'. Even the crumbling weed-edged concrete in
the yard had been overlaid with herringbone brickwork.

The receptionist looked ready to repel boarders, but mel-
lowed when I announced myself and, with an air of importance,
spoke into a phone as soon as the doctor was 'between
patients'. He would be entirely free in twenty minutes, she
relayed, and if I'd like to wait in the house I'd find Mrs
Hampton there, who would be glad to give me some coffee.

Making my way towards the house, I felt a strange sense of
unreality, as though I were stepping backwards into a dream. I
noticed a few changes – the side path had been bricked over
and partially rerouted, the climbers clipped closer to the wall,
two magnificent stone lions guarded the door – but the house
itself was as solid and steady as ever, a mellow-bricked three-
storey cube supported by low leaning wings like buttresses,
with matching curved bays under the startled gaze of the semi-
circular eye-windows beneath the roof.

As a child I had loved this house because it was my home,
yet for most of my teenage years I had also thought of it as my
mother's prison, and then it had seemed an altogether sadder
and more difficult place.

Ringing the bell, I prepared myself for the revamped interior
Edward had warned me about.

'Alex!' Anne Hampton swept me in with a show of pleasure
that was a little too effusive to be comfortable. 'How lovely to
see you! Come in! What a wind! What a storm! Come in!

Gosh, how nice of you to—' She pulled up short with a sudden exclamation. 'Of course, it must be ages since you've seen this place! We've done the odd bit. I hope you'll *approve*.'

In the hall I was confused to recognize the central lantern and wall sconces and realized my parents must have sold them with the house.

'It's mainly this side of the house,' Anne said. 'Come and see.' I followed her across the hall into the kitchen and was immediately confused again, this time because nothing was in the slightest familiar. Even the view through the bay window was distorted and diminished by a distance it had never had in my day, a distance achieved by removing an entire intervening wall. It was as if a hand had reached in and wrenched the core from the centre of the house. I felt I was looking through the wrong end of a telescope. A bright modern kitchen now led into a bright modern dining area. The old sitting room, so lovingly decorated by my mother, so warm and serene in the morning sun, might never have existed. The eau-de-nil panelling had gone, the pale chintz curtains too; now there were white walls and blinds and spotlights, no tranquillity in the space any more, just modernity.

'Can I look around the rest of the house?'

'Of course! Let me show you!'

'Would you mind if I went on my own?'

She laid a hand on my arm and narrowed her eyes sympathetically. 'I understand!' she cried. 'Childhood memories!'

I went upstairs to my mother's bedroom. New wallpaper, new curtains, yet the past was still here, in the light, in the wide windows, in the chair placed to catch the best of the view. During the long years of her illness, my mother had always been torn between the sunlight and the sea. While she could still manage the stairs, she would spend most of the morning in the sitting room taking warmth from the morning sun, before coming up here to sit and read and watch the afternoon light on the marshes. She liked it best when the air was dry and clear, when, far out under the sky, beyond the line of the dunes, she could see the long glittering ribbon of the sea.

When the first symptoms of her illness appeared my mother hadn't said anything to my father. She hadn't wanted to worry him, though I had often wondered if, as a doctor's wife, she hadn't feared his disappointment too. Instead, she went to an old friend of my father's, a GP with a large practice in Cambridge, who told her that the weakness in her muscles, the pins and needles in her legs, the depression and loss of memory were just symptoms of anxiety, the result of an inability to cope. He told her she had simply taken on too much; she must learn to take life more calmly.

My mother said no more for a year, not until her right foot began to drag and she tripped in Burnham Market and fell heavily on top of her shopping. The raspberries in her bag stained her dress the colour of blood.

My father was a diligent and humane doctor; he would make endless visits to the sick, the bereaved and terminally ill. His manner was cheerful and uplifting, his compassion practical and unsentimental, he believed in the power of positive thought and the avoidance of gloom. Nothing in this rather simplistic philosophy prepared him for my mother's illness; nothing could disguise the fact that none of the magical drugs in his considerable arsenal was able to cure her. As the years went by his cheerfulness acquired a brittle edge, his optimism became an exercise in determination. He found it hard to come to terms with the changes in my mother's personality. In those days the treatment consisted of large doses of cortico-steroids whose side effects were terrible, both demeaning and distressing. Over time my mother suffered massive weight gain and oedema. Her body grew bloated, her face almost unrecognizable. She became easily upset, uncharacteristically angry and hopelessly depressed. For a time my father was confused and angry, then, slowly but resolutely, he withdrew behind a veneer of detachment and cheerfulness.

Nowadays they hardly ever prescribe steroids in the treatment of multiple sclerosis.

My old room had been decorated with floral wallpaper and matching curtains and fitted with built-in cupboards. Standing in the doorway, random images flickered through my mind, a jumble of years and seasons and activities, through which a sense of my own unconcern and optimism meandered like a thread. While my mother's health had not been deteriorating too obviously, while Edward had been small and not yet angry with life, I had never imagined anything would change, certainly not our future in this house.

I glanced into the other bedrooms before going downstairs again to peer into the drawing room and what had been our dining room, now a study.

'Well?' Anne cried from the kitchen door. 'What do you think? We wanted to put a conservatory at the back but in the end – well, we live in the kitchen. We felt it'd be rather a waste.'

She showed me to a seat in the breakfast area. As she chattered on, I had the illusion that she was speaking in two voices, the one I'd heard on first meeting her at Marsh House, and the one I'd heard on the answerphone message. I wanted to ask if it had been her on the machine, but something made me pause. It was possible the message had been entirely innocent, the supportive words of an old friend. It was also possible that my more imaginative suspicions were correct, and from my work I knew that if you don't want to hear the answer then you don't ask the question.

The skin of her cheeks was less vivid today, as if the allergy had temporarily subsided. This had the effect of making the yellowness of her hair less obvious, and she looked pretty in an open unaffected sort of way. Nothing could stem her flow of talk, however, nor her inability to pause and listen. She had a nervous jollity which wore away at you like a constant rubbing on the same spot. I wondered how Grace and she had become such friends.

'. . . *Such* a support, you know. Just when I needed her. You don't find many people like that, do you?'

'No,' I replied vaguely, supposing we were talking about Grace.

A door slammed, followed by a low call of greeting. Julian Hampton strode in and introduced himself with the brisk smile of the busy doctor. 'Shall we repair to the study?' he suggested firmly, as if to forestall argument, and I couldn't help thinking that he repaired to his study rather more often than Anne Hampton would have liked.

He led the way across the hall to a room containing a large desk, a TV, several shelves of videos and an easy chair incorporating head and footrests.

Julian Hampton placed a chair in front of the desk and gestured me towards it. He was a tall man, six-three or -four, slim and straight-backed with a receding hairline and brown hair fashionably cut and carefully brushed. He wore an immaculate grey suit, a blue and white spotted bow tie and matching blue shirt. He had a bony face with a long nose and small blue eyes behind rectangular gold-rimmed spectacles. He looked more like a senior consultant than a GP; the suit was certainly expensive enough.

'I'm representing the Deardens,' I began, as he took his place behind the desk.

'So I gather,' he said in the same rather brisk manner as before.

'I wouldn't ask you to break patient confidentiality, but I was wondering if you could give me some idea of whether you believe the police are right to rule out suicide.'

'You mean, was Grace depressed?' He had a way of staring directly at you without blinking or averting his eyes. 'The answer is no, she wasn't. I would say they're fairly safe to rule out suicide.'

'And intentional disappearance? I mean, as a result of psychological problems?'

His gaze slid away at last. 'Unlikely.'

'And there was no medical condition that could have resulted in an accident of any kind? No history of blackouts, fainting fits, epilepsy or a heart condition, that sort of thing?'

He remarked in passing, 'Not a doctor's daughter for nothing.'

'There have to be some advantages.' I added a smile.

He said in a weighty professional tone, 'There was no condition like that. Nothing that could account for a sudden blackout.'

I shrugged. 'I just thought I should make sure.'

He leant forward and, resting his elbows on the desk, made a steeple of his hands. He hesitated slightly. 'You didn't know Grace, did you?'

'Not really, no.'

'She had extraordinary . . .' He chose his word carefully. '. . . *energy*. She had . . .' Another small pause, a testing of the atmosphere, as though he wasn't sure how much he could safely tell me. '. . . a great appetite for life.'

I was careful not to show too much interest in my face. 'Oh?'

We eyed each other, I waiting, he coming to a decision about something. 'Speaking as a friend rather than a doctor,' he ventured cautiously, 'from what I knew of her personally, so to speak . . . I would say she was a . . . *restless* spirit.' He frowned at the description, as though marginally dissatisfied with it, but appeared to find nothing better.

I waited again, in case he said more. Finally I murmured, 'A searcher, then.'

We seemed to be getting each other's drift. 'Yes,' he replied quietly, 'a searcher.' Another inner debate and he ventured, 'Very beautiful, of course. Much noticed. Much admired.'

Again I waited. Again he seemed to be in a state of indecision. Finally he said, 'But beauty isn't always enough, is it?'

'For those who have it?'

'Indeed. For those who have it.' He stood up suddenly, as if he had said enough. When he shook my hand at the front door he raised his voice against the wind and said, 'Wish I could have been more help.'

It was only as I got into the car that I realized he had talked about Grace in the past tense.

I drove up to the village, which was little more than a ribbon of cottages and shops strung haphazardly along the main road. The weather had kept most people away. A woman scuttled out of the fishmonger's-cum-café and dived for her car. A man trudged the pavement with his collar up and head down, accompanied by a dog with wind-blown fur and flattened ears.

A lone car came from the opposite direction and I recognized the now familiar four-wheel drive of Barry Holland. It drew up in front of the hardware shop and, passing it, I glimpsed Barry in the driver's seat. By the time I had parked outside the post office he had disappeared into the shop.

The post office still bore the name Evans on an amateurish hand-painted sign over the door, but the interior had been modernized and extended. In addition to newspapers, sweets and birthday cards, it now offered travellers' food and emergency groceries. Among the bread, milk and eggs, there was even a choice of Perrier or Evian. The young woman who took my money had been a child when I had last seen her; I didn't try to introduce myself. But her mother, appearing from the back room with an armful of stock, said immediately, 'Well, hello, Alex! How are you?'

I smiled, 'I'm all right, Mrs Evans.'

She was a cheerful woman with wiry grey hair and round cheeks, who had lived in the village all her life. While she filled a shelf with chocolate bars we talked about how long it had been, and where I was living, and the dreadful weather. Pausing behind the counter, Mrs Evans said how sorry she had been to hear about my father's death.

'Your father was sorely missed when you all moved away,' she said solemnly. 'A real old-fashioned doctor. Used to come out at all hours. When Cherry got the asthma' – she tipped her head towards her daughter – 'he was round at three in the morning, no questions asked. Not like now. Now you get phone advice from some stand-in bloke you've never met.' She shrugged philosophically. 'But then the whole village has changed, I suppose. Newcomers, weekend types, commuters. Get the lot now.' She smiled abruptly. 'So what brings you back? Visiting your brother?'

'Partly.'

'Don't see much of him in the village. But then he's off and away quite a bit, isn't he?'

'I suppose he is, yes.'

A pause while she eyed the stack of newspapers I had bought. 'Terrible thing about Grace Dearden. Such a lovely person. Always a smile, you know. Always a nice word.' Her open face assumed a pessimistic expression, she lowered her voice respectfully. 'Can't help thinking it doesn't look good.'

'No?'

'Well, someone like that – so full of life, wasn't she?'

'I didn't know her that well.'

'Oh, always bright and cheerful. Always the busy one. Organizing things. Rushing about. Getting the whole place going. Lovely little Charlie. No reason to up and off of her own accord.'

I made a show of taking this in. 'No, I suppose not.'

'Dreadful for Will Dearden, of course,' said Mrs Evans in a tone of sympathy. 'They go searching, he and the men, almost every day. All over.'

I tucked the newspapers under my arm. 'Nice to see you again, Mrs Evans.'

'Don't forget your chocolate.'

Chocolate was meant to be a banned substance – I was prone to migraines – but I weakened whenever I was cold or stressed. Sitting in the icy car, I quickly ate my way through half the bar before starting on the papers.

I went through the down-market tabloids first. With growing disbelief, I searched them a second time. Only one had covered the appeal at all, four lines hidden away on a middle page; none had printed a picture of Grace. Presumably her disappearance had been deemed too dull for their readers and – I took a guess – her status too up-market. Yet the broadsheets were almost as bad. Only one had published Grace's picture, while the others carried the story as a minor item on the home pages. Alone out of the nationals, the *Mail* had given the story real space. Opening it, I was immediately transfixed by the main picture. It showed Grace and Will arriving at some function, Will in a dinner jacket, Grace in a pale clinging dress that looked as though it had cost a packet. The neckline was low, the straps thin, the wide expanse of neck offset by a wide choker of pearls. Her hair was swept up into an elaborate knot which accentuated the perfect heart shape of her face. Under the effect of the flashbulb her eyes, subtly accentuated by makeup, were doe-shaped and beguiling, while her mouth was set in the sweet shy smile that was so characteristic of her. She was triumphantly beautiful. By no stretch of the imagination did she look like a farmer's wife. I could see the angle the paper was going for, I could see why they had given it almost a whole page. A woman this beautiful was bound to get into trouble, a woman this well dressed could only bring financial ruin to a man of anything but ample means. *Ergo*, this disappearance was not as simple as it seemed. *Ergo*, the decision to show Grace and Will together so that the readers could make up their minds about what had really happened.

The picture did Will no favours. His eyes were narrowed, his mouth pulled down into an irritable line, miserable, no doubt, at being dragged out to a black-tie affair. To a stranger, though, he would look bad-tempered and mean spirited and jealous, someone with a fundamentally antagonistic view of the world, who probably ran on an extremely short fuse.

The second smaller picture showed Will at the press conference. He was looking troubled, but a cynic might say that he didn't seem all that heartbroken.

The story itself said nothing and everything, treading the

narrow line between truth and insinuation so beloved of certain newspapers. Grace was popular, a leading light on the social scene, newspaper-speak for being much admired and having plenty of opportunities to fall for someone else; she was known for her charity work, a saintly exterior being a good front for strong passions; finally, she was not believed to have had any worries, which meant that suicide was ruled out. Will, on the other hand, was a tenant farmer, and thus a bit of a yokel; he had been forced to sell off some of his land, which meant he was broke and had killed Grace for the life insurance; and he had made a televised appeal which, read against the rest of the story, meant that the police knew he was guilty.

Plunged into gloom, wondering what could have persuaded me to pressurize Will into making the appeal against his judgement, I ate my way doggedly through the rest of the chocolate.

A shadow darkened the window, someone tapped on the glass, and I looked up to see Jilly huddled under the hood of a Barbour.

'I didn't know you were still here,' she said when I had wound down the window. 'Edward thought you'd gone back.'

'I stayed on. Not working today?'

'No.'

I could never remember quite what Jilly did in Cambridge. Something to do with language tapes, or perhaps information technology.

'Will you be staying tonight?' Her breathless voice was scooped up by the wind. 'The bed's still made up.'

'Thanks, but I'm okay.'

'Oh, well.' She gave a nervous little smile and glanced away before coming closer to the window. She seemed to be gearing herself up to say something. 'Terrible weather,' she offered rather desperately. 'There's a flood warning.'

When we had agreed on this, she searched around for another topic. 'No more news . . . ?'

'No.'

Gathering her courage, she finally got it out. 'Just as well you're not staying, actually. Edward's in a frightful state.'

'Why?'

'Will Dearden's refused to sign the transfer.' When I failed to react, Jilly explained rapidly, 'The sale of the Gun Marsh, it's all off! He says he's not prepared to give it up after all! Edward's furious. I've never seen him so angry.'

'Well, these things do happen.'

'He gave no reason, Will Dearden, no reason at all. Not so much as a letter.'

I had the feeling I knew where this was leading. 'He doesn't have to give a reason.'

'Oh, but perhaps it's something that could be sorted out. Something *silly*.' When I didn't help her along, she said, 'You couldn't . . . well . . . you know . . .' It was a terrible effort for her to say it. 'Have a word with him?'

'No, Jilly. It's nothing to do with me. I couldn't interfere.'

Her face fell. 'I just thought . . . I mean, if we just knew the reason . . . And you'll be seeing him . . . Just a hint of why . . .'

'I really couldn't, Jilly. Under the circumstances, it would be totally inappropriate.'

She tried to look resigned to this but only succeeded in looking wretched.

'Edward will survive it, Jilly. It's not the end of the world.'

She stared at me as though I had understood nothing. 'But he won't!' she cried. 'He won't!'

'Jilly, he'll *have* to. There's nothing he can do about it!'

'He won't,' she repeated miserably, and for a moment she seemed close to tears.

I reached through the window and patted her sleeve clumsily. 'Don't let Edward take it out on you. Don't let him bully you.'

She blinked. 'It's not that.' Then, as though the full meaning of my words had only just sunk in, she straightened up and said defensively: 'It's not that at all!'

Chapter Seven

———•———

MAGGIE'S CAR was parked outside her cottage, but when I knocked there was no answer. I tried the handle but the door was locked, and I knocked again. Thinking my raps might have got drowned out by the gale, I peered through the sitting-room window, then, braving the full force of the wind, went down the side of the cottage to put my eye to the small pane set into the kitchen door. The breakfast dishes still stood on the draining board, the coffee cups on the table, while Maggie's uneaten melon lay unwrapped on the counter.

At the first touch of the handle, the kitchen door caught the wind and flew open, banging against the stop. Closing it rapidly behind me, I called into the quiet, 'Maggie?'

I kept calling as I walked into the passage and up the stairs.

She was lying on her back on the bed with a towelling wrap pulled roughly over her. In the meagre light she looked so still and so cold that she could have been dead.

Abruptly, she turned her head, though not enough to look at me.

'Maggie – are you all right?'

'Tell me,' she commanded, 'what did the police say?'

I took her hand and it was like ice. 'You're not well.'

'Tell me,' she insisted, in a voice that contained both impatience and entreaty.

'It was mainly old ground,' I reported obediently, sitting on the edge of the bed. Folding her hand in mine, I gently rubbed the parchment skin to bring the circulation back. 'They asked Will to go through everything that happened that Wednesday.

Times, places, the problems with the sluice, why he had to stay up most of the night, that sort of thing.'

The moment I paused, she looked at me swiftly and her hand tensed in mine. 'What else?' she demanded.

'There was one new thing,' I told her, choosing to forget Grace's alleged visit to the solicitor. 'They think they have a sighting of Grace that day. A witness who saw her driving down Salterns Lane in this direction at about five forty—'

She snatched her hand from my grasp and drew it against her side in a fist. 'Damn him! *Damn him!*'

I watched her face. 'Who, Maggie?'

'Damn him!'

'You know who this person is?'

She couldn't speak the name.

But I was already there. I remembered the conversation I had interrupted between Maggie and Barry Holland, the sound of their voices as I put my hand to the knocker, and Maggie's distress when she opened the door.

'Barry Holland?'

She affirmed it with a despairing lift of her eyes.

'He told you yesterday?'

'He wouldn't listen. I said he was not right, but he wouldn't listen. No, no! He knew best! He said he must go to the police. I knew it would be a bad thing. I *knew* it.' She shook both fists.

'Hang on a minute, Maggie. Hang on. He could have been mistaken. He could have got the time wrong – anything. But tell me – just to get it straight – Grace brought Charlie over at about four, is that right?'

She dropped her hands. 'Yes.'

'And she left within ten minutes?'

'Two minutes. *Two.* But, Alex, I tell you – she didn't come back again! She did *not* come back. And now this stupid man goes to the police and says these things! So they will think Will has been lying or I have been lying, or *both* of us have been lying!' I recognized the despair in her voice; it was the despair of someone worn down by deep tiredness and unremitting stress and endless days waiting for news that never came.

'Maggie, listen – it was dark, Barry Holland might have been some distance away. Did he say where he was when he thought he saw Grace? Did he say if he was in his house or his car?'

She gestured uncertainty.

'And how well did he know Grace, anyway?'

'Oh, he—' She pulled up abruptly, with an exclamation, a hiss against her teeth. 'He knew her well enough.'

'But in the dark? Maggie, there's a wealth of difference between *thinking* you've seen a person and being *sure*.'

She considered this for a while, she closed her eyes as if to impose some sort of calm before pushing the robe away from her body. With an audible intake of breath and a brief grimace, she lifted her legs and swung them over the far side of the bed. She sat up very straight with her back to me, motionless, as though drawing on scarce energies. 'He is certain,' she said dully.

I went round the bed and perched on a small chair in the corner where I could see her face. 'Grace's car is a grey Volvo estate, isn't it? Well, there must be dozens of people in this area with almost identical cars. Someone in a Volvo might have been visiting one of your neighbours, someone with blonde hair . . .'

She turned her head into profile. 'I tell you – he says he is *certain*.'

I took a long breath. 'Okay . . . Maybe Grace *did* come back. Maybe she came back to tell Charlie something or to bring him something or . . . And maybe you were elsewhere, in the loo or the bathroom or whatever, and she came and went very quickly without your knowing it.'

This brought an adamant rejection. 'No, that's absolutely not possible. No – Charlie didn't see her. No, it couldn't have been that way!'

'Perhaps you were both out of earshot.'

'No.'

'Grace couldn't have been visiting anyone else in the lane?'

'No.'

But for all her refutations I could sense that she was starting to open her mind to the possibilities, starting to realize that this evidence might not be as incontrovertible as it seemed.

In the pause that followed, I went and sat beside her and put an arm round her shoulders. 'Maggie, what are they doing about these gallstones of yours? There must be something—'

She made a *pah!* sound and frowned.

'Can't they take them out?'

'Oh, sure. The knife, they love the knife, but they cannot promise anything at the end of it.' She lifted a hand and tilted it one way then the other as she chanted, 'You may be better, you may not . . .'

'But—'

She patted my knee. 'Alex, it's nothing. I tell you, the smoking will kill me long before the gallstones.' And she laughed gently.

Something told me it would be futile to tackle her about the smoking. From my years with Paul, I recognized the self-destructiveness behind her addiction, the sheer determination to continue against all advice, though in her case, unlike Paul's, I couldn't imagine what had caused her to turn her energies against herself. In the old days Maggie had burst with a zest for life; now she seemed contemptuous of the damage she was wreaking on herself.

'And still it blows,' she sighed, lifting her head to the storm.

We listened, and I thought I could make out the thunder of the waves beyond the dunes, thought I could hear the sea as it drove against the defences, and it seemed to me that the water was very high. But then you could hear anything in a wind like this. If you let your imagination run wild, you could hear the sea breaking through the dunes and cascading over the marshes towards you.

Touching my hand, offering me a fleeting smile of

unhappiness, Maggie stood up. 'I suppose I should think about this flood.'

'Is it going to flood? I thought—'

'No, no. There will be no flood. But I feel I should go through the motions. Eh? Go through the motions.' She rolled the expression around her tongue.

I followed her towards the door. 'Let me know what I can do.'

'Just a few things to come upstairs.'

'Give me a list.'

'Dear girl.' She turned and embraced me solemnly. Drawing back a little, she fixed me with fervent eyes. 'I knew you would not let us down.'

And, touching a hand to her hair, she pulled a strand back from her face, smoothed her sweater and, drawing a breath as if for battle, led the way slowly down the narrow stairs.

'How long do we have?' I asked.

'They said eleven tonight.'

There were easy things, like rugs and books and photo albums, there were objects that were going to be far more difficult, like cabinets and chairs and sofas, and there were totally impossible things like dressers and bookcases. The books took longer than I'd thought because there were so many of them and few horizontal surfaces at a safe height close by. In the end I carried them through to the dining room and stacked them on the table. Maggie kept wandering in from the kitchen where she was dealing with the food and saying, 'Oh, darling girl, leave them, leave them . . . That's enough, really . . . enough.'

I found a home for the last pile of books as an early dusk closed around the cottage, bringing an uneasy gloom. I had just carried a pretty little button-backed chair upstairs when a car horn tooted outside and the cottage door banged and I heard Will's voice.

Seeing me, he exclaimed, 'Alex!' He seemed disorientated

for a moment, as though he couldn't think how I had got there. Glancing around, he saw the books and the rolled-up rugs and dining chairs standing on the table. 'You . . .?' And when he looked back at me, he smiled with gratitude and affection, and before I could stop myself my heart squeezed with foolish pleasure.

Turning away, I said, 'I wasn't sure what to do with the sofas and the rest of the heavy stuff. Whether they were to go upstairs . . .'

And then for a brief moment he laughed, an explosive sound that creased his eyes and showed his even teeth. I had not seen him laugh like this since we were young. The strain fell from his face and he looked twenty again, just a handsome carefree son of a gun.

I laughed too, though I had the feeling I was being teased.

'I'm sorry, I'm sorry.' He tried to suppress a smile. 'It was the thought of you trying to get the sofas upstairs. Sorry . . .'

I grinned back at him. 'You mean, you doubted me.'

'I didn't doubt you'd *try*.'

Charlie appeared unexpectedly in the doorway.

I said, 'Hello, Charlie. Not at school?'

He was solemn and pale and unlaughing. His eyes flickered up to mine, a greeting of sorts.

'More use here,' Will said, and laid a hand on his head.

A car door slammed, and Frank Yates and John Simons arrived to help with the furniture. They greeted me warmly, as though I were a valuable and much missed friend, and I thought how very long I must have lived in the city to think this unusual.

The men started in the hall, with a small antique table that wouldn't tolerate the water.

'Do you want to help me with the curtains?' I said to Charlie.

He looked around for his father, faintly alarmed.

Will called, 'You help with the curtains, Charlie. We'll shout if we need you.'

Charlie followed me reluctantly to the dining room. I showed him how to lift each curtain off the floor and tie it in a giant knot.

I said, 'Did your father tell you about the flood that happened years ago, when he was a young man?'

A small nod.

'Of course it was different then. They hadn't reinforced the dunes. It's much safer now.'

His expression told me he wasn't worried about the dunes. Crossing the hall, standing aside for the men as they carried a cabinet upstairs, we moved on to the long curtains in the sitting room.

'The whole village turned out,' I told Charlie. 'Your father and I went to help in one of the Salterns cottages. Did he tell you that when the men were moving the furniture they got a dresser stuck half-way up the stairs?'

He was intent on pulling the tail of the knotted curtain through, but he was also listening.

'Couldn't move it, and the old lady who lived there was stuck at the top, wailing blue murder.' We finished the curtains and stood back to inspect our work. 'The more upset she got, of course, the more solidly the dresser got wedged.'

He fixed me with an unblinking gaze, and I thought I had never seen eyes quite so pale and clear before. They were the colour of ice, far paler than his mother's which in all the photographs looked closer to sapphire. I tried to remember what Veronica Bailey's were like, if Charlie could have got them from her.

'So there it was,' I said, 'the dresser wouldn't go any further up the stairs and they couldn't very well leave it where it was, not with the old lady stuck on the landing, so it had to come down again. A big chunk of plaster came with it, I seem to remember. And by the time they'd finished there might have been one less banister, too.'

He was waiting for an ending to the tale.

'The only thing they could do with it was to plonk it on top of the outhouse.'

He looked uncertain about that. 'Was it all right?' he asked eventually.

'Oh, safe as houses. Or safe as outhouses.'

It was an awful joke, but he had the kindness not to groan.

I cast around. 'Well, what next, Charlie? What d'you reckon?'

This threw him for a moment. Then, thinking hard, he said, 'Down here.'

He led the way to a cupboard, whose lower shelves contained photo albums and board games.

As we began to gather them up, Charlie asked, 'Was it high, the water?'

'Quite high,' I said. 'Seven cottages got flooded. I think it was seven, anyway. But all the important things were saved. Cats, budgerigars, chickens, books, valuables, food. The flood didn't come till morning, you see. We had all night to move everything upstairs and get the people to safety. There was only one old chap who wouldn't move, wouldn't let anyone lay a hand on his furniture, but it didn't matter in the end because the flood stopped just short of his door, he managed to keep dry. Your father and I sat up all night, though, keeping watch.'

Charlie appeared satisfied with this, though nothing seemed to lift his air of general apprehension.

He carried the albums out of the room, leaving me to memories of the flickering candlelight in old Mr Kemp's kitchen, of Will's profile as we sat beside the old-fashioned range in the dead of night, of my sense of complete and perfect happiness. A storm had seemed romantic to me then, I had been intoxicated with the drama of it, with the idea of danger and rescue. The wind had made an extraordinary noise – I could remember it even now, a whistling that was sometimes a moan, sometimes a drumming – and I saw again the flimsy curtains shifting restlessly, I heard the ill-fitting windows rattling in their frames. Soon after Will and I had arrived, the power had failed. Old Mr Kemp had thought this funny. Chortling with delight, boasting that he knew all about surviving storms, he had lit a stump of a candle and poured tots of whisky, one each for Will and me, and a succession of large ones for himself 'according to age and need'. When he fell asleep in his chair Will and I had huddled round the stove, giggling like conspirators. Alive with the excitement of the storm, fired by the whisky, it was some time before we stopped laughing, and then we'd sat shoulder to shoulder, talking quietly, and I was aware of a new mood between us, as though in the progress of a single day Will had come to realize that I was virtually grown up, not so very far from him in age after all. When we had touched fingers and held hands, when we had lightly kissed, I had thought with the simplicity of youth that there was hope for me after all.

Charlie returned.

'What next?' I said.

After careful consideration he suggested, 'The cushions?'

'Sounds good to me.' We began to strip the sofas. 'How was school today?' I asked brightly.

He shrugged.

'You like school?'

Still he didn't answer, but his frown said a great deal.

'Not so great, eh?'

The frown deepened.

It occurred to me that school must be very hard for him at the moment, with his mother's picture all over the TV news.

'I remember thinking school was a real pain sometimes,' I offered. 'And then it got better again. In the end I quite enjoyed it. Do they give you much homework?'

He scooped up a cushion and gave a single shake of his head.

'What, none at all?'

He stood stranded in the middle of the room with a large

seat-cushion tucked under each arm and shot me an uncertain glance, assessing the risk of going further. 'I'm dyslexic.'

'That must be a nuisance for you. Do they give you extra tuition?'

He nodded.

'Where are we going to put these?' I asked from over the pile of cushions, which reached almost to my chin. 'Upstairs?'

As I followed him, I said chattily, 'They have teachers trained in dyslexia nowadays, don't they?'

He didn't reply.

We dropped the cushions in a corner of Maggie's bedroom, next to a stack of dining chairs.

'So much better than the old days,' I meandered on. 'At least it's recognized now. Some friends of mine send their son to a special school in London. The kids use these sunglasses, except they're not really sunglasses. They filter out parts of the colour spectrum. Something like that. Have you heard of them?' I was so sure I was on safe ground that it took me several moments to realize that Charlie was locked with sudden tension, eyes frozen on the floor.

'Charlie?' I took a step closer. 'Something the matter?'

He twisted his head away and would probably have escaped if I hadn't been standing between him and the door.

'Was it something I said?' But of course it was; I could have bitten my tongue off. I had thought Veronica's scornful talk of sending Charlie away to a special school was malicious invention, but now I wondered if the idea hadn't been a serious consideration and a source of terror to Charlie.

'I'm sorry, Charlie. I didn't mean to say anything wrong. I know nothing about dyslexia. Nothing. I was just . . . talking.'

He lifted his head a little.

'It was a day school, the school this boy went to,' I continued lamely. 'And he was happy there. Terribly happy.' I was making no ground. Giving up, I touched his arm lightly and said, 'Shall we go and see if there're any more cushions?'

He didn't need a second invitation to hurry from the room.

'There you are!' Maggie cried from the hall below, looking first at Charlie as he swung past her, then at me as I followed down the stairs. 'What have you been doing?'

'Cushion removals.'

She was watching me closely and when Charlie had disappeared in the direction of the kitchen she whispered urgently, 'You didn't say anything to Charlie, did you?'

'You mean . . .?'

'About his mother. About . . .'

'*No.*'

'It's just that . . . he cannot talk about it. You understand? He cannot hear about it!'

'Maggie, I wouldn't say anything, I promise you.'

Her face cleared a little, only to cloud again. 'I worry about him, you see,' she explained unnecessarily. 'He is so . . .' But she couldn't find the words and finished with a gesture of deep feeling, a fist pressed against her heart.

'Of course.'

'He is the one who matters,' she said. 'He is the one we have to protect.'

I would have said something more to reassure her but we were interrupted by the boom of voices as Frank and John emerged from the kitchen and took their leave.

'You don't have to stay,' Will said, and there was a note of challenge in his voice, as though he were testing me in some way.

'Can't I be of use here?'

'You might get wet.'

'I've run the risk before.'

But Will was too preoccupied to catch the allusion, and I was too shy to spell it out.

I said, 'I'll be quite happy to sleep on some cushions.'

He nodded vaguely, then, with an urgency that bordered on brusqueness: 'But we should eat before it gets too late.'

Maggie was sitting at the kitchen table, reading a story to Charlie in the monotonous voice of deep exhaustion. She barely glanced up as I opened the fridge, and nodded rapidly when I held up eggs and ham and salad.

No one ate much. No one talked much either. Maggie had no appetite at all and, though she spoke to Charlie now and again, cajoling him to eat, fussing generally over his health, the conversations soon foundered. The moment we had abandoned the meal, she lit a cigarette, the first of several, and drew on it fiercely.

Will stared grimly at his plate, emerging from his thoughts only to squint into the darkness beyond the window. Once I glanced up to find him gazing at me with unfocused absorption and slight puzzlement, as though he were trying to work something out and at some point along the way his thought processes had led him to me. Coming to, he smiled slightly, and a look of fellowship passed between us.

As I cleared the plates, Will stood up and announced that he was going outside to have a look around.

Charlie's cry was so sudden, so shrill, that I jumped, the plates slithered out of my hands and across the draining board.

Charlie screamed, '*Don't go! Please don't go, Daddy!*' His panic was as overwhelming as it was absolute. For an instant Will stood immobile with astonishment, then, reaching out towards Charlie, he dropped onto one knee by his chair and said soothingly, 'It's only for a minute, Charlie. I'll be back in no time—'

'*Don't go! Please don't go!*' Charlie sobbed, his dread inconsolable.

Scrambling to her feet, Maggie threw her arm around Charlie's shoulders and shook him slightly. 'Charlie, listen – it's all right! *It's all right!* You hear me?'

'*Please don't go ... please ...*' The child's face contorted into agonies of unhappiness, his cheeks ran with tears, he kept crying, *'Don't go ... don't go ...'* over and over again. Nothing that Will or Maggie could say seemed to have any effect; Charlie refused to be contained or placated. His body stiffened, he twisted his head from side to side, he tried to wrench himself free of their hold.

Temporarily defeated, looking stunned, Will dropped his arms and fell back.

I said to him, 'I could go and have a look around for you, while you stay here.'

'Don't go! Don't go!'

I said again, *'I* could go, Will. Let me go!'

Will shook his head and, coming to some sort of decision, stood up and tried to draw Maggie away from Charlie. 'Mum, go next door for a minute, would you?'

'What?' She clutched Charlie's shoulder tighter. 'No, no.'

Gripping her arm, he said in his firmest voice, *'Maggie* – go next door.'

She glared at him. *'No!'*

His eyes flashed with exasperation. He pulled her bodily away and growled, *'Do as I say!'*

Maggie's face crumpled. She repeated, 'No,' but now it was a cry of capitulation rather than defiance, and, eyes lowered, she followed me out of the room and down the passage. There were no seats left on the ground floor, the sofa frames had been upended against the walls, so we sat on the stairs.

It was colder here and, taking off the long wool cardigan I was wearing, I draped it round her shoulders. 'He'll be okay, Maggie.'

But she turned away and, leaning her forehead against the wall, sat with one hand over her face.

And still we could hear Charlie sobbing in the kitchen.

I remembered a corner cupboard in the sitting room with drinks and glasses. There was whisky and brandy and a fearsome-looking Italian liqueur. I poured a small brandy then added another half-inch for good measure.

Maggie accepted the glass wordlessly and took a sip.

'Perhaps Charlie needed to talk,' I said. 'Perhaps he needed to talk to his father.'

Maggie shivered with fresh anger and retorted in a sharp voice, 'No! *No*.'

I kept quiet after that. Fetching a brandy for myself, I sat silently on the bottom stair, at Maggie's knee.

In the kitchen the sobbing trailed off at last, and, though we listened for a long time, it didn't start again. The only sound was the buffeting of the wind and, somewhere in the sitting room, the insistent scratching of a branch against a window.

Finally Maggie gave a long sigh, which seemed to contain all the sadness of her life. 'Tell me ...' she began in a low voice. 'Tell me about the people who come to you, Alex.' She was leaning back against the wall, eyes half closed.

'My clients?'

'What is the worst they do? Are they robbers? Murderers? Tell me how they get caught, tell me what happens to them.'

I floundered for a moment – where to begin? what to cover? – before explaining that the bulk of my work was petty crime, with a bit of assault, a smattering of robbery and the occasional murder thrown in. I told her about the increasing use of knives by young men, and how a knife could kill far more easily than the kids ever imagined, and how, when they found out, it was always too late and someone, often a kid of their own age, had died. I told her about the professional criminals, the ones for whom burglary was a career and prison a way of life. I told her about the real villains, what made them different from the rest, and immediately thought of Ronnie Buck.

I wouldn't have known Maggie was listening but for the occasional murmured question. When I told her that it was the petty thieves and the hardened criminals who were most likely to get off, she asked: 'And you help in this, Alex?'

'Most of the time they simply don't get caught, let alone charged. But when they do – yes, I do my best to get them off.'

'The bad ones too?' she asked in a low drifting voice. 'You get them off?'

A moment of truth. A moment in which I acknowledged the extent of my self-doubt. 'Yes. The bad ones too.'

'But usually . . .?' She lifted her fingers in the beginnings of a gesture.

'Sorry?'

'You said . . . usually the bad ones don't get caught.'

'That's right. The people around them get too frightened to talk. Witnesses get bought off.'

'They never get caught?' she asked in the distracted tone of someone filling time.

'Oh, in the end. They make a mistake. They get careless, leave evidence. Or someone talks – a partner, an employee, a girlfriend, someone who's gone sour on them. Even then . . .' I sighed openly. 'Even then they can get off with the help of a smart defence.' And I recounted the story of Ronnie Buck and the policeman half killed in his garden. I told her about the plea of self-defence, and how it would never have succeeded without the crucial witness, the witness who was in all likelihood bought and paid for.

I paused there. I couldn't bring myself to talk about the unknown investigator Paul had hired to find the crucial witness, or to voice my worries about Paul's involvement with Ronnie Buck.

The silence drew out. I glanced up to find Maggie staring into a distance of her own making.

The kitchen door sounded. Shoving her brandy into my hand, Maggie clambered rapidly to her feet.

Will came down the passage. 'He's okay,' he said briskly.

Maggie slid past him towards the kitchen.

Will continued to the front door and began to pull on a warm jacket.

'Would you like me to come with you?' I asked.

It was a moment before he took in what I had said. 'No . . . If you could keep an eye on things here.'

'Are you going to be long?'

'Twenty minutes. Less, probably.'

'You've got the phone with you?'

He patted his pockets absentmindedly, then, pulling on boots and an old woollen hat, finally found the phone in the inner compartment of his jacket and held it up to me. As he opened the door he glanced back over his shoulder as though to speak, only to change his mind and turn away without a word.

Soon afterwards, Maggie led a subdued Charlie up to bed, whispering, 'I am tired, Alex. I will see you in the morning.'

I waited in the kitchen, drinking coffee, sitting at the scrubbed pine table that had been the centre of life at Marsh House, remembering the meals I had eaten there, the heavily laden pizzas, the meatballs in spicy sauce, the tomato and basil salad, dishes that stood three Michelin stars above the sludgy stodge that Mrs Hill was giving us at home. The sun had seemed to shine more often then, too – a trick of childhood memory; just as the hand-painted china on the dresser in front of me had seemed a more brilliant blue. Even the winter storms had been washed with a romantic light.

Listening to the storm now as it drummed against the cottage, I thought I heard the sea again, and went to the window a couple of times to peer out into the darkness.

Will had been gone ten minutes. To help pass the time, I fetched my notebook from my bag and brought my notes up to date.

I wrote down Barry Holland's name and the time he claimed to have seen Grace: six p.m. And added: *Mistaken ID? Wrong day? Wrong time? Wrong car? Bad vis/dark?*

Under this I wrote: *If not mistaken, where was Grace going?*

Turning to a fresh page, I began to draw a rough map, with a long straight line across the page, west to east, for the marsh edge – though in reality it was far from straight – and another straight line running parallel to it some distance below, for the main coast road. I drew Quay Lane as an inverted U standing on the coast road, its top marking the extent of the quay. Off the right-hand corner of the quay I added a small blob for Marsh House.

Going back to the main road, I went east and drew another line leaving the road at right angles to go due north, a line that did not loop anywhere but petered out near the marsh edge. This was Salterns Lane. I marked Reed Cottage at the end of this lane, and the Salterns cottages away to the left, and, back at the beginning of the lane, just short of the junction with the main road, Barry Holland's house.

I stared at the map for a while, then for want of anything better to do I drew a line showing the Gun Marsh embankment where it left the marsh edge just to the east of Reed Cottage and headed out towards the dunes. Drawn like this, it could almost have been an extension to Salterns Lane. To the left of the embankment I sketched a suggestion of creeks and wrote 'salt-marsh', and to the right 'Gun Marsh', though strict logic should have demanded 'fresh-water marsh'. A short way up the Gun embankment I also marked the position of the first sluice with a cross, while along the marsh edge I indicated the footpaths with dotted lines.

It was tempting to go on doodling, but none of it was going to get me any closer to guessing where Grace might have been going at five forty that evening. Salterns Lane was a dead-end road. She had already said goodbye to Charlie. She wasn't on particularly friendly terms with any of Maggie's neighbours, excepting Barry Holland. She hadn't been coming to help with the sluice because, according to Will, she never went near the marshes.

It seemed strange to me that anyone could live in this part of the world and not go near the marshes. A fear of water, perhaps. Or – I pictured Grace's photographs, the immaculate face and hair – a dislike of wind and winter cold and muddy feet and blazing summer sun.

I paused. I had missed something. And only just now, one

or two thoughts ago. I retraced my steps, and still I missed it. Back again, more slowly this time.

I got there at last. What had Grace been told about the sluice? And who might have told her? It couldn't have been Will – he'd got no reply from Marsh House when he'd called. That left Maggie. Maggie, who might have sounded panicky, who might have led Grace to believe that the trouble was far more serious than it actually was, might have made Grace feel duty-bound to drive back to Reed Cottage and offer support, however ineffectual.

I ran through this scenario several times and found a succession of problems, not least the fact that, having been seen to enter Salterns Lane, which was neither long nor hazardous, Grace had failed to reach Reed Cottage.

The latch of the front door sounded, a draught chilled the air. I went into the hall to find Will pulling off his jacket.

'How's it looking?' I asked.

He wore one of his darker expressions. 'Can't be sure for a while. The tide could be late. There could be a surge.'

He went upstairs to check on Charlie. When he came down again I offered him a brandy, which he accepted vaguely but didn't immediately touch.

'Charlie all right?'

Sliding his elbows onto the kitchen table, he propped his head in his hands and closed his eyes tightly for a moment. 'Well . . . he's asleep.'

'I think I put my foot in it earlier,' I confessed. 'I said something about special schools for dyslexics.

Will squinted at me. 'Why on earth did you say that?'

'I don't know. It just sort of . . . came out. Had you considered it, in fact, a special school?'

'Not me! *Grace.*' His tone was sharp, his look too. 'Charlie hated the idea. He didn't want to go. And he was dead right. It was an absolute dump.'

'A boarding school?'

'Oh, *yes.* That was part of the attraction for Grace. She

wanted him shaped up. That's what she called it – *shaped up*.
Meaning she wanted him to be more *manageable*, more *obedi-
ent*.' He gave a harsh sigh, and I saw again the barely
suppressed fury of his feelings for Grace.

'This was recently?'

'A year or so ago.'

He rubbed his eyelids energetically, then straightening up,
focused on his drink for the first time, and, swilling the brandy
round the glass, drained it in one. The worries chased across
his face, he almost spoke several times. Finally he said tightly,
'This sighting of Grace – I just can't work it out, Ali. There
was no reason for her to come back.'

'Could it have been the sluice? Could she have thought the
problem was far more serious than it really was, that the
cottage was in danger? Felt she had to come back and help
Maggie and Charlie?'

He nodded at me, and kept nodding. 'I can't think of
anything else.'

'The only problem with that is that Maggie and Charlie
would have seen her, and they didn't.'

He threw me a meditative glance. 'Yes . . . *yes* . . . Unless
Grace thought they were out on the marsh and went straight
there . . .' But almost as soon as he'd said this, he waved the
idea firmly aside. 'No, no . . .' He leant forward and, jabbing
his fingertips against his forehead, gave a great shudder, as if
to clear his mind.

I said, 'But don't forget, there's always the chance that
Barry Holland was mistaken—'

His head shot up. '*Barry Holland?*'

'I thought you— Yes, that's who it was, apparently.'

Understanding spread slowly over his face. He exclaimed
ironically, 'Of *course*.'

'Why of course?'

'Well, it had to be him, didn't it?'

'Why?'

'Because—' He shrugged impatiently. 'Oh, because Grace

was after him for sponsorship money. Cultivated him. Chatted
him up. I think he was a bit smitten by her. What am I saying?
I *know* he was smitten by her. Under her spell, just like the rest
of the world.' He lowered his voice, and added more reflectively, 'It's amazing, you know, how she could work her trick
on people. I've never understood how they couldn't see through
it.'

'What was her trick?'

'Oh, fixing them with an admiring gaze, hanging on their
every word, searching them out all the time, making them think
they were dead special to her. And then the moment they were
out of her sight she'd forget about them. I mean, *instantly*. Go
back to making her plans. That was the only time she'd ever
think of them again, when she was planning how they could be
useful to her.' He lowered his voice still further, as if aware of
Charlie asleep above our heads. 'So cold, Ali. So bloody cold.'

'She's been seeing quite a lot of Barry Holland then?'

'A *lot*? No. Just *enough* to charm the pants off him. To get
the money.'

'So not a lover, then?'

He laughed drily. 'What, *Barry*? No – not Grace's style.
Rich enough, sure, he's absolutely rolling in money, but far too
rough around the edges. A criminal record in the family? God,
no, she wouldn't have liked that at all!'

It seemed to me that he was protesting too much, that he
wasn't absolutely sure about this or anything else, and it was
the uncertainty that really frightened him.

We lapsed into a troubled silence, accentuated by the
growling of the wind. I made more coffee and slid a cup in
front of him. Abruptly, he looked at the time. 'Is it half past
yet? I should go and check the tide again.'

'You've still got five minutes.' While I had his attention, I
said lightly, 'Someone told me that you'd decided to keep the
Gun after all.'

'Huh?' He was about to give one answer when he remembered whose sister I was and gave another reply altogether.

'Edward isn't too pleased with me, I'm afraid.' He raised an eyebrow, making no effort to pretend he felt terribly concerned about it.

'You hadn't signed the transfer?'

'No.'

'An agreement?'

'No.'

'Well, then, there isn't much he can do about it.'

'He's muttering about a verbal contract.'

'Verbal contracts are almost impossible to enforce in property deals. People break them all the time.'

'Well, he doesn't seem too worried about the finer points. He's talking about suing.'

'You know what he's like. He'll simmer down in time.' Though even as I said this, I had serious doubts. The concept of surrender was anathema to Edward, an indignity that weak people were forced to endure because they'd been feckless enough to be outmanoeuvred. For him, every slight, large or small, real or imaginary, was like an open wound; it gaped, raw and painful, it stung unbearably, until the moment when he could turn the tables and get the upper hand again. At the best of times there had never been any love lost between Edward and Will; for Edward, this reversal would be a red-hot barb in his flesh.

'Well, I wouldn't worry about it now,' I said. 'Even if Edward does decide to pursue it, it'll take months and months to get the action off the ground.'

'Can't have you as my lawyer, I suppose?' And a wry grin twitched at his mouth.

'Wouldn't do you any good, anyway. Hopeless at contract law.' And I smiled back. 'May I ask . . . why did you change your mind about the Gun?'

He stirred his coffee roughly, so that it almost spilt. 'Couldn't let it go, Ali. Just couldn't. Would have finished the farm, would have finished *me*. So . . . I'm restructuring the finances instead. New mortgage and all that.' He met my eyes with a touch of defiance.

'I'm glad.' I was glad about the marsh, very; but, far more than that, I was glad he wasn't relying on luck or the vague hope of a windfall to cover his debts. It would have looked bad, and this wasn't the time to be looking bad.

There was a pause. The wind thrummed its warning on the window.

He glanced at his watch. 'I must go.'

I followed him to the front door. He pulled on his jacket and boots again and, with a short wave, went off into the darkness.

He was gone for only five or six minutes, but it was long enough for the last of his nervous energy to have given way to exhaustion. Throwing off his jacket, he sprawled on a kitchen chair, legs extended, head dropped back, eyes closed. 'God, I'm tired, Ali.'

'Why don't you sleep for a while? Let me keep watch.'

'If I go to sleep I'll never wake up again.'

'Well, sleep, then. I don't mind staying up. How much longer is the tide high? An hour? Two?'

'An hour.'

'I can last that long. Easily.'

'Ali . . .' He whispered my name softly, with the languor of fatigue or affection. 'Ali . . .'

I felt a pull high in my chest.

For an instant I thought he'd fallen asleep there in the chair, but then he murmured, 'Remember the storm? In seventy-eight?'

'I remember.'

'Old man Kemp, pie-eyed on all that whisky. If the place'd flooded I don't think we'd have been able to shift him, I don't think *anyone* would have been able to shift him. I think he'd have slept straight through the whole thing. Or drowned. What a wild old boy!' When I didn't reply he turned his head and squinted at me.

'I was in love with you that night,' I said.

His gaze didn't waver, he stared at me with great seriousness, and said in a tone of fond bewilderment, 'I missed that. How did I miss that?'

'I think I made it rather obvious.'

He echoed, 'How did I miss that?' And this time he smiled.

'Long time ago.'

'I was nineteen. You were . . .'

'Sixteen.'

'Bad at picking up signals, I suppose.' He sat up and regarded me with an expression that was both teasing and shy. 'Just that one night, that you loved me?'

'It could have been two.'

'Oh, Ali. What happened?'

'What happened was that you went away to college, then I went to college . . . And when I came back . . .' I splayed a hand.

'Grace.' The shadow descended again, and there was no going back for either of us.

Getting up suddenly, Will took the brandy bottle from the side and, offering me a glass, poured himself another measure.

'She set out to get me, you know,' he said.

'Sorry?'

'The car in the ditch. She did it on purpose. Driving ahead of me back from a party, she simply drove into the ditch. She was laughing when I pulled her out. She'd gone in slowly – just a shallow ditch – never any danger of hurting herself. The car wasn't even dented.' He smiled darkly. 'Made for a good story, though. And Charlie . . .' He looked down at his hands. 'She said she was on the Pill, got pregnant straight away, probably that very night . . . Oldest trick in the book, you might say. Married within two months.' He threw some brandy down his throat. 'What you might call a whirlwind job!'

'Still, you have Charlie.'

'Yes,' he agreed softly, 'I have Charlie.'

He looked exhausted again.

'Let me stay up,' I said.

Beyond argument suddenly, he nodded and, sliding forward over the table, dropped his head onto his arms. By the time I turned off the brighter lights he was asleep.

Alone with the storm, my mind began to paint a landscape of rising water and flooding banks. I found a warm hat of Maggie's and a pair of boots one size too big, which I padded out with extra socks, and, in the pocket of Will's jacket, a powerful torch. Emerging from the shelter of the cottage I thought at first that the wind had eased a little, but when I climbed up onto the embankment it was like a giant hand pushing at my face and grabbing at my clothes and snatching the air from my mouth. Leaning my weight into it, I shone the torch downwards and saw water that surged and clawed restlessly against the bank, like an echo of the giant breakers on the dunes.

The water was high but I couldn't tell if it was dangerous. I walked west along the marsh edge, past the Salterns where windows also blazed, until I could make out the blurred lights of the houses above the quay. Sometimes the water seemed much closer to my feet, sometimes it touched the path itself, but nowhere did it actually threaten to cross the bank. Near two spots – a small bush, a raised stone at the side of the path – I pushed a twig into the bank to mark the water level, and it occurred to me that somewhere along this stretch of bank Will had probably done the same.

Retracing my steps, I went back along the marsh edge, past Reed Cottage and the light glimmering in the kitchen window, and onwards until I reached the Gun Marsh. Climbing up onto the embankment I shone the torch downwards onto the Gun, and made out clumps of reed and patches of meadow but no sign of water that shouldn't be there.

I turned to face the full blast of the wind. Behind, the warmth of Reed Cottage was just two minutes away. Ahead, the long arm of the Gun Marsh embankment stretched away into the darkness for one and a half miles to the sea.

Not sure what I was hoping to achieve, I lowered my head and started along the embankment.

To the left, the salt water lapped and worried at the bank, emitting the occasional fierce ripple, a hissing note that rose briefly above the bass of the wind. To the right, the low expanse of the Gun meadows stretched away into the darkness.

I came to the first sluice.

I shone the torch into the tunnel and saw the tide high against the brickwork. On the Gun side, small rivulets flowed down the slots that held the gate, while from a point high up in the mounting a tiny jet of water spurted out at an angle into the darkness. The total leakage amounted to no more than a trickle which collected in the pool at the foot of the gate and oozed away towards the drainage ditch. Whatever repair Will had made, it had been a good one.

There was no point in going further, and I wasn't feeling that brave anyway. Out here, the storm had a dark and lonely sound. Heading back with the gale hard on my shoulders, I was pushed along almost faster than I could walk. With the wind roaring in my ears, my mind on the events of the day, I was oblivious to everything but the torchlight on the path ahead, a pale cone dividing two worlds of darkness.

I faltered, I wasn't sure why, and looked up. Off to the right I could see the lights of the Salterns glimmering above water, and further to the right, the lights above the quay, hanging like lanterns in the night. Ahead, there was only blackness.

I started off again, only to stop a second time with a dart of alarm made sharper for having no obvious cause.

The darkness ahead seemed to move and break up. My senses reached out. I jerked the torch beam higher.

A shadowy figure loomed out of the darkness, head down, approaching fast.

The head came up. Will's face met the beam of light and, flinching, ducked down again.

My relief was rapidly overtaken by anxiety. 'Is something the matter?' I called.

He barely paused as he walked past, slowing only to make sure I had turned to follow him.

'What is it?' I cried.

If he spoke I didn't hear him.

'Will?'

'Just come with me, Ali!' he shouted. 'I just need you to *come with me.*'

His voice was blunted by the wind but I caught enough in his tone to make me follow without another word.

He walked fast and I had a job to keep up. He was carrying a long wooden pole on one shoulder and a short angled metal bar in his right hand. I recognized the sluice handle. It occurred to me that he might think the sluice was broken again, that I should tell him it was all right, but something told me he wouldn't listen, and we were almost there anyway.

As the sluice came into view, Will transferred the handle to his shoulder and reached back to take the torch from me. Leaning over the gate, he flashed the light downwards and around the sides of the sluice. Almost immediately he straightened up again and, before I realized it, he was off at the same rapid pace, heading further along the embankment towards the dunes.

I didn't attempt to stay abreast of him this time, but followed in line behind, led by the outline of his body silhouetted against the pool of light on the path ahead.

It was some way to the next sluice, perhaps a quarter of a mile, and I soon fell into the mindless rhythm of keeping pace.

Above the rushing of the wind I began to pick out the faint reverberation of thunder. The sound seemed to merge into the wind for a time, only to rise above it and grow steadily, a deep resonant roar that slowly filled the air. There was something terrible and thrilling in the sound of such a sea, a sea of nightmare and destruction, a sea which beat and dragged incessantly at the dunes, seeking an opening.

Will slowed up and moved the torch to his other hand. In the dance of the beam I glimpsed the frame of the second sluice ahead. Striding up to it, Will leant over the side and shone the torch down the front of the gate for perhaps three or four seconds.

When he spun round, he turned so abruptly, with so little warning, that he almost knocked me over.

'Hold the torch, would you?' he yelled.

Taking it from him, I saw in the gleam of light that his expression was very grim.

'I'm sorry about this! I'm sorry!' he cried, and now I saw that his face was contorted with something far more terrible, like dread.

'What is it? What do you mean?' I shouted.

'*God help me, Alex, but I have to look! I have to look!*'

My stomach tightened. I felt a lurch of fear. I stared at him, I tried to speak, but before I could say anything he swung away and, striding towards the sluice, jammed the handle onto the spindle and began to crank it with fierce energy.

Dazed, uncertain, I forced myself to go to the edge of the sluice.

'Shine it down, Alex. *Down.*'

I echoed weakly, 'Down,' and, gripping the sluice frame, shone the light down over the surface of the gate. The pool at the foot of the gate was already gurgling and stirring as water began to flow underneath the gate. As the slab of metal rose further, the pool erupted into a gushing spout that pushed a cascade of water out onto the meadows of the Gun.

Staring at the hypnotic rush of water, I tried to persuade myself that I might be looking for anything at all, but the chill in my stomach, the dryness in my throat told a different story.

And still the gate came up. Now the water was spewing out in a massive torrent, straight onto the meadows.

A glimmer of white appeared, deep down under the gate, deep under the water. The torch shook in my hand; I steadied it.

A white *something*.

Oh, God.

I shouted then, I shouted Will's name.

He came and crouched at my side. He had the long wooden pole in his hand. He pushed the pole down into the cataract, down towards the white thing. The pole had some sort of hook on the end of it and he tried to get it under the white thing. He missed once, twice. I heard him shout, then he twisted round and lay full length on the ground, and, his shoulders hanging precariously over the torrent, tried again. This time the hook found something to catch onto. The white thing rose up, took shape, became—

I felt a rush of horror, I dropped my head onto my chest, I forced myself to look up again.

A leg, and behind it, rising slowly but inexorably, as though freeing itself from the ooze beneath, the rest of her body.

Will gave a great bellow. I shouted too. Someone was crying, '*Oh, God! Oh, God!*' and it might have been him or me or both of us.

I grabbed the torch so that the scene below was plunged into darkness.

I heard him moving, I heard him scrabbling, but in the dim light from the deflected beam it took me a moment to understand what he was doing. By the time I realized, he had one foot over the edge and was lowering the other, ready to jump down into the water.

'*No!*' Abandoning the torch, I grabbed his shoulders and tried to hold him back. We struggled. He threw up an arm, trying to elbow me away, trying to slip downwards out of my grasp. Dropping onto my knees, I hooked an arm around his neck and pulled against his throat, and somewhere, as though at a remove, I heard myself crying again and again, '*You mustn't! You mustn't!*' It sounded wrong, there were better things to say, but before I could say any more he was clawing at me, trying to pull my arm away from his neck. With one last effort, finding a strength I didn't have, I gave a powerful wrench and managed to force his head back. Suddenly he gave in, there was no resistance any more and he fell back, half on top of me.

We lay entangled for a moment, panting hard, then I wriggled from under him and clambered to my feet.

I picked up the torch and went and shone it down into the pool again. Rushing water, no whiteness. Nothing at all. The body had gone, swept out onto the meadowland of the Gun.

I shone the light back towards Will. He lay on his side, face turned into the ground, retching and sobbing.

Then, sobbing a little myself, shivering violently, I went unsteadily to the sluice handle and began to lower the gate.

Chapter Eight

'IT'S TOO much, Alex! *Too much!*' Maggie exclaimed in sudden exasperation. She had been monosyllabic until now, almost withdrawn; her outburst came from nowhere.

We were sitting side by side at a white-topped table in a bare interview room at King's Lynn police station, sipping machine coffee out of plastic beakers while we waited for Ramsey, who was now ten minutes late.

'I warned him we wouldn't wait long,' I said firmly. 'I told him you weren't up to it.'

She tore her eyes from a point above my head and gave me an uncomprehending look. 'What?' Following her gaze, I realized that her irritation had been directed not at the time but at the no-smoking sign on the wall beside me.

Tutting defiantly, shooting the notice a last reproving glance, she pulled a cigarette from her bag and, lighting it, drew on it hard.

I found a battered tin ashtray on the window ledge and slid it onto the table in front of her. It pained me to hear the wheezing in her lungs, the loose cough, the breathlessness that mingled with the inhalations in a series of rasps. Yet within moments the nicotine had begun to work its magic on her, she exhaled with a sigh of contentment, and a calm of sorts spread over her face. 'They go too far, these people,' she muttered at the non-smoking world in general.

Taking another lungful, she emerged from the last of her trance. 'Alex, this will be the end, yes? This will give them what they want?'

This was the sort of question that was almost impossible to answer. 'I would hope so, yes.'

'And Will? Do they have all they need from him?'

'I think so. For the moment, anyway.'

'And then . . .?' She lifted her brows wearily, wanting reassurance, expecting none.

'Early days yet, Maggie.'

She gave a small nod of acceptance.

It was four days since Grace had been found. The preliminary post-mortem findings had been inconclusive, which, short of a stomach full of barbiturates, was exactly what I had hoped for. There was a bruise on the side of the head, but it could have occurred in a fall; there was no evidence of violence. The final report was awaiting some lab tests. I knew from a drowning case some years back that after long immersion there was a good chance that the lab results would produce nothing significant; I also knew from experience that it would be unwise to bank on it.

From the way Ramsey's investigation was proceeding, I guessed that he too was finding little of significance. Scene-of-crime officers and forensic specialists were still drifting in and out of Reed Cottage and Marsh House and the barns at Upper Farm, examining or removing cars, clothing and miscellaneous objects in what appeared to be haphazard fashion. All this gave me reason for hope, though, once again, I wasn't counting on it.

Maggie cast me an apprehensive eye. 'You won't let me say anything I should not say, will you?' She grasped my arm and pleaded with strange intensity, 'Please . . . kick me or something. If I say the wrong thing. You will? Yes?'

I was looking for an answer when the door opened and Ramsey came noisily into the room. 'I'm sorry to have kept you waiting, Mrs Dearden,' he said. 'Roadworks on the way from Norwich.'

Sweat gleamed at his temple, his collar was crooked, his little eyes danced with excitement. He ignored me completely until I said, 'I would remind you that Mrs Dearden was admitted to hospital three nights ago with breathing difficulties. Her doctor doesn't want her subjected to unnecessary stress.'

'I understand.' He waved his team into the room impatiently, as if they had been responsible for keeping us waiting. There was Barbara Smith again, and the languid DC Wilson, along with an officer we hadn't seen before, an older man with an embittered face and a bad complexion.

Ramsey took the seat opposite Maggie and placed some typed pages on the table in front of him. Wilson sat at his side with a statement pad and pen.

Ramsey wiped a limp handkerchief over his forehead and straightened his tie before positioning his plump hands precisely at the edges of the typed sheets and saying, 'Mrs Dearden, in the light of subsequent events I need a more detailed statement from you concerning your daughter-in-law's movements on the eighteenth of February.' He inclined his head solicitously. 'DC Wilson will take it down for you, if that's all right?'

Maggie glanced briefly in my direction for approval and nodded.

'No problem. Then we can get it typed up and, once you've read through it, we will ask you to sign it, if that's acceptable.' Without waiting for an answer, he gave a fleeting smile that didn't touch his eyes. 'Coffee?'

Stubbing out her cigarette, lifting her chin, Maggie gave a regal shake of her head that didn't entirely conceal her nervousness.

While Ramsey leant across and murmured something to Wilson, I tried to work out why he was so animated. A combination of excitement and fear, I guessed. Excitement at having what he hoped was a murder, fear of messing up the investigation. Live on your fear, I found myself thinking combatively. Get used to it, because if you try to get Will in your sights I'm going to block your every move, I'm going to use every trick I know.

Paul's voice sprang into my mind. *Too involved, Lexxy. That's your trouble. Too emotional.*

'So . . . Ready to start, Mrs Dearden?'

Maggie nodded and pulled another cigarette out of the packet in front of her.

Ramsey picked up the first of the typed sheets. 'This is your previous statement, Mrs Dearden. I thought it might be helpful to have it in front of us.' He glanced at it. 'You are Margherita Claudia Dearden, of Reed Cottage, Salterns Lane, Deepwell Staithe?'

It wasn't until he reached the evening of Grace's disappearance that Maggie stopped him.

'No,' she interrupted abruptly. 'No – Grace arrived with Charlie at *four*. She stayed just two minutes, just two, three, then she was gone again. Gone by five past.'

'Ah.' Ramsey's little jaw emerged from the folds of his plump neck. He frowned with the air of someone who wished to be absolutely clear. 'So, not four *fifteen* as you said previously?'

'That's right.'

'And she was gone by four five p.m.?'

Wilson bent over his pad and took it down slowly, in a schoolboy's script, everything well spaced, almost nothing joined up.

Referring to Maggie's previous statement again, Ramsey said, 'So then at about five fifteen you discovered that there was a flood on the meadows.' Ramsey looked up. 'Is that correct?'

'Yes.'

'You saw this flood, did you?'

Maggie blew out a slow plume of smoke. 'Yes.'

'From your cottage?'

'The top windows. You can see from there.'

'It wasn't too dark?'

A tiny shrug. 'There was still some light. But I went out to see. To make sure.'

Ramsey surveyed the transcript and put on an expression of puzzlement. 'You went out to *see* . . . Did you mention this before?'

'Perhaps. I cannot remember.' Her tone was deliberately offhand.

Ramsey's eyes skimmed the page and the next. 'No,' he said heavily. 'You didn't mention it. So . . . at five fifteen you saw the flood from the upper window, then went out to have a look.'

'Yes.'

We were forced to wait again while Wilson got it down. Bent low over his writing, lips pulled in, I was again reminded of a schoolboy, doing his best to be neat.

'And then?' Ramsey prompted.

'Then I came back for the sluice handle. I—'

'One moment . . .' Wilson's pen moved ever more slowly across the page.

Eventually Ramsey was able to say, 'And then?'

'I found that the sluice was not working.'

'When you say not working?'

'It was broken.'

'Could you explain where this sluice was exactly?'

'The first one. On the embankment of the Gun Marsh.'

'What about the second sluice?'

She looked blank.

'Did you go there at all?'

'No. It was the first sluice that was broken.'

He regarded her for a moment before taking up her story again. '*I called my son to tell him about the flood.* Is that right?'

'Yes.'

'You called his mobile telephone?'

She drew the end of her cigarette slowly across the bottom of the ashtray, scraping off ash. 'First I tried the house, to know if he was back from Norwich.'

Another search of the transcript, another frown. 'You called the house first?' Ramsey echoed, as though he were fated to repeat everything that wasn't in the script.

Maggie nodded.

'And when you called the house, was there any answer?'

Maggie's eyes narrowed, she quivered slightly: irritation or nerves. 'Grace answered.'

Ramsey repeated with heavy emphasis, 'Grace Dearden answered?' He looked conspicuously at the transcript, but he already knew he wasn't going to find it there. 'Why didn't you mention this before, Mrs Dearden?'

'I thought I did.'

Ramsey shook his head slowly. 'No.'

'I thought you understood this, when I said I called my son.' She made a gesture implying a certain lack of intelligence on Ramsey's part. 'It was Grace who told me Will would be in the car. That is why I called the car.' She added, in an offended voice, 'I did not think I had to explain this!'

Ramsey stared at her. He couldn't make out whether she was being purposely obscure, or whether it was simply in her nature to be equivocal. 'Mrs Dearden, if Grace answered the phone she must have been in the house.'

Maggie looked for the catch in this statement and found none. 'Of course.'

'And what time did you make this call?'

Maggie waved a hand. 'Something like five thirty.'

Letting it go for the moment, looking unsettled, Ramsey went back to the typed sheet. 'So then you called your son in his car?'

'Yes.'

'This was when?'

'Well . . . straight away.'

I interrupted, 'According to the Cellnet records the call was logged at five thirty-six p.m., and the mobile was within range of the Costessey transmitter on the outskirts of Norwich.'

There was a pause while Ramsey eyed me coolly. 'Thank you for that information.' He returned his attention to Maggie.

'And what did you say to your son?'

'Say?' She searched her memory. 'I said . . . the sluice was broken, the meadow was flooding. He must come quick. Something like that.'

'And then?'

'Then . . . I tried Frank Yates, at the next farm. He was not there. So then I could do nothing. So then I waited for William.'

'And he arrived at six thirty?'

'Six twenty, six thirty. Some time like that.'

Ramsey gestured to Wilson, who picked up his pen again. They began to record the new material, Ramsey checking each sentence with Maggie before Wilson set it down on paper. When the task was done, Ramsey pushed the transcript aside and rocked back in his seat in a conspicuous attempt to set a less intimidating tone. 'Did anyone come to the house during the time you were waiting for your son?'

With a quiver of impatience, Maggie stated, 'Grace, you mean? No. Though I was out some of the time looking at the flood, so it's possible that she . . .' She left the remark hanging in the air.

I felt my lips give an involuntary twitch.

Uncertainty stole back into Ramsey's face, he sat forward again. 'You went to look at the flood a *second* time?'

'I took Charlie, yes.'

I was careful to hold on to my expression, to maintain a neutral gaze aimed at a point somewhere over Ramsey's right shoulder.

'I would like to understand correctly, Mrs Dearden . . . At some point between telephoning your son in his car and the time he arrived at your cottage, you took your grandson out to the marsh to look at the flood a second time?'

'Yes.'

Barely containing his irritation, Ramsey said briskly, 'Mrs Dearden, why didn't you tell us this before?'

I looked towards Maggie as she replied, 'You did not ask me.' She made one of her Italian gestures, a raised shoulder, a spread hand, a widening of the eyes. 'I did not know it was important.' There was openness in her expression, but also obduracy.

Ramsey's button mouth tightened still further. 'What time was it, then, when you went out to look at the flood?'

'After I spoke to Will.'

He asked, 'So it could have been five forty?'

'It's possible. I cannot be sure.'

'And you didn't notice Grace's car, either when you left or when you returned?'

She gave the question consideration. 'No,' she said, 'I did not notice any car. But, then, we went out by the kitchen, Charlie and me. We came back the same way. If the car was at the front, well . . .' She shrugged. 'But I think if Grace had come back, she would have come into the house. She would have come to find us. No?' She looked to me as though for confirmation. 'I think so,' she stated ingenuously to the room at large. 'I think she would have come in.'

'And later, when your son arrived?' Ramsey asked. 'You didn't notice Grace's car then?'

'I did not look at the front, so . . .'

Ramsey exhaled heavily. He was getting the picture. 'So Grace could have come and gone and you wouldn't have been the wiser?'

Maggie frowned slightly, as though this idea was new to her. 'That's right.'

'But you were aware of your son arriving?'

'Yes. I heard the horn, I followed Will out to the sluice.'

Maggie's energy was ebbing visibly, her eyelids were dipping, she seemed to be sinking lower into her chair.

'You followed immediately?'

'Yes, I follow his torch along the sea bank. I arrive at the sluice just after him.'

Ramsey took a steadying breath. 'Then?'

'I stayed with him,' she replied, rediscovering the past tense.

'Maybe fifteen minutes, maybe a little more. Until he saw what the problem was, you know. Until he went to bring tools from the barn.'

'This is the barn at Upper Farm?'

'Yes.'

'He went by car, then?'

She sighed, making no attempt to hide her weariness. 'Yes, in the Range Rover.'

'How long was your son away?'

'Ten minutes. Fifteen maybe.'

'You saw him return?'

'Oh, yes.'

'Then?'

'Then he worked on the sluice. I helped him.'

'And how long did you help him for, Mrs Dearden?'

'Until he finished. Almost three hours, I think . . . Though I came back to make sure my grandson was all right. Twice I came back.' Her lids drooped again, a vein like a knotty thread beat at her temple, she touched a hand to her neck.

I bent towards her. 'Would you like a rest?'

'Yes,' she breathed instantly.

'Some coffee would be welcome,' I said.

Barbara Smith and DC Wilson got up, took our orders and went out. Ramsey surveyed Maggie thoughtfully before beckoning the older, sour-faced officer towards the corridor.

While everyone was in motion, I murmured to Maggie, 'Are you okay to go on?'

'Have I said anything wrong?' she whispered anxiously. 'Tell me.'

Something sank inside me as she said this. 'I don't think so.'

'I'm so nervous that I will say the wrong thing.'

'Just stick to what you know.'

'Yes, but sometimes I can't remember, Alex. Sometimes I get in a confusion.'

I was moved by the sort of helplessness you feel when someone you love is in trouble and there's nothing you can do to extricate them. 'You're doing fine,' I said.

She cast me a doubtful look. 'You'll remember everything I say, won't you? So that I make no mistakes.'

'We'll read through the statement carefully before you sign it. We can take all the time in the world, we can amend anything we like.'

The coffee arrived. As soon as everyone had reassembled, Ramsey went through the additional material and clarified a few details while Wilson took it down in his laborious longhand. After fifteen minutes we moved on.

'So . . .' Ramsey's animation had been replaced by a rather sullen look. 'Apart from when your son went to fetch the tools, and from the two times that you went back to the cottage to check on your grandson, you were with your son from the time he arrived at six twenty or so until the time the repairs were completed at nine thirty.'

'Yes.'

'And then?'

'My son came in to have a bath and to eat, then he went back to drain the marsh.'

'He could do this on his own, could he, the draining?'

'It's an easy job.'

'What does it involve?'

'Involve?' She frowned at this strange question. 'You open the sluice at low tide. You empty the water out.' She spoke in a deliberate tone, with pauses, like a teacher who suspects her pupil might be a bit slow. 'Then you close the sluice again. Yes?' She waited for Ramsey to show he had understood.

'Your son came and went during much of the night, then?'

'Came and went?' Maggie repeated in a cold voice, getting his drift all too well. 'No. Just three times he went. He went once at ten thirty to open the sluice. He went again at half past midnight to close it again. Then he checked the gate at four to make sure it was holding against the tide. He was away just minutes each time.'

Ramsey looked towards the high-set window, as if something had caught his attention there. 'Just minutes?'

'Yes.'

He looked back at her. 'You saw him leave and return, did you? Each time?'

She hesitated while she gauged the dangers in the question. 'I saw him go out at ten thirty and return a few minutes later. Ten minutes he was gone, that is all.' She paused as if to examine this statement for flaws. 'Later, at twelve thirty, I heard him getting ready to go out. I went to the top of the stairs, I spoke to him as he went out . . .' She inhaled, drawing her cheeks in against her teeth, looking frail. 'I heard him return later.'

'*Heard* him?'

'It's very small, the cottage. You hear everything.'

'How long was he out that time?'

Her long fingers twitched and shifted in her lap. 'I . . . It must have been . . . I . . . Yes . . . Before one. Yes, I think – ten minutes before one.'

Ramsey watched Wilson write this down. Maggie's hand stole across and touched my leg. Her eyes followed: a plea, a lament.

Taking my cue, I asked, 'Are you feeling all right? Would you prefer to stop?'

'Almost there,' said Ramsey easily. 'If you can bear with us for another minute or two, Mrs Dearden.'

Maggie looked from me to Ramsey and back again, recognizing the opportunity for escape yet seemingly unable to grasp it.

Ramsey said with false cheer, 'Literally another three questions, Mrs Dearden.'

'But not if you're not up to it,' I said.

Mutely Maggie signalled her willingness to go ahead.

'So you were awake when he returned at ten to one?'

'I heard him, yes.'

'Later, during your son's last outing, the one in the early hours, you say he went out at four?'

'Yes.'

'You know it was definitely four?'

'Yes, I heard him. I looked at the time. It was close to four. Perhaps five minutes before. Five minutes after.'

'When you say you heard him go, you heard what exactly?'

'I heard the door,' she said firmly. 'I heard him go out.'

Ramsey's eyes glinted momentarily. 'And his return?'

'I heard him come back also.'

'A door again, was it?'

'Yes.'

Ramsey sat back and arranged his face into the semblance of a smile, a motion that pushed his fat cheeks upwards and creased his eyes but conveyed no suggestion of sincerity. 'Thank you, Mrs Dearden.'

Maggie stiffened abruptly. 'Not just a door,' she protested. 'Not *just* a door! Other things. The bolts on the inside, they make a big noise. And the bathroom door ... the water running, the loo. Other things! Please ...' She pointed a fierce forefinger at Wilson's pad. 'I want it there, in the statement.'

Ramsey slid a nod towards Wilson. 'As you wish.'

'I *wish*.' Her indignation gathered momentum. 'Because I can see how you are trying to make it sound like.'

Ramsey assumed a look of puzzlement. 'I wasn't trying to make it sound like anything, Mrs Dearden.'

'I think you were!'

I cut in, 'Have we finished, Inspector?'

'I just need the time your son left in the morning,' he said to Maggie. 'And how you heard of your daughter-in-law's disappearance. What searches were made.'

It took another five minutes of Wilson's interminable handwriting to get everything on paper. At long last, Ramsey pushed back his chair and stood up. 'If you could bear with us while we get the statement typed.'

There was a release of tension in the room, people coughed and stretched and got slowly to their feet.

The officers drifted out into the corridor. As soon as we were alone, Maggie gave a long ragged sigh. '*God*, Alex . . . *God.*'

'You did fine.'

'But you know what they are trying to say, don't you?' She turned her beautiful ruined face towards me.

'I don't think they're trying to say anything at the moment, Maggie.'

'What do you mean?' she protested fiercely. 'They are trying to say he went out in the night to kill Grace. *That*'s what they're trying to say!'

'Maggie, they don't even know how Grace died yet. They may never know. They have nothing to go on so far, nothing at all. They're just trying to cover everything, to investigate every angle. It's something they *have* to do.'

Absorbing this slowly, wanting to believe it against her better judgement, she breathed reluctantly, 'I suppose . . .' By the time Ramsey and Wilson returned she was calm again. She read through the typewritten statement with great concentration, muttering the words aloud, pausing occasionally to go back over something. For a brief moment she became agitated again, wanting more on the telltale sounds that had placed Will inside the cottage during the night, but once she had been allowed to add and initial two explanatory sentences she seemed satisfied, and signed the statement in silence.

On our way out, Ramsey caught my eye, and we let Maggie and DC Smith move ahead.

'Your statement, Mrs O'Neill. There was one thing I wasn't clear about. How was it that *you* had the torch? How was it that you were the one to look down into the water and see the body? Why wasn't it Mr Dearden?'

'I think I gave you the answer to that in my statement. Mr Dearden was checking the mechanism.'

'Without a torch?'

'Yes.'

Ramsey's button eyes gazed at me in open appraisal, as though he still couldn't work me out. 'And what made you shine the torch down into the water?'

'As I said, I was looking at the gate, looking for leaks.'

'But that particular spot in the water?'

'I wasn't looking at any particular spot, Inspector.'

Coming to a swing door, he led the way through and held it open for me. 'And this visit to the sluice, it was just a routine thing?'

'That's right.'

'No special reason?'

'As I said in my statement, it's normal practice to check the sluices in bad weather.'

'Aha.' He nodded thoughtfully. 'Normal practice ... Is that what Mr Dearden told you?'

'It's what I know.'

'What you *know*. Of course ... You yourself come from Deepwell, I gather?'

'Yes.'

'So you know these things?'

'Yes.'

'Does everyone know these things?'

'I can't answer for everyone.'

Reaching the entrance hall, he waited for me to say more, but I didn't speak and he knew better than to press me. There was nothing either of us could teach the other about the value of silence.

The portable incident rooms had finally been removed, along with the lengths of fluttering blue and white tape which had sealed off the Gun embankment from the public. All that remained were the flowers: bouquets in cellophane with garish bows, bunches of early daffodils tied with string, a clump of tawdry pink carnations, drooping blue hyacinths, forming a carpet of fading colour over the side of the marsh bank, the cards and labels stirring softly in the wind, looking at a distance like a shifting patchwork.

In the cottage I put a cold meal on the table for Maggie, turned up the heating a little and slid a hot-water bottle into her bed. I also left a message on Frank Yates's answering machine to ask him if he could come the next day and return the last of the furniture to its proper place. I had already unrolled the rugs and replaced most of the books.

Maggie followed me to the door and gave me a perfunctory embrace. 'How long, do you think, then, Alex?'

I wasn't sure what she meant. I had already explained that it would be months before the inquest was held, maybe just as long before Grace could be buried. 'Till what, Maggie?'

'Till they are finished. Till they leave us alone.'

'They'll be waiting for the forensic tests, and the final post-mortem results, and—'

'Yes, yes,' she said, as though all this were immaterial. 'But once that is out of the way . . .'

'I couldn't say, Maggie. I'd be lying if I said I could. It could be anything from a few weeks to a few months. It all depends on what line they decide to take. Whether they keep open the possibility of foul play.'

But she didn't want to hear about foul play. Whenever it was mentioned, however obliquely, something came over her face, a shutting down. 'A few weeks,' she repeated firmly.

'Or months, Maggie.'

'I want them to have a holiday, Alex. I want them to get away. I have a little money. I want them to use it for a holiday. To begin to start again. This is important, Alex. They must get away.'

'There's no reason why they can't go on holiday.'

'Yes?' Her spirits lifted a little. 'You really think so?'

'Of course.'

As I drove away, I thought how very differently people were affected by death. I had seen relatives cry for weeks and others who didn't cry at all. Some went into shock, as Maggie had done that first night, fighting for breath, sending us into a more immediate panic until Julian Hampton arrived with some sort of antidote; others went into a kind of overdrive, becoming lucid and hyperactive and alert to everyone else's needs, as Will had been for the first two days. When the initial shock wore off things changed again. Some people, such as Maggie, took refuge in practicalities like holidays, planning ahead to the time when life would return to normal; others, like Will, became increasingly disturbed. When I had seen him early that morning he had looked like a sleep-walker, numb and disorientated. Charlie, on the other hand, had remained frozen throughout, a rigid, silent creature with downcast eyes.

Turning into Quay Lane, I stopped at the side of the road and switched on my mobile for the first time in almost a day. I picked up messages from Corinthia and Ray. There was nothing from Paul, and I remembered rather guiltily that I hadn't spoken to him in two days.

I tried Ray first, but his phone was switched off and I left a message.

Paul was in the office.

'Hahh! Lexxy!' He sounded pleased, or at least benevolent.

I explained how tied up I'd been with the Deardens, how difficult it had been to get to a phone.

'They managing, the family?' he asked.

Just four brief words, but I heard the burr in them, the lilt of the drink. I felt the weary tug of disappointment, but also a sort of rage. It was barely three in the afternoon.

I said shortly, 'They're managing.'

'Is it murder?'

'The PM's inconclusive.'

'What think you?'

What thought I? In the early days this question had been a

precious ritual between us, an opportunity to express opinions too candid to be voiced within anyone else's hearing.

'I think she might well have been murdered.'

'And?'

'Nothing beyond that.'

'Husband main suspect?'

'They'd like to.'

'But nothing on him?'

'No.'

'Looking good, then, for the moment?'

'We'll see,' I said. 'And how are things with you?'

If he heard the coolness in my tone, he didn't show it. 'Oh, fine, fine!' His voice was a little too high, his jollity a little too forced. 'No problems! Ahead of the game for once.' He gave a small chuckle.

'I'll be home tonight,' I said. 'Not sure when.'

'Marvellous!' he sang. 'Food? A meal?'

'Whatever's in the fridge.'

'No, no! I'll make something! Salmon? A steak?'

It was hard to think of food. 'Salmon,' I said, going for the easiest thing. 'But cold will be fine. A salad, something like that.'

'No problem! Take care, now, on that road.'

At this, something caught at my heart, a touch of old affection. Then I heard the drink in his voice, and the love turned bitter and cold.

'You take care as well.' I rang off, wondering if he still drank to escape from himself, or whether it was me he couldn't take.

I set off again. A few yards down the lane I saw a sporty red car coming towards me and recognized Edward's Mercedes.

We stopped alongside each other.

'I was looking for you,' Edward said in a tone that suggested I should have kept in touch. 'Listen . . . I know you must be busy . . .'

'I am,' I agreed bluntly.

'The thing is, could you drop in? When you have a moment, I mean?'

'What's it about, Ed?'

'Oh, just that legal matter, you know.'

I knew exactly what he meant, but for some reason I wanted to hear him say it. 'Which legal matter?'

'The—' He was about to snap at me but thought better of it. Modifying his expression, he said casually, 'The, er . . . business about Father's money.'

I suppressed my impatience. 'Can't it wait?'

'Of course, of course. Just when you have a moment.' When I didn't say anything, he ventured, 'Any news?'

'About?'

'*Grace.*'

'No.'

'They near to charging anyone?'

'It's not a question of charging anyone. They don't even know how she died.'

'What do you mean, don't know?' he scoffed. 'How else could she have died, for God's sake?'

'That's for the police to find out.'

'Oh, come *on*. She has to have been killed – they must have got *that* far.'

'Ed, I really can't talk about this.'

'And don't tell me they haven't got a suspect in mind,' he crowed viciously. 'Don't tell me they haven't homed in on Will.'

'Ed, you're wrong, quite wrong.'

'Really?' His voice rasped with sarcasm, and I felt a moment of despair for this brother of mine, whose petty animosities could so completely overshadow his compassion.

'Goodbye, Ed.' I put the car into gear.

'They must know he was there, for God's sake! They must know he was there on the marsh, fiddling about with those gates, just when Grace disappeared.'

'So?'

'So they can't be so completely dense that they haven't worked it out! How else did she get stuck underneath the gate?' He raised his eyebrows in a show of incredulity. 'How else did she get pinned down?'

I didn't say anything.

'Oh, for God's sake, Alex,' he continued in a cold fury. 'He was terrified of losing the farm. Terrified she'd up and leave and take half of everything.'

He had my attention again. I slid the gear back into neutral. 'What makes you say that? Did you know? Did you hear?'

'Stands to reason, doesn't it?'

There was something very ugly about Edward in a vengeful mood, and I held on to my temper with difficulty. 'You're saying they were splitting up?'

He gave me a narrow look, full of meaning. 'I'm saying she had a lot to put up with. Everybody knew he was playing around!'

I didn't try to hide my astonishment. 'This is the first I've heard about it.'

'Shocked, Lex? Your saintly Will, running another woman on the side. Well, *there you are*!' he said with undisguised relish.

'Who was this other woman, then?'

He didn't like the question, mainly because he didn't have an answer to it. 'Well, she wasn't going to announce it, was she?'

'Who wasn't – Grace? But you just said everyone knew about it anyway.'

His gaze shifted angrily. 'Enough people knew.'

'Who, exactly? Who told you?'

'Christ, I don't know! *Someone*.'

And this was the person who never listened to gossip. It seemed to me that Edward had let his resentment for Will get completely out of hand.

'Careful,' I warned. 'Be very careful what you say, Ed.'

'*Me*? Why the hell should *I* be careful?'

'Because you're making particularly wild and dangerous statements.'

'They're not *wild*! They're true!'

'In that case you should be going to the police with them, shouldn't you?'

'I bloody will, at this rate.'

Without warning I reached some boundary, the anger came over me in a sudden heat. '*For God's sake*, Ed! It's just a piece of land, for heaven's sake! Why can't you let it go? Just let it go!'

His eyes sparkled ominously. 'Just a bit of *land*?'

'Isn't that what this is all about?'

His face seemed to bulge, he shivered with resentment, and for a moment his fury blocked his words. 'Go to hell, Lex!' he hissed finally. 'Just go to hell!' Flinging a last savage look in my direction, he gunned the throttle and the car shot off in a shriek of revs.

I turned off my engine and sat in the quiet of the lane for a few minutes, thinking what a very eventful journey this short trip was proving to be. When I felt calm again, I drove slowly on to Marsh House.

For once there were no shady figures waiting outside the house, no lizard-limbed reporters easing themselves out of their cars to ask for statements and interviews, no photographers angling for pictures of 'the grieving husband'.

Letting myself in by the kitchen door, I called Will's name and had no answer. Calling again, I went through into the passageway and found him in the sitting room, slouched in a wing chair, head propped on one hand, staring into the unlit fire.

'Hi,' I said, hearing the false cheer in my voice. 'How're you doing?'

He glanced up briefly. 'Hi.'

I sat near by. 'Well,' I said in an energetic tone, 'Maggie gave her statement. So that's one more thing out of the way.'

If he appreciated that Maggie had provided him with the closest thing he was going to get to an alibi, he gave no sign.

'Now we wait for the forensic tests and the final PM results.'

He asked, 'What's the time?'

I looked. 'Three twenty.'

'I must go and fetch Charlie in a minute.'

'I can go if you like.'

But he turned the offer down, as I knew he would. It was the domestic routine that provided some shape to his days, the round of meals and driving Charlie to friends and TV and bedtime.

Still mesmerized by the fireplace, Will asked, 'When are you going back to London?'

'Tonight, unless you want me to stay. I'll come back as soon as I can, Friday at the latest.' I said again: 'Unless you want me to stay.'

'I'd like you to stay, Ali,' he murmured in a distant voice. 'I'd like you to stay for ever.' His eyes remained blankly on the hearth. 'But,' he continued in the same dreamy tone, 'I know you have to go.'

'I'll be back every few days or so.'

Shaking himself free of his trance, he sat forward with his elbows on his knees and ran a hand savagely down his face. He looked rumpled and lost and deeply tired. With his wild hair, red-rimmed eyes and dishevelled clothes, he might have been a traveller living rough.

'There was one thing before I go,' I said. 'Would you mind if I went through Grace's papers again in more detail?'

He turned to me with a vague expression. 'What?'

'Her desk, her papers.'

'Sure. Sure. Anything.' Making another effort to concentrate on the present, he asked, 'What did the police say?'

'Nothing, really. They don't seem to have anything definite so far.'

'They haven't, umm . . .' He looked away again. 'They haven't asked about the sluice?'

'No. And we've all made our statements now, so . . .' I left the rest in the air, unspoken.

A pale smile flickered over Will's face. 'Loyal Alex. What did you say?'

'I just said what you'd said, really. I told them that we went to look at the sluice because of the flood danger. I told them it was a routine thing.' For an instant I was thrust back into the blackness and noise of the storm, I saw again the gleaming white limb in the water below me. 'I said I shone the torch down to check the gate while you were at the mechanism. That was it, really. Nothing that wasn't true.'

But, as we both knew, plenty that had been omitted.

Held by some self-punishing mood, Will murmured, 'My witness, my partner in crime.'

My stomach tightened with unease, but also, confusingly, with something close to joy. I gave a nervous half-laugh.

In the pause that followed I lost a battle with my better judgement, I ignored a primary rule of my training, which was never to ask a question that might give you an answer you didn't want or need to hear, an answer that, far from helping your client, was likely to detract from his defence. 'What made you want to look, Will? What made you decide to go just then?'

He considered this intently, as though he himself had been giving it deep thought. He said, 'You know, I'm still not entirely sure.'

The silence stretched out unbearably. I said at last, 'You hadn't thought of looking there before?'

'Well, yes, but . . .' He amended this with a lift of one hand. 'I'd got so fixed on the idea of the salt-marsh . . . the creeks . . . the idea that she'd got swept towards the sea . . . that I couldn't think of anything else. But then – that *sighting*. It was the *sighting*, the fact that she'd gone back towards the Gun. Gone back and not been seen by Mum or Charlie. I began to think, Where could she have got to? Where could she be?'

Listening to this, I realized that a still more daunting question loomed ahead. I heard myself ask, 'How could she have got under the sluice, Will? How could she have got under the gate?'

He pressed a knuckle against his mouth. 'They didn't ask that, did they?'

'No,' I whispered.

'I don't think they grasped . . .'

'No.'

'I think they thought . . .'

'Yes.'

They thought the body had been swept against the gate by the force of the water.

He gasped, 'Alex, the awful thing is she must have been *there* . . .' His voice became desperate. 'She must have been *there* all the time.'

I waited. Somewhere outside a car engine drew closer and stopped. A moment later a car door slammed. I said urgently, 'You mean, she was there from the very beginning?' I knew the answer, but I needed to hear it from him.

His eyes glittered violently. 'Ever since I closed the gate . . .'

He meant: on top of her.

And still I needed to be absolutely clear. 'That gate – the second gate – you opened it that night?'

'To drain the marsh quicker. To get the water out.'

'How long was it open?'

'Five hours. Six . . .'

'And what time did you close it?'

'Four in the morning. Just after.' He thrust his head into his hands. '*God* . . .'

Going to him, I dropped onto my knees and put an arm round his shoulder. 'She was dead,' I pointed out. 'She was

already dead.' Somewhere outside I heard what might have
been the latch on the garden gate.

'But she was *there*! Whatever I felt about her, whatever bad
things happened between us, I can't bear to think . . .'

'You weren't to know she was there.'

'But I should have looked. I should have *looked*.' His back
bowed further, his head sank deeper into his hands.

Tightening my grip on his shoulders, I said what I could to
reassure him and, when the words ran out, leant my cheek
against the head of wild dark hair.

The sound behind me was tiny but distinct. I twisted around.

Anne Hampton stood in the doorway. 'Sorry,' she said in a
voice that was unusually sharp and low. 'I didn't mean to
disturb anyone. I did knock.'

Will dropped his hands hastily from his face and straightened up. I let go of his shoulder and stood up.

'Charlie!' Will exclaimed abruptly. 'I must go.' He scrambled to his feet and, with the briefest glance at Anne, hurried
out of the room.

'What's happened?' Anne asked, pink cheeks flaming.

'Nothing.'

'But he's so upset.' It was almost an accusation.

'It wasn't anything in particular.'

'Not Charlie?'

'No.'

'Not the police?'

'No.'

'You would tell me, wouldn't you, if something had
happened?'

'It wouldn't really be for me to say.'

'Yes, of course. Of course,' she said hurriedly, as if she had
given herself away. 'I just thought . . .' She smiled awkwardly.
'It would be dreadful if he was alone – you know, when there
was bad news.'

I wondered what sort of bad news she had in mind. I said,
'I'll do my best to make sure that doesn't happen.'

Perhaps I let something show in my voice, perhaps I had sounded a warning, but she gave a nervous smile.

'He's lucky to have you,' she said, and I wasn't absolutely sure of the spirit in which this was intended.

Two days' post had accumulated in the hall. As soon as Anne Hampton had left, I carried it into the drawing room and opened it at Grace's desk. More than twenty letters of condolence, three letters from crazies, which I tore up and put in the bin, an offer of counselling and support from a bereavement support organization, five bills, and a letter from a solicitor in King's Lynn, headlined 'The Gun Marsh Tenancy', informing Will that the other side were threatening to sue for breach of contract but he advised no action until and unless they looked serious about going to court.

No call breakdown from the telephone company yet. I cursed them; they had promised it for today.

I put the mail aside and contemplated Grace's desk. I had already located her will, which was lodged with a solicitor in London. I had pointed the police towards her desk diary and the kitchen address book, which they had dutifully removed. Now I wanted to look beneath the carefully polished image.

Once, when I was first qualified, I'd represented a retired army officer on a shoplifting charge. He was a sad dignified man with a drink problem and no friends. It was his first arrest, the result, he swore, of a complete misunderstanding. Held in custody overnight, frantic about his dog, he'd begged me to go and see to the animal which, he assured me, was small and docile. I was young then, I believed what people told me. As I'd faced the growling Alsatian-cross and tried to edge my way towards the dog food, I couldn't help noticing that the one-roomed flat was stuffed from floor to ceiling with shirts by the hundred, sweaters and trousers by the dozen, coats, jackets, underclothes, all new, most in cellophane wrapping: a magpie's nest, an old man's cry for help. Once the dog had been fed and aired on the tiny balcony, I'd locked the door and rushed away.

Facing Grace's desk, I had the sense of entering another secret world, of searching for things she had not intended anyone to find.

I started with the upper drawer. In one corner lay a bundle of used chequebooks held together by an elastic band. In a rush of memory I saw Paul's knowing face in the mirror: *Money's always important.* I saw his mouth shaping the words with cynical relish, I heard my own vehement argument: *These are country people. Money isn't that important to them.* It had been an absurd thing to say of course, no one was above money, and some would say that farmers understood that better than anyone, but I'd resented the way Paul had swept the whole population into the same greedy boat, the way he'd thrown in the people from my past, as if to diminish them in my memory.

The cheques had been issued against a joint account in the names of W.R. & G.S. Dearden. The stubs showed a stream of household payments: heating oil and newspaper deliveries and Peter Jones and Barclaycard. Nothing out of the ordinary. I went back through six sets of stubs until I reached the previous February. The outflow of cash had been much heavier then: for three months running the Barclaycard payments had come in at around two thousand pounds, and one month the bill had been more than three thousand.

I found the Barclaycard statements in the lower drawer, stored in a small clip file. Most of the payments in the high-spending months seemed to have gone to fabric suppliers and interior design shops whose names I vaguely recognized, as well as Harvey Nichols and a variety of expensive clothes shops in Sloane Street. Up until the previous July there had been regular restaurant bills too, all in London, though none at the Brasserie.

I did a rough calculation: the Barclaycard payments alone

came to over fifteen thousand for the year. A legal secretary's salary; a rich man's expense account.

I searched the rest of the lower drawer and found a folder of fabric and carpet samples, estimates and quotations. Another folder contained a thick batch of brochures for fitted kitchens, kitchen appliances and heavy-duty chrome bathroom fittings. A file labelled *Garden* had leaflets for conservatories, summer houses and gazebos of every shape and style.

Much of the upper drawer was taken up by the music festival: a file of financial projections, costings and estimates; a second with contractors' correspondence and estimates; and one marked *Sponsors*. I put this last file on the flap of the desk and drew out a thick sheaf of papers.

Large numbers of requests for sponsorship had gone out over Grace's name, perhaps two hundred in all, to national companies, international companies, local companies. Her success rate had been about one in ten, which I imagined was quite good. There were fifteen offers of free products and four of cash, including the one thousand pounds and loan of three cars from the Volvo dealer.

Flicking through the duplicate requests for sponsorship my eye was caught by a large cross in fluorescent pink highlighter at the top of one sheet.

The name Barry Holland swam out from the page, above a company called Clawfoot Productions of London W1.

The letter began: *Dear Barry, Herewith the formal proposal as promised!* The rest followed the usual format, describing the festival, extolling the benefits of sponsorship, asking for, in this case, five thousand pounds.

I looked for a reply, but either it hadn't been filed in date order or Barry had never answered. I went back through the earlier correspondence in case it had been misfiled, but there was nothing there either. Presumably they had used the phone.

I moved on to the pigeonholes.

Unusually – but significantly, perhaps – Grace had stored

the bank statements in less than immaculate order. Each sheet had been roughly folded and jammed into a pigeonhole which was already overflowing. The statements revealed an overdraft, which six months ago had been as high as £15,000 but more recently had settled around the £10,000 mark, with hefty associated interest and bank charges.

In the next pigeonhole I found more bank statements, as well as banking correspondence, stockbroker accounts and building-society statements. I had never grasped the subtleties of finance – VAT and fraud cases always went to Paul – but for once my failure to make sense of these statements had nothing to do with the figures and everything to do with my having failed to take note of the account numbers and account titles at the top of each sheet. Once I got these straight I realized that Will and Grace had a second joint account at the same bank, also with an overdraft, though this one wasn't so large as the first, at around the £5000 mark.

There was a year-end statement from the building society, summarizing the monthly payments for a mortgage which, going by the interest charges, had to be in the region of £125,000. At the same building society there was a high-interest savings account with a credit of £32,000. However, while the mortgage was in joint names, I noticed that the savings account was in Grace's name alone. Will hadn't mentioned this to the police, but then high-interest accounts were usually difficult to access, any withdrawals requiring something like a week's notice.

The stockbroker's account was also in Grace's name. I couldn't find a portfolio valuation, but going by the trading statements, the broker had in the last three months alone purchased Grace shares worth over £50,000, against sales of only £15,000. So, if I had this right, Grace and Will had joint liabilities of at least £135,000, while Grace, in her own name, had assets of at least £65,000, probably more. Will had hinted at this situation, it was more or less what I'd expected, yet something bothered me all the same, a sense that I'd seen something and missed its significance. I went through the statements again, but couldn't find whatever it was that I was looking for.

Grace was no letter writer. She had kept clusters of thank-you notes from dinner guests, but only four newsy letters from friends, and the women who had written – old schoolfriends, it seemed, or former flatmates – made no mention of having received any sort of written communication from Grace.

Grace may not have written letters, but she most certainly used the phone. But though there were various household bills in the desk, I could find no phone bills, and it occurred to me that they might be entered as a farm expense and kept in Will's office across the yard.

In the miniature drawers under the pigeonholes I came across bundles of redundant diary sheets from a Filofax; three years' worth, each year held together with its own miniature bulldog clip. Looking through the last year, I saw that Grace had used these pages solely to record engagements and meetings; no tradesmen got a mention, nor any lists. The entries were in the same neat hand. Times, places, initials or first names. Dinner parties, drinks, visits to London. No sign of AWP. And only one lunch at the Brasserie early in the year, though she had lunched elsewhere in Knightsbridge regularly, as well as places around Covent Garden, Belgravia and Chelsea. I noticed immediately that she had put first names or full names next to each and every lunch date – mostly female, none met with too regularly – until roughly six months ago, when she had suddenly consigned her lunch companion to anonymity.

I looked at this from a variety of angles, I tried to think why she might have done this, but I always came to the same conclusion. It had to be the same person she was seeing every time, it had to be someone whose name she wouldn't even entrust to her private diary.

I realized, too, that once the companion had become nameless, she went to London more often, every week instead of every ten or fourteen days, and that the restaurants got closer to Knightsbridge and began to repeat themselves until, ultimately, the Brasserie triumphed.

It could only be Mr Gordon of Hans Place.

I went back to July, the last month in which Grace had named her lunch companions. There was a Sarah, a Diana R, and, for the first time in her diary, a person identified not by name but a single initial: T.

Mr T. Gordon? Tony, Tom, Tim.

It was immediately after T appeared that, excluding time off for a short holiday in France, Grace had begun to make weekly visits to London and to have afternoons which were marked 'shopping' or simply left empty, without plans or appointments.

After Christmas, she had started going to London less often again, had lunched at the Brasserie only three times in six weeks. Love cooling? Or love interrupted in some way?

I put the diary pages into my bag for safekeeping. Safekeeping was, in this instance, a relative term. Should the police decide to treat Grace's death as suspicious and issue a search warrant, I wouldn't withhold the diaries, but short of that happening I wouldn't offer them up either.

Will's office was locked. Returning to the kitchen, I hunted through the key rack above the phone, but none of the key tags said 'office'. Then, remembering the favourite justification offered by housebreaker clients – *but the key was there for the taking* – I went back across the yard and upturned stones and drain-lids and ran a hand along the underside of the outhouse eaves and over the window frames until I found the key secreted on the ledge of a ventilation brick high up on the side wall.

Will's desk had accumulated even more detritus than before, in an even greater state of disorder. Avoiding this, I went to a shelf lined with lever-arch files and found the phone bills in a binder marked: *Receipts – Office Expenditure*. There were two telephone lines, it seemed, one for the office and one for the house, both paid through the farm. The back-up sheets with the itemized long-distance calls were missing, however. I went back through the last year, but in every instance only the summary sheets had been filed.

Returning to the desk, I faced the undulating landscape of paper. Trying not to disturb whatever order might lurk within the chaos, I peered under letters, read corners of bills, leafed through stacks where stacks existed. After a while I began to make out a pattern of sorts. The top leaf-fall of paper had no pattern to it at all, as though Will had chucked the incoming mail onto the desk at random, but the piles of paper beneath were arranged more or less according to subject. Suppliers' catalogues; Ministry of Agriculture bumph; orders and invoices; correspondence. Finding the bills, I had a clean sweep: not just one but two bills from British Telecom, one for each line, as well as a Cellnet bill for Will's mobile; and with the list of itemized calls still attached.

Within a couple of minutes my excitement had evaporated. No calls to the Hans Place number. No single number, in fact, that she'd called long distance with any regularity. Not even, I noticed, her mother. In the three months covered by the bill there were just two calls to Veronica, and they were several weeks apart. With a growing sense of futility, I made a note of the other three long-distance numbers that Grace – or Will – had called more than once from the house line.

The office line was even less revealing, with few long-distance calls and only two to London numbers, which I didn't recognize.

I wasn't sure which was worse, the suspicion that I had missed something, or the suspicion that there was nothing to miss, and that Grace had no secrets after all.

With a curiosity that wasn't solely professional, I glanced through Will's Cellnet bill. The majority of the calls had been made to Marsh House, with Reed Cottage a close second. Five or six calls had been made to a place in Norwich, with the remainder scattered over a variety of mainly local numbers.

Combing through the list, I realized there was only one local number he'd called with any regularity: a number I had seen or used recently but couldn't place.

There was a phone book beside the desk. I leafed through it with a sting of anticipation. Hammond, Hampson ... *Hampton Dr J., surgery* was listed but, following modern practice, no home number.

I hovered over the phone, then, wishing I didn't feel driven to such measures, incapable, it seemed, of stopping myself, dialled quickly. The number rang for what seemed a long time, until a female voice answered, a voice with a hint of a local accent.

'I'm sorry,' I said, 'I'm not sure who I'm speaking to.'

'This is Carol Yates.'

'Mrs Yates!' I gave a nervous laugh. 'Of course. I'm sorry to bother you.' Pulling a ready-made excuse out of the air, I said I was calling to see if it was convenient for Frank to move the last of Maggie's furniture the next day.

Ringing off, I dialled the number with the Norwich code. It was answered by an agricultural merchant.

The relief crept over me. Will had no lover. No traceable full-blooded lover, at any rate, which was the only sort that mattered. No man could have a full-time lover and not communicate with her; no man could maintain an illicit relationship without giving his lover the reassurance of regular calls. And while a man might be forced to call his lover from his office now and again, all his instincts would draw him to the mobile. The mobile, irresistible, clandestine, was the medium of the modern affair.

My relief grew sharper: if I couldn't discover evidence of another woman, then neither would the police. For the police, people's lives were a series of clichés and the possession of a lover was more than enough reason for a man to kill his wife, more than enough reason to close their minds to all the other possibilities.

There was only one problem with all this, and I had been

trying to avoid it. If lovers needed to talk so badly, then how had Grace managed to communicate with Mr Gordon of Hans Place? How had she survived the separations between lunch dates?

I tried Ray on his mobile.

He answered to a background of traffic noise. 'Where are you?' he asked.

'Norfolk.'

'I've been trying to reach you.'

'Mobile turned off. Listen, I'm desperate for that Hans Place information.'

'Right-ho. Got a bit more. The trust which owns the place is controlled by a family called *Aubrey*. The trust is Guernsey-based, like I told you, but no indication of where the family come from, and a bit difficult to find out. You know what these Guernsey lawyers are like.'

No Mr Gordon. I suppressed my disappointment. 'Keep on it, would you, Ray? I need a name, a workplace number, some way of talking to them.'

'I'm on to it,' he promised. 'Would have given it more time, but had a panic on.'

'Oh?'

'Paul. Lost a witness. But, listen, I *have* got a name for your Regent's Park geezer.'

'What?'

'25 Avon Court on Prince Albert Road is leased by' – he paused, as if to check his notes – 'a Mr Barry Holland, who runs a company called . . . hang on, got it here somewhere—'

'Clawfoot Productions.'

'You know the guy?' Traffic droned through the earpiece, then Ray's voice said, 'Hello? Alex? Hello? You still there?'

'I'm here . . . Thanks, Ray . . .'

'Enough on Mr Holland, then?'

'Plenty. Just stay with Hans Place.'

I put the phone down, my brain filled with images of Grace and Barry Holland. Sponsorship business? Other business?

Friendship? Love? Adventure? For a wild instant I wondered if he might keep a second flat in Hans Place, but it seemed unlikely.

Lovers. I tried to imagine the two of them together. Barry, the boy-made-good pop promoter whose hair would always be a little too slick, suits a little too broad-shouldered, aftershave a little too powerful, and the elegant classical-music-loving Grace with her effortless fastidious style and – Jilly's words came back – her grand manner. I couldn't think of anything they could possibly have in common, although that of course had never prevented people from being drawn to each other. Yet, even allowing for sex and the power of money, I simply couldn't see them as an item. Barry's relative lack of refinement, his rather flashy veneer, would have repelled Grace. It came to me with new clarity: Grace had been a snob, and not the harmless sort who clings rather desperately to her own kind, rather the type who aggressively seeks higher social ground.

No, it had to be a simple matter of money that had brought Barry and Grace together, a subject on which they were both, in their separate ways, experts.

I realized that I didn't even know if Barry was married or otherwise attached.

Before leaving Will's desk, I couldn't resist moving a couple of stray bills onto the appropriate piles, and then it seemed a simple matter to sort the rest of the paper-drift into some kind of order.

You don't see things, and you see them. Putting a letter on the correspondence pile, I hardly glanced at it, yet I found myself pulling it back towards me and reading it in more detail. It must have been the numbers that had caught my eye, the sheer size of the sum. The letter was from Will's bank manager, to say he was prepared to offer Will a mortgage of £250,000 against the value of the house and farm tenancy. He realized that this was below the £300,000 that Will had wanted, but it was the absolute maximum he could offer.

Chapter Nine

———

PAUL'S CAR was parked neatly outside the house, parallel to the kerb. The porch lantern was on, and through the spare-room window I could see the glow of the landing light. I found it impossible not to tick these things off in my mind, just as I found it difficult not to notice that two days after the dustmen's visit the rubbish bins were still out of their cuddy, their lids upside down on the paving, and that a new telephone directory lay uncollected by the flower urn. Such tiny things: I was angry with myself for even noticing.

I let myself in and called a greeting.

Paul appeared from the living room, a fluid smile on his face. 'Welcome home, stranger.'

As we put our arms around each other I savoured the moment of homecoming, though in the same instant, rising in the same emotional breath, I felt a familiar ache of foreboding.

'You're late!' Paul cried, holding me at arm's length.

'Am I?' I tried not to look too closely into his face in case I should see the signs. 'Had we said a time?'

He wagged a finger in mock reprimand. 'Dinner. You were going to be here for dinner. Still, it may not be spoilt yet. I hope, anyway.'

The drink lay thick on his voice and in his eyes, and I looked away.

Guiding me by the shoulder, he led me towards the kitchen, to a table laid as though for guests, with candles, napkins and best wine glasses. I was touched by the trouble he had taken, but uneasy too.

Playing the waiter, he pulled out my chair with a flourish and, protecting his hands with a dishcloth that was far too thin, slid a plate precariously out of the oven and almost dropped it.

'Careful!'

'No, I'm there! I'm there!' Grimacing at the heat, he rushed the plate onto the table and, rearranging the dishcloth around the edges, placed it in front of me.

'I wasn't expecting hot.' It was salmon with peas and fried potatoes.

'Ah ha!' he declared flamboyantly. 'It's hot you've got!' Pouring some wine, he sat opposite and gestured me to eat.

'What about you?' He had laid a place for himself.

'Big lunch,' he said breezily. 'Not hungry.' He motioned me towards the food again.

'Salmon. Didn't your pa used to call it a poacher's dinner?'

'A poacher's *feast*, he used to say!'

'A feast indeed,' I said. 'Thank you.'

He grinned modestly but evasively, his eyes continually slipping away from mine.

I ate a little only to find that I, too, wasn't hungry. 'Well, what's the news?' I asked lightly.

'The news?' He made a show of thinking about it. 'We're fine at the office. Ahead of the game. A bit of a struggle the other day. But really fine now.' His smile was very quick and very bright.

'And?'

'And?' He gave me an ingenuous look. 'Nothing, really. No, that's it.'

'No problems?'

'No, no.' And still his eyes wouldn't settle on my face.

'But Ray said you'd had a panic?'

'Oh, just for a moment there. Lost an alibi witness in a burglary.'

'Ah.' I left it a moment before asking, 'And what about that GBH? Munro, wasn't it?'

He didn't quite manage to conceal the edge to his voice. 'What about it?'

'I just wondered when it was coming to court.'

'Oh, not for ages yet.' His voice was casual but his body was delivering quite different messages.

'Nothing you want to talk about?'

'No. Why should there be?'

'It was just . . . I don't know, I got the feeling you weren't happy about it. That there was some problem.'

'Why do you always think there has to be a problem?' he blazed suddenly. 'Really, Lexxy, you always manage to see doom and gloom as far as I'm concerned.'

I lowered my fork. 'Doom and gloom? No, darling. No, I was just asking, that's all.'

'The way you talk, I feel like *I'm* the one who's done something wrong!'

I laughed falsely. 'Don't be silly.'

'Well, I'm telling you, that's how you are! You always manage to make me feel bad.' His face was flushed, his eyes glaring. Even allowing for the drink, his indignation was beyond all reason. He cried suddenly, 'Oh, for God's sake!' and, pushing his chair back, stomped out of the room.

Stunned by this switch of mood, I sat absolutely motionless.

He returned a moment later with a large whisky which he deposited on the table with a clunk. Sitting down again, he shot me an aggrieved glance. 'And don't give me that look!'

I said helplessly, 'If I'm looking, it's only because I don't know what to say.'

'Well, don't pretend you don't know what I'm talking about! Don't pretend!'

A bubble of indignation surfaced, I felt a sudden heat. 'I think I'd better leave you to your drink.' Getting untidily to my feet, I found my way out of the room and upstairs to the bathroom where I turned the taps on full blast. When Paul appeared a few minutes later, the bath was almost overflowing and I was sitting on the chair, staring at the wall.

Turning off the water, Paul sat awkwardly on the edge of the bath and fumbled for my hand. 'God, and now you're crying. I'm sorry, I'm sorry. I don't blame you, Lexxy. Really I don't. Sometimes I just feel . . .' He groped for the thought. 'I feel . . . that somehow you're judging me all the time.'

'I judge you when the drink does the talking, I judge you then all right.'

'And I can't blame you. I can't.'

I looked into his face. 'You can see, then? You can see what it does to you?'

'It's only when things get tense, that's all . . . I get carried away. When things get tense.'

'It's *not* just then, Paul. It's all the time.'

'I'll cut down. I promise. Really I will. Cut right down.'

'But you won't stop.'

'I will if you want me to.'

'It's not what *I* want. It's what *you* want that counts.'

'You're right, Lexxy. You're always right.' The way he said this, it sounded like a reproach.

'Why do you do it, Paul? Why? Is it us? Is it our marriage?'

'No, no, Lexxy. No.'

'What, then?'

'There's nothing wrong. Really. Nothing at all. I'll cut down, I promise. Right down.'

We were silent for a time, then he sighed heavily and said in the tone of a boy owning up to a misdemeanour, 'I'm going to lose my licence.'

I stared at him uncomprehendingly. 'What?'

'They stopped me the other night, two uniformed guys.'

It was a moment before I managed to take it in. 'How far over the limit?'

He laughed, shame-faced. 'Three.'

'*Three times*. God.' A car was absolutely essential for our work, for getting to police stations late at night, not to mention the more distant courts during the day.

He said airily, 'I'll use cabs.'

Cabs would never work, and we both knew it, but I bit the comment back. 'You could take all the work close to home. Give the night duties to the others,' I suggested, knowing that we didn't have enough qualified staff to cover the nights.

'The cabs'll be fine once I get them organized.'

I didn't have the heart to argue. Slumped on the edge of the bath, Paul looked much older suddenly, and, for all his weight, more insubstantial. His eyes were puffy, his skin colourless, his hair drab. I saw a man who'd lost his confidence and self-regard, and with it his capacity for optimism and joy, leaving a dull shadow of himself.

'We'll manage somehow,' I said. 'Sturgess is ready to do some of the easier stuff.'

His eyes shifted uneasily, he was tense again. 'We have to talk about Sturgess.'

'What about him?'

'He's going to have to go.'

I stared at him. 'Go? Why?'

'Oh, it's a real saga,' he said rapidly. 'Let's just say he's not with us in spirit, not at all. Making mistakes. Overstepping the mark.'

'But *how*? What's he done exactly?'

Paul made a dismissive gesture, as if the business were far too complex to discuss in detail. 'Oh, failed to follow instructions. And more than once, too. Nearly landed one client in shtuck. Keeps getting himself into situations—'

'Situations? What sort of situations?'

He met my eye with difficulty. 'Oh, asking questions he shouldn't ask. And, worse still, getting the answers, for God's sake. Making it impossible to represent people. Oh, but there've been plenty of other things too, Lexxy. A whole bundle of things. Been building up for some time. No,' he said fiercely, as if I'd been arguing against the idea, 'he has to go, and that's all there is to it.'

'If you feel that strongly.'

He stood up. 'He has to go!'

'Okay.'

He looked surprised at my compliance, and a little uncertain, as though he distrusted such an easy win. Eventually he mumbled, 'Your dinner's probably died a death.'

'I wasn't that hungry, to tell the truth.'

'I'll chuck it, then.' He paused in the doorway. 'You'll be going back to Norfolk, will you?'

'Yes.'

'Soon?'

'As soon as I can.'

He eyed me thoughtfully, sadly, as if I had just confirmed something irrevocable for him, before nodding and turning away.

I bathed and washed my hair and stood under a cold shower for as long as I could bear it. Filled with the nervous energy that cold water and tiredness can bring, I went down to the study to tackle the mail. From the kitchen I could hear the clink of plates as Paul padded about, clearing away. Shutting the study door behind me, I put some Mozart on the CD player and started on the accumulation of bills and letters. Sorting through old papers, I found myself staring at the notes I had made when I had got Will's original message all those evenings ago. Checklists, procedures for missing persons, then at the bottom of the sheet: *Medical problems? Emotional problems? Secret life?*

Staring at 'Secret life' it struck me that Will was right, that if Grace had had a lover then she had conducted the affair with quite extraordinary secrecy, more secrecy than most women would ever have managed or indeed wanted. She had confided in no one, it seemed, not Anne Hampton, who appeared to have been her closest woman friend, and not – though this was less surprising – her mother. She hadn't given the smallest hint, so it seemed, to anyone at all. There had been no rumours about her, not so much as a breath. Either she had been immensely self-controlled or immensely anxious not to be found out.

My view of Grace shifted again, and again, a flickering picture that wouldn't hold still. Was she the cold-hearted conniving wife that Will had described? Or simply worried about the repercussions of being discovered? It was hard to imagine Grace anxious about anything or anybody. Unless – it came to me suddenly – she had been worried about scaring the lover off. Or – an even more promising thought – it was the lover himself who'd insisted on absolute secrecy, who'd had too much to lose from being found out. Perhaps he'd insisted on doing all the phoning and forbidden Grace from making any calls.

I went through the mail and paid the bills. When I'd sealed the last cheque I entered the amounts on the bank statement and calculated the new balance. The account was in credit: it was always in credit; Paul couldn't bear the thought of an overdraft. All the utilities were paid monthly by direct debit, while insurance premiums and other large bills came out of a special savings account. As a result of this stringency, our monthly expenditure hardly varied. Neither of us had the time to spend much on luxuries. Even when we'd carpeted and furnished the house Paul had planned it meticulously so that, by economizing on holidays and restaurants, we'd been able to pay for everything out of current income.

Grace hadn't budgeted at all. Grace had gone for what she'd wanted when she wanted it, and what she'd wanted was the very best. Will had told me that Grace had paid for the over-expenditure out of her own money. Yet unless I'd missed something in the bank statements, unless she'd transferred money by a circuitous route, it appeared she hadn't paid for very much at all. I wondered what had prompted Will to make this remark, whether he'd said it out of a lingering sense of loyalty or because for some misguided reason he'd believed it to be true.

It was another half-hour before I'd scribbled instructions to the cleaning lady and written the last note. I came out of the study into silence. No squawking from the TV, no light from the kitchen. The living room was in darkness too, though in recent months this hadn't necessarily meant it was uninhabited, and peering over the back of the sofa, I found Paul stretched out, snoring gently, mouth gaping wide, looking the picture of a drunk. I was tempted to leave him for once, tempted to let him wake in the early hours, cold and alone, yet there was nothing I could teach Paul about loneliness, nothing that a childhood in a hard-drinking household hadn't already taught him.

I went round the sofa and shook him gently by the shoulder. 'Come on. Time for bed.'

He groaned and pulled his shoulder away.

I tried again, a little more firmly.

His arm came up, as though to protect his face from the blows of an aggressor. 'Leave me alone! Just leave me alone!' His voice was rough and slurred.

I straightened up and looked down at him with a numb and distant heart. Pity runs dry in time, and for me the time had stolen up and rushed past. Paul didn't need me any more, except to cover for him, to collude by default in his addiction.

I fetched a blanket and pulled it over him. I locked up and went upstairs and lay in bed, wide awake.

It was almost midnight when the phone rang, and for a moment I wondered if Paul was Duty Solicitor and had forgotten to tell me about it.

'Yes?'

'It's me.'

I felt a rush of pleasure. 'Will.'

'Is it too late?'

'No, no – I was awake.'

'I wanted to talk.' He sounded dispirited.

I propped myself up on the pillows. 'Of course.'

'Nothing particular.'

'That's all right.'

'Charlie was a bit upset tonight. Couldn't talk to him at all.'

'What about finding a therapist for him? A counsellor?'

He gave a dry laugh. 'This is Norfolk, Ali, not London.'

'Yes ... Of course. A family friend, then? Someone he trusts.'

'No, he wouldn't want that. He wouldn't want to talk to them.'

'What about Maggie? Can't he talk to her?'

'No.' There was irritation in his voice, a note of disapproval. 'She treats him like a small child. It's all "your mother's gone to heaven" stuff. She can't see how confusing it is for him, can't see that it does no good.'

'Well, he still has you. He'll listen to you.'

After a pause he murmured something I didn't quite catch, something that might have been: '. . . wish he would.' Then, in an altogether brisker tone: 'I had a look at the tides, by the way.'

'The tides?'

'For that night. To be absolutely sure.'

I took a guess. 'The current, you mean?'

'It was ebbing fast when I opened the sluice. Two hours into the flood when I closed it again.'

A silence. I suggested, 'So anything lying on the Gun would have been swept away?'

'No – *not at all.* No, the point is that she couldn't have been swept in from the creek. *That's* the point. She couldn't have come from *that* side of the sluice.'

There was obviously some great significance to this, which I hadn't grasped. 'And if she *had* come from the creek side, what difference . . .?'

'Well, then, she could have come from anywhere, couldn't she? From right up by the quay, the house. *Anywhere.*'

I was getting there: the ebb ran fast through the creeks; a body might be carried a long way on the tide. 'So you're saying she must have fallen on the Gun side?'

'Yes.'

'And not far from the sluice.'

A reluctant pause. 'Yes.'

'But then, when you drained the marsh, why wasn't she—'
I caught myself on the point of saying 'flushed out' and changed
it to: 'carried out into the tide?'

'The flow was too sluggish, just a trickle, it wouldn't have
carried her . . .'

'Far.'

'Far.'

He was saying that she had fallen on the Gun side, near the
second sluice; he was saying that her body hadn't travelled very
far, if at all.

'She could have tripped,' I ventured, for something to say.

He murmured under his breath, 'But why was she there?'

In the silence that followed, I thought I heard him give a
sigh of hopelessness.

'We can go through it again when I get back,' I said.

'When's that, Ali?'

'Tomorrow, in the evening.'

'You'll be able to stay for a while?'

If I stayed for more than a day it would be Friday, and then
it would hardly be worth going back to London until after the
weekend. Taking a decision, I said, 'I'll stay for a while.'

'Otherwise it'll be the whisky bottle.' He attempted a laugh.

'Don't even think about it,' I said.

Heavy rain and a broken-down lorry had brought the one-way
system around Camden Town to an early standstill. On the
dismal pavements mothers wielding flimsy umbrellas dragged
their children to school, teenagers sloped along, heads down,
hoods shielding their faces like aspiring bank robbers, two
scowling workmen hurried past clutching bags of McDonald's.
I did not love the city at times like this, perhaps did not love it
deeply at any time. If it hadn't been for my work, I could have
lived in the country very happily indeed. Years ago, hunting
for my first job, I'd applied to a firm in Plymouth, imagining I

could rent a country cottage above the Tamar, not too far from my parents' new home, and get the best of both worlds. But the firm hadn't done much crime, just the occasional shoplifting, and, young and arrogant as I was, I'd thought my talents would be better used elsewhere.

My only arrogance now was to think that my clients might miss me if I wasn't around any more.

I had woken to an empty house and a note from Paul to say that he was at Ealing Magistrates Court for the day. He hadn't come to bed during the night and I hadn't heard him leave in the morning. The phone had rung very early, some time before dawn, but the ringing had stopped or been answered before I'd managed to roll across the bed to pick it up. When I got up I realized from the damp towels and discarded underwear that Paul had showered and dressed in the guest bathroom. Separate bathrooms: by such small degrees does one grow apart.

The traffic began to move at last. By one of those strange quirks of jams, the road ahead cleared rapidly.

The mobile rang. Expecting Corinthia, I called a bright, 'Good morning!'

I heard traffic noise through the earpiece and the muffled sound you sometimes get from another mobile. A male voice said, 'Alex?'

'Yes.' Whoever the man was, he was breathing heavily. 'Who is this?'

'Gary.' His voice was high.

'Gary. What's the matter?'

'I've got to see you. Straight away.'

'I'm on my way into the office. Where are you?'

'Farringdon. Station.' This was just two minutes' walk from work.

'I'll meet you at the office, then. I'll be there in fifteen minutes.'

'No. Not there.'

I thought I understood then: this was about Sturgess's

future with the firm and Paul's determination to fire him. 'That new café on Clerkenwell Green, then? The Italian place with the black blinds.'

'I know.'

I parked in my bay beside the office and, taking an umbrella from the boot, picked my way back along the rain-soaked Clerkenwell Road to the café. Sturgess was sitting hunched at a corner table. Spotting me, he jerked as if on strings and fixed me with a fervent stare.

'You okay?' I asked.

'Something's happened,' he gasped.

I sat down. 'The job? I'm sorry if there've been problems.'

'The job?' He was momentarily baffled. 'No, something's *happened*, something bad.'

'What?'

'It's Munro,' he explained urgently. 'The GBH case.'

'I remember.'

'He's dead, Alex! *Dead!*'

My first thought was suicide. However vigilant prison staff tried to be, remand prisoners regularly found new and desperate ways of doing away with themselves. 'I'm very sorry.'

'They found him this morning!'

'I'm really sorry.'

'But it's my fault! My *fault!*' He was almost in tears. 'He didn't want bail! He didn't want it! It was only because I told him it was okay— He *knew*, for God's sake! He knew!'

I asked quietly, 'You got him bail?'

'Yesterday. But he didn't want it! He knew they were going to get him. He knew!'

Understanding came at last. 'You're saying he was murdered?'

Sturgess nodded mutely.

'Let's just go through this slowly, Gary. One fact at a time. You're saying that Munro knew he was at risk?'

'Christ, yes. He was shit scared. Fucking terrified. He kept asking me, is it okay for me to walk, you sure it's okay, sure my name's not posted? *Knew?* Christ, he knew better than anyone. And it was me that went and told him, wasn't it? Told him – *Jesus* – his face contorted – '*told him it was okay.*'

The waitress came up and stared at Sturgess with open curiosity. I ordered two espressos. As soon as she was out of earshot I held up both hands as if to quieten things down, but really to give myself a chance to think. 'But what are you saying, Gary? Are you saying he was expecting you to know whether it was safe for him or not? To have some sort of inside information?'

He gave me an odd look, a blend of shame and caution. 'Yeah. Well, I guess so. He kept asking me, is that the message? Are you saying it's okay? Are you sure?'

The implications of this hung uncomfortably in the air, and for the moment I didn't pursue them. Instead, I said, 'Did he say who he was frightened of?'

'Sure. Told me the whole bloody lot. Couldn't stop him. Chapter and verse. The whole bleedin' story. I didn't ask for it! Didn't want it!'

'But he insisted?'

'Yeah.'

The waitress brought the coffee and stared again.

I said, 'He wanted you to know, then.'

Sturgess grimaced. 'To be his insurance policy, you mean? Jesus, fine bloody insurance!'

I felt a moment of sympathy for him. Nothing in his training could have prepared him for this.

'So who was out to get him then?'

'Ronnie Buck. He was one of Ronnie Buck's men, and Ronnie had the frighteners on him.'

I absorbed this slowly, with surprise, but not, perhaps, so much surprise as all that. 'Okay,' I said in my calmest voice. 'Let's decide how to—'

'There's more,' Sturgess announced abruptly. 'Worse.' He leant forward and I noticed two spots of heat burning high on his cheeks. 'I saw them pick him up.'

'What do you mean?'

'After Munro got bail, I had another case. When I finally got clear, Munro'd gone. Well, I *thought* he'd gone. But then I'm on my way to the Tube and I see him ahead of me. Making for the Tube too – well, that's what it looked like, we were a street away. Then this car draws up. Merc, big one. Munro takes one look at the driver and starts walking like hell. The car drives along with him, and the driver and Munro are having a conversation, and it's definitely not a happy one. Suddenly Munro tries to scarper but the car overtakes and the driver and this other geezer jump out and the next thing, they're pushing Munro in the back seat. *Shit . . .*' The memory made him wince. 'I ran after them, but the car was off like a shot . . .'

'You got the registration number?'

He shook his head.

Suddenly I was impatient with him. 'What, none of it?'

'I was too bloody gobsmacked! Too *freaked*. I couldn't believe it – the way they'd just scooped him up, in broad daylight. And I felt so bloody sick, Alex. Part of me *knew* what was going to happen, you see. Once I saw the driver I bloody knew!'

'You recognized him?'

'Oh, yeah, you bet I did! It was Russell, the driver was *Russell*.'

'Russell?'

'Ronnie Buck's driver.'

I felt a flutter of excitement. 'The guy who stood trial with Ronnie for the attempted murder?'

'Yeah.'

'You're sure?'

'Christ, I spent six weeks in court looking at him every day. Yeah, I'm dead sure.'

'How far were you from the car?'

'Oh, twenty feet and closing. And he turned towards me, full face. No mistake, Alex. No bloody mistake.'

A lot of things went through my mind as I heard this, some

electrifying, most of them unsettling. Only one thought emerged with any clarity. 'You'll have to go to the police with this. You realize that?'

He fiddled with his coffee cup. 'Yeah, I suppose.'

'There's no option, Gary.' Saying this, I forced myself towards the final question. 'The bail – I just need to understand – what made you go for it?'

There was a heavy pause. 'Told to.' He kept his eyes on his cup.

I hardly needed to ask: 'By Paul?'

'Yeah.'

Having got this far, I went on coolly, 'Did you tell him about Munro's worries?'

'Yeah.'

'And what did he say?'

'He said it was okay.'

'That was it?'

He shifted slightly in his seat. 'Well . . . more or less.'

'Give me the conversation, Gary, would you? In detail.'

He didn't want to tell me, but I pressed him. Finally he murmured, 'When Paul said to go for bail, I said are you sure, because Munro's dead worried about what'll happen to him when he gets out. And Paul sort of shrugged it off, and said, oh he's worrying about nothing, or there's nothing to worry about, something like that. And I said again, are you sure it's a good idea because he's shit scared. And Paul sort of made out I was questioning his judgement. I don't know – he made me feel I was making a fuss about nothing. He just told me to get on with it and then he was busy with something else and I didn't get the chance to talk to him again.'

'Thank you,' I said rather formally.

We sat for a while, locked in our own thoughts, then I said, 'I think as far as the police are concerned it might be best to stick to the basic facts.'

'Don't worry,' he said immediately. He was quick, Sturgess, he seemed to be way ahead of me, but I had to be certain.

'Just what you saw,' I said.

'Yeah. Just Russell and the car.'

'Anything else would . . .'

'Make it too complicated.'

We exchanged a look of complete understanding, and I thought that Paul hadn't done much to deserve such loyalty.

Sturgess hesitated. 'I'll have to tell them that Munro was dead frightened of Ronnie, though. I mean, he was shit scared, the poor bastard. He *knew*. I'll have to tell them that, Alex.'

'Yes. That would be the right thing to do.'

'But I'll say . . . I'll say . . .' He agonized over it for a moment. 'I'll say he was aiming to go into hiding when he got bail. Keep it simple. Otherwise they'll want to know why I went for it, you know. Why I went for bail.'

Suddenly I hated Paul for making conspirators of us both, for landing this can of worms in Sturgess's lap. 'You mustn't say anything you're not comfortable with, Gary.'

'Look, I'm not going to drop Paul in it, am I? I'm sure he didn't mean Munro any harm. I'm sure it wasn't a *message* he was giving me as such. Nothing – you know – *definite*.'

I wished I could be so certain. 'It would certainly keep it simpler,' I said, guilt building on guilt. 'How was Munro killed, by the way? Do you know?'

'Shot.'

'And how did you hear?'

'Corinthia. She called me this morning.'

'Did she say where it happened? Which CID we're dealing with?'

'She may have said . . . I can't remember.'

I glanced at the time and called Corinthia on the mobile.

'Lewisham,' she told me.

'Who's the investigating officer?'

'DI Barrett.'

'How did you hear, Corinthia?'

'How?' Faint surprise sounded in her voice. 'Well – Paul.

He called me first thing this morning. He said they'd contacted him in the night.'

The call before dawn.

'Did Paul leave you any instructions?'

'He said to find next-of-kin if I could. But I've been through the file, and I'm pretty sure we don't know of any relatives.' She was flustered; she was talking a little too fast. 'I don't know why he should think we did.'

'When are you expecting Paul back from Ealing?'

'Noon.'

I looked across at Sturgess, whose face still paraded myriad emotions. I asked Corinthia, 'What's Gary got tabled for today?'

I heard her flipping the pages of the central appointments diary. 'Nothing in court. Meetings with clients this afternoon, at two and three thirty.'

'Can you find someone to stand in for him? And I won't be available today, either.'

Corinthia was trying to work out what was going on. 'Are you going to be contactable?'

I thought about that. 'No.'

'What shall I say?' She meant: to Paul.

'Say I'll call in later.'

I snapped the phone shut and paid the bill.

'It's Lewisham,' I said to Sturgess. 'We might as well go straight there.'

'What're they like at Lewisham?'

I thought of Dave Adamson. 'One of them's okay.'

'One?' Sturgess showed some of his old spark. 'Oh, well, nothing to worry about, then.'

It was three in the afternoon before DI Barrett's team were ready to take a written statement. It was always flattering to believe that success in the law came from a blend of tenacity and talent, but I had long since recognized that the main requirement for a criminal solicitor was an ability to endure long periods of crushing inactivity in small airless spaces. Sturgess hadn't been encouraged to leave the interview room – the reasons for not showing his face hadn't needed to be spelt out to him – and while we'd chatted desultorily between interviews Sturgess wasn't exactly in the mood to chat. At one point I'd gone in search of Dave Adamson, but they'd told me he was off duty until later in the day, and I'd resorted to consuming large quantities of canteen coffee, which had left me with jittery nerves and a mouth tasting of old tin or worse.

The written statement, once started, was not to be hurried either. We were still soldiering through it at four when I was passed a note from Dave Adamson to say he was in the building. We met in the passageway forty minutes later.

'Have I heard right?' he asked with unconcealed excitement.

'Depends what you've heard.'

'You've brought in a witness to the Munro killing?'

'Not quite to the killing, not quite as good as that.'

'To the grab, was it? *Still.*' He made a triumphal fist and fixed me with a beady eye.

'Long way to court, though, Dave. Long way to proving anything.'

'But at least we've got Ronnie back in our sights!'

'Ronnie Buck still happens to be a client of my firm, I should remind you.'

'Ah.' Dave gave me an ironic smile. 'But the driver, Russell? Not one of yours?'

'He's represented by a firm in Catford somewhere, so I believe.'

'Bad luck for him.'

'It would be unprofessional of me to comment on that,' I said, deliberately choosing to misunderstand him.

'They tortured him first, you know.'

I stared at him. 'I didn't know.'

'Ugly stuff. Poor blighter.'

I decided not to tell Sturgess about this quite yet. He was feeling guilty enough already.

'It's got Buck written all over it.'

'I hope you get him,' I said, giving up all attempts at lawyer–client detachment.

'We'll give it a bloody good try.'

We fell silent as some officers walked past.

On a lighter note, I asked ingenuously, 'Am I in your good books again, then?'

His smile was conditional.

'Enough to ask a favour?'

His expression became both wary and attentive. 'Ask away.'

'There's a flat in Hans Place, Knightsbridge, owned by one of those private trusts based in Guernsey. The trust's controlled by a family called Aubrey. But I need to know who lives there, who actually uses the place.'

Dave pulled a questioning face. This was such simple stuff that he was looking for the catch.

'I've even got the phone number.'

He raised his palms. 'That's it? Just who lives there?'

'Or uses it regularly.'

'Knightsbridge . . . Not someone who's likely to be known to us, then?'

'No.'

'Not someone who might be known to Special Branch?' he said, going through the danger points.

'Very unlikely.'

'Not a diplomat or enemy alien?'

'No.'

'Tomorrow okay? I'm on duty till late tonight.'

'Tomorrow'll be fine.'

He made a fist again. 'Know something? I'm only ever truly happy when we're going after Buck.'

*

'I'm meant to let him know the moment you arrive,' Corinthia announced in a purposeful tone, jerking her head towards Paul's office.

It was after five thirty; the rest of the staff had gone home. In a voice that wouldn't carry, I asked, 'Anything for me?'

Corinthia glanced towards the table where the immediate-action files were kept. 'Plenty for you, but it's all been dealt with.' She had her cool voice on, and I knew it was because I had kept her in the dark about the day's events.

'Thank you,' I said with suitable humility.

'DI Ramsey from Norfolk CID called to say he'd like to see Mr Will Dearden tomorrow morning at ten. At the Dearden home. If that's okay.'

'Tell him that's okay.'

'You're going back there?'

'Tonight.'

'Returning?'

'Not sure.' Saying this, I realized that I had taken the decision to stay on in Norfolk until after the weekend. 'Sunday night?'

'Right,' said Corinthia, already planning the logistics. 'And Gary?'

'He'll be back tomorrow.'

'Aha.' Now she was openly curious.

'We had to go and sort something out.'

'Oh?'

A door opened and footsteps sounded in the passage. It could only be Paul.

I said quickly in the same low voice, 'Can't talk about it. Not allowed to.'

Corinthia's expression lifted; she liked a bit of intrigue. 'A security thing?'

She was near enough. 'Yes. Not a word, Corinthia. Not even to Paul.'

'*Right.*' She gave me an old-fashioned look, all pride and discretion.

Paul appeared in the doorway, looking rumpled in shirt-sleeves. 'You're here,' he said accusingly.

'Just a minute ago.'

'Where've you been?' His lids drooped darkly, his stare contained a childish rebuke.

'Goodnight, Corinthia.' Waving to her, I led the way down the passage to Paul's office.

'Why didn't you call?' he said, at my shoulder. 'I've had one hell of a day, what with this Munro thing. One hell of a day. You heard?'

'I heard. Where was he found?'

'Oh, somewhere near Lewisham.' He followed me into the room.

'How did he die?'

He pushed some papers across his desk to clear some space. 'Shot, they said.' As he perched side-saddle on the desk the weight he'd put on during the last year showed in the bulge of his stomach, the tightness of his belt. His shirt was terribly crumpled and I realized he must have taken it straight from the ironing basket this morning rather than come into the bedroom and risk a conversation.

I went back to the door and closed it. 'An execution, was it, then? A gangland affair?'

He waved a hand, he averted his gaze. 'I guess so.'

'They must know by now.'

'Nothing yet.'

'Did he know he was a marked man?'

'Eh? What?' He put on a show of incomprehension, but I could see that he was giving himself time to think, to un-scramble his brain from the lunch-time drinking session, and in that moment I felt a wild mindless rage at his weakness, at the fatal flaw that had led him to this pass. 'What?' he repeated absentmindedly. 'Know? Oh, well – he *muttered* something, you know, about being on the wrong side of someone, of worrying about the sort of treatment he might get when he came out. But they're all in trouble, aren't they, the Munros of this world? I didn't take it too seriously. Especially when we said we were going for bail and he didn't *object*, didn't instruct us *otherwise*. I mean, he didn't *say* not to. You know?' All this was delivered at breakneck speed, as though to discourage interruption.

'Which gang did he belong to?'

Paul affected the expression of exaggerated innocence that always told me when he was about to lie. 'Who knows?'

'Someone said it was Ronnie Buck's.'

An expansive shrug this time. 'Listen, I never asked. Safer that way, you know?'

'But you must have realized.'

'What do you mean?' he flared defensively. 'Why should I have realized? Since when was it a good idea to know something like that?'

My anger rose steadily. 'Oh, come on, Paul. Don't tell me Munro was paying his own legal fees.'

Paul's expression became indignant. 'He was on legal aid. He was always on legal aid! What are you getting at, Lexxy? What are you trying to say here exactly?'

I sat down heavily in a visitor's chair. 'I was just asking.'

But I must have sounded unconvincing because he protested furiously, '*No*, you're saying something here. You're saying something that I take exception to!'

The phone rang. Glaring at me, he ignored it for a while until, with a gesture of remembering something important, he swept it up and conferred with the barrister on a blackmail case listed for the Old Bailey in the morning.

When he rang off he was more subdued. Eyeing me circumspectly, he said, 'So where've you been all day?'

'Something came up.'

'With Gary?'

For an uneasy moment I thought he might know. 'Gary came along with me, yes.'

'So?' he demanded. 'What was it?'

'I can't talk about it, I'm afraid.'

His mouth gave a twitch. 'What?'

'I'm not free to talk about it.'

He affected a laboured expression of amazement. 'Not *free* to talk about it? What does that mean, Lexxy?'

'I can't discuss it on professional grounds.' I couldn't prevent myself adding, 'Nor on ethical grounds, for that matter.'

'Hang on, hang on!' He reached out a hand, as if to stop this foolishness before it went any further. 'Professional grounds? Well, I'd like to hear why. I mean, I think I'm entitled to hear the *why*, aren't I? And *ethical*? For Christ's sake, Lexxy, what does *that* mean? *Ethical*?'

'Professionally, it's simply that we have a conflict of interests, nothing more.'

'But who's your client? At least I can know who your client is, can't I?'

'It wouldn't actually be in my client's interests for anyone to know who he – or she – is.'

He froze a little, his eyes took on an injured look. 'Not in your client's interest even for *me* to know?'

'Even you.'

His mouth worked furiously, he controlled himself with difficulty. 'Okay,' he said with a supreme effort at patience. 'Okay. Let's move on, then, to this *ethical* business. Why wouldn't it be *ethical* to talk about it, for God's sake?'

'I can't answer that.'

He clutched a hand to his forehead in a theatrical gesture of impending madness. 'You can't answer.'

'My client needs anonymity as a first priority.'

'Anonymity I understand all right,' he said in an aggrieved tone, 'but I didn't think it applied to us, you know? I thought we could tell each other anything.'

'Not in this case. I've promised. I've given my word.'

Behind his spectacles, his eyes glinted with suspicion. 'This is nothing to do with Munro, is it?'

I felt no compunction about lying, not with Sturgess's safety on my conscience. 'No,' I said, calmly holding his gaze. 'But, Paul, I don't want to get into guessing games on this.'

'Ronnie Buck – it's something to do with him, then?'

I stood up. 'No guessing games, Paul.'

'Fine,' he said, backing down instantly with a lift of both hands. '*Fine.*' He was breathing heavily, a rivulet of sweat glistened on his cheek.

I said, 'Go home. Get some rest.'

He pulled off his spectacles to rub his eyes. 'You're not coming home, then?'

'I'll be away till Sunday night, maybe Monday.'

'Norfolk?' He made a feeble attempt at lightness: 'Can't compete with Norfolk.'

It was like a goad, this pull on my emotions. I felt a pang of responsibility and guilt. I said, 'Try not to drink tonight.'

He gave a sardonic laugh. 'Oh, sure, sure.'

He didn't make any promises, I noticed. We had passed the point where we felt we had to spare each other's feelings.

The lift had the aura of the Arab palace, with pewter mirrors artificially distressed with gold veining, a marble floor and a brightly gilded control panel. In the fourth floor passageway there was an ornate carpet patterned in a quasi-eastern design, a series of fancy chandeliers and mock-Louis-XVI side tables with extravagant flower arrangements in gilt-encrusted vases. The apartment door had an elaborate gilt knocker and a bell set in a gilt shell. I chose the bell.

Barry Holland opened the door in the sort of suit you see media stars wearing in press photographs, dark and casual and beautifully cut, worn with a simple white open-necked shirt and slicked-back hair. This look – the international promoter, the metropolitan man-about-town – fitted him much more easily than the country squire.

'Come in.' He stood back to reveal a hall with yet more distressed mirrors and marble and chandeliers and flowers, as though the designer from the passageway had been let loose in here too.

The living room was large and dimly lit. I walked across an uncluttered space to wide windows and looked out over Regent's Park. Above the dark canopy of trees the lights of the city were bright against a troubled sky. Below, headlights chased each other around the Outer Circle, and through the first rank of trees a light reflected darkly off the canal.

'A drink? I've some champagne open.'

I asked for water. On his way out of the room Barry turned on another light and I saw a room furnished in much simpler style than the hall, with minimalist armless sofas, low transparent plastic tables and splashy modern pictures. The walls were white, the carpet smoky blue. Tall wafer-thin speakers stood in each corner, emitting what I would have called mood music.

I sat on a sofa facing what had once been a fireplace and now contained a large bronze of a dolphin. Barry brought the drinks and sank onto an adjacent sofa facing the windows. Here in his own surroundings, sipping champagne, he possessed the polish and confidence and sense of power of the self-made man with serious money.

'So what can I do for you?' He asked it pleasantly though with a suggestion of reserve.

'Basically, I'm trying to fill in some of the gaps in Grace's diary—'

'Haven't the police done that already?' he argued mildly.

'Possibly. But it's always best to be sure about these things.'

He asked, with the same air of polite enquiry, 'You think they might have missed something?'

'It's always possible.'

'And what might they have missed?' If he had intended to take charge of the conversation, he was succeeding effortlessly.

'Well, that's the point – you can never be sure.'

'But what are *you* looking for?' He tempered the question with a faint smile. 'You must have some idea of what you're

looking for.' For all his politeness, there was a quiet relentlessness to his tone, and I couldn't make out if it was a habit of
his, to get the answers he wanted, or whether he had reserved
this approach specifically for me.

'It's really to eliminate everything that isn't relevant.'

He studied this idea with interest. 'Aha.'

I felt bound to explain, 'The family simply want to know
everything there is to know. There's nothing on cause of death
yet, you see. It's all a mystery.'

'The *family*?' This seemed to puzzle him. 'I thought you
were acting for Will Dearden.'

'Will and the family.'

He nodded thoughtfully. 'Ahh.' Fixing me with indolent
eyes that missed very little, he continued smoothly, 'So you're
filling in the gaps.'

'There was an entry in Grace's diary for the Thursday after
she disappeared. A six thirty meeting at this address.'

'That's right, but we cancelled it.'

'Any particular reason?'

'Because I was going to be in Deepwell the previous day
and it seemed easier to meet there.'

'And did you meet in Deepwell?'

'We were going to fix something for the Friday when
she was back from London, but by then, of course . . .' His
gesture suggested unfortunate events. 'So – no, we didn't
meet.'

'May I ask what you were meeting about?'

Taking a sip of champagne, he observed me over the rim of
his glass and when he spoke again it was with the air of
someone who has decided to be a little more forthcoming. 'We
were meeting about the music festival. My company were – *are*
– putting up some sponsorship money. Five thousand pounds,
to be exact. Grace and I had a few details to discuss. The
billing, the advertising, that sort of thing.'

'I see.' I made a show of taking this in. 'And who is AWP?'

'Come again?'

'Grace had put the initials AWP against the appointment. Above this address.'

'AWP?' He pulled his mouth down. 'No idea at all.'

'There was no one else due to come to the meeting?'

'No.' He was still very sure, then a glimmer of realization crept into his face. 'Unless . . .' Dropping his head briefly, he smiled to himself. 'It just could have been Grace's sense of humour at work. It could have been the nickname she used on me a couple of times.' He smiled again. 'She used to call me Amazingly Wealthy Person. To my face. She had a way of doing that, of being right up-front. She was a bit wicked that way. Yes,' he mused, 'that would be it. Amazingly Wealthy Person.'

'You'd had meetings before?'

'What, on the festival? Yeah. Two or three.'

'Here?'

His eyes narrowed, his expression contained a mild warning, as though I were straying into matters that were really none of my business, and I wondered why he should be so defensive – or protective – on the subject of Grace.

'We met in Deepwell once,' he replied. 'And once at my company offices. And once here.'

'Otherwise, you knew Grace and Will socially?'

'I saw them a bit, yes. But not that often. I like to be a bit of a hermit in Norfolk. Go there for a quiet time. Not too mad about the socializing.' And touchy about his status, I would have guessed, sensitive about the doors that might be closed to him because of his background.

'When did you last see Grace, then?'

There was an abrupt pause, a moment of appraisal, while Barry tried to work out if I knew he was the key witness to Grace's baffling last journey, that he was the one who'd seen her returning to the marshes.

I amended, 'I meant, last see her to *talk* to.'

'To talk to.' He thought back. 'It must have been three weeks ago, I suppose.'

'And she seemed all right? Normal?'

'Normal?' For some reason this question made him frown. 'Well, she was on sparkling form, no problem about that.'

Sparkling form.

Impulsively I sat forward. 'Tell me about her, Barry. Tell me what she was really like.'

'*Really* like? Blimey, there's a question. A bit of a mystery, really, like most women. Bit of an unknown quantity.' He slid me a mischievous look. 'Known quite a few women in my time, but can't pretend I ever got as far as *understanding* them.' He chuckled contentedly, a man who still relished the challenge. 'Really like?' he echoed. For a while I thought he was going to palm me off with something superficial, but he took his time, he considered his answer carefully. 'She was a funny old mixture, all sweetness and light on the outside, but tough on the inside. You know what I mean? Confident and clever. Not *bright*, exactly, but . . . yes, *clever*. And very together. Organized, efficient. In fact' – he narrowed his eyes – 'a bit obsessive, if you know what I mean. The details she wanted to pin down – like what sort of guests I'd be bringing to this festival, what sort of clothes they'd be wearing . . . *Nothing* was left to chance. Of course, she was a really classy dresser herself. Always looked great. *Great.*' He gazed past me while he pulled more thoughts out of the air. 'Beyond that . . . ambitious, definitely. And I don't mean that in a bad way. Nothing wrong with a bit of ambition.' He raised his eyebrows to show that ambition certainly hadn't done him any harm. 'Wanted things from life. Knew where she was going. Very . . .' He considered the word. '. . . shrewd. Yes, and strong. Used to getting her own way, you know? Used to getting what she wanted.' He added under his breath, 'Though she didn't *always* pull it off, so they say.'

'No?'

He waved the comment away. 'Just something I heard. From the old days.'

'Tell me.'

'Listen, this was years and years ago. A mate of mine, he told me Grace had a big thing for him then. In fact, no reason not to tell you – it was Dan Elliott, the actor.' I remembered Veronica telling me about him, how he'd been in love with Grace. 'They had a big bust-up. He ditched her. Dan's a bit of a shit that way, a real lady-killer until the going gets serious, then he's off like a shot – and Grace, she cut up rough, according to him. Gave him a hell of a time, he says. A real virago. Pursued him, threatened him, wouldn't let go. Tried the overdose trick – the lot.'

'A serious overdose?'

'*No*,' he scoffed emphatically. 'Just a few pills to get Dan to her bedside. You know the sort of thing. Anyway, then Grace went off and married Will on the rebound. Well, that's Dan's story anyway. A big relief for him. Though he says he met her again not so long ago and she was fine about it. No bad feelings. But that's Grace. Get on with life, put on a show. Yeah,' he went on reminiscently, 'Grace had her share of knocks all right, just like the rest of us. But she was a battler. A real goer. No quarter asked, none given.' He gave a grin of approval. 'I have to say I thought she was one hell of a girl!'

'You got on?'

'Oh, *what*!' he exclaimed. 'You bet. House on fire. We understood each other. We spoke the same language, you might say. She didn't have to pretend with me, didn't have to pretend she was anything but what she was. I knew what she was about, and I admired her for it.' The curiosity must have shown in my face because he cast me a sharp glance. 'And the answer to the next question is *no*, there was nothing between us. She was a very lovely lady, but it wouldn't have been right. I would've felt I was taking advantage.'

I tried to keep the amazement out of my face. 'Advantage?'

'She wasn't happy, was she? A bit desperate, really. And ladies don't know what they want when they're in a state, do they? You can't just wade in, you get a whole heap of problems. She wanted a bloke with all the trimmings – commitment, future, joint account. I thought it best to keep clear.'

Struggling to come to terms with this vision of Barry as the generous-spirited Lothario, the charmer who felt bound to fend off women to protect them from themselves, I mumbled, 'I didn't realize. I thought . . . But you said she was so confident, so together.'

He gave me an old-fashioned look, as if he suspected me of playing the innocent. 'The marriage was in trouble, though, wasn't it?'

'Well . . . all marriages have problems.'

'But she was having one hell of a time.'

Suddenly I began to get the picture. 'Was she now?'

'Our Will was a bit of a nightmare, wasn't he?' He waved his glass to encompass a whole host of problems. 'Money. Other women.'

'That's what Grace told you?'

He caught my drift instantly. 'You think it wasn't like that?'

'I think she might have enlarged on the truth when it suited her.'

Unexpectedly, the thought seemed to amuse him. 'I wouldn't have put it past her. That was half the fun with her, the games she played. But having said that, everyone knew Will was up against it financially and that Grace had all the money. It was common knowledge.'

'Really?'

'You're looking doubtful again.'

'Because as far as I can gather Grace didn't have that much money. And if she contributed anything financially to the marriage, it was probably a long time ago.'

Barry looked away thoughtfully before draining his champagne. 'If she lied, she was a bloody good liar.' There was admiration in his tone.

'But *you* – you didn't make a mistake about seeing her that evening, driving down to the marsh?'

'No.'

'Were you far away?'

'No. Just a few yards. I was going out, stopped at the gates, saw this car coming like hell. Glimpsed her face as she went by. It was her all right. Recognized the car too. No mistake.'

'Why did you wait before going to the police?'

'I was in Hong Kong and LA. Left that Friday night. Didn't know Grace was missing till I got back.'

When I didn't speak, he looked away towards the window and chuckled quietly to himself. 'Interesting about the money. She looked so classy, you'd think she had it coming out of her ears.'

'She said she was rich?'

'Yeah.' And he smiled again in admiration.

'What else did she tell you?'

'What, that mightn't have been true?' He raised a palm, which suggested everything and anything. Then, as another thought came to him, he grew very serious. 'There was one thing. She dropped a big hint that Will had roughed her up a bit.'

I stared at him, aghast. 'Have you mentioned this to the police?'

He pulled a face. 'Thought it was the right thing to do.'

I finished my drink hurriedly and Barry saw me to the door.

'Just for the record,' he said, his hand on the latch, 'I think she'd got a bloke lined up somewhere.'

'Why d'you say that?'

'Call it instinct.' He turned his lazy, roué's gaze on me. 'A bloke like me, I can always tell. Women give out signals, you know. Whether they mean to or not. To begin with, back last summer, Grace was on the hunt. Couldn't miss it, the way she eyed me, the way she eyed other men. She had wicked eyes, you know. Innocent but sort of wicked. Determined, too. She wanted *out* from her marriage, I could see that, clear as day. Then later in the summer she got another look in her eye, a sort of I'm-in-the-frame look, a sort of I've-found-the-guy look. You know?'

I pretended I did.

'Then . . . it must have been September, when we had this meeting at my office, her mobile rang all of a sudden. Some arrangement for meeting up later.' His eyes took on a foxy glint. 'But she definitely wasn't talking to a girlfriend, you know what I mean?'

There was an accident at the beginning of the M11 and a ten-mile jam. By the time I reached Deepwell it was eleven thirty, though it might have been far later, the village was so dark and so still. Marsh House looked as though it had been locked up for the night. There were no outside lights and nothing showing in the downstairs windows, just the glimmer of a light upstairs.

The front door was locked but, feeling my way round to the side of the house, I found the kitchen door open. Turning on a light, I looked for a note and found none. In the hall I called out softly and heard deep silence.

I went into the drawing room and touched the switch. Grace's world of lemon and blue silk sprang coldly into life. Sitting at her desk, I began to search for the one thing that I must have missed.

There was nothing on the bank statements. Mobile phones had to be paid for by direct debit, strictly monthly, yet the only direct debits were for interest payments and insurance premiums. I went through the cheque stubs, just to be sure, though I knew that none of the phone companies permitted payment by cheque. I found Grace had made only one regular monthly payment without an identifiable recipient marked on the stub. Every month since the previous July Grace had paid between £29.38 and £36 to 'SP'. On no fewer than five occasions the amount had been for exactly £29.38, which – I allowed myself a small measure of hope – suggested a fixed-time tariff she hadn't, in those particular months, exceeded.

But 'SP': the initials matched no mobile phone company I knew of. I could phone each company in turn, but if the account wasn't in Grace's name it would be a hopeless task. I looked back through the stubs once more and noticed that the entry on the July stub hadn't been quite the same as the others. The payment had been made not to 'SP', but to 'S–P'. I went back further, to the June stubs, and found a payment for £58.76, which – I calculated it quickly – was exactly double the minimum monthly payment she had paid subsequently. The payee had been entered on the stub as: 'Stephen M.'. I chased back through my memory, but I was fairly sure that only one Stephen M. had ever been mentioned in relation to Grace: the accountant-cum-treasurer of the music festival, Stephen Makim. Making further connections, I translated the subsequent S–P as 'Stephen – phone'.

Back in the kitchen, I flicked through the local directory and found Stephen Makim's number, with an address in Fakenham. As I noted it down, I heard a faint bump somewhere in the house. In the quiet of the night, it sounded like something falling. Closing the address book, I went quietly into the hall and stood on the wide flagstones, listening hard, hearing nothing.

Eventually I went back to the drawing room and, putting the cheque stubs away, closed the desk and turned off the lights. I paused again in the hall, my senses reaching out into the house. Then I caught it: the faint but unmistakable rhythm of a man breathing in sleep, dragging heavily on air, almost but not quite snoring.

He was stretched out on the sofa in the unlit sitting room, and I couldn't help thinking that I seemed destined to know men who had difficulty in making their way to bed at night.

'Will?' He lay on his side, his head cradled on the bend of one arm. He looked beautiful in sleep, the line of his eyebrows, the curve of his mouth, the frame of dark hair. I crouched beside him and, in the shadowy light from the hall, watched him silently, like a lover in the night.

I watched him for a long time before I called his name again.

He stirred and mumbled. He opened a slit of one eye and peered at me uncertainly.

'It's Ali,' I said.

'Ali.' He laughed softly. '*Ali.*' Eyes closed again, he reached an arm out to me and, sliding a hand round the back of my head, drew me towards him. I dropped forward onto my knees, I let myself be conveyed, I told myself there would be no harm. As my cheek came up against his, as his arm fell to my shoulders and pulled me tight against him, he murmured dreamily, 'Ali, I was *waiting* for you. Waiting for *ever.*'

'I'm here now.'

'Waiting . . . Had some wine for you. But . . .' He gave a groan of mock rebuke. 'Drank it all.'

'Yes.' I had smelt it on his breath, I knew he'd had too much.

'Good wine, though. Thought I'd better drink it before the bloody *dragon* got it.'

His cheek was warm against mine. I drew in the smell of his skin, the faint blend of soap or spice and some elusive indeterminate masculine scent. 'The dragon?'

He growled, '*Veronica.* Bad, sad, *mad* Veronica. Sent me a nasty letter.'

'In what way nasty?'

'Says bad things. Says I'm trying to steal Grace's money.'

'I'll look into it in the morning. I'll deal with it.'

His hand moved slowly over my back, stroking it in what might have been a caress or a search for reassurance. 'She's mad *and* bad,' he mumbled. 'How can anyone be mad *and* bad?'

'Forget about it now. Don't think about it.'

He sighed, agreeing or dozing off.

'Ali?' he whispered from his half sleep.

'Yes?'

He sighed again, but more contentedly. 'Such a . . . strange . . . thing.'

'What is?'

'*You.*'

'In what way?'

'Here . . . Back here . . . with us.'

He squeezed me closer, he moved his cheek affectionately against mine. 'Back here . . . with us.' His mouth brushed against my ear.

The moment for unreality had passed. I pulled away.

He opened both eyes blearily and squinted at me. 'Where are you going? Don't go.'

I sat back on my heels, I removed his arm gently from my shoulders. 'You should go to bed,' I said.

'Don't go,' he pleaded. 'Please don't go.'

'I'll stay in the house tonight. I'll be here.'

'Promise?'

'Promise.'

'Such nightmares, Ali.'

'No nightmares tonight.'

He reached for my hand and, tucking it close against his chest, would have fallen asleep again, but, needing no instruction on how to get a man to go to bed against his wishes, I soon had him on his feet and on his way towards the stairs.

He muttered morosely, 'Was thinking, Ali . . . We waste it all. *Waste* it.'

'What?'

He climbed two stairs before halting. '*Time. Life.* Everything.'

'Nothing's ever wasted.'

'Her life . . . Mine . . . What was it all *for*?'

'Big questions, Will.'

'Big answers.' Then: 'No answers.'

I urged him on to the first landing. 'Tell me,' I said, striking a casual note, 'did you ever find a mobile belonging to Grace?'

He paused with a foot on the next tread, he surveyed me with glassy eyes. 'Mobile? She didn't have a mobile.'

'Couldn't she have had the use of one, though?'

'No, no.' He waved a jerky uncoordinated arm. 'She didn't have a mobile. No, no.'

We started up the last flight only for him to slow up again. An almost comical expression of puzzlement came over his face. 'Why d'you think she had a *mobile*, for heaven's sake?'

'Someone said they'd seen her with one.'

His hand flipped through the air. 'Never had a mobile.'

In the bedroom, I persuaded him to take a few clothes off. As he rolled into bed, he murmured, 'I'm drunk, Ali. Drunk . . .'

'Nothing to be done about it now.'

'But I hate drinking too much. *Hate* it. Wouldn't do it if . . . No good at being *alone*. After Charlie's in bed, can't stand it, Ali. Being alone.'

My heart tightened, I said briskly, 'Can't Maggie move in for a while?'

'Keep seeing her . . . This dream. Keep seeing her. All that water . . . So cold, so *cold* . . .'

'Perhaps you and Charlie should go and stay with friends for a while.'

'Stay. Don' wanna stay . . .' His eyelids had given up the battle. 'Julian's a pompous prat . . .'

'Julian?'

He grunted, 'Anne . . . keeps asking us to go . . . stay as long as we like.'

I wasn't sure which was more disturbing, the thought of him staying in my old home, or sleeping under the same roof as Anne Hampton. 'I was thinking of further away. Another part of the country.'

'Can't ask Frank to keep doing the farm . . . Can't . . .' He yawned, he lost track, he dug his head deeper into the pillow. 'So good, Ali.' His voice drifted gently. 'So good . . . Don't go . . .'

'I won't go.'

I looked around the room, at the dressing table littered with perfumes and cosmetics, at the banks of wardrobes, at the long silk scarves hanging from the cheval mirror. The bed itself was dominated by a majestic awning of flowered pink and green chintz that rose from the matching headboard in pencilled pleats to a rail suspended above the foot of the bed, from where it hung in a deep pelmet.

When I looked at Will again he was asleep.

I was on my way down the stairs when the phone rang, very shrill in the stillness. I ran quickly into the hall and picked it up.

The silence was long and deep.

'Hello?' I repeated several times.

A click as the person rang off. I looked at the time: well past midnight.

I dialled 1471. The disembodied voice informed me of the time of the call and the number which had called me. I stabbed my finger on the rest, and dialled 1471 again, but there was no mistake: the call had come from Wickham Lodge.

Chapter Ten

———•———

THE HOUSE stood in a neat cul-de-sac on the outskirts of
Fakenham, one of six or seven identical mock-Georgian homes
with columned porticoes and sash windows and disciplined
lawns edged with daffodils. Three of the homes had BMWs
parked on the garage aprons. Stephen Makim's had a Lexus.

He looked much as I'd imagined from his voice, an energetic
man of about forty-five, as neat and trim as his house, wearing
large spectacles, a salesman's grey suit with a crisp white shirt
and sports club tie.

'I did tell the police,' he said as he showed me into a living
room with a raspberry velveteen three-piece suite and matching
curtains. 'I said Grace had been using a Cellnet phone for her
work. I did tell them.'

There were sounds of breakfasting from the back of the
house, young voices arguing and being urged to hurry up. We
sat opposite each other on identical armchairs.

'The phone was registered to you, though?'

'Oh, yes, it was *my* phone, but I hardly used it any more,
you see. I'm based at head office now, don't travel like I used
to, and Grace needed it for the festival, so she took it over for
the duration, so to speak. Insisted on paying for the phone
itself, and wouldn't charge for any of the calls. I kept trying to
tell her she could get the festival calls reimbursed from sponsorship funds, but she said it was too much bother to separate out
the personal calls from the festival calls. Life was too short, she
said.' He blinked rapidly, and said in a voice muffled with

emotion, 'I did try to persuade her, but she insisted on paying for the lot. She said maybe she'd charge the calls around the time of the festival itself, when she'd be using the phone a lot. She said then it would make sense.' He blinked some more, and rearranged his mouth.

'She didn't have a phone of her own, then?'

'Oh, no. That was the whole point. She didn't want one. After the festival she said she wouldn't have any use for one. And they're not cheap, you know,' he informed me gravely, 'not cheap at all.'

'Would you have any of the bills I could look at?'

'The statements, you mean? Well, no. You see I forwarded them unopened to Grace. No point in my checking them myself, no point at all. I wouldn't have known if they were correct, would I?' The thought of not being correct struck deep at his accountant's soul. 'No – Grace said not to bother with them. Just forward them to me, she said. She'd check them herself.'

'I need to get a copy of the last statement, Mr Makim. Could you call Cellnet and ask them to fax you a copy of the last statement as a matter of urgency?'

'I don't have a fax here. But I suppose . . . if they'd agree to send it to the office. But what reason should I give them, do you think? Should I tell them the full story?'

'Perhaps not. Just say it's urgent. Offer to pay if necessary.'

'*Urgent*, yes . . .' He clasped his neat white hands, he looked a little uncertain. 'And the phone itself . . . what shall I say? Shall I say it's lost?'

'It *is* lost, I'm afraid. So far, anyway.'

'I could report it missing, then, couldn't I? I could say that's why I needed the statement.' He looked happier with this solution, a man for whom veracity was everything. 'But I don't quite understand why the police haven't followed this up. They never even asked for the number, you know. They never asked for any details at all.'

'They'll probably get round to it in time.' Far more likely

they had overlooked it, but I didn't mention that in case Stephen Makim should take it on himself to remind them.

He asked politely, 'How's the family coping?'

'Well . . . you can imagine.'

'And Charlie? Poor lad. He's at school with our son, you know.'

'I didn't know.'

'Smashing chap. Good with his hands, artistic. He's been here for tea once or twice.'

'A happy boy?'

The question caused him a moment's pause. 'Well . . . you'd have to ask my wife. A bit quiet, I'd say. Shy with strangers. But then they often are at that age, aren't they?'

As if to contradict him, a child shouted furiously in the hall. He sighed ruefully, 'Well, *some* are.'

A woman's voice issued a reprimand, feet thundered up the stairs.

With a start, Stephen Makim sprang to his feet. 'I'll need to move my car. I'm usually gone by now.' He moved purposefully towards the door where he cocked an ear towards the movements upstairs. Relaxing a little, he turned back. 'She was amazing with Charlie, you know,' he offered solemnly. 'He's dyslexic, quite badly so. Did you know? But she was so patient with him, read to him for hours, encouraged him no end. She'd got him into this special school. World famous, apparently, with an enormous waiting list. Places like gold dust. But Grace, she fought tooth and nail to get him accepted, wouldn't take no for an answer—' His emotions threatened him again, he swallowed rapidly. 'She was a fine woman.'

I followed him to the front door, we looked out over the daffodils at a departing BMW.

I said, 'I hadn't realized Charlie had got a place.'

'Oh, yes, in the autumn. It was all set. Charlie was thrilled.'

*

I took the long way back, along narrow lanes with no markings and blind bends. A morning mist lay low over the land in a damp haze. Cresting the last rise, the ground sloped away in a sweep of undulating fields towards the marshlands, lying in thin ribbons under the margin of the sea. A short distance to the east, I could see the corner of Upper Farm, with fields of cereal and beet and, tucked into the corner of a turnip field, two large barns set at right angles to each other with a silage store on the third side, and beyond them, a railed paddock with a small stable block. A short track led to the barns, but if Will was there then the Range Rover was out of view.

The lane descended between tall hedgerows that offered no further view of the barns until, rounding a bend, their angular roofs rose above the hedges, some twenty yards ahead. The entrance appeared suddenly, a sharp turning through an open gate.

The track was compressed shale, smooth and soundless. I saw the Range Rover almost immediately, parked on the wide concrete apron in the angle of the barns. I accelerated a little, only to slow again.

There was another car, parked just inside the open doors of the larger barn. I slowed further, I looked again, feeling disorientated. It was a little blue Golf. Jilly's. I corrected myself: a car *like* Jilly's.

I stopped and parked beside the silage store. Walking across the apron, the lowing of the cattle was raucous, magnified by the metal walls of the barn. The interior appeared very dark until, reaching the doors, pausing by the Golf, I looked down the aisle and in the cones of light from the roof panels saw clearly the cattle in their pens, the trolley with its load of feed, and at the far end, Will leaning back against a railing, arms folded, in conversation with a woman who was unmistakably Jilly.

I stood motionless, held in the trance of an unwitting observer. I watched as Will dropped his chin onto his chest and spoke, as Jilly listened and, gliding closer, raised a hand and rested it on his shoulder. A solicitous hand? An affectionate hand? A hand that touched a shoulder.

She turned her face a little towards me, and still I couldn't move, as though by staring long enough the scene might yet turn out to be a trick of the imagination.

Jilly bent her head forward. From where I was standing, their heads could have been touching. Her hand still lay on his shoulder, heavy with meaning. I watched with a blend of curiosity and desperate foreboding, as one watches two friends enacting a disturbing event one is powerless to prevent.

Above the braying and shuffling of the cattle, a hoof kicked against metal with a sudden clatter. I drew back furtively, I turned away and walked quickly to my car. I drove down the track and into the lane, the worm of suspicion twisting in my stomach.

The press crows had settled around Marsh House again. One was sitting inside his car, another lounging against the car door chatting through the open window. I hadn't seen them before but I recognized the breed all right, the rapacious eyes, the sly gestures, the smooth advance like two crabs sidling up a slope.

'Mrs O'Neill?' the first called – they always knew one's name. 'Wondered if Mr Dearden was thinking of a new media appeal . . .

'. . . a piece about bereavement, how he's coping . . .'

'. . . how he feels about her killer . . .'

Killer. They almost had me there; the temptation to ask what they knew was very strong. 'Killer' suggested that the police had decided on murder, that the investigation was shifting into a different gear. The press were often the most reliable source of this kind of news; just as they were experts at using half-truths and distortions to inveigle people into talking when it wasn't in their interests to do so.

As I closed the gate behind me and started up the path, their tone became more strident. 'Is it true that Mrs Dearden was considering divorce?'

'Is it true that Mrs Dearden's life was heavily insured?'

'No comment at all,' I threw back, wondering what had brought them here so conveniently close to Ramsey's arrival, thinking darkly of a tip-off.

The kitchen door was as I had left it at seven: latched against intruders. Putting my face to the window I saw Charlie at the table eating breakfast, and rapped softly on the glass.

His head came up a little, he stopped eating, but didn't look round.

I called, 'It's me, Charlie. Could you let me in?'

With infinite slowness he turned his head, only to pause in profile, as though his mind were on something else altogether. I tapped on the glass again. Seeming to hear at last, he turned towards me, though when his eyes found their way slowly to my face there was no flicker of recognition.

'Charlie?' I called through the glass.

Eyes down, he rose slowly to his feet and came towards the door. I stationed myself in front of it, ready for the sound of the lock, but there was nothing. With my mouth close to the jamb, choosing my most reassuring tone, I called again.

The catch sprang back at last.

'Thank you, Charlie.'

As I went in he was already heading back to the table where he resumed his breakfast, spooning cereal mechanically into his mouth.

I paused close by, searching for something to say. 'Dad's up at the barn, is he?'

He didn't reply, and I was acutely aware of being an unwanted visitor in his house, a stranger who must seem to bring nothing but bad news. Since his mother's body had been found I had been careful to keep my distance from Charlie, careful not to impose. In the last five or six days I probably hadn't exchanged more than a couple of words with him.

I said rather too brightly, 'You don't mind if I have a coffee while I'm waiting?'

His expression had the quality of registering little, of feeling even less, as though he were existing in a dream.

I made myself a strong coffee and, placing myself carefully at the other end of the table, worked on my notes for the day.

Charlie finished his cereal and stared at the empty dish. After a time he picked up the carton of fruit juice and poured it into his glass. His movements were slow, his eyes unfocused. Again, I had the sense of a trance-like state. Over the years I'd seen people in trauma, I'd seen kids in shock, but this was different, more elusive. A realization floated just out of reach, tantalizing, unformed, but important in some way I couldn't quite identify.

A lock turned, a door opened at the front of the house. Going into the hall, I found Maggie closing the front door with a firm thud.

She rolled her eyes furiously and jerked her head towards the reporters. 'Those people! I have told them they had no right to be here! I have told them to leave!'

'They're not breaking any law, unfortunately.'

'But how dare they say these things to *me*! They ask me about Grace wanting a divorce, about big life insurance! How dare they!'

'Just trying their luck, I'm afraid.'

She was more upset than she'd first appeared. Her mouth trembled, her eyelids fluttered in distress. 'But how do they *know* these things, Alex? Tell me.'

'They don't know.'

'But they *do*! They *do*!' Then, seeming to grasp what I was saying, she retreated with an odd glance. 'You're right. Of course. Yes ... They don't know ...' The glance again, the pulling up short, as though she'd remembered something perfectly obvious. With a thin nervous smile she lifted a bird-like wrist to her face and looked at her watch. 'What time are the police coming – nine thirty?'

'Ten.'

'Well, Charlie and I must be off. We're going to Norwich for the day. A hamburger, you know. Ice cream. A film!' Caught up in a whirlwind of her own creation, she made for the kitchen.

'Maggie?'

She paused unwillingly.

I said in a voice that wouldn't carry, 'Charlie seems rather . . . *low* this morning.'

Her eyes sparked briefly. 'Why do you say this? Did he say something?'

'No, no. Just the way he looks.' I chose a neutral word. 'Exhausted.'

'Ah! Don't tell me,' she agreed lavishly. 'He has bad dreams, poor baby. He is so frightened in the night. And *Will*! He doesn't hear him, he doesn't get up! I know he doesn't!'

'Why don't you move in, Maggie? Why don't you take care of them for a while?'

She said casually, 'Because Will does not want me here.'

I frowned my disbelief. 'But why on earth not?'

'He's angry with me.' She gave a shrug, as if these trials, though unfathomable, were to be endured stoically.

'But this is *mad*, Maggie. Can't you sort it out?'

She made a gesture suggesting that, if left to her, the whole business would be instantly forgotten, before swinging resolutely away and hurrying into the kitchen.

Following, I found her stooped over Charlie, whispering in his ear. Charlie was listening with desperate attention, struggling to emerge from whatever constrained him. Watching him closely, I saw again the clouded gaze, the dreaminess, the disconnection from the world. The realization, when it finally came to me, was so striking and so obvious that I couldn't think why I hadn't thought of it before. Charlie was under sedation.

I remembered that Julian Hampton had come to the house several times in the hours and days immediately after Grace had been found. He could easily have prescribed something then, though I would have thought sedation rather a drastic remedy for a child.

I looked at him again, I wondered if I was wrong; and all my instincts told me I wasn't.

After Maggie had led Charlie to her car and driven away, I watched the pressmen at the gate with growing unease. Pressmen did not usually wait around unless they were expecting what they liked to call 'developments'.

When at nine fifty-two more cars drew up and disgorged heavily equipped photographers, my fears finally raced away with me. I snatched up the phone and dialled Will's mobile, hoping against hope that he would have it with him and would answer, that he wasn't even now approaching the house.

He answered at the fifth ring.

'Where are you?'

'At the barn,' he answered flatly. 'Just packing up.'

'Stay there. Don't move till I tell you.'

'What's happened? What's wrong?'

'Trust me. Just do as I say.'

'Charlie—?' he asked in sudden agitation.

'Gone with Maggie. No, it's – I just don't want you around, that's all.'

'But if it's the police, I'd rather get it over with.'

'*Not now*, Will. Trust me.'

'But I know why they've come, Ali.'

'Never mind that—'

'They know I was there on the Gun, they know Grace went to stop me—'

'We'll talk about this later,' I snapped fiercely.

'But—'

'*Don't argue with me.*'

A pause, and he yielded with a harsh sigh. 'I'll stay here, then, shall I?'

'Until I call. Until I find you.'

Ramsey arrived on time at ten. There were four of them in two cars: another indication of intent.

'Urgent business?' Ramsey repeated with quiet fury when I told him Will wasn't available. 'Business he wasn't aware of yesterday?'

I said, 'That's right.'

Ramsey regarded me with the cold eye of scepticism. At his shoulder, Wilson and Barbara Smith stood impassively,

'And you can't say where he's gone?' Ramsey asked again.

'No.'

'Meaning – do I understand correctly – that you don't *know* where he's gone?'

'I'm not actually sure, no.' Inside the barn, outside the barn, in the paddock.

The officers were standing just inside the hall. I wasn't going to ask them to sit down.

'And you don't know how long this urgent business is going to take?'

'No.'

He asked sourly, 'Are we talking hours here, do you think? Or days?'

'Oh, hours, I'm sure.'

In the grey light from the fanlight Ramsey's skin had the pasty malleable look that comes from a diet of junk food and sweet drinks, but now his cheeks were livid with silent anger.

'The boy's at home, is he?' Ramsey cast around as if to catch sight of him.

I had a good idea of why he was asking, and I didn't care for the implication. 'I'm sorry?' I asked ingenuously. 'I don't quite see what that has to do with this.'

Ramsey didn't mind putting it more bluntly. 'Did Mr Dearden take his son with him?'

'As a matter of fact Charlie's spending the day with his grandmother.'

Ramsey pulled down the corners of his little mouth. 'It's

unfortunate that Mr Dearden is not available.' He made a gesture, supposedly of regret but actually of annoyance. 'We would have preferred to inform him of the latest developments ourselves rather than have him hear about it elsewhere.'

I asked calmly, 'And what *are* the latest developments?'

Ramsey shifted his considerable bulk more evenly onto both feet and pulled in his chin. 'It is my duty to inform you that we are now treating the death of Mrs Grace Dearden as murder, and that we have stepped up the investigation accordingly.'

So it was true. I dropped my head to hide my disappointment, a disappointment made more acute by having allowed myself to believe that things might not get this far. When I looked up again it was to show the appropriate dismay. 'This is terrible news,' I said.

'Terrible indeed,' Ramsey agreed pedantically.

Professionally, I was still regaining my breath. 'So what's happened, Inspector? What's brought you to this conclusion?'

'I cannot reveal that at the present time.'

'But in general terms what are we talking about? The forensic results? Or new information of some sort?'

He gave me an obdurate look. I was well aware of his problem. I was representing the family; but I was also representing Will. As the family's solicitor, I had the right to be kept informed of progress on the case, but as Will's lawyer I was another animal altogether, a person to be kept as much as possible in the dark. It was a dilemma, but not one I was going to help him with.

'Not the forensic results alone,' he ventured.

'You're saying there *is* something in the forensic tests, then?' When he didn't reply, I pressed on, 'And something else besides?'

'New information,' he admitted at last.

'A witness?'

'It would not be appropriate for me to say.'

'Do you have a suspect?'

He managed to hold his expression. 'That is unanswerable at the present time.'

'Well . . . is an arrest imminent?'

He gave himself away then: I caught the glint of anticipation in his eye. 'I can make no comment on the progress of the case.'

I pushed harder. 'Can I take it, then, that there's no likelihood of an arrest at the moment?'

His knowing look, his hostile silence were a confirmation: he had come to arrest Will on suspicion. Everything had pointed to it: the press hanging around the gate, the two police cars, his anger at being thwarted.

I turned up my hands in appeal. 'So, what shall I tell the family?'

Ramsey indicated Barbara Smith. 'DC Smith will be available to the family for liaison and support virtually on a round-the-clock basis for as long as necessary. At the same time she will be able to keep them informed of developments.'

'I'll let them know.'

'DC Smith will be happy to wait until they return.'

I had no doubt she would. 'They won't be back for some time.'

'She can wait outside in the car.'

'With the press at the gate? Is that wise?' I remarked innocently. 'They might get the wrong idea.'

Ramsey's gaze did not falter.

I said with great puzzlement, 'Strange, them coming back today. Strange that they should turn up just now. Almost as if they knew . . .'

He studiously ignored the innuendo. 'So, when do you suppose Mr Dearden will be available?'

'I can bring Mr Dearden to the station later today.'

We understood each other perfectly then: I was going to bring Will in without fuss and Ramsey was to be denied his dramatic publicity coup.

'Could you give me a time?'

'Not at present.'

Ramsey arranged his face into a poor imitation of appreciation. 'As soon as you can, then. I'd be grateful for as much notice as possible.'

Will did not answer his phone, and when I tried again a couple of minutes later the mobile was out of range or switched off.

I left the house with my briefcase and a stack of documents, as though for an appointment. DC Smith had settled into her unmarked car near the gate, prepared for a long day. A last photographer loaded his gear into a four-wheel drive before sweeping off across the hard. I drove away quietly, taking the east lane, eyes on the rear-view mirror, watching not for Ramsey's people, who were accustomed to waiting games, but for the press, for whom a snatched photograph of a frowning suspect was worth a hundred words. Reaching the main road, I went in the opposite direction to Upper Farm, towards Burnham Market, and did not turn off until I was sure the road behind was empty. The little side lane wound between tall hedgerows, no one could follow unseen, but I still pulled into a gateway after half a mile and listened for other furtive engines. Starting off again, I drove much faster with a sense of being pursued by other more urgent problems, like time.

Completing a long southerly loop, I approached the barns of Upper Farm from the same direction as before, and almost missed the entrance again. Coming onto the apron, I saw no sign of the Range Rover. Casting about in slight panic, I parked hastily and sounded a short rhythm on the horn.

The hail came from some way off, blanketed by buildings, and it wasn't until I rounded the corner of the large barn that I spotted Will by the stables, unloading bales from the Range Rover.

As I crossed the paddock towards him, he called out: 'That was quick.'

'Ramsey didn't stay long.'

Working with energy, Will lifted a straw bale and chucked it into a loosebox. 'So, what was the panic?'

'The press. They were hanging around, looking for a story.'

He shot me a narrow stare, scenting evasions.

'The police were going to ask you to go to Norwich with them. I didn't want you photographed in the back of a police car.'

'Like a suspect, you mean?'

I didn't deny it, and in that moment his face stiffened, he seemed to understand what was coming.

I announced, 'The police have decided to treat Grace's death as murder.' I gave him a moment to absorb this before delivering the rest of the bad news. 'And I can't be absolutely certain, but I think they're going to arrest you, as a formality.'

'A *formality*?'

'So that they can question you under caution, so that anything you might say is admissible as evidence. It's a way of covering themselves. It doesn't necessarily mean they have any hard evidence against you, it doesn't necessarily mean that they're going to charge you with anything, or keep you in custody.'

A succession of expressions passed across his face, shadows of alarm and dread and grim acceptance.

I said, 'I've told Ramsey we'll come and see him in Norwich later today.'

Will threw the last bale into a loosebox and shut the door.

Somewhere close by an animal snorted softly, there was the rustle of bedding, and a handsome bay pushed his white-flashed nose over the half-door of the adjacent box.

'Yours?' I asked.

'Grace's. Her *hunter*.'

'I didn't know she hunted.'

'She didn't,' he said rapidly. 'She and the horse couldn't agree on how to take the fences. I was going to sell him last year, but Grace started to get enthusiastic again. Her enthusiasm generally peaked around the time of the hunt balls.' He screwed up his face in an expression of self-disgust. 'I'm sounding bitter,' he stated solemnly. 'I'm sounding mean-spirited. And she doesn't deserve that. Whatever else she was, she wasn't . . . *bad.*' He struck his palm softly against the door as if to confirm this in his own mind.

'So . . .' He gave a desolate, explosive laugh. 'They're going to arrest me. Presumably they don't arrest people for nothing.'

'It could be the smallest scrap of circumstantial evidence.'

He shook his head firmly, suspecting otherwise. Slamming the tailgate shut, he leant back against the vehicle with a force that made it rock, and crossed his arms fiercely. 'You took on a bad bet with me, Ali.' His eyes gleamed with some fiery emotion I couldn't read.

'No one's a bad bet to me.'

'No?' he cried. 'Well, you could just change your mind, you could just regret taking me on!'

'I don't think so.'

'They're going to say I lied, Ali. They're going to say I lied about all sorts of things.'

'But they're always going to—'

He thrust out a staying hand, he raced on, 'No, no, they're going to be *right*, you see. I mean, about *some* of it. The thing is, I *have* lied to them, Ali. Oh, not about everything – I mean, I didn't kill Grace. Minor point!' He gave the strange bleak laugh again, his voice rose another notch. 'Small unimportant detail! But they're not going to be too concerned about that, are they? One lie's much like another, really, if you think about it . . .' He grimaced briefly. 'No, I've lied, and they know it. And I won't be able to deny it.'

'You have the right to deny anything,' I interrupted more harshly than I'd intended. 'Or to stay silent. Don't even *think* of admitting anything yet! We need to go through it first, step by step. For heaven's sake, promise me you won't even *think* of saying anything yet!'

Chastened by my outburst, he yielded a little, he gave the suggestion of a nod.

'Right,' I said more coolly. 'Tell me how they might challenge your story. Tell me what you think they might know.'

'What I *know* they know.'

I conceded briskly, 'Okay.'

'What I *know* they know is that Grace heard what I was planning to do and rushed out to try and stop me.' He explained heavily, 'She'd found out that I was going to flood the Gun, she went to find me and stop me.'

'But you weren't going to flood the Gun.'

'*Ah* . . . .' He made a contrite face, and a chill tightened around my heart.

'What are you saying?' I asked incredulously. 'That you *wanted* to flood the Gun?'

'Yes.'

'But . . . *why*?'

He attempted a flippant gesture, a sharp jerk of one shoulder. 'To cover it with salt! To ruin it!'

'To ruin it,' I echoed helplessly. Then, trying to make sense of this: 'Because you didn't want . . .' The thought clarified: 'Because of *Edward*? You didn't want Edward to have the Gun?'

'Something like that.' He spoke crisply in a tone intended to deter further comment.

I took a long breath. 'So . . . have I got this right? You were aiming to flood the marsh . . . Grace found out . . . Grace came and tried to stop you?'

'Grace got it wrong. She thought I was already there, opening the sluices, and when she didn't find me she went off again. Disappeared.'

'Hang on, hang on . . .' He had left out far too much, and I turned him back. 'How did she *know* you were intending to flood the marsh?'

A silence like a shadow. He looked away. 'A phone call.'

'The call from Maggie, you mean?'

'No, from me.'

I waited for him to explain.

'When I called from the car, I told her what I was going to do.'

'You spoke to her from the car? You didn't get the answerphone?'

'I spoke to her. I told her what I was planning. She went ballistic, of course. She didn't stop to listen, she didn't realize I was still in the car. She shot over to Reed Cottage.'

'But . . . according to Maggie the marsh was already flooding! Long before you got there!'

'Ah.' The penitent look again. 'The truth is . . .' He hesitated, looking doubtful as to the benefits of truth. 'Maggie was just trying to help. She thought it would keep things simpler if she said it was already flooding. An accident. The broken sluice. We . . . well, we sort of *decided* on it. Agreed that it was the best story.'

I wondered if the situation could get any worse, if there were any more disastrous revelations to come.

'So . . .' I searched desperately for firm ground. 'You told Grace that you were intending to flood the marsh . . . Grace thought you were doing it then and there. She rushed out.' I halted, I said almost to myself, 'Do we *know* that Grace rushed out?'

'Oh, yes.' Will dropped his head. 'You see . . .' He delivered the words with dark emphasis: '*Grace was not alone*. She had company at Marsh House. That was what Jilly came to tell me about earlier. You were here, weren't you? You saw her?'

I nodded briefly.

'Well, she came to tell me that Edward was there with Grace at Marsh House, that he'd dropped by to see her about the festival, to have *tea*. Knowing *I* wouldn't be there, of course. Knowing better than to risk seeing *me*!' He shivered with brief tension before hurrying on, as if to get the whole miserable story out in the open as quickly as possible. 'It seems that Edward was there when Grace took my call. She told him that I'd gone totally mad or words to that effect, said that I was hell-bent on destroying the marsh, that I'd opened the gates – some sort of stuff like that. And then she rushed out of the house and jumped into her car. Oh, and . . .' He waved a careless hand. 'According to *Edward*, he then had a fit of conscience. Thought he'd better make sure Grace was all right.' He commented in a scornful undertone: 'More worried about the Gun, if you ask me. More worried about seeing his precious investment flooded! *Anyway*,' he went on scathingly, 'according to him he drove over and heard a row. Thought he'd better keep out of it and retreated. Well, that's what Edward has gone and told the police. Something like that. He went yesterday, according to Jilly. Doubtless that's why they've leapt into action.' He flourished a hand to mark the end of the tale, and frowned into the distance.

My first reaction was amazement, my second – far more intense – was disbelief. 'This is *mad*, Will. It doesn't make sense! Why didn't Edward come forward before? Why's he waited all this time? No – it's crackers!'

'It was Jilly . . .' Stepping away from the Range Rover, he straightened up and thrust his hands in his pockets. 'Jilly talked him out of it.'

'But . . . why?'

He said, with soft irony, 'The goodness of her heart?'

Another connection that took me by surprise. 'Jilly . . .?'

But he offered no further information and I was left with a jumble of conflicting information. Desperate for understanding, I reached back to the beginning of the puzzle, to the first mystery, and asked again, 'The marsh . . . You really intended to *spoil* it?'

A definite hesitation. 'It seemed a good idea at the time.'

'But you weren't serious about it?'

'Oh, yes, totally serious.'

I tried to picture him flooding the marsh, but I couldn't see it, couldn't imagine his mood at the time. 'But . . . the Gun would be worthless if it was ruined.'

The hesitation again, another frown. 'Yes.'

'So what were you hoping to achieve?'

'I wasn't thinking too straight that night. I was angry at having to sell it. I just . . . went mad.'

Again, something about this image bothered me, I couldn't make it come to life. 'Okay . . . Just take me through what happened when you finally arrived at Reed Cottage.'

'What? Oh, then I opened the sluices.'

'Both of them?'

A pause. '*Yes.*' He spoke very deliberately, aware of the implications. '*Both* gates.'

'Then?'

He made a gesture, suggesting it should have been obvious. 'I left the marsh to flood.'

'How long for?'

'Oh, I don't know . . . an hour or so.'

'And what about Grace? Where was she?'

'No idea. She'd come to look for me, then disappeared again, driven off. I never saw her on the marsh. I had no idea she'd even been there.' A sound escaped him, an abrupt gasp, half laugh, half desperation. 'Not that anyone's going to believe *that*, are they?' He glanced at me, smiling grimly. 'Eh?'

Needing to hear the worst, I asked, 'What about this row that Edward heard? The raised voices?'

'It was Grace yelling at Maggie. Not having me to shout at, she shouted at Maggie instead.'

'So just to be sure I have this absolutely clear – you didn't see Grace at any time that afternoon or evening?'

'No.'

I took a long breath, I got my bearings again. 'So . . . what happened after you opened the gates? Where did you go? What did you do?'

He took his time, he had to think about it, and a part of

me stood back and saw him as Ramsey would see him, with a critical eye, and it seemed to me that this kind of uncertainty would count heavily against him, that he would need to get his story much straighter in his mind before facing the police.

'I walked,' he said at last. 'I walked for miles. I was angry, you see. Furious. With myself, with life, with the money problem, with having to sell the Gun. You name it. I walked out to the dunes and along the sea bank, around the other side of the Gun and back along the bottom path.'

'Where did you go then?'

'Reed Cottage.'

'What time did you get there?'

'Oh . . .' His brows sank deep over his eyes, he brushed the question aside. 'Not sure.'

'You must have some idea.'

He sighed, 'Eight?'

'And you didn't see Grace?'

'No.'

'You didn't see her car?'

'No.'

I had already asked it, but I had to ask again, 'And there was no row between you?'

'No.'

'And what about the sluices? When did you close them?'

'Shortly after I got back. When I realized how *stupid* the whole thing was.' He shook his head in disgust, and kept shaking it. 'When I realized I was cutting off my nose to spite my face. Ruining perfectly good land. Destroying any chance of selling it! Loathing the thought of selling it at all!' He lifted his handsome face to the sky. '*Stupid. Mad.*'

'And then?'

'Then?' He frowned as if the answer were self-evident. 'Then I had to wait for the tide so I could begin to drain it away.'

'You stayed at Maggie's?'

'Yes, yes,' he said dully. 'Drank too much wine, fell asleep on the sofa. Felt so *bad*, Ali. It was all such a bloody mess! Money ... crisis after crisis ... marriage ... Everything *looming*. I just wanted to bury my head in the sand – or a gas oven. There were times that night when I wasn't sure which was the most attractive.' He flashed me a rapid humourless smile, denying his words, but not so strongly that I didn't appreciate what he had gone through that night.

I looked out over the fields, towards a lone copse of beeches standing sentry duty on a distant hill, and the landscape seemed very bleak and very cold. 'So I'm Ramsey,' I said at last. 'I'm listening to all this, and so far I have the following ... You phoned Grace from the car to tell her that you were intending to flood the Gun Marsh, you arrived at the Gun at six twenty or six thirty, you went out to the sluices, you opened them. In the meantime, Grace had turned up, found you weren't there, had a row with Maggie and disappeared again. You never saw her. The moment Grace was discovered to be missing, you and Maggie concocted a story whereby the marsh flooded of its own accord and no one saw Grace at all, not even her car ...' I turned to him, I threw up my hands, I said in utter despair, 'This is nonsense, Will! Complete nonsense!'

'Why? I wish it were.'

'Well, you certainly mustn't admit to any of it.'

'Oh, but I have to.'

'But there's no reason to.'

'I'd rather get it out of the way.'

I paced off, I did a small circuit while I attempted to control my exasperation. Facing him again, I said very deliberately, 'This story will do you the most terrible damage, Will. This story' – I spelt out each word – '*will get you charged*!'

'But they know about the call, they know I was planning to open the sluices. Edward's told them.'

'Listen.' I put my face close to his, I fixed him with my sternest gaze. 'This story is *madness*. This story is going to put you in the wrong place at the wrong time, *without* an alibi, *with* a motive. This story,' I repeated urgently, 'will get you charged.'

His expression hardened, his jaw worked furiously.

'My advice,' I said, 'in fact, more than my advice – my firmest possible recommendation is to stick to what you said before, to add *nothing* to your original statement, to change *not a word*. If the police suggest you opened the sluices deliberately, simply point out that it wasn't in your interests to do so, quite the reverse in fact – it could only ruin the land just when you were about to sell it, just when you wanted the highest possible value for it. If they say Grace was coming over to stop you opening the sluices, simply point out that you weren't there, you were still in your car miles away and we have the mobile phone records to prove it. Offer no further comment. Offer no explanation for Edward's statement. Look puzzled – whatever you like.' Sensing his growing resistance, trying to pre-empt it, I argued, 'There's no come-back on not knowing, Will! There's no danger in saying nothing. The danger's in telling them things they don't need to know, things which will give them *entirely* the wrong idea!' I pleaded, 'Believe me! Trust me! Just stick with what you've said. Or rather, don't alter it. That's what I mean – just don't *alter* it. Don't say anything about getting it wrong. And *certainly* don't say anything about lying, about cooking up stories with Maggie.' I came to a halt, I gave a deep sigh, I lifted both arms. 'I beg you.'

He wasn't quite there.

I grasped his arm. 'If you're charged there'll be no going back. Do you understand what I'm saying, Will? *No going back*. The charge will hang over your head for months. There'll be a trial. You'll be dragged through the trauma of a long case, day after day in court, terrible things being said, every detail of your personal life dragged through the tabloids, people pointing their finger at you *for ever*.'

He was looking frightened, but not so frightened that he was quite at the point where he was going to give in.

I played the emotional card. 'And there'll be Charlie, you'll have to explain things to Charlie. You'll have to tell him why everyone thinks you killed his mother. You'll have to tell him that you may not be around for him in future.'

Will shot me a blazing look, as though I were playing foul.

'This is my best advice, Will, and I urge you very strongly to take it.' Then, absurdly, desperately: 'It's the best advice you'll ever get.'

I walked away again to give him time. I looked out at a line of black rainclouds lying across the northern sky. The bay snorted and pushed his head further over the stable door, trying to nudge my arm. I ran a hand down his nose and over the velvet of his nostrils.

'You should get another opinion anyway,' I announced without looking round. 'In fact, you're going to have to.' I voiced the realization that had been growing on me ever since I'd heard about Edward's involvement. 'I should stand down, you see. I won't be able to represent you in the future.'

'Why?' he exclaimed angrily. 'Because I want to tell it my way?'

I walked back to him. 'It has nothing to do with what you decide to say or not say. It's because of Edward.'

He made a gesture of incomprehension.

'Whatever else Edward may be, he's still my brother. There's a conflict of loyalties,' I explained. 'Technically speaking, I shouldn't even—'

'You're not serious? You can't be serious?'

'Standing down is the correct thing for me to do. In any other circumstances I wouldn't dream of it, believe me, but Edward could be a crucial witness. It would create an impossible situation—'

'But you're not even *close* to Edward,' Will argued indignantly. 'You hardly ever see each other. He's not even nice to you!'

This argument was so disarming, so irrelevant that at first I couldn't think of anything to say. 'Maybe not. But that's not quite the point. The point is, if it came to court, if it came to a trial, then it would be my job to look for ways of discrediting his evidence, even of discrediting him personally. It would be—'

'What do I have to do to make you stay?'

'It's not that simple, Will.'

He grasped my shoulders. 'But I can't get through this without you, Ali. I can't!' His eyes were very dark and very intense. 'Don't give up on me, please! Please!'

He could see I was weakening.

'I can't *face* this thing without you! I can't . . . Look – all right!' He dropped his arms abruptly, he screwed up his face with misgiving. 'I'll . . . think about what you say. I'll . . .' Another internal battle. 'I'll say what you want me to say!'

'It *is* the right thing, Will. Believe me.'

He looked at me pleadingly. 'But you'll stay, won't you, Ali? You will stay?'

Drained of argument, I couldn't fight him any more, and perhaps a part of me didn't want to. 'For the moment, then.'

He embraced me as he'd embraced me on the marsh that first day, suddenly and overwhelmingly, but this time he held on to me for a long time.

There was a message from Dave Adamson on my answering service. His mobile didn't respond, so I tried his office, then his home before tracking him down to a gym in South London. I had to pass myself off as a colleague before the staff would call him to the phone.

'Trying to lose ten pounds,' Dave explained, panting hard. 'It's the second five that doesn't want to shift. D'you think it's the beer?'

'Which answer do you want to hear?'

'There's a lawyer speaking.'

'You have something for me, Dave?'

'*News*. Russell was charged with Munro's murder a couple of hours ago. It's not quite as satisfactory as nabbing our Ronnie, but tomorrow's another day, you know what I mean?'

'And Hans Place, Dave?'

'Ah! Got a name for you.'

'*Dave*.' I breathed his name like a lover's, and at that moment he could have been my dream man, I felt such affection for him.

'19D Hans Place is owned by something called the Esme Aubrey Family Trust, but the people who actually pay the bills are called Hampton.' When I was silent, he called, 'Alex? Hello? You still there?'

'*Hampton*.'

'That's it.'

'Got a first name?'

'Just an initial. Hell – it's in my notebook, but going by memory, I think it's a J. Yes, J. Hampton. Any good to you?'

Ringing off, I sat in the car for some minutes before driving slowly into the village. I wasn't sure which took more getting used to, the fact that Grace had fallen for the restrained charms of the patrician Julian Hampton, or the convincing display of indifference that the doctor had managed to put on when I'd questioned him about Grace. But then, some people were born to lying and concealment, while others spent a lifetime giving themselves away.

A heavy drizzle was falling as I parked outside the surgery. I declined the receptionist's invitation to join Anne Hampton for coffee in the house, and waited beside a hugely pregnant woman with two small children and a numbered green disc in her hand. After ten minutes a door with a matching green light above it opened and an elderly woman shuffled out, closely followed by the elegant shirt-sleeved figure of Julian Hampton, gold-rimmed spectacles perched half-way down his nose, a fistful of papers held high in one hand.

The receptionist directed his attention towards me. He

peered at me and without blink or hesitation called out my name like a patient's. As he led the way down the passage to his room I noticed his height again, and the way he stooped slightly from a lifetime of low door frames.

The room had a new window which looked out onto the dark shrubbery where as a small child I'd built a secret camp. The shrubbery had been pruned or thinned out: you could see right through it to the lawn beyond. There was a large desk in front of the window, an examination area with a couch and a curtain against one wall, and, opposite, a lighted alcove with a number of framed photographs of Julian and Anne and their children – two boys – one group posed in the drawing room, another in the arbour my mother had installed at the bottom of the garden and covered in climbing roses. In the various pictures everyone was smiling confidently. Happy families.

Julian Hampton waved me to a seat and settled his rangy frame behind the desk. His hair looked a little less immaculate today, his eyes rather watery, and I noticed a distinct kink in his long nose, as though in his distant youth it had been knocked off-true on the rugby field.

'You said it would only take a minute?' The quick professional smile, attentive but distant.

'Hopefully. I was wondering if you could tell me about Grace Dearden's visits to Hans Place?'

He turned his head slightly as though he'd misheard. 'Visits?'

'Her regular weekly visits.'

He went through a show of puzzlement, a drawing together of his brows, a ranging of his eyes. 'Weekly visits? But she didn't.' He gestured mystification. 'I think there's a mistake.'

If he was lying, then once again he was making a good job of it.

'It *is* your flat, number 19D?'

'A family flat, not mine. Left to us by Anne's grandmother.'

'You use it regularly?'

'Hardly ever.'

'Once a week or so?'

He laughed outright. 'I don't manage to get *anywhere* once a week, let alone London. A GP in an overstretched practice! Ha! That'll be the day! No, I suppose we use the flat once every six or eight weeks. When there's some event, when we go to the theatre.'

'Does anyone else use it?'

'One batch of cousins, but they're living in France, hardly ever come over. But tell me . . .' He made a neat steeple of his hands, he narrowed his eyes in an expression of solemn enquiry. 'What makes you think Grace went to the flat? And once a *week*?'

'She used the phone number there. She left it with restaurants.'

Frowning, he reached for his address book and flipped through it. He read out a phone number that matched the one given to the Brasserie.

When I'd confirmed the number, he closed the address book very slowly, he pulled his mouth into a tight line, his long fingers fluttered in agitation. 'I can only think . . .' He cast me a glance that contained both realization and displeasure. 'I think you'd better talk to Anne,' he announced finally.

Now he had taken me by surprise. 'Anne?'

'She ran the flat. She was in charge of it. If anyone'll be able to answer your questions it'll be her.'

Staring at him, I began to appreciate the extent of my mistake.

He stood up briskly and moved towards the door, the disquiet still apparent in the pucker of his mouth.

I got up more slowly. I spoke my thoughts aloud. 'Who could Grace have been meeting, then?'

Raising a sharp eyebrow, he said with dignity, 'Well, it certainly wasn't *me*.'

There was a transparent honesty in his face, an obvious distaste for the situation, which confirmed his words.

I made a gesture as if to take back my original suspicions. 'So you have no idea . . .?'

'None at all! You will really have to ask Anne.'

I started up the path to the house, wondering how I could have let myself jump to such careless conclusions, how I could have missed what now seemed so obvious. Anne Hampton may have liked Will, may even have hungered after him a little, but her overwhelming loyalty and devotion had always been to Grace: to the Grace she had admired, the beguiling magical creature without fault or flaw, the accomplished hostess who had positioned herself so triumphantly at the heart of local life. Anne had been honoured and flattered to be Grace's friend, had been in awe of her too, no doubt, and a friend who lives in another's shadow can never do enough to please.

And what tokens of friendship Anne had been able to offer! The perfect meeting place for Grace and her lover, a place Anne had made available, so it appeared, as often as required, the arrangement sealed by a commitment to secrecy, a secrecy Anne had been prepared to maintain after Grace's death. Such loyalty. Such generosity. And, I couldn't help thinking, such power too. For the other side of the coin of loyalty was the potential for betrayal, a possibility that would have been unvoiced and probably vehemently denied, but nonetheless real. The more I thought about it, the more it seemed to me that Anne's silence had been her most potent offering of all.

Approaching Sedgecomb House, it occurred to me that she might not feel bound to talk even now. Seeking ammunition, I walked on beyond the porch and, standing in the drizzle, pulled out my phone.

Stephen Makim sounded strangely subdued, almost reluctant. Yes, the fax had arrived from Cellnet. Yes, he had it on the desk before him. Yes, it included a fully itemized list of calls.

'Well?' I demanded.

Nine out of ten calls had been made to the same number, he told me. He relayed the number to me just as Anne Hampton came out of her door, car keys in hand, and, spotting me, uttered a small whoop of surprise.

'Hello!' she cried brightly. 'Were you coming to see me? Would you like a quick coffee?'

I stared at her, it was an effort to speak. 'No,' I muttered. 'Thank you very much, but no . . . I don't have the time.'

Chapter Eleven

———•———

THE RED Mercedes was nowhere to be seen, but Jilly's Golf stood confidently in the centre of the gravel sweep in what I had come to think of as Edward's parking place.

Jilly appeared at the front door almost immediately, as though she had been listening for a car.

She blinked in agitation. 'Alex.'

I said a breezy hello, and just as casually: 'Edward around?'

She searched my face keenly. She was trying to work out if I had spoken to Will yet, if he had told me about Edward's visit to the police. 'He should be back in the next half-hour.'

'I'll come back later, then.'

'No, stay!' Her hand flew towards my arm, only to halt in mid-reach as though startled by her own impulsiveness. 'I want to talk to you. Can I? Will you . . .?'

Closing the door rapidly behind me, she led the way across the hall, glancing over her shoulder a couple of times to make sure that I wasn't in danger of changing my mind.

In the sitting room there were lamps lit against the drab morning light, and an open fire. Jilly waited for me to choose a chair, then sat on the edge of the nearest sofa, hands clasped tightly on her knees. For once she was wearing almost no mascara, her eyebrows were hardly pencilled, and the blonde streaks in her hair seemed mellower. The effect was to make her look pretty in a pale elfin sort of way.

Plucking up her courage, she confided in her wispiest voice, 'Edward's been to the police.'

'I know.'

'Ah! I wasn't sure, you see! I wasn't sure if Will had told you.'

'He told me.'

'I'm so terribly sorry about it!' she cried passionately. 'I did try to stop him, you know. I did try to persuade him.'

'Why?' I wasn't quite sure what had made me ask this, but now it was out I very much wanted to hear the answer.

Her eyelids fluttered, she stared at me, not understanding, or possibly understanding too well. 'Sorry?'

'Why did you try to stop him telling the police?'

She cast around, as if for outside assistance. 'Well, I . . . Because . . .'

I gave her no help, I was past the point where I felt I had to save people's feelings.

'I thought it might be bad for Will,' she offered at last. 'And I thought it was a terrible responsibility for Edward. I mean, *terrible*. I thought he might live to regret it.'

'I don't think that's quite right.'

She said in an unsteady voice, 'I don't know what you mean.' But she knew only too well what I meant, I could read it in her face.

'You didn't want Edward's affair with Grace made public. You didn't want the whole thing to come out.'

Her thin smile froze on her face, she thought about denying it, then the pretence fell away, she lowered her gaze and when she looked up again her expression had hardened.

We eyed each other warily, gauging the next step.

'Well . . . I did what I thought was right.'

'Right for *him*, you mean?'

Jilly pushed her chin out in rare defiance. 'For everyone.'

My exasperation got the better of me. I exclaimed hotly, 'I don't understand how you can let him walk all over you the whole time, Jilly! Why don't you tell him to take a running jump, for God's sake? Where's your pride? Where's your self-respect? He's a *bastard*! And I say that as a sister – he's a cold-hearted bastard!'

'But you don't understand!' she argued vehemently. 'You don't understand at *all*! He's never been able to get over his childhood! Never! He's always been so *tormented*.'

I gave a derisive laugh. 'Jilly, really! *Tormented* makes cheating on you and having an affair with someone else's wife all right all of a sudden? *Please*.' I made as if to get up.

'No!' She tipped forward and, doubled over into a crouch, stretched out a hand as if to hold me back. 'You don't understand! You don't realize!' She settled back slowly on the edge of her seat. 'He was so damaged! So angry! And he couldn't make sense of it all, couldn't find a way out. Grace was just a way of *freeing* himself.'

I was in no mood for this sort of half-baked psychological rubbish. I had spent too much of my life defending clients for whom damage and anger had real meaning after childhoods of abuse, neglect and abandonment. In my book Edward had long since run out of the few mild excuses he'd ever had for his selfish behaviour.

I was about to voice harsh things when Jilly held up a trembling hand. 'He never told you. He never told *anyone*. He kept it to himself for all these years. Bottled it all up! Feeling so *desperate* all that time, so full of misery.'

'Never told anyone *what*? Look, Edward may have had his troubles, but they weren't so terrible, believe me. He's just never learnt to let go, never learnt to take responsibility for his own life. I know all about the problems with Father. The rows. I know Father didn't deal with it too well. He was never a great communicator. Never good at heart-to-hearts. I know he used to walk away all the time. I know Edward used to seethe. I know all that! But *really* – compared to some . . .'

Jilly drew in breath to speak, only to pause and go through the process again. At the third attempt she finally blurted out, 'Edward saw something when he was young. Something . . . terrible. For a child, I mean. He . . . saw your father . . .' She faltered.

'Saw Father what?'

'With Maggie Dearden.'

I stared at her. I was very still.

'He saw them together . . . I mean, actually in the . . . act of . . .' She examined her hands hurriedly. '. . . making love. Up at the, er . . . barn at Upper Farm.'

The words caught me like a blow, they left me reeling. I felt a lurch of astonishment, a sharp snatch in my stomach, my throat was suddenly dry. 'My God . . .' For a moment, all I could think of was the barn. The *barn*. 'But . . . was this . . .? Had they . . .?' It was a moment before I could pull a coherent thought together. 'Was this a . . . long-term thing?'

Still avoiding my face, Jilly pulled her clasped hands tight into her lap. 'I couldn't say . . .'

Another lurch, and I was overtaken by a powerful sense of unreality. So many sensations rushed through my mind, so many conflicting emotions that I wasn't sure what I was feeling any more. Astonishment certainly, hurt – yes, quite a bit of that – but also something like wonder, at the capacity of life to deliver such massive surprises, at the way it could so quickly cut the ground from under one's feet.

A part of me was desperate to know more. 'When was this again? When?'

'Edward was nine.'

'Nine . . .'

It was the year I had taken my A levels, the year I had gone backpacking. I tried to remember what life had been like at home then, if it had been so very different from before. I searched my memory for clues, I looked for momentous events, and found none. I tried to picture Father as he'd been then, and it seemed to me that he was his usual benign self, always busy, occasionally overtired from the night calls, but never less than calm and equable, rarely to be seen without the expression of mild amusement he liked to present to the world, rarely without a quip or aphorism on his lips, for he had loved words more than anything, the neat parcelling of them, the pinpointing of meaning. I saw a man who had seemed contented with his life, a man for whom a good crossword, a glass of claret, a satisfying dinner conversation had seemed quite enough to round off the day. I saw – and the thought brought a fresh stab of incredulity – a man without great passion, a man with an apparent distrust for what he had called 'romantic nonsense', a man for whom courtship and love had been a necessary path to marriage but not a major consideration thereafter. If anything he had seemed reticent in his dealings with women, polite, engaging, but essentially reserved.

The sense of wonder returned, the astonishment at how little you may know or guess about the people close to you, at how determinedly they guard their secret selves. At that moment I felt that I'd hardly known my father at all.

And a barn! I tried not to let this image get too firm a grip on my mind – it was too disturbing by far – yet I couldn't help remembering how fastidious my father had been about his clothes, the way he had brushed his jacket every morning before leaving the house, the way he had polished his shoes. A barn! The straw, the dust. God – the roll in the hay. To have committed such a terrible cliché in middle age seemed the ultimate affront.

More stabs of realization as it came back to me that Mother's health had been particularly bad that year, that she had deteriorated suddenly and taken months to make any sort of recovery. We knew that the cycle of relapse and remission was part of the illness, we'd seen it often enough, we knew there was never any obvious cause for the relapses, yet now I imagined causes aplenty for her deterioration. The thought that she had known about Father's affair was so excruciating that I winced visibly, I gasped aloud.

'Oh, I'm sorry!' Jilly cried miserably, in a frenzy of nerves again. 'I've done the wrong thing – I shouldn't have told you. Oh dear, I *knew* I shouldn't have told you! Oh dear!'

'No, no . . .' I was regaining my breath. 'I'm glad you did. Glad.'

'Really? *Really?* But you won't tell Edward, will you? I think it would be a mistake to tell Edward.'

But I couldn't think that far, I couldn't think far in any direction at all. I felt as though I was on a slippery slope looking for handholds.

Jilly pleaded, 'But now you see, don't you, why he was so desperate about everything to do with the Deardens?'

She was talking very fast, I was only half listening.

'Why he was so furious about the Gun Marsh. I know he got it out of all proportion, I *know* he did, but he couldn't help it! Coming on top of the money, coming on top of all that! Well, he felt he'd been cheated again! You can see that, can't you, how he'd feel cheated? And these things are like *death* to Edward. His pride, you know! Such pride! Everything destroys him, everything! But you do see, don't you, how it was, coming on top of everything else?'

Now I knew I was lost. 'Everything else?'

'Well . . . Oh dear!' Her eyes flitted around the room in a new fit of agitation, she squeezed her arms close against her sides, like someone caught in a draught. 'Oh dear, I've said too much again. Oh dear . . .'

'The money,' I prompted as her words came back to me. 'You said, "coming on top of the money".'

'Oh dear . . .' But she was relieved to be telling me, she was glad to have let it slip. With a gesture of giving in against her will, she whispered, 'Your father's money – the money missing after his death? Well, Edward is convinced it went to Maggie Dearden.' She waited in vain for a reaction from me before bracing herself to discharge the rest of the secret. '*And* . . . he thinks she got a whole lot of money from your father *before* that, when your parents moved away. He thinks that's how she managed to buy her cottage!'

Strangely, my reaction when it finally came was one of relief. Despite the barn, this had obviously been no brief impetuous fling. No, this affair had lasted for years and years, maybe – the calculation came as another small shock – as many as eight or ten, if one assumed the affair started when Mother began to be seriously disabled – I didn't want to imagine it had started any sooner – and ended with my parents' move to Cornwall. A relationship, moreover, that would seem from the gifts of cash to have been one of deep commitment and obligation. This thought consoled me perhaps more than it should. But in life – and certainly in my work – I had always found it hard to condemn people for taking happiness as they found it, had always proclaimed that a little love never did any harm so long as no one got hurt along the way.

In this case someone *had* got hurt, though. Perhaps someone always got hurt.

Jilly exhaled suddenly, her shoulders slumped. 'Well, I've told you now,' she cried in her little mouse voice. 'I just hope I've done the right thing.'

The door banged open and Edward strode in, hair damp from the rain, face stormy from life.

Glowering, he demanded aggressively, 'What are you doing here?'

'I came to see you.'

Edward threw a dark look at Jilly who immediately jumped to her feet and, eyes averted, scuttled past him and out of the room.

'Well?' He struck an exaggerated pose of impatience, hand gripping the edge of the door, body turned towards it, as if to conduct me off the premises at any moment.

'I know about you and Grace.'

His expression didn't alter. He said gruffly, 'What about me and Grace?'

'Your relationship. The lunches at the Brasserie, the flat in Hans Place, the four or five calls a day.'

He didn't move for a long time. Then, his face fixed in a

cold mask, he pushed the door closed and came and stood in front of the hearth, glaring down at me, arms tightly folded. 'So?'

'Don't you think you should have told the police?'

'Why?'

'Oh, come on, Ed!'

'My relationship with Grace had nothing to do with her *death*!' His rage was as abrupt as it was furious. His arms flew out, his skin grew red, his neck bulged. 'Nothing! Forget about me and Grace! Just go and talk to Will Dearden about what happened to Grace! Go and talk to your beloved *Will*!'

'Ed, for heaven's sake! You must know that you can't keep this sort of thing—' But this was a futile path, it would only antagonize him, and I began again in a more reasonable voice. 'The moment you decide to become a witness, then I'm afraid your relationship with Grace gets to have everything to do with it. You're not an independent witness any more, you're an interested party – and that's putting it mildly.'

'You're going to tell the police, then?'

'Ed . . . They're going to find out sooner or later.'

'Fine,' he barked. 'Doesn't bother me!'

He twisted away and kicked the fire with the toe of his boot, sending a shower of sparks up the chimney. Fury unquenched, he picked up a couple of logs from the basket and threw them onto the embers with equal force.

I said quietly, 'I gather you were there with Grace that day at Marsh House. That you were there when this phone call came. Could you tell me about it?'

Jamming a forearm against the mantelpiece, fist tightly clenched, Edward stared fiercely into the fire, until, containing himself with an effort, he growled, 'Which version?'

I wasn't sure what he meant. 'Whichever.'

'Well, the *official* version then—' Breaking off, he bit savagely on his lip as though to forestall some powerful emotion. 'Yes . . .' he rasped. 'Yes . . . We were having tea,

Grace and I. *Tea.* We were talking about the *festival.* The phone rang. She answered. I could see it was something serious. She was very upset. Hysterical. Ranting down the phone. When she rang off she said, "He's opened the sluices! He's trying to flood the Gun!" And then she—' Disturbed again by some painful thought, he swung his head away and gave a cough that sounded like choking. When he looked back at the fire and got started again, his voice was low and rough. 'And then she was in a frantic rush, pulling on her coat, grabbing her car keys. I offered to go with her, but she wouldn't have it. She could be bloody stubborn when she tried. Bloody stubborn!'

'She didn't say who it was on the phone?'

Straightening up, he dug deep into his shirt pocket and pulled out a cigarette packet. 'Well – no.'

'You didn't ask?'

'It didn't come up! There wasn't time! She was out of the house before we could talk!'

'And did she say anything else before she left?'

He jammed a cigarette into his mouth and grabbed some matches off the mantelpiece. 'Nothing. She was speechless. Couldn't believe what he was doing. Couldn't—' He cut himself short with a jerk of his cigarette.

'She was angry?'

'What difference does it make if she was angry?' he shot back at me without warning. 'That was no bloody excuse for what happened to her, for God's sake! She had every right to be angry! Christ!'

Selecting a deliberately neutral tone, I said, 'I'm not saying she hadn't every right. I'm not saying anything. I just want to build up a picture, that's all.'

He eyed me darkly, not entirely convinced that I wasn't trying to outmanoeuvre him in some devious way. 'She was angry,' he admitted grudgingly. 'Bloody furious, in fact. But what the hell difference *that* makes I really don't know!'

With this last salvo, he seemed to lose his energy for

hostilities. He lit his cigarette and, throwing himself into the chair opposite, tipped his head back so that I could hardly see his face.

'Should have stayed with her. Should have stayed,' he declared roughly. '*Did* to begin with . . . Worried what he might do to her, the bastard. Thought he might give her a hard time. Drove round, got near the cottage, stopped short, got out of the car, stood and listened. Heard this almighty racket. A screaming match . . .' He tightened his lips, he inhaled sharply. 'But then it died down and, well . . . Knew Grace wouldn't be at all pleased if I bowled up. Knew Will would probably try to kill me. So . . . thought I'd better keep out of the way.' Abruptly he brought his head forward and slid a hand over his eyes. When he let it fall again his expression was desolate. I had never seen such feeling in his face before, not since he was young and had first learnt to despise everything that might touch him.

The fire crackled and hissed. Beyond the window, the rain fell steadily and silently.

I asked, 'Did Will know about you and Grace?'

He was staring into the distance, lost to another world. It was a while before he heard my question. 'No. Grace didn't—' He pulled himself up short as if he had been in danger of saying too much, and took a long drag on his cigarette. 'No, Will didn't know. We were very careful that he shouldn't know.' He added defensively, 'But it wasn't just any old affair! It wasn't like that. It was something . . . *else*. Something . . .' A brilliance leapt into his eyes, his lip trembled, and again I was taken aback by the depth of his feeling.

'She wanted to leave him, you know. She was desperate to leave him! She was very unhappy!' He gave me a searching glance, gauging my response. Then, unwinding a little further, he said in a more confiding tone, 'She would have left him months ago, *months*, but all her money was tied up in the farm and the house and Will's disastrous financial *mess*. She couldn't escape. Not without losing everything. And then there was the boy – custody and all that. She knew she was going to have a battle on her hands. She was trying to sort it all out. Trying to get *clear*.'

I nodded silently.

'She was very unhappy,' he repeated, as though I needed convincing on this score.

'I knew she'd seen a lawyer.'

'And pretty useless *he* turned out to be!'

'You were obviously very fond of her,' I said.

Even now he found it hard to admit to anything as powerful as an emotion. 'Impossible not to be,' he conceded tightly. 'She was . . . well, she was . . .' He fanned out his fingers, he jabbed his hand impatiently into the air, searching fruitlessly for some expression that lay outside his reach. 'Quite *amazing*. Quite . . . *stunning*.'

I leant forward a little, as if to hang on his words.

He struggled again. 'She was . . . not like other people. You know? Went for life flat-out. Full of energy. Full of ideas. Swept you along. A real whirlwind!' His frustration intensified as he attempted another, more elusive thought. 'She had this way of . . .' The hand with the cigarette did several jerky loops. 'Making you feel good, you know? Making you feel sort of – number one.' Dissatisfied with this, or possibly embarrassed by it, he barked, 'I don't know!' and withdrew to the comfort of his cigarette.

I wondered what Grace's ambitions had been for this relationship, but I suspected I already knew. Grace would never have invested so much time and trouble in clandestine visits to London and up to five phone calls a day if she hadn't been aiming for marriage and occupation of Wickham Lodge. Edward was the closest thing to the man of her ambitions, if not her dreams. A bona fide landowner, an undisputed member of the gentry, owner of four farms in addition to the one he rented to Will, with a healthy income that even Grace's extravagances would have been hard-pressed to exhaust, and a large house which only needed total renovation to make it into a spectacular base for entertaining. No, Edward was a good catch. He was six years younger than Grace, but that wouldn't have bothered her; it might even have added to the attraction.

I asked, 'Did the two of you have plans?'

Edward gave me a superior look, as if to show he wasn't going to get caught as easily as that. 'If you're suggesting we were going to run off together, the answer's *no*. Grace wanted to get clear before we thought about anything like that. She wanted to sort everything out as fairly and honourably as possible. Keep things civilized.'

I bet she had. She was, beyond everything else, a great planner. She'd have realized what a long and bitter battle she faced if Will ever discovered she was leaving him for Edward. The humiliation for Will would have been too great, the idea of Charlie coming to live here in Edward's house too terrible. No, she knew she had to get 'clear' with her money and the custody agreement before she delivered her bombshell. The only thing I couldn't work out was why she had waited this long before starting divorce proceedings. Perhaps there had been a problem. Perhaps she hadn't been quite sure enough of Edward to make the leap.

'But there was an understanding between you?' I prompted.

There was conflict in his face, and irritation. 'We'd talked about the future, yes. Of course we had. I told you – it wasn't a casual thing!'

Abruptly, and for no apparent reason, I remembered the Gun Marsh, and wondered if this was the real cause of the delay. Perhaps Grace had been waiting for the sale to go through. Or Edward had made her wait. The more I considered this, the more likely it became. Edward would have wanted her to wait until the Gun was safely in his hands because, deep down, he still trusted land and possessions far more than people, because revenge was a more dependable objective than love. For Edward, the true prize was the Deardens' humiliation at losing the land they had farmed for a hundred years, Grace the more uncertain icing on the cake.

I stood up. 'Thanks for telling me all this,' I said rather formally.

Edward threw his cigarette into the fire. 'You going to tell the police, then?'

It was a good question. 'Not at the moment anyway.'

'No. Wouldn't look too brilliant for Will, would it?' Having delivered this remark, he seemed to appreciate just how true it was, and a look of calculation came over his face, his eyes glinted with possibilities. Watching him then, I thought what an irredeemably cold-hearted person Edward could be when he really tried. It occurred to me that he and Grace would have been ideally suited.

I remembered something. 'Just now, you talked about the official version of that afternoon. What was the unofficial version?'

'Did I say that?' He affected a look of bafflement. 'Mistake.'

He didn't get up when I left.

Jilly was waiting in the hall, and, though I walked fast, she managed to get to the door ahead of me. Hand on the knob, blocking my way, she whispered insistently, 'If it hadn't been Edward it would have been somebody else, you know. Grace was that sort.'

'But, Jilly, it *was* Edward,' I said.

I drove through the rain without thought or direction. Eventually I stopped under some trees and, winding down the window, let the damp air rush against my face. The rain fell from the overhanging branches in uneven salvoes, beating tattoos on the car roof.

A dazed and overladen mind goes its own chaotic way, and the string of revelations, the succession of surprises seemed to have filled all the available space in my brain, I couldn't begin to make sense of anything. I kept seeing Father and Maggie together over all those years, meeting in secret places, and nine-year-old Edward standing at the barn door, judgemental, unforgiving; I saw Will opening the sluices with destruction in his heart, and Grace shouting at Maggie, with rage in hers; and everything in my understanding of people seemed to have been turned upside down.

Worse still, in all the confusion, I couldn't escape the suspicion that I was missing the one simple fact which would keep the police off Will's back; that if only I could find a way through the minutiae cluttering my brain I would be able to home in on the unarguable piece of evidence that would set him free.

I closed my eyes, I let my thoughts drift, I tried to push the contradictions and inconsistencies to one side and concentrate on what seemed clear.

What seemed absolutely clear was that Will's story was nonsense. Every instinct told me so. Almost nothing rang true. The phone call to Grace – why warn her of what he was about to do? – the opening of the sluices, an act that would harm no one but himself, the sudden change of mind and the decision to reclose the gates. I couldn't imagine it, I couldn't see the point of it. Remembering Will's uncertain delivery, the lack of detail, I could only think he had made the whole thing up.

Except for one thing. The raised voices, the row between Grace and Maggie. It seemed to me that this was the only part of the story that might be true. Unless Edward was lying about following Grace to Reed Cottage – and I knew him well enough to think this unlikely – who else could he have heard?

I wound up the window and started off again, heading, I thought, for Marsh House, only to find myself driving past the road to the quay and turning down Salterns Lane. Maggie was in Norwich, but I would leave an urgent message for her.

The hunched grey outline of Reed Cottage emerged through the steady downpour, its windows dark and secretive under the dripping eaves. I looked twice, I peered hard, but there was no mistake: Maggie's Citroën was there, parked at the corner of the cottage.

In a surge of anticipation, I began to rehearse my questions; I didn't stop to think why she hadn't gone to Norwich.

Pulling up as close as possible to the front porch, lifting my jacket up over my head to make a dash for it, I didn't glance in the direction of the Citroën again, I didn't notice the figure in the front seat.

I gave the bell a quick ring and was just reaching for the door handle when it turned, the door opened and Charlie appeared, face pale, hair wet as though he'd just come in from the rain.

'It's Granny,' he panted in a small voice. 'She needs her pills.'

He had something clutched in his hand but still I didn't make the connection. 'Can I help?'

He didn't say anything, but dived past me and ran towards the Citroën.

At last I saw Maggie through the streaming car window. She was lying in the driver's seat, head lolling against the rest, mouth slightly open, eyes swivelled towards me.

I reached the door as Charlie pulled it open. 'What is it?' I cried. 'Are you ill?'

She said calmly, 'Get me inside, Alex.'

Her skin was drained, greyer even than the day, her eyes were half closed with pain or illness. I looked for something to cover her head, but there was nothing, and, drawing her coat lapels more securely around her neck, I hooked her arm over my shoulders and helped her out of the car. She leant heavily on me, Charlie took her other arm, but still she couldn't walk at any speed and by the time we reached the cottage door her face was running with water, her hair was plastered to her head.

I got her into the dining room, to the nearest chair, and sent Charlie to fetch a towel. She sat with her head resting on the chair back, eyes closed, arms splayed out over the sides.

'Let me get you to bed,' I said. 'And then I'll call the doctor.'

'No doctor,' she gasped. 'Just my tablets.'

Charlie produced the bottle of white capsules on his return and I held them up to her. 'Two.' She nodded.

Charlie fetched water and steadied the glass while Maggie washed the capsules down. She wanted to rest, but not on her bed, so we helped her through to the sitting room. With one hand propping her elbow, the other gripping her waist, I couldn't help thinking of other arms that had circled her, had held her body while it was still strong and vital, had clasped it with passion, maybe love. I couldn't help thinking of Father in this cottage, moving around these rooms, climbing the stairs, lying next to Maggie in the bed in the small white room; in this cottage that he may have paid for, or helped to pay for. I thought, too, of the early years of the affair, when Maggie was still living at Marsh House, when people dropped in all the time and Will was a student with long vacations, and I couldn't help wondering how the relationship had stayed secret for so long. Had they always met in barns and out-of-the-way places? My father had led such a busy, organized life that it was hard to imagine him ever having the time. Had they simply been immensely careful? Followed some apparently innocent routine?

I helped Maggie out of her coat. She lay down on the sofa and exhaled with a soft shudder. 'Five minutes, some tea . . . I will be fine.' Her eyes fixed on me sternly. 'No calls, Alex. No doctor. Promise?'

I promised, subject to review.

I left Charlie hovering uncertainly beside her, but as soon as I came back with the tea he moved towards the door. Maggie put out a hand as if to detain him.

'We'll go in half an hour,' she called after him. 'Half an hour, Charlie!' Her arm fell, she listened as he banged noisily up the stairs and went into his room. 'Poor Charlie!' she breathed. 'I am no good to him like this. No good.'

'Is it pain?' I asked.

She pulled a dismissive face, she wasn't going to be drawn as easily as that. 'These doctors, they know nothing.'

Leaving her to rest for a while, I went into the hall and made some calls.

Will's voice contained a note of reproach. 'Where are you? I've been trying to get you.'

I would have preferred to tell him the truth, but I didn't want Maggie disturbed until I'd had the chance to talk to her. 'I'm going into Fakenham,' I said. 'Stephen Makim has a list of calls Grace made on the mobile.'

'Mobile?' He sounded baffled and mildly exasperated. 'But she didn't have a mobile.'

I explained about the borrowing of the handset, the use of Stephen Makim's number, how she'd made six or seven calls a day. If Will thought it strange that Grace had kept the mobile such a secret, he didn't comment on it.

'When'll you be back?' he asked. 'I've got DC Smith in the kitchen, wanting to fix a time for us to go into Norwich.'

'Say you can't possibly arrange anything until I get back. And go out for a few hours if you can. I don't want Ramsey knowing you're there, thinking he can turn up again.'

'How long are you going to be?' He was sounding unsettled.

'An hour, maybe two.'

'Then we'll go into Norwich? I want to get it over and done with, Ali. As soon as possible. I want to get Charlie back to a normal life.'

I realized he had failed to appreciate the danger he was still in, or that I had failed to spell it out to him.

'It might be best to wait until tomorrow.'

'Why that long?'

'I just want to check out a few things first.'

'But what things?'

'Let's talk about it when I get back.'

'You're sounding worried.'

'I'm sounding cautious, Will.'

'Ali, don't frighten me.' And he gave a nervous laugh.

Ramsey wouldn't hear of leaving Will's interview to the next day. We haggled over a time for that evening. I wanted seven, he pressed for five, I politely stuck to seven. I told him Will was busy on the farm all day and couldn't possibly get away any earlier.

Ringing off, I tried to work out how much time this left me and, whichever way I calculated it, it wasn't enough.

I made another cup of tea and took it quietly into the sitting room, but not so quietly that Maggie didn't hear me and turn her head. The pills appeared to have done their work, the pain had cleared from her face.

'So, Alex!' She gave me a sharp appraising look. 'What happened with the police?'

She still looked so frail that I wondered whether this was the moment to tell her. But she needed to be warned of the dangers ahead, and perhaps I wanted to frighten her a bit so that she would tell me something nearer the truth.

'Someone has gone to the police with new information,' I said. 'Apparently this person was with Grace at Marsh House that last afternoon. Apparently Grace took a call while this person was there, a call informing her that – as she thought – Will was in the process of opening the sluices. Then—'

'He said *this*!' Maggie pulled herself upright, vibrating with indignation. 'Your brother, he said *Will* opened the sluices?'

I stared at her. 'You knew it was Edward—'

'How could he do such a thing?' she exploded. 'How could he tell such *terrible* lies?'

'You knew about Edward?'

'Oh, I *knew*! I just did not *believe* he could do such a thing! I did not believe he could tell such *lies*, Alex! Such lies!'

'How long have you known?' I asked, wondering if we were talking about the same thing.

But she was carried away by the force of her own outrage. Shivering with anger, she railed against Edward for some moments before giving in to exhaustion and sinking back against the cushions. Patting the sofa, casting about the room, she hunted fruitlessly for cigarettes.

I urged, 'Tell me about Grace. Tell me what happened when she came over.'

'My bag, Alex. My bag.'

I didn't argue but went out into the rain again and fetched her bag from the Citroën.

When I got back she was a little calmer. Shaking a cigarette from the packet, she echoed one last time, 'How can he *say* this, Alex? *How?*'

'Maggie, whether it's true or not, the police have decided to act on it. I have to tell you they're now treating Grace's death as murder and . . .' There was no easy way to say it. 'I'm afraid they're going to arrest Will.'

She paled, she searched my face for confirmation, then she was very still, very contained.

'Tell me what happened when Grace arrived.'

But she was caught up in her own thoughts again. She started to nod distractedly, and kept nodding for some time. Lighting her cigarette at last, she pulled the smoke deep into her lungs and stared at the window. The rain cast a pall over her face, a deathly whiteness that emphasized the withering of her body. Drawing another long gasp of smoke, she seemed to arrive at a decision.

'There is no choice, then,' she announced in a gruff voice. 'I will tell them.'

'Tell them what?'

'The truth.'

As always, the truth sounded a loud note of alarm in my mind. 'Well, let's just see what we need to tell them, shall we?'

'No,' she declared firmly, 'they will have everything.' A tremor passed down her body, as if the enormity of her decision was only now coming home to her.

'Why don't we just go through it first?' I coaxed gently. 'See what needs to be told.'

'No.'

'Maggie, you must trust me on this.'

She spread a hand. 'But, Alex, you will not like what I say, you will try to stop me.'

'Absolutely right,' I agreed emphatically. 'Because you may not understand all the implications. You may end up saying things that do as much harm as good.'

She gave this a lot of thought. 'There's time?'

'There's time.'

'Though I tell you now, Alex' – she raised a warning finger – 'you will not stop me.'

I was distracted by a sound that seemed to come from the other side of the door. I got up and opened it. The little hall was empty. I listened for a moment. Above the steady drone and dribble of the rain I could make out the faint repetitive squawk of Charlie's computer game upstairs. I peered out of the dining-room window and saw nothing but my car and the Citroën and the rain.

Going back to the sitting room, I waited until Maggie had taken a gulp of tea before prompting, 'So, what happened, Maggie?'

She turned her gaze to the window again. 'It was me,' she announced flatly. 'It was me who opened the sluices.'

She glanced at me and shrugged. 'I opened them.' She paused as if to gauge my reaction before going on in a matter-of-fact tone, 'I did it so that the Gun Marsh would be no good to Edward Woodford. I did it so that he would get nothing but black fields stinking of salt.'

'But, Maggie, the marsh hadn't been sold. It didn't belong to him.'

The point appeared to catch her off-guard. 'But I didn't know this. I thought it was finished, done, *sold*. I didn't know this.'

I found this so extraordinary that I had to press her. 'You thought the sale had gone through?'

'Will told me so. He said it was all finished.'

Still puzzled, I nodded slowly. 'And why *then*, Maggie? Why that afternoon?'

Her eyes hardened. 'Why? I tell you why. Because I understand many things that evening.' She made a cone of one hand, pressing the thumb and fingertips together, and circled it towards me to emphasize the bitterness of her words. 'Many, *many* things.'

'Tell me. Everything.' I added, thinking of a possible witness statement to come: 'From the beginning.'

'The beginning?' She was breathing unevenly, and when she drew on her cigarette the smoke caught in her lungs, she coughed suddenly and violently, and went on coughing for some time. 'There is too much for a beginning! Where is the beginning?' She threw this remark disdainfully to the world at large.

'The events of that afternoon, then.'

'The *events* . . .' she echoed seriously, as if to impose some sort of order on herself. Stubbing out her cigarette, she coughed again with the deep rasp of the habitual smoker. 'Yes! Grace dropped Charlie off. She did not stay long, she never stayed long. A minute, no more.' She was speaking at a gallop, as if to get through distasteful memories in the shortest possible time. 'Charlie had his tea. I asked him about homework. He had forgotten it, left it at home. He wanted not to do it, of course. But no, I said he must do it. Charlie, he said he would go and get it, but it was a dark day, I wanted a walk, I did not want him to go. So I left him watching TV, I went to Marsh House along the path.'

She reached for another cigarette but, still coughing now and then, thought better of it and settled for turning the packet over and over in her long fingers. 'I come to the house, I see the red car, Edward's car. I think: Ah, the festival! Well, that is what I *try* to tell myself.' She rolled her eyes sardonically. 'I go in by the kitchen, I hear voices in another room somewhere. I leave them to talk. I look for Charlie's homework. Nowhere.

There is nothing I can do – I must go into the hall, I must look in the other rooms. I realize the voices are upstairs. I go up. Yes, *yes*,' she argued wearily, as though I had challenged her. 'I know this is putting my nose in what is not my business! Being like a fish-wife! Yes, *yes*, I know this! But you see, Alex, half of me already knew what I would see. In my heart, I *knew*. It was just *who*, you understand. I had never been sure of *who*.' She made a wide gesture, as if to paint in the rest of the story. 'So! I saw them! I knew, then! I knew who it was!'

Finally she succumbed to the lure of another cigarette. Between the mechanics of lighting up, the reaching for the lighter and firing it, she kept raising a hand as if to stay a barrage of comment. 'Let me tell you about Grace! Let me tell you! Grace, she thought only of one person in all her life – and this was *Grace*. She had no problem with this idea, no problem at all. The centre of the world, it was Grace. Everyone else – they were there for *her*. You understand? For *her*. And one day – three years ago, four maybe – she looks around and she decides that her life is not good enough for her. She decides she deserves more money, more beautiful things, more *expensive* things. She decides she would like a house where she can have the lords and important people to dinner and pretend to be a grand lady. And what she wants she always gets – you understand this, Alex? Grace has to have what she wants. *Always*. So she begins to buy things, to make Marsh House into this *palazzo*. Marsh House! It is never designed to be a *palazzo*! It is a farmhouse. It does not want silk walls and' – her hand windmilled, the cigarette with it – 'furniture that is too big, and paintings of ugly people sitting on horses. Ah, but she has fixed her mind on this. She begins to spend money like there is no tomorrow. How she spends money! Every time Will tells her to stop, she says it is her money. *Hers*. Never! I tell you, Alex, it is never her money. She says she will pay it back, but never once does she pay it back. Well, maybe once at the beginning. Just *once*. But after that, nothing. Never again. *No*, because by this time she has other plans.' She gave a throaty scoff of contempt. 'She has better ideas!'

She pressed her fingers into the hollow of her temple as if to stem an incipient headache before reaching for her cup, which she held absentmindedly, without drinking. 'No, she decides it is not enough to have a house like this, she must have a better house, a proper country house, a *grand* house.' Making a contemptuous gesture, she almost spilled her tea. 'And a new husband to go with it, a husband who is not a farmer getting up to feed the cattle in the morning, not someone who *rents* his land. No, she wants someone who *owns* the land, someone who can give her this beautiful life that she wants, with the house, the money, the people at dinner . . .'

'I didn't know about Edward until today,' I volunteered, needing to justify myself to her. 'I didn't know before.'

'Yes – Edward,' she stated coldly.

We contemplated this fact in silence for a second or two, then Maggie went on hurriedly as if time were running out. Her breath quickened as her words gathered momentum. 'But she does not leave straight away. No, no! Not before she has made Will sell the Gun Marsh to Edward. This is her farewell to him, you understand!' Her voice rose suddenly in anger. 'Already she has done her best to ruin him, she has spent all his money, now she tries to make him sell his land to her lover!' Not trusting herself to say more on this, Maggie shook her head vehemently and replaced her cup in the saucer with a loud rattle. 'She is making plans for Charlie too! It is not enough that she is a bad mother, that she is unkind to him. No! She plans to get the custody and send him away to this special school, to make him into what she wants him to be! To make him *obey* her. I ask you, Alex, what kind of woman is this?' She repeated despairingly, 'What kind of woman?'

'And who knew about all this? Who knew Grace was planning to leave?'

She stubbed her cigarette out in the saucer with small

stabbing motions. 'No one! She is clever, *clever*. Like a fox. She says nothing. She is secretive. No one knows. But me – *me* . . . I *feel* many things.' She drove a fist against her heart. 'I *guess* many things. I see Will miserable, I see the money going out, out, *out*' – she flipped a hand into space – 'I see Charlie so unhappy. Oh, *Alex*, he is so nervous all the time, so full of bad feelings, and wanting his mother to be good to him. And I watch Grace. And I see there are no problems for her. No, no! She is happy! She is full of herself! And then I *know*. Don't ask me how, Alex, but I know. And I *pray* she will leave! I want her to leave! *But*' – she pointed a finger at me and squinted down it, as though down the barrel of a rifle – 'not with the Gun Marsh! Never with the Gun Marsh! This would kill William. This would kill his pride for ever.' She threw her head back, she gave a harsh sigh.

'So,' I said, urging her quietly on, 'you went and opened the sluices?'

'I opened the sluices.' The passion fell away, her voice became devoid of tone or emotion. 'I took the handle, I went and opened them. The first was hard. Stiff. Heavy. I had to work at it, really work. The second, it wasn't so hard, quite easy in fact. But the water – I have never seen water like this, Alex. So much water, coming so fast.' The memory horrified her a little, but also gratified her; she couldn't keep the gleam of triumph from her eyes. 'Then . . . I came back here.'

I sat forward on the edge of my chair. 'But . . . the call to Grace.'

'It was me. I called her. Just like I said to the police. Just like I told them.' She was tiring now, her eyelids were drooping.

'And what did you say to her?'

'I asked if Will was back. I said that the marsh was flooding. No,' she corrected herself. 'No . . . I said it was flooding *badly*.' She added forcefully, 'There was no talk of *Will* opening the sluices. This would be mad. Why would I say a thing like this? I was wanting to know if he was back. Why would I ask for him at Marsh House if he was here with me? No, Edward is *crazy* to say these things.' The thought of Edward sent her into a new fit of agitation. 'Why would he say a thing like this? Will, he was still in his car then. Still far away. No, Edward has this *totally* wrong.' She tapped a finger against her head to indicate madness. 'He *heard* it wrong. Ha! Or he *wanted* to hear it wrong! He is saying this just because he wants to hurt Will.'

I sat back, puzzled again. 'But why did you make the call, Maggie? Why did you want to find Will?'

She put on a look that was both sheepish and defiant. 'I began to think . . . perhaps I had done the wrong thing. Perhaps I had been too . . . quick. That I had been thinking with my heart and not my head.' She was glancing away all the time, not avoiding my eye exactly but not meeting it either. 'You see, there was so *much* water, Alex. It came so fast, it covered everything just so quick. I began to think that I had done too much. That I should call for help.'

I asked, 'You didn't think of trying to close the sluices yourself?'

'Of course,' she asserted rapidly. 'I was going out to try and do it, to close them, when Grace arrived. Yes, I had the handle with me, I was walking. Yes . . .'

'There was a row?'

She blew loudly through pursed lips, a sound of disbelief. 'Grace was in a rage . . . I tell you, Alex – such fury! She was *shaking* with anger. Quite mad.' Maggie fixed me with a firm gaze and raised an eyebrow. 'I do not say this too strongly, Alex. *Mad.* She hit me, she kept hitting me. On the arm first, then the side of the head. She was *wild* with rage. There was blood, I thought my ear was broken inside! I thought . . .' With a small motion of her hand, she left this thought behind. 'I tell you, Alex, never have I known anything like this! Then . . . oh, we said many things, many bad things, many things we had wanted to say for a long, long time!' She laughed abruptly, a short biting laugh. 'Then ... when the words were over, she went off to close the sluices. She marched off with the handle.' Her voice fell. 'I did not see her again.'

She fell silent, and we both looked away to the window.

'What did you do then?'

'Me? I was recovering myself. It is many years since anyone hit me like this, Alex. Since I was a child. In fact, I think never has anyone hit me in this way, around the head. I was ... shocked. I could not breathe. I stayed there until I felt better.'

'Where?'

'By the outhouse.' She waved towards the back of the cottage.

'And then?'

Another shrug, another descent into exhaustion. 'I came inside to wash, to sit, to recover more.'

'And Charlie? Where was Charlie all this time?'

'Inside,' she replied briskly. 'Watching TV. I had put a video on, his favourite, so that he would not see me opening the sluices.'

'When did Grace disappear? What time roughly?'

She pulled the corners of her mouth down, she raised a palm. 'Oh, before six. Maybe ten minutes before six. I don't remember.'

'Quite a long time before Will arrived, then?'

She went through the motions of testing her memory again. 'Yes.'

'And you never saw any sign of Grace after that?'

'No.'

'When Will arrived, did you go out to the sluices with him?'

She lowered her head and nodded.

'And you said nothing to him?'

'I said nothing.' She kept her head down. 'I was ashamed. I didn't want to tell him it was all my fault.'

I sat forward in my seat. 'But the *car*? Grace drove around in her car.'

'I took it back myself. Later. I didn't want anyone to know she'd been there.'

'How much later?'

Another cigarette appeared from the packet. As she occupied herself with the business of lighting it I noticed that her hands were trembling. 'Later, later – when Will was busy with the sluices. Ten, maybe.' She gazed at me levelly through the smoke and said with a show of calm, 'So, there we are. That is what happened, Alex. I am not proud of it, but that is the story.'

A dozen questions rushed into my mind. 'You never thought of telling anyone that Grace had gone off onto the marshes?' I asked incredulously.

Her expression grew defiant. 'I didn't care what had happened to her. I didn't care if she was lost, wet, hurt . . . I didn't care *if she was dead*. In fact, the thought made me happy, Alex. I have to say, it made me happy.'

'You didn't even tell *Will*?'

'Especially not Will! Tell him that she was unfaithful? Tell him she was leaving him for Edward Woodford? Tell him she was taking the Gun Marsh as a wedding present to her lover? She boasted about all these things, she was proud of it! Tell him some of the things she said – terrible, terrible things that should never be said? No, *no*! I said nothing!'

I said in a tone of greatest reluctance, 'Maggie, I have to tell you that the police may not accept all this . . . Not without corroboration. They may think that you're saying this simply to protect Will. Is there any way you can support your story? Anybody who can back you up? What about Charlie? Surely he saw something. Heard something.'

'Charlie saw nothing,' she cried immediately. 'He knows nothing. He must not be upset again! He must not be told this!' Something came over her then, faintness or pain or sickness, and she screwed up her eyes suddenly, she clutched her stomach. 'My pills, Alex! Could you . . .?'

I fetched them for her. 'Is it okay to take more so soon?' I took a glance at the label.

Brushing the question aside with a quick gesture, she took two of the capsules and washed them down with the dregs of the tea. 'Five minutes, Alex. Just five minutes . . .'

I stood over her, looking down at the pale ravaged face. She seemed cold and I brought a dry coat from the hall and laid it over her.

As I closed the door behind me I heard her give a slight gasp.

The door was unlocked, the interior low and narrow under a sloping roof with a small skylight. Immediately ahead of me I saw the hook that Will had carried to the sluices on the night of the storm, the hook he had used to pull Grace's body from under the gate. Beside it were gardening tools and seed boxes, and beyond, a stack of rotting deck chairs, an old lamp, and a pile of bulging cardboard boxes.

The sluice handle was attached to the near-side wall. I wrenched it from its clips and was stepping backwards when I noticed a second handle clipped to the back of the door. The two appeared identical, so I left the second handle where it was.

I strode towards the Gun embankment and climbed the grassy slope. Reaching the path, I walked even faster. A wind was blowing sideways off the salt marsh, the rain fell coldly against my face. I passed a couple of dog-walkers in hooded anoraks who looked at me curiously: at the lack of a proper waterproof, at the handle gripped in my fist, at the look in my eye probably, too.

Reaching the first sluice, I faced the mechanism and, grasping the handle in both hands, jammed it into the socket. I prepared to throw my weight into the first turn, only to find that the handle spun freely without resistance: it had failed to engage the worm gear. Rattling the end of the handle, thrusting it deeper into the socket, I felt it slide in and engage the thread. I began to wind.

The mechanism was very stiff or the gate very heavy, but it was all I could do to make the handle turn. I began to pant slightly, to feel my muscles protest. It was half tide – I heard the water starting to trickle in. After six or seven turns, I peered over the edge of the tunnel and saw that the gate had lifted no more than a foot.

I lowered it again. It went down much more easily than it had come up.

Still breathing hard, I tucked the handle under my arm and walked quickly back.

I climbed the stairs softly, stepping on the outside of the treads to reduce the chance of noise. The landing was more difficult, it creaked under my weight, but the rain and Charlie's computer drowned out much of the sound and when I paused to listen there was no sudden movement from the sitting room, nothing from Maggie at all.

I tapped gently on Charlie's door. The computer squawks stopped. I tapped again and opened the door a few inches. 'Charlie,' I called without showing myself. When he didn't respond, I called again and put my head around the door.

He was sitting in front of the computer screen which was displaying garish red figures bouncing around a schematic green maze.

'I'm afraid Granny's still not feeling too well,' I told him. 'I think perhaps you won't be going to Norwich today.'

Looking back at the screen, he accepted this without a word.

I stepped into the room. 'Do you mind if I ask you something?' I said it kindly, but not quite so kindly that he felt he could refuse.

Instantly, he hunched a little, he lowered his head, so that the white-blond hair fell forwards over his forehead.

I moved further into the room. 'Has this happened to Granny before?'

Unable to escape some sort of response, he gave a minimal nod.

'Is it always this bad?'

But he wasn't at all sure about that, he frowned uncertainly, and I left it alone.

Drawing up a chair beside the desk, making myself at home, I stole a closer glance at him and it seemed to me that he was far more alert today, that if he was taking tranquillizers they weren't having nearly such a drastic effect as before.

'Charlie, can I ask you something? Just a small thing, but I thought you might be able to help me out.'

The vivid pale eyes remained fixed on the bouncing red figures in a solemn glare. The computer continued to emit loud squawks and whoops.

'Would you mind?' I gestured towards the game.

He pressed a button and there was an abrupt silence.

Crossing his arms tightly across his chest, he didn't look at all happy at the idea of questions, but he didn't protest either.

'The thing is . . .' I paused, anxious to explain myself clearly without talking down to him. 'You know what I'm doing here, don't you, Charlie? You know what my job is? I'm here to represent your family – that is, you and Dad and Granny – in your dealings with the authorities. To help sort things out with the police, the coroner's office, all those sorts of people. Now, representing you and your family has a very particular meaning. It means that I'm completely on your side. In every situation. Whatever happens. It means that I'm here to protect your interests the whole time.'

He was utterly still apart from his eyes, which travelled from one unpromising side of the table to the other, in search of escape.

'The thing is, I need your help, Charlie.' I spoke diffidently, like an old friend asking an important favour. 'You see, if I'm to look after you and Dad and Granny *properly*, to the very best of my ability, then I need to get a couple of things clear in my mind. About *when* things happened that night – the night the Gun flooded, I mean.'

Tension rose rapidly into his face, a tide of alarm. He tightened his arms.

I continued easily, 'I just need to know whether certain things happened *before* other things or *after*. You see, Charlie, it's important for me to get the time-scale right. Well, it's important for *Dad*, actually.' I hadn't intended to say this, but now it was out I left it hanging in the air for a moment where it would do no harm to my cause. 'It's been explained to me – in fact, several times – but somehow I still haven't got it straight in my mind. I was hoping you could put me right.'

The pale eyes flickered towards my face and darted rapidly away again.

'For instance' – I made a show of searching my mind – 'when Mum heard about the flood and came rushing back here, was that *before* dark, or *after* dark?' Wanting to give him plenty of time, I added in a matter-of-fact tone, 'I thought your memory might be better than Granny's, you see. She was a bit hazy about all that, about whether it was before dark, or after dark.' I affected the look of someone who needs to be helped out on a puzzling point. 'It's to help Dad,' I explained again, to fill the silence.

When he finally spoke, his voice was so soft that I almost missed the word. 'Before.'

'Before dark? Well, you see I *thought* it must have been,' I said companionably. 'Yes, I *thought* so . . .' I might have been shrugging it off, I took it so lightly. 'And Dad – that's the other thing I'm not clear about. When Dad arrived, when he went out to the sluice, that was . . .' I was the dim-wit now, touching the side of my head as if to jog an inadequate brain. 'That was . . . *later*, wasn't it? When it was getting dark?'

He nodded rapidly, as if this might encourage me to cease the torture sooner.

'In fact, *night*, wasn't it? I mean, pitch black?'

Tucking his chin down further, Charlie nodded again, a single tense jerk of the head.

Outside, the rain fell dully against the sill and dripped heavily onto the ground below.

'Well, that's all!' I said, wrapping things up. 'I'm sorry to have bothered you. I just hadn't got it quite straight in my mind.'

I watched some of the tension drop away from him.

'Oh . . .' I narrowed my eyes in concentration, I fluttered my fingers, as if a last niggling question were just coming back to me. '*Yes* . . . One other thing. Not important, just my curiosity, but . . . you must be very strong, to open the sluices on your own.'

His reaction caught me by surprise, it was so sudden and so intense. He shot me a brief horrified stare, then his face puckered into an expression of misery, and a tear appeared from nowhere, followed in quick succession by several more, spilling down his cheeks as if from a concealed tap. He hunched his shoulders and ducked his head to hide his face.

I leant forward, I reached a hand tentatively across the table, only to hold back. 'Charlie, it's all right,' I said soothingly. 'No one's blaming you. No one at all. I promise you.'

I found a clean tissue in my pocket and handed it to him. Crushing it into a tight ball, he dragged it hard across his eyes, rubbing them mercilessly.

I echoed, 'No one's blaming you, Charlie.'

The worst of the storm passed almost as quickly as it had begun. His face emptied, his tears dried up, he seemed subdued by the strain of it all.

'You thought you were doing the right thing, I can understand that.'

I sensed him closing himself off, dropping the shutters again. I added quietly, 'I knew it had to be you, Charlie. But you see, I haven't mentioned it to anyone till now, not a word, because I didn't think we'd ever need to tell anyone. But now we have to tell them, Charlie. You know why? Because otherwise the police are going to get it all wrong.'

His expression was blank; I felt I was talking against glass.

I took a deep breath. 'They're going to think that Dad is guilty of bad things. They're going to think that Dad hurt Mummy.'

He glared at me in such abject horror that I said hastily, 'But once they've heard what you have to tell them, they won't think that any more, Charlie. They'll understand what happened, and then they won't think bad things about Dad any more.'

He was breathing hard, I wasn't sure he had understood me.

'Shall we go through it first, Charlie? Just to make sure we've got it right. Well – to make sure *I've* got it right, really. Is that okay? You don't need to say anything. Just let me do the talking, and you just stop me if I get it wrong. All right? Just stop me with a shake of the head. That's all I need – just shake your head.'

He was still in a daze, but he was listening now.

'Okay. Mummy dropped you at Granny's,' I began slowly. 'You had tea.'

I waited quietly for a second or two. Charlie was utterly motionless, his head low, his eyes fixed on the table.

'But you'd forgotten something. You went back home to get it. Along the marsh path.'

He was so still now that he might not have been breathing.

'You saw Mummy there with Edward Woodford . . .'

He began to gulp air, his head jerked slightly, for an instant I thought he was going to deny it, but his head did not move.

'You didn't think it was right for Edward Woodford to have Dad's land, you knew Dad didn't want to sell it, so you came back and opened the sluices.'

When I paused this time it was with a sharp sense of anticipation. But he didn't move, he may even have nodded slightly, and I continued with the sense of having reached the downhill stretch.

'Then . . . Granny saw the flood. She tried to find Dad to help close the sluices.'

Again I paused, again the small tense figure made no sign. I reminded him gently, 'Just shake your head if I've got anything wrong, Charlie.'

His chin rose a fraction, his shoulders eased a little, but still he didn't shake his head.

'And while Granny was waiting for Dad to arrive, Mummy came over and went out on the marsh to try and close the sluices herself.'

Unexpectedly, he spoke. His voice seemed to come out of the ground, it was so faint. 'I wanted to help her.' Tears were close behind, another sudden stream, and he dropped his head again. 'I wanted to *help*!'

'Of course you did. Of course, Charlie. You mustn't blame yourself.'

'I only wanted to *help*!'

'Of course.'

But for the moment he was inconsolable. I found another tissue. When he had blown his nose and his breathing had subsided a bit, I said, 'You wanted to go with Mummy and help her close the sluices?'

He nodded fervently.

'But she wouldn't let you go with her?'

His dismay was an answer in itself.

'You saw her go off to try and close the sluices?'

He nodded.

I said, 'You're doing fine, Charlie. Just fine. Just tell me if I've got the rest right. Dad came over much later, after Mum had been out on the marsh for some time?'

Charlie half raised his eyes and gave a slight nod.

'And when Dad went out to the sluices, did he go alone?'

'Granny . . .'

'Granny went with him?'

He nodded instantly.

I smiled gently. 'This is very important, what you're telling me, Charlie.'

He met my eyes at last.

I said solemnly, 'Now all we have to do is go and tell the police.'

He gave a small dip of the head, and the relief swept over me like a balm. At long last we were home and dry.

Chapter Twelve

THE RAIN had not let up and the roads were covered in mirrors of shifting water. Just short of the entrance to Wickham Lodge a small lake had formed in a dip. I negotiated it cautiously and was just turning in through the gates when the red Mercedes came screaming out of the tunnel of laurels and, failing to see me until the last minute, braked with a violent lurch, swerved slightly and halted just inches from the gatepost.

Through the blur of the wipers I saw Edward throw up both hands and cast his eyes heavenward in an appeal for deliverance from the idiot drivers of the world.

He backed up a little then eased his car between mine and the gatepost.

I motioned for him to wind down his window.

Lowering it no more than an inch, he called, 'Can't stop.'

'I must talk to you. It's very important.'

'Can't stop!' he repeated as if I were deaf or stupid, then, looking away implacably, he raised the window and charged off in a shower of gravel.

The anger swept over me in a white hot sea. Reversing rapidly, yanking the wheel hard over, I shot back into the lane in time to see the Mercedes speed through the lake at full pelt, sending up great arches of spray. Jamming my foot flat down, I set off in pursuit, taking the lake at a rate that left the wheels planing and the steering dead in my hands.

Edward drove like a madman, but by then I was touched with madness too. I hung on grimly through the high-banked bends, keeping the bobbing red tail of the Mercedes in my sights, relying on Edward's course to warn me of an approaching car. Once I brushed the grassy bank, once I felt the back wheels slip, and once my heart hammered against my chest as I saw the Mercedes lurch across the road almost out of control.

Reaching the main road at last, Edward turned left then almost immediately left again into the lane that led to his shooting land among the inland hills. He slowed a bit, then a bit more, until he was meandering along at a ludicrously leisurely pace. I knew this game: he was pretending he didn't care, pretending that his childish tantrum had never happened. But my own anger was still burning bright and, coming up close behind him, I hung on his bumper, I almost touched him. Only when he gesticulated at me did I fall back to a sensible distance, feeling petty and foolish.

Passing through the low-lying hills, reaching the long wooded valley where he raised his pheasants, Edward paused in front of a five-bar gate and jumped out to open it. He was back in his seat and driving off again before I had the chance to stop him. I followed him down a leafy track to a clearing of dripping trees with a dark hut and a row of pheasant pens.

'You are the absolute end!' I declared as we emerged from our cars.

'Whatever the hell it is, I just don't want to know, that's all.' He pulled a cap out of his pocket and jammed it on his head.

'I said it was important.'

'What's important to you probably involves the Deardens, and I don't want anything more to do with them, thank you very much. I was very fond of Grace, and now she's dead, and I don't want to hear any bloody sob stories.' He stomped off past the hut to the pens and ran his hand along the mesh, examining it for damage.

I strode up behind him. 'I came to tell you that someone saw you that afternoon. With Grace.'

He frowned, not understanding, or perhaps not wanting to understand. His fingers plucked at the wire.

'That last afternoon,' I repeated impatiently. 'Someone saw you together.'

His glance flickered briefly. 'So?'

'I assume . . . making love. You *were* making love?'

He shifted awkwardly, he was on the point of denying it, but at the last moment he tightened his mouth and sighed harshly in affirmation. 'Bloody great!' he growled. 'People creeping about, spying. Nothing better to do in this damn village! Who the hell was it, anyway? Have they dared to come out of the woodwork? Bet they bloody haven't!'

I hesitated and, catching this, he gestured impatiently. '*Well?*'

I examined my feet for a moment. 'It was the child.'

His expression did not change. He stared at me blankly, as though I were a moron who'd got it hopelessly wrong. 'He wasn't *there*.'

'He'd forgotten something. He came back from Maggie's.'

'Nonsense! He couldn't have.' Edward wore the bloody-minded look I knew so well.

'He came by the marsh path.'

'No, *no!*' he insisted fiercely.

'Well, he did, I'm afraid. And he saw the two of you together in a situation which upset him very deeply.'

Edward turned away abruptly with a truculent gesture. 'We would have *heard*. We would have known! Oh, for God's sake – Grace locked the bloody doors!'

'There must have been a spare key,' I suggested. 'Or Charlie saw you through a window.'

'No, no! It's all rubbish. Complete bloody rubbish!' This sort of stand-off was typical of Edward, who always aimed to block out unpleasantness by sheer force of willpower and obduracy.

I grasped his arm, I forced him to face me. 'Charlie was the one who opened the sluices. He went and opened the sluices because of what he *saw*.' I shook his arm slightly. 'Because of *you* and his mother.'

Edward recoiled, his lips tightened into a thin white line. 'I don't believe you.' But he did believe me, I could see by the revulsion in his face. 'You're just saying it to get your precious Will off the hook! You're making the whole thing up!' He turned on his heel and strode along the side of the pens, dragging his hand savagely along the mesh.

I followed more slowly. The rain had drenched my hair and had begun to seep down my neck. Edward swung a kick at a section of loose mesh and cursed, 'Bloody foxes!' He kicked the wire again, and this time his kick was full of pent-up anger. Finally he stood hunched and still, waiting for me to catch up.

'How do I know it's true?' he said defensively.

'The boy told me.'

'Well, he could be lying, couldn't he! Put up to it by his father!'

'Children don't lie.' Then, because it was the moment for all sorts of truths: 'You should know that.'

His head snapped round, he glared at me with a mixture of shock and uncertainty.

'Children tell small fibs to avoid blame sometimes,' I went on, 'but they never lie about traumatic events. They simply don't have the imagination.'

The word 'traumatic' got to him, and perhaps I had meant it to. He kept thinking about that, he got more and more emotional. 'Christ. *Christ.*' A last wrestle with his doubts. 'You're sure? Absolutely sure?'

'Yes.'

'And the sluices?' he asked in a fading voice.

'It was Charlie.'

Turning his back on me, he moved away a couple of steps and faced the dank dark wood. I heard him gasp, once he sighed, now and again he shook his head fiercely.

Swinging round, he cried fiercely, 'We never usually met at her house! Never! Christ – another man's house! And everyone knowing my car! It was crazy. We *never* met at her house, not until that afternoon. I mean, never. It was *her* idea, Lex! Honest to God, *her* idea!'

I didn't say anything.

He shuffled back, driving each foot hard into the ground, sending up small eruptions of mould, like a small boy shambling through leaves. 'I should never have agreed! Never!' He shuddered with fury and self-disgust. 'Jesus . . . *Jesus* . . . ' He leant his elbows on the edge of the cage and dropped his head in despair.

'The phone call,' I said. 'Grace never gave a name, did she? She never actually said it was Will opening the sluices?'

Edward's head came up with a jerk, he searched his memory feverishly. 'She— I *thought* she—' Breaking off, he clutched a hand to his forehead as if he were going mad. 'She said . . . She said *he* was opening the sluices. She was so furious, she was cursing so much, I didn't hear properly . . . I thought it had to be—' He closed his eyes as the full impact of his mistake came home to him. '*God.* I never dreamt . . .' He added in a tone of self-justification, 'How could I? She was so angry, so furious! I thought it *had* to be Will. I mean, the way she spoke, the language she used. You know – *bastard*, things like that. I thought . . . *God* . . .'

'It's not too late to put it right.'

He was still deep in his memory. 'There was one moment when . . . well, I *thought* I heard her say "bloody little bastard", but, well, I didn't think anything of it. She was babbling so much, sort of *raving*, that I thought I must have got it wrong. I mean, she was so *furious*, Lex. Sort of hissing under her breath and rushing about picking up her car keys, her jacket, all that stuff. It was hard to make *any* sense of what she was saying.'

'But you heard her say "bloody little bastard"?'

He nodded slowly.

'You're sure?'

He exhaled unhappily, and nodded again.

'You can put this whole thing right,' I said again.

'You mean, go back to the police?'

'Explain that you got it wrong. It often happens. People often change their statements.'

His expression hardened, he said darkly, 'But Will was still around, wasn't he? On the bloody marshes. I mean, he met up with her, didn't he? Don't tell me he didn't!'

I made him face me again, I made him look me in the eye. 'Will arrived later,' I said slowly and deliberately. 'A long time after Grace. He wasn't there, Ed. He wasn't there when you heard the screaming. He was still on the road and it can be proved he was still on the road. The Range Rover wasn't there when you got to Reed Cottage, was it? You didn't see it there?'

He looked defensive, and I guessed he'd said something about this in his statement.

'You told the police you saw the Range Rover?'

He was angry at being caught out: the small boy again. 'They kept asking me if I'd seen it,' he admitted crossly. 'I *thought* I had. It was pretty murky, you know. And I wasn't that close.'

'These things happen. Just say you made a mistake, that you realize his car wasn't there after all.'

For an instant he looked as if he'd argue. 'Who did I hear, then?' he asked helplessly. 'Who was screaming?'

'Grace and Maggie.'

He set this against his memory and grappled with it.

I said, 'You heard female voices, I take it.'

He caved in with a harsh sigh. 'Yes, *yes*. So what happened, for God's sake? What happened to Grace?'

'Grace went out onto the marshes to try and close the sluices. She went on her own. She never came back. She must have stumbled, fallen.'

His gaze met mine. 'Alone?'

'Maggie was too ill to help. Too weak. And they'd just had a fight. And I mean a fight.'

'How could she have fallen?'

'Very easily, I think. Those gates are heavy. It takes a lot to wind the mechanism. I almost keeled over myself.'

He looked at me closely, searching, as he was always driven to search, for signs of honesty and straightforwardness. 'I'll go to the police,' he agreed finally in a tone of near despair. 'I'll tell them I got it all wrong.'

Knowing what a big thing this was for him, knowing how hard it was for him to admit to even the smallest mistake, I said, 'It's the best thing, Ed.'

'What about the child, though?' he asked, in a gruff voice. 'He's not going to get dragged through a whole lot of stuff by the police, is he?'

'I think he *wants* to tell them what happened. I think it'll be a weight off his mind.'

Edward shifted awkwardly. 'Yes, but . . . not the bit about Grace and me, for God's sake.' Another uneasy movement. 'It would be too . . . unfair.' His eyes slid up to my face and away again, and once more I saw the small boy at the barn door. 'It's not that I care a damn about what people think of *me*!' he declared hurriedly. 'I don't give a bugger! It's just . . . well, you know . . . Not fair on the child. Shouldn't have to . . .' He finished the sentence with a sharp gesture.

'I'll try to find a way round it. Come to an arrangement with the police.'

He examined my face again. 'You can do that?'

'I would think so.'

He snorted slightly, he lifted a hand and dropped it again. 'Good.' Appearing to notice my dripping hair for the first time, he added, 'You're wet,' and we began to walk back towards the hut.

'Tell me about Grace that day,' I said. 'Tell me what sort of mood she was in.'

'Mood?' He thought about that. 'Well . . . a bit hyper. A bit edgy.' Then, in the tone of someone who's fixed on just the right word: '*Touchy*. Yes – touchy, you know? My doing, it seemed. I'd told her I couldn't go to London. Phoned and told her the day before, and she wasn't at all happy about that. Sob stuff. Ruffled feathers. That's how she'd got me round there.

Managed to make me feel guilty. Said there was something important she had to tell me.'

'And was there?'

'No,' he scoffed. 'No, it was all the usual stuff. How Will was spending all her money. How he had other women. How she had to get out. How she—' He broke off, looking embarrassed. 'How she couldn't live without me.' He gave a derisory grunt at the absurdity of this notion, having long ago judged himself unworthy of anything resembling devotion. 'The Gun Marsh was *meant* to be the urgent thing. But we'd been through that before, it was nothing new. She said she wasn't sure she could get Will to sign the transfer. Well, I knew that score all right. She was trying to dangle it in front of me as a sort of bait. Trying to get me to promise things – you know, in exchange for getting Will to sign. Well, I wasn't having any of that, Lex. I don't like being crowded. The Gun Marsh had nothing to do with Grace and me anyway. It was *business*. She just couldn't get that straight. It was *business*.' He added with a touch of his old ruthlessness: 'I wanted Will to settle on my terms or not at all.'

'So you talked about other things?'

'Oh, *she* wanted to talk about the future – she always wanted to talk about the future. When we'd be together, all that sort of stuff. Wanting me to name the day when she'd move in. Laying on the pressure, boxing me into a corner. Virtually had us married off, for God's sake! Oh, don't get me wrong, Lex. I mean, it wasn't that – that—' Unable to articulate the thought, he circled a hand in frustration. 'I mean, I was fond of her, Lex. *Very fond*. We had good times together and all that. Seeing her in London, away from everyone – that suited me fine. Just fine. Couldn't see why we couldn't leave it at that – you know? Just go on the same way. Not doing anyone any *harm*.' The mention of harm made him wince with some expression I had never seen in him before, something like remorse or regret. He hung his head.

'To be honest,' he said, in the tone of the confessional, 'she was too much for me, Lex. You know what I mean? A bit *overpowering*. In fact . . . well . . . she frightened me, the way she had everything worked out. I could see her taking over my life. Trying to change me, trying to make me into this other regular sort of chap. You know what I'm like, Lex – a bit of a slob,' he said disarmingly. 'Like my fry-ups and my fags and my home comforts. Nothing too fancy. Don't want to change. Don't want to be brought up to scratch, have the house all tarted up. Don't want to – you know – have to *behave* all the time. Just not *me*, Lex.'

'No.'

We reached the hut. Before stepping under the eaves, Edward lifted his head to the sky and blinked as the rain fell full on his face. 'She got bloody tricky when I tried to back off.' He gave a nervous laugh as he ducked in out of the wet. 'Hadn't seen that side of her before. Oh, cool and sort of foxy on the outside, but inside . . . *Christ*.' He blew out his lips and gave a nervous shudder.

We stood side by side under the eaves, looking out at the rain. 'She was angry?'

He rolled his eyes. 'Definitely. I'd sort of *tried* to tell her it was all getting a bit much, oh, two or three times. You know, let's cool it a bit, that kind of thing. But she always managed to ignore it somehow. Sort of said, don't worry about a thing. I felt I could never get *through* to her. It was like . . .' But words had never been his strong point, and he abandoned the thought with a shake of his head. He tried the hut door and finding it locked absentmindedly patted the pockets of his Barbour for the key. Giving up almost immediately, he went back to his story.

'Well, I finally plucked up courage that afternoon. Finally came out with it straight, no interruptions. Actually said, I don't think it's such a good idea, us getting together. She was angry. Hid it well, of course. She always hid it well. But I could see. Those eyes of hers got a flinty look. A woman scorned, and all that. And then . . . well, she started on the usual spiel –

how brilliant we were together, how happy I made her, all the things we'd do together. She made it sound quite good, I have to say that. Sort of tempting. But all the time ... well ... I felt she was too much for me, Lex. Definitely a bit too much.'

'And then?'

He said sheepishly, 'Then I, er, got side-tracked. Same as always. She, er ... got me the way she always got me.' He shambled out into the rain again and studied the weather. 'She was a ... er, a bit hot in that direction.'

'So you kissed and made up?'

He lifted a helpless hand.

'And when she got the call and rushed out she thought everything was all right between you again?'

He turned his head into profile. 'I suppose so.' Then, with a sharp look: 'God, you weren't thinking—' He gave a dry laugh. 'Oh, she'd never have got upset about *me*. God, no! Only ever saw her cry once, and that was when she thought it was the thing to do. No, no ... Grace wouldn't have been upset about *me*. No—' He looked startled as some memory came back to him. He turned to face me. 'No, it was Charlie she was upset about.' One memory seemed to trigger another. He said in a tight voice, 'No ... After she got the call, when she was rushing around ranting and raving, she kept saying, "I'll kill him! Wait till I get my hands on him, I'll kill him!"'

We were quiet for a time, the only sound the rushing and pattering of the rain.

'Who was T?' I asked, thinking of Grace's old diary. 'Was it you?'

Edward looked shifty. 'Yup.'

'Ted?'

His face told me it was worse still.

'Teddy?'

'Told her I didn't like it, but she wouldn't listen. That was her, Lex – never really knew what I was about.'

*

Ramsey sat immobile in the corner of the car, staring through a small patch of window that he had rubbed clear of condensation. 'We have facilities,' he said at last in a distant tone. 'The victim interview suite. Comfy chairs, pictures, pleasant colour scheme. Video camera behind glass. We're quite proud of it. One of the best.'

I asked, 'And you have someone trained to interview children?'

He turned towards me. 'There's a child psychologist we've used. Haven't dealt with her myself, but she's meant to be good. Teams up with a woman detective constable.'

'And it can be arranged soon? While it's still fresh in his mind.' I didn't add: And while he's still willing to tell it.

With an ironic gesture of being the last person wanting to hold things back, Ramsey said, 'First thing in the morning, if it can be arranged.'

'And I'd like to have a quick word with the psychologist before she sees him, if that's okay with you.'

In the last half-hour Ramsey's manner had progressed from open doubt to grudging acceptance to something very like cooperation. Now he said mildly, 'About?'

'There're a couple of things she should know, a couple of things that she should avoid if she's to get him to talk freely.'

'Such as?'

My instinctive reaction was to disclose nothing, then I remembered that we were both after the same thing: to expedite Charlie's journey towards the truth. 'There was a special school his mother was threatening to send him to – that's a very difficult subject for him. And what he saw between his mother and her lover – I feel that no child should be asked to describe that.'

'Between his mother and Mr *Woodford*,' Ramsey stated with deliberate emphasis.

'Yes.'

'Your brother.'

'Yes.'

'It was on the strength of his evidence that your client almost got charged.' He sounded resentful all of a sudden, as if it were somehow my fault.

'I realize that.'

He seemed on the point of making some comment, only to shake his head and move on. 'I don't see a problem with you talking to the psychologist.' Then, with the air of someone who could not be reassured too often: 'He saw his mother go off to the marsh alone?'

'Yes.'

'He's sure about that?'

'Yes, absolutely sure.'

'And she was going to close the sluices?'

'Yes.'

Lost in thought, Ramsey rubbed at the condensation again with his plump finger and peered out at the rainswept quay.

After a while I prompted, 'So . . . once you have Charlie's statement, that'll cover everything, will it, Inspector?'

He raised an eyebrow, he cast me a knowing look, as if to give me full marks for trying. 'Look here, Mrs O'Neill, whatever Maggie Dearden's intentions might have been – and I accept that she might have *thought* she was acting for the best – the fact remains that she seriously misled us, she denied us vital information. She has singlehandedly been responsible for the most enormous wastage of police time – a truly enormous wastage! Fifty officers in the search, three assigned to the incident room, up to twenty as of yesterday. No . . . I can't say to you that it'll be allowed to pass. I can't give you that sort of undertaking because it's not in my power to do so.'

'She's not a well woman.'

He made a gesture of regret. 'It's simply not in my hands.'

'So, what's going to happen?'

'She'll have to give us another statement, for a start. A full and *accurate* statement. I'm going to need to be satisfied on several points. Like' – his round shoulders hunched in a fresh wave of disapproval – 'why she couldn't at least have pointed us in the right direction at the beginning. Towards the marsh. We spread the search ten miles in every direction – a complete waste of time.'

I kept an expression of polite sympathy on my face.

'And then the *car*. Moving Grace Dearden's *car*. I will need to be satisfied as to *why* she moved the car. And *why* she didn't choose to say anything about it.'

'She'd just been subjected to an attack by Grace,' I suggested quietly. 'Quite a furious one. She's not a young woman. She's not well. She may have been a little disorientated.'

Ramsey considered this with the air of someone who feels duty-bound to give each and every idea a fair hearing, and I found myself warming to him. 'Yes, well ... maybe,' he acknowledged. 'But didn't it occur to her that Grace Dearden might be in trouble out there? Wasn't she concerned when Grace didn't come back?'

'I think she was too busy calming the boy. Calming herself. Everyone was very upset.'

Ramsey's face reflected a number of expressions, among which disappointment, weariness and anxiety were clearly visible. 'I'm not at all sure,' he murmured, pulling in his thin lips.

I didn't ask him what he wasn't sure about.

'How sick is she?' he asked.

'I don't know. I would have to speak to her doctor.'

'And the boy?'

'Sorry?'

He leant across and lowered his voice, as though in the midst of the rain we were in danger of being overheard. 'We're not talking about a child who's disturbed, are we? Medically speaking, I mean?'

'No,' I said. 'What made you think that?'

'A child that you would wish to protect?'

'I don't quite follow.'

'A child who might have been ...' He tightened his lips, he frowned. '... more deeply involved.'

I looked him straight in the eye. 'I believe that we have the complete story, or as close as we'll ever get. I believe that Grace's death was an accident pure and simple. I believe she was in a blind rage, and that her rage, combined with the effort of closing the gates, could have caused her to black out or maybe to stumble or fall. Charlie wasn't there, Inspector. Of that I am sure.'

Ramsey pulled back and eyed me pensively for some time, before nodding and reaching for the door handle. 'So . . . we're ready then, are we?'

He might have been ready, but I realized that I hadn't even begun to think of how I would explain this to Will.

'I forbid my son to make a statement.' Will's voice was ice-cold and ferocious.

Ramsey said gently, 'I'm afraid we're going to have to insist, Mr Dearden. But, as Mrs O'Neill has explained, it will be done in congenial surroundings, by a trained expert, and, under the code of practice, you yourself have the right to attend, or' – he glanced towards me – 'your designated representative could attend on your behalf.'

Will resolutely ignored me, as he'd ignored me since I had broken the news. He said stiffly, 'You're telling me you're going to interview him anyway, whatever I say?'

'It's a matter of the law, Mr Dearden. When we receive information of such a significant nature we have no choice but to follow it up.'

'And where did this *information* come from?'

Ramsey looked down at his feet before glancing in my direction.

'It came from me,' I said quickly. 'Charlie told me everything.'

And still Will did not look at me. He said starkly, 'I will be accompanying my son to the interview, Inspector. No one else.'

'Hopefully it won't be any later than tomorrow morning. But we'll call and let you know.'

'Call *me*, Inspector. No one else. All communications are to come through *me*.'

'As you wish.'

Shivering with anger, Will spelt it out. 'Mrs O'Neill won't be representing us any more.'

Ramsey took a small step back, as if from a dispute. 'I'll call you very soon, then, Mr Dearden.'

Will made to stop him. 'My mother,' he said in fresh agitation. 'You won't need to—?'

'We'll have to take another statement from her, Mr Dearden. There's a great deal to be explained.'

'But she's ill.'

'We'll try to keep it as simple as possible.'

'But her illness – it's serious. It's . . .' Will's voice rose hoarsely. 'She may not have long.'

There was a pause in which I felt my throat seize, my eyes burn. A part of me had suspected how bad it must be ever since that morning I had seen her, grey and haggard, in the kitchen at Marsh House; at the same time a part of me had kept hoping I was wrong. Certainty was altogether more brutal, and the sorrow pulled at my heart.

Ramsey said solicitously, 'We'll certainly bear that in mind. Should we speak to her doctor, perhaps?'

Will gave a sharp nod, and Ramsey, with a muttered farewell, walked off across the hall and let himself out.

The moment the door had shut, Will thrust out a fierce hand as though to push me as far away as possible. 'You'd better leave *now*.'

'I'm sorry about Charlie but, Will, there was no other way. If there'd been any other way, I would have taken it, believe me.'

His face contorted with anger, his eyes blazed, he could hardly speak. 'You did this behind my back! *Without telling me!* You did this without even—' He swung away and raised clenched fists in a gesture of fury and impotence. '*For God's*

sake, what do you think I've been trying to do all this time?'
He spun back. 'Trying to protect Charlie! Trying to keep him
out of it!'

It was a moment before I understood all the implications of
what he was saying. 'You knew it was Charlie who'd opened
the sluices?'

He shouted, '*Yes!*'

'You knew *why*?'

He wrestled with this, he flung out an arm. 'Well, I *guessed*!
Didn't take a lot of guessing! I knew – *knew* – it was all to do
with the Gun Marsh. She kept pushing me to sell. *Pushing,
pushing, pushing!* Thought she was being so subtle, so clever.
But I could always see through her when she was after
something she wanted! Always!' he scoffed in a tone of deep
bitterness. 'Didn't take a lot of working out after that! No! I
mean, two and two made four several times over. *Edward!*' He
almost yelled it: '*Edward! God!*' He took another furious turn
and when he faced me again his eyes were glittering harshly. 'I
wanted Charlie *out of it*! That was the whole point – I wanted
Charlie *kept out of it*!'

The realizations came quickly then, one after another: his
intention to keep me in the dark, his duplicity, the lack of trust.
I stood dumbly, abruptly and unexpectedly close to tears. 'You
should have told me about Charlie,' I said painfully. 'How
could I help you if you didn't tell me?'

'That was the *whole point* – I thought you'd be able to keep
them away! Stop them bothering us! I thought you'd know all
the tricks! I didn't think you'd do *this* to us! I didn't think—'
But his anger got in the way again. He wheeled a hand as if to
sweep me from his sight.

My breath came in a tight shudder, I blinked the heat from
my eyes. 'You didn't trust me,' I said.

'No!' he cried with despair. 'I trusted you too *much*! *That*
was the trouble! *Too much!*'

More realizations followed, more lurches of understanding
that pulled at my pride as much as my heart.

I took a step back, I turned towards the door. 'You should have told me about Charlie,' I murmured again.

He made another wild gesture, a bewildered upward jerk of both hands, before marching into the kitchen and slamming the door behind him.

I spotted Paul's car further along the street – parked hurriedly, by the look of it – but the porch was lit, the hall too.

I was about to slide the key into the lock when the latch sounded and the door flew open to reveal Paul on his way out, wearing a sports jacket, sweater and casual trousers.

We faced each other in mutual surprise.

'You're back!' he exclaimed with a rather sudden laugh. 'Thought you were gone till Monday.'

'Didn't you get my message?'

'Ah!' He made an exaggerated face of contrition. 'Have to confess, didn't call in and collect any messages. Thought, what the hell, it can all wait till Monday! New philosophy – weekends to be weekends. No more work allowed!'

He'd already had a drink or three, I reckoned, possibly a liquid lunch that he'd topped up during the afternoon. 'I left a message on your mobile too.'

He gave a wince. 'Stuck in meetings all afternoon. No time to check.'

Stepping past him into the hall, I saw a bulging holdall on the floor and gave him a questioning glance.

'Ha!' He put on his jaunty Irishman. 'I thought, since my wife was abandoning me for the weekend, I might as well go and get fit. Get the old forehand up to Wimbledon standard.'

'What, tonight?'

'Well, tomorrow. A tennis clinic. Intensive weekend.'

'Oh.' I knew nothing about tennis clinics, intensive or otherwise. 'Is it far away?'

'Ah, well, you see . . .' He made an expansive gesture. 'Thought that while I was about it a bit of warmth wouldn't go amiss. A bit of sun – well, *hopefully* – and a bit of good food and wine and—'

'Spain.' Warning bells sounded, echoes of unease.

'*Espagna!*' Paul attempted a flourish. 'Bit of R and R, bit of a tan and improve the old backhand at the same time.' Catching my expression, seeing that I was having trouble with this story, he said briskly, 'For God's sake, a last-minute thing, Lexxy. Fixed this afternoon. Thought it'd do me good to get away. You know – fresh air, exercise, all that sort of stuff. Going with a couple of the lads, that's all.' He spread his arms, the picture of innocence, though his shifting eyes told a different tale.

I was feeling so demoralized, so defeated, that I would have done anything to avoid a confrontation, but when I glanced at the hall table there was no note. 'You've left a number?'

'With Corinthia.'

'But you'll leave it for me as well?'

'Sure . . .' He went through the pantomime of patting his trousers, of fishing into his breast pocket, he put on an expression of mystification, but I knew it was all a show, a way of marking time until he could announce that he couldn't find it. Glancing out of the open door, his expression lifted with almost transparent relief. 'Ah! The transport's here!'

A car had drawn up, the kind the hire firms like to describe as an executive car, long and silver with a driver in a suit.

'The number, Paul.'

'Not sure where I've put the blasted thing. Look, would you get it from Corinthia, sweetheart? Have to go – late already.' Scooping up the holdall, he planted a kiss on my cheek and would have marched down the path if I hadn't held out a hand.

'The name of the hotel, then.'

'I've told you.'

'You didn't give me a name, Paul.'

'Oh, for heaven's sake, Lexxy, I can't remember!'

'Ronnie Buck's booked it for you, has he?'

Paul gave an overblown sigh and rolled his eyes.

'Or are you staying at his place?'

His expression grew sullen, his eyes gleamed with something approaching hatred. 'It's just a tennis weekend!'

'Courtesy of Ronnie Buck?'

'Well, what's wrong with that, for God's sake?' he argued scathingly. 'He's a client, he pays his bills on time – which is more than can be said for most of our customers, the Legal Aid Board included. It's *normal* to accept hospitality from a client. Everyone does it, for God's sake, except, it seems, for *us*. We're too grand! We're above such things!'

I stepped aside to let him pass. 'Go, then.'

The abruptness of my retreat unsettled him. He retorted sarcastically, 'So I have your approval?'

'You do what you like, Paul. You know my feelings, you knew them when you decided to go.'

'Fine. *Fine.* So I'm damned for ever, am I? Not to be forgiven?'

I hadn't realized I'd come to any sort of decision until I heard myself say, 'I'll be gone when you come back.'

He knew what I meant, but he needed to hear it again. 'Gone?'

'I'll have left. Moved out. I think we both need a break, don't you?'

He lowered the holdall, he gave me a reproachful look. 'And this is the time to be discussing such a thing?'

'Yes, it is actually. Yes, this is the time.'

'So!' With a theatrical gesture, he indicated the path. 'I walk down here, I get in the car, and that's it!'

Everything seemed confused and clear all at the same time. 'I think so. For a while at least. Why don't we say a month? And then we can talk about it again.'

For an instant he looked at me fiercely, as if I were to blame for creating this crisis, before lifting both hands in a gesture of bewilderment and impotence. 'I'll stay, then,' he said heavily. 'I'll *stay.*'

But that wasn't the answer and we both knew it. We stood in silence for a time, then he picked up the holdall again and said sadly, 'We'll talk when I get back, then. Eh, Lexxy?'

'Yes.'

He paused a moment longer, then with an awkward nod walked towards the shiny silver car.

Chapter Thirteen

THE HEAT hung over the streets in a hazy pall of orange light. There was no movement in the air and no likelihood of any. Fumes billowed out from the crawling traffic and went nowhere. Diners abandoned the pavement tables for the more familiar hazards of the smoky interiors; cyclists wore masks with skull-and-crossbones motifs. For a week the media had been broadcasting air-quality warnings, and the forecasters saw no immediate prospect of an improvement. It was ninety degrees in the street, and not much less in the claustrophobic second-floor office on the Gray's Inn Road. When I had agreed to take the place, in the bracing winds of a particularly crisp April, the rent had seemed very reasonable.

Across the room Sturgess sat with rivulets of sweat at his temple and damp Romanesque curls across his forehead, clutching a phone to his ear, trying to extract information from a police station on the other side of town. Lisa, the third member of our team, sat in the next room, transcribing a taped interview onto the WP.

I was studying the monthly balance sheets and profit-and-loss statements for the partnership of O'Neill & Sturgess. At various times in the last three months the accountant had tried to explain how these figures should be read, but I still found it baffling that the balance at the bottom of the page bore no relation to how much cash you had in the bank, and the profit-and-loss statements failed to reveal whether you were making money or not. I wanted to know if we were going to break even this month, but had few clues so far. All I knew was that

Gary and I were taking on all the work we could get, the duty shifts that the other firms didn't want or couldn't do, last-minute jobs, referrals, pass-me-downs. If we weren't starting to make money then there was something seriously wrong. One thing was certain, with accommodation like this we couldn't accuse ourselves of going mad over the fixed costs.

The phone rang and Lisa called through the open door, 'Jason Hedley for you, Alex.'

My first reaction was pleasure that he should have tracked me down, my second – and more prudent – was to brace myself. 'And how are you, Jason? What can I do for you?'

'Thought you'd gone away when they said you wasn't there no more,' he complained mildly.

'I've set up a new practice, that's all. But otherwise it's business as usual. When did you get out, Jason?'

''Bout three weeks ago.'

'Pentonville, wasn't it? Treat you okay?'

'Yeah. Okay.'

'In trouble again?' But I already knew from his voice.

A long pause. When he finally spoke, it was in a tone of despair. 'Didn't mean to, Mrs O'Neill. Didn't know what they was planning. Never thought they was goin' to go for the bloke. Never would've agreed otherwise. The truth, Mrs O'Neill.'

I got what details I could. The nick was Lewisham, the charge – so far – robbery: two hundred quid from a petrol station. Some injury had been done to the attendant, but from Jason's garbled account I couldn't tell if the man had been pushed, shoved or cracked over the head. The only thing I did manage to establish was that no weapons had been involved. At this stage I was grateful for small mercies.

I told him I'd try to be there within the hour. Jason didn't need to be instructed not to say anything until I arrived, but I reminded him anyway.

'Robbery charge,' I told Gary when he came off the phone. 'Lewisham.'

'Known to us?'

'Jason Hedley. Small stuff till now. Chickens from super-markets. Funny, but I had hopes for him. Thought he'd got a chance of sorting himself out.'

'You're just an old romantic, Alex.'

'An optimist,' I pointed out darkly.

'Same thing?'

'So much to learn, Gary.'

He offered in a more sympathetic tone, 'Perhaps a big one'll finally do the trick.'

'What, three years inside?'

He raised both hands, demonstrating possibilities. Watching me load my briefcase, he added, 'You'll let me know a.s.a.p., won't you, if it looks like running into tomorrow so I can sub for you?'

'I don't think we want you showing your nose in Lewisham just at the moment, Gary.' The Russell trial was only a month away; by now the two sides would have exchanged final documents, with Gary's statement prominent among them.

Gary brushed this aside. 'Yeah, but we don't want *you* sweating in a hot cell with a common-or-garden robbery when you're meant to be doing heavy family duty at your brother's wedding, do we?'

The wedding. I still hadn't got a suitable hat. I hadn't even begun to think of what shoes I should wear with the blue suit I had bought in haste as soon as Edward gave me the news. Somehow, with all the changes in my life, the unstructured evenings, the baffling choice of ways to fill them, I seemed by some curious evolution to have far less time for mundane tasks than ever before, as if the absence of a domestic routine had undermined every other organizational instinct. I had failed to collect my laundry for three weeks running; there was never any food in the fridge – though in my present state of mind, this was a sort of freedom; and I hadn't managed to get to the hairdresser for over two months. Instead, I filled my spare time with films and plays and suppers with friends, or semi-business evenings with Gary and his girlfriend. I didn't spend much time at my rented one-room flat at Chalk Farm: too inept at being alone, too disorientated, too unhappy.

As I went out through the door, Lisa called, 'Enjoy the wedding.'

It was too late to find a hat now; the cream straw with the curvy brim would have to do service yet again, and I hoped I had remembered to pack my only suitable shoes in the two suitcases I'd brought from the house.

The shady side of the street offered little relief from the heat and by the time I reached the car park I could feel the sweat running inside my shirt. The air conditioning in my car had broken some weeks ago and in the heatwave the repair companies laughed at the idea of fixing it this side of Christmas. The road to Lewisham was slow: there was a traffic-light failure on the Old Kent Road. By the time I reached Lewisham police station, my face was bright pink, my hair dank.

The cells were stuffy with the scent of too many people with too many problems jammed into too little space. The air smelt of stale sweat and greasy food and cheap disinfectant.

The month in Pentonville had changed Jason in the way prison changes everyone: he seemed harder and brasher and more cynical. I got more details from him, the date, time and place of the offence, the names of the other boys, their histories, the drugs situation – all three of them high on cannabis and booze – and the story of the robbery itself. Jason said he hadn't realized what the others were planning. He'd only gone along for the ride. It was the least original defence in the book, but with the benefit of familiarity and plausibility.

I advised him to co-operate at the forthcoming interview, to tell the police everything, and he agreed.

'Blown it this time, eh?'

'It'll be a custodial sentence, that's for sure. Can't say how long, not yet. But you could look on it as a beginning, you know, not an end.'

'Yeah,' he sighed sarcastically. 'Sure. Like this time was goin' to be.'

'Have faith in yourself, Jason. Take a leap. Go on a youth training scheme, get a skill, move out of the city. Think big, think possibilities.'

He glared at me, hardly knowing whether to scoff or grimace, before bending his head low and shaking it slowly.

'And while you're on bail, we'll see if we can't get you on a course of some kind, get you started before you go inside. What d'you fancy? Carpentry, arithmetic, reading and writing, plumbing, bricklaying?'

He was shaking his head again, but less forcefully.

'And I'll send you stuff when you're inside. Books and tapes and ideas for when you get out.'

'Jesus, Mrs O'Neill, I dunno. I . . .' He sank his head almost to his knees and covered his face with his hands.

I patted his shoulder. 'I know all right.' Though all I knew, really, was that he needed someone to believe in him.

There was the usual delay before Jason's interview could start: one of the detectives was unavailable. While waiting, I took my mobile out into the street and called Ray Dodworth. I was asking him to check out Jason's friends when I vaguely noticed a car sweep into the kerb, a large shiny Jaguar with tinted windows. I paid more attention when all four doors opened and Ronnie Buck emerged from the back seat, his stocky figure looking cool and uncreased in the sort of light-weight silvery grey suit that gangsters wear in American films. I was so busy watching Ronnie that it was a moment before I realized that Paul had got out of the other side and was walking rapidly round the car to join Ronnie on the pavement.

Ray's voice said in my ear: 'You still there, Alex?'

'Speak to you later.' I turned away and hurried back into the police station, but not before I saw Paul glance towards me and do a perfect double-take.

Jason's interview took an hour, the statement another forty minutes. He was scheduled to appear at Clerkenwell Magis-

trates Court on Monday morning when I would make the first
of what would probably be a number of bail applications.

By the time I got outside again, it was six and a little cooler.
Whatever had brought Ronnie Buck to Lewisham police station
it hadn't detained him long: the Jaguar with the tinted windows
had gone.

Walking head down, wondering if I still had time to find a
hat, I didn't notice the car door opening ahead of me, the man
stepping out, until Paul's voice called my name.

'I was hoping to catch you.' He smiled a quick, diffident
smile. 'Was hoping you might be on for a drink.'

He seemed larger, smarter, grander, though I couldn't at
first make out why.

I said, 'I have to get back.'

'Just ten minutes. No time. A quick glass on the river.'

The car was the latest Mercedes. The driver wore a crisp
shirt and red tie with a logo I couldn't read. Following my
gaze, Paul laughed rather awkwardly.

'Oh, hire him by the hour.' Then, hastily, as though to
justify himself: 'Got a good deal. Shopped around. You know.'

I saw now that he had been shopping for clothes as well.
His suit was a new one, lightweight medium-grey and beautifully cut with hand stitching on the lapels: Jermyn Street, by
the look of it. His cufflinks were new too, chunky and gold. He
looked prosperous and not too worried about showing it.

'Just ten minutes, Lexxy.' He said it lightly, but there was a
hint of purpose in his eyes, a suggestion of an agenda.

'I have to get to the shops before they close.'

He tilted his head to one side, he gave me a look of warm
entreaty.

We went to a place on the river with a terrace and
umbrellas. It was crowded, every table taken and the railing
lined with knots of young people. We walked to the far end
and found a small space with a view. In the thick haze the
dome of St Paul's was a distant outline, but the silvery water,
rippled by the current, gave the illusion of space and air.

Paul was a long time buying the drinks, eventually returning with a bottle of white wine and some mineral water to mix spritzers.

'Well, then.' He raised his glass. 'Cheers.'

'You look well,' I said. And he did. It was six weeks since we had seen each other. If anything he had put on more weight, but there was colour in his face and more shine in his hair, though it occurred to me that this too might have been procured in Jermyn Street.

I asked, 'What brought Ronnie in today?'

'Oh, a formality. Nothing more.'

'The Munro case?'

But he wasn't going to answer that, and he tipped me a smile for having asked.

'So?' I said. 'There's something you wanted to talk about.'

His eyes darted away, he shifted awkwardly. 'Oh, just wanted to know how you were, Lexxy, that's all.'

He had always had difficulty in approaching certain subjects directly, anything to do with emotion, anything that activated his insecurities, so we talked about the law for a while, about the staff at Clerkenwell, about some of the cases I'd handed over to the other partners on my resignation.

Eventually, downing his second glass, he summoned his courage, he gave a nervous laugh. 'The thing is, Lexxy . . . I was wondering what you thought about the house. I have to say that I'm finding it a bit much on my own. You know, a bit of a handful.'

I tensed suddenly. 'You want to sell it?'

'You wouldn't mind?' He said it with such alacrity that my instincts reached out, my imagination raced away with me. I saw another woman, I saw him happy with someone else.

I managed to say, 'If that's what you want.'

He brightened. 'You're sure?'

Sure? How could one be sure about ending something that had gone on for so long and which, for much of the time, had brought us both happiness. I felt my lip tremble, I felt my heart beat high in my chest. I forced a smile. 'It's probably the sensible thing to do, isn't it? Where would you go?'

'*Me?*' he protested a little too forcefully. 'Oh, my heavens, plenty of time to worry about that. Oh, all the time in the world!'

He flipped a hand, a gesture that avoided much, yet, in my state of heightened awareness, seemed to tell me everything. With the certainty that comes from instinct I said, 'You're going to live with someone else.'

His head jerked up, he gave me an indignant look, he blustered, 'No, no! No plans at all.' He laughed falsely. 'No, goodness me . . .'

I felt a stab of possessiveness, a pang of loss that belonged to another time. 'Well,' I said in a voice that wasn't entirely steady, 'I hope she looks after you.'

'No, no, there're no plans, nothing decided— It's not—' He was set to bluff it out but, catching my eye, he made a gesture of submission. He said, 'Oh, it's early days yet, you know. We'll see. We'll see.'

'But she's all right? I mean, she'll look after you?'

He nodded bashfully. 'Oh, yes. She cooks and all that.'

The last of my love for him welled up in the blend of regret and relief I felt. There could be no going back, but it was still painful.

He added, 'I didn't mean to . . . I wouldn't have . . . if I'd thought there was a chance, you know . . . of you and me . . .'

We looked at each other, and a moment of truth passed between us: there would be no second chance.

He said, 'Well, then . . .'

We kissed each other on the cheek. When I looked back Paul raised his glass in salute or farewell.

The band were packing up their gear and lugging it out through a flap in the marquee wall. The waiters were making a final round of the tables, removing the wine glasses that were not in the grasp of more determined hands. The few remaining guests sat doggedly at their tables, chattering raucously, or stood in clusters in the floodlit garden, waylaid by friends on their way towards the car park. One man sat abandoned at a table, sleeping soundly, mouth open, cigar drooping from slack fingers.

I wandered into the house, longing for sleep, but knowing that it would be at least another hour before the bride and groom left for the hotel where they were spending the night, before the helpers departed, and I could lock up the house and get to bed. Bypassing the kitchen, which was still full of staff and equipment, I made for the sitting room, where I found Edward alone in his favourite chair with a large whisky clasped to his chest.

'Where's Jilly?' I laughed. 'Haven't lost her already?'

'She's somewhere about,' he declared breezily. 'Rabbiting to an old schoolfriend last time I saw her.'

I sank into a chair with a sigh. 'Great evening,' I said. 'Great day.'

'Went all right, didn't it?' Edward remarked matter-of-factly.

'More than all right.' The weather had been sunny without being overbearingly hot, the service beautiful, Jilly had appeared radiant in a simple ivory dress with a Victorian lace veil handed down from her grandmother. Even Edward had looked half pleased with events, as though life might yet surprise him and turn out not quite as badly as he'd expected.

'Hasn't everyone gone yet?' he asked.

'Not quite.'

'Kept the wine flowing too long. Can *never* get the devils to leave then.'

'It was fabulous wine.'

'Well, didn't want to stint. Never hear the last of it otherwise.'

While he was in a benign mood, I asked, 'By the way, did you hear back from the Falmouth solicitors about Pa's money?'

He screwed his face up as if to dredge his memory for
something rather inconsequential. 'Oh, *that*. Yes, stupid bligh-
ters tried to palm me off again. You know how they are – blind
you with legalese, tell you everything was done in pukka
manner, all above board. Tell you to piss off, basically.'

'So what have you decided?'

He made a disowning gesture, a wave of his glass. 'Oh, I've
handed it over to my chap to deal with. Issue a writ or
summons or whatever it is. No, can't be dealing with these
bloody stupid people. Drive you mad.' He rolled his eyes.
'Life's too short, for God's sake.'

He was going to drop it, then. Being Edward he would
never admit to it, would rather die, but I could read the subtext.
I knew better than to comment, however; I knew better than to
say he was doing the right thing.

There were sounds from the hall, the rustle of silk and Jilly
floated in, smiling and breathless and very pretty, despite, or
because of, wearing almost no eye makeup at all.

'God,' exclaimed Edward. 'Can't imagine why you're looking so pleased with yourself – you're married to *me*!'

She laughed her little-girl laugh, though I fancied I saw a
new glint of confidence in her eye. 'I'll survive!'

'More than *I* will, probably.' He winked at me, and I
thought what a very good thing it was that he had finally
committed himself to Jilly, that he'd come to appreciate that in
most respects she suited him very well indeed.

Jilly told him some people were asking for him and with a
grunt he got dutifully to his feet and rambled off towards the
hall.

'Well!' I grinned at Jilly.

'There we are!' she cried, clasping her hands to her chest.
Then, in a confidential tone, 'Thanks for sorting it all out.'

'What out?'

'You know – the Grace business.'

'I don't think I sorted anything out.'

She took this as false modesty. 'The *inquest*. Thought it'd be ghastly. The press and all that. But there was almost nothing in the papers.'

'That wasn't my doing.'

'And Edward not having to say anything about – you know, him and . . .'

'Jilly, that wasn't me. That was the coroner.'

She said knowingly, 'Yes, but . . .'

'The coroner investigates cause of death – nothing else – that's the only reason.'

But she refused to be persuaded. Touching my hand in gratitude, she smiled brightly again. 'There we are, then! All ended happily.'

There was no answer to this, and I didn't attempt one.

Jilly swept off again, and I followed more slowly.

In the hall an elderly man was casting about, asking anyone who was passing if they'd seen his wife. Edward and Jilly were in the drive shouting farewells to departing cars. I stood in the porch, thinking again of bed.

A woman's voice sounded at my elbow. 'There you are! Hardly seen you all evening.' Anne Hampton was wearing cerise and pearls, and had her yellow hair pulled back in a black velvet bow. Her cheeks were flushed a uniform pink, from the dancing or the wine. 'Hasn't it been a *wonderful* party? Nothing like a good hooley to get the neighbourhood going.' She was smiling but she was watching me closely too. 'Seen Will?' she asked lightly.

'Not recently, no.'

'Oh? You haven't been up at all?'

'Not since the inquest.'

'I thought you'd be at the funeral. Weren't you able to come?'

'I understood it was family only.'

Her eyebrows shot up. 'Oh, I don't think it was ever— Well, anyway, quite a few people were there. Friends, some of the neighbours – you know. People who really loved Grace. A pretty decent turnout. Considering, I mean. Even her *mother* came. Wouldn't speak to Will, of course, but then we all knew that was going to happen. Nice service, terrific sermon.' Her voice rose in sudden emotion. 'Everyone wept buckets.'

I thought: Poor Will.

Anne sniffed, 'I must say, I still miss Grace. Still can't believe she isn't coming back.'

I asked, 'And Maggie?'

'No, not at the funeral. Didn't make it. But then' – she lowered her voice in sympathy – 'she's in bad shape, you know. They say . . . Well, they say it's only a matter of weeks. At the very most. Maybe days.'

'She's in hospital, is she? I've been trying to contact her.'

'Oh no, not in hospital,' she said, with the air of someone imparting valuable news. 'She's at Marsh House. Aiming to stay there, apparently. Until the end. Poor *poor* thing.' She gave a long sigh, then added for no apparent reason, 'Charlie was at the funeral, you know. I thought that was a bit unnecessary, I must say.'

She wanted me to ask why, and though a part of me didn't want to give her the satisfaction, I had to ask: 'Why shouldn't he have been there?'

'Well . . . because of everything. You know.'

'No,' I said simply. 'I don't know.'

She laughed with pretended awkwardness. 'Well, we know he was' – she spoke the word delicately – '*there* with her.'

'There?'

'On the marshes. When she died.'

I kept all expression out of my face. 'What do you mean *there*? You mean, he saw what happened? He watched her?'

She shrank a little, as though she was far too discreet to repeat rumours of an unreliable and damning nature.

'Come now, Anne,' I said coldly. 'Don't be coy.'

She caught the criticism in my tone, she bristled. 'It's not *me*,' she said in a tone of injury. 'I'm just telling you what some people said, that's all!'

'And?'

She replied stiffly, 'They say he was there, that's all! Nothing else!'

I looked into her pink face and said quietly, 'Well, you can take it from me, they're quite wrong. Absolutely wrong.'

She blinked rapidly. 'I see.'

'Perhaps you would set the record straight. When you can.'

'Of course. Glad to. Of course.' She gave an uncomfortable laugh. 'I'm so pleased. For Charlie's sake. And Will's.'

I would have turned away then, but I had to ask: 'You've seen Will recently? Is he managing?'

'Haven't seen him for a while. Not for some time, actually. No one has. I've tried to call him, oh, dozens of times. But he won't talk. Says he's busy. Rings off. Won't answer the door. A bit of a hermit at the moment. It's the shock, I expect. The grief. Takes time, doesn't it, if you lose someone?'

I looked into her untroubled face, free of any thought that by conniving with Grace in her affair she might have contributed in some small way to the tragedy, and it seemed to me that Will was very wise to keep his distance.

I woke in a sweat at five, unable for a split second to remember where I was. Throwing off the covers, I slept fitfully until six, when I got up and, choosing the stateliest bathroom in Wickham Lodge, a grandiose room with cracked marble surrounds and a baroque mirror, took a bath in a claw-footed cast-iron bath of battleship proportions, raised on a platform to give a fine view of the garden and the marquee. I fed Edward's dog and took it out for a short walk, then, as soon as the band of cleaners and clearers began to arrive, drove quietly away through the village and down to the quay.

I couldn't decide how to approach Marsh House: a ring at the front door might not get answered, while a walk round to the kitchen might disturb the family at breakfast.

The problem was solved by the absence of the Range Rover; I went up the side of the house and peered in through the kitchen window to see no people and no signs of breakfast. The door was unlocked, and I walked through the kitchen into the hall, calling softly as I went.

A voice answered, and the sound led me towards the sitting room. Most of the room was in shadow, but a faint light from a partly drawn curtain illuminated a dressing-gowned figure on a bed which had been placed close by the window.

'I'm intruding unannounced,' I said.

Maggie said, 'So you are, Alex. Well, since you're here you can open a curtain and go and make me some tea.'

I drew a far curtain.

'No, this one, Alex, then we can see when Will returns.'

I opened the one nearer to her.

When I turned to look at her, she said, 'I was trying to reach you, Alex. I was trying to call.'

'Well, I'm here now.'

'It's the China tea I like. But strong.'

I brought it in a pot with the best porcelain cups and saucers, and poured it through a strainer.

'Tell me about the wedding.' She had pulled herself higher on her pillows. She didn't look as bad as my imagination in all its fears had painted her, though she was painfully thin and her eyes seemed to be set deeper and more darkly into her head. Her voice had changed too: it was husky and pitched higher.

'The wedding went very well.' I described the dress and the service and the speeches. I told her who was there, and who had danced wildly, and who had knocked wine over a woman's dress.

She listened distractedly, her eyes on the windows, nodding occasionally, smiling faintly once or twice. 'A good day then. A pity, though, that your father couldn't have seen it.'

'Yes, he would have been pleased.'

'Edward was always a worry for him, I think.'

'Yes.' A pause, and I asked in a level voice, 'Tell me about you and Father.'

She cast me a long gaze containing emotion and mild

surprise. 'I have so many confessions to make, Alex, but I think
this is my one happy confession, the confession for which I feel
no shame or sadness. I hope you are not cross that I am happy
about it? That I cannot be sorry? I was careful not to do your
mother harm, you know. Always I made sure there was no
harm. It was only at the end . . .' She sighed softly. 'I regret
that your mother found out. After so long, too. And that she
was not happy to let things stay the same, that she made your
father move away.' She added with a touch of her old incredulity: 'To *Cornwall*. No, Alex, I regret very much that it ended
like this because for many years there was no hurt, no harm.
Everyone was happy. *I* was happy. And your father . . .' She
smiled slightly. Her hand rose and fell to the unfinished
sentence. 'There was no reason not to go on in the same way.
You would think that after so long there would be no harm.
But no . . . she would not allow it. And then, he never came
back, your father. When your mother died I thought he would,
you know.' She gave one of those gestures I loved so much, the
overturning of one hand, the opening of the palm as if to
question the powers above, but now it was a listless gesture,
without conviction. 'But perhaps he felt it would not be the
same. And, you know – perhaps he was right.'

'Did you manage to see each other often?'

'Oh, almost every day, more or less. Not always for long,
of course. Sometimes we would walk, on the fields at Upper
Farm, somewhere like that. Sometimes we would just talk on
the phone. We loved to talk, Alex – we were great talkers!
Great endless talkers! You understand, it was not just attraction, more than love. We were the best of friends also.'

Unexpectedly, I felt a sharp pang of envy, the envy that
springs from the wounds of one's own unhappiness, from the
feeling that such a complete love will always remain beyond
your grasp. I asked reticently, 'But how did you manage to
meet? Where did you go?'

'Ah,' she whispered in her hoarse voice, 'mostly we would
be at Reed Cottage. Your father would walk along the marsh

path late in the evening, or early in the morning, or he would come between house calls, or for tea.'

'But before you moved to Reed Cottage, when you were still here?'

She said softly, 'Ah, but you see there was always Reed Cottage, Alex. Always.'

I shook my head. 'What do you mean?'

'Your father rented it for many years. Before it was bought.'

It took me a moment to absorb this, and the idea disturbed me, it seemed so very calculated, so terribly organized.

Reading something of this in my face, Maggie said, 'It was just a little happiness, Alex. Just a little happiness now and again. In a difficult life, when things are not right, it is something very important, very special, to be given a little happiness. You must take it where you find it.'

I nodded quickly and breathlessly.

Maggie reached to the other side of the bed, to a table cluttered with bottles and glasses and tablets, and fiddled with something I couldn't see. When she turned back, I noticed that there was surgical tape strapped across the back of her right hand and some sort of connector coming out of it, leading into a transparent tube, which snaked away across the bed to the table. 'I choose the dose,' she said matter-of-factly. 'I use less than they say, then I can know I'm still alive.' She laughed a little, to ease the moment along. 'I gave up smoking, you know.'

'About time too.'

'Well, I knew what was on the score, Alex. I thought, why not smoke? It will make no difference. The end will be the same anyway.' She dismissed the whole business with a derisive grunt.

'Crazy thinking, Maggie.'

But her thoughts had moved on. She fixed me with a sombre gaze. 'So, Alex, will you do me this favour?'

'Sorry?'

'I need this favour.'

'If I can, of course.'

She was gasping slightly, she seemed to be struggling, though whether with pain or general distress I couldn't tell. 'I thought I had done it fine, but now, Alex, now I don't think I did it so well. It's on my mind. It worries me.'

I poured her more tea. As she drank, I noticed her hand was trembling and she had to steady the cup.

'Alex, this is what I ask you to do for me. I ask you to go to Reed Cottage. You take the spade – you will find it in the outhouse, to the right, inside the door – you go and dig by the corner between the outhouse and the wall, where there's a rose and a clematis. But closer to the rose, you need to be closer to the rose. You will find the handbag there, and the jacket, Alex. Be sure to get them both, yes?'

My hesitation lasted no more than a second. 'Of course.'

The matter was over so quickly, it had been so straightforward that Maggie immediately searched for difficulties. 'The handbag – maybe something fell out. You will check?'

I said I would check.

'And the jacket – if there were things in the pocket . . .'

I said I would sift through the earth to be sure.

'And nearer the rose than the clematis.'

'Nearer the rose.'

She seemed reassured at last. She gave a long sigh. 'Ah, Alex, that was the stupid thing – to take the car back, to pretend she had never been there. *That* was a stupid thing – not the handbag. I did not think that Barry Holland would see her . . .' She inhaled slowly, her mouth turned down bitterly. 'But the biggest mistake of all, Alex? How could I do this? Tell me – *how*? I told Grace that Charlie had opened the sluices. My God! Why did I do this, Alex? What could make me do this? I still don't know why I should be so *crazy*!' She gave a heartfelt sigh of regret and despair. 'Poor Charlie, his grandmother is a crazy fool! Crazy!'

Then, as though to answer her own question, she said, 'I was so *angry*. *That* was why I said this to her, Alex – I was so angry. Charlie was so upset, I have never seen him so upset. I knew it had to be Grace that had done this – I *knew* – so I shouted at her down the phone. I asked to know what she has done to make him so upset.'

'Tell me about it, Maggie,' I invited quietly. 'Tell me what happened.'

She became composed, her expression grave, and it occurred to me that she had been preparing herself for this moment for a long time. She gazed out towards the window, she said in her hoarse voice, 'What happened was that I killed Grace.'

'Grace dropped Charlie off. She did not stay long, a minute, no more. Charlie was in a happy mood, he had done a project at school, the teacher had given him top marks. He was proud of his marks. He wanted to show me the project with its marks, but he had left it at home. After tea he wanted to go and fetch it. I said I would see it next day, it could wait – but no, it could not wait, he had to show me then. So he ran off home to fetch it.'

Her calm did not completely conceal the emotion beneath; she took a steadying breath. 'He was gone so long. I was worrying. I could not think what was happening. He had been by the path many, many times. It was so quick. What – five, six minutes? But it was half an hour. More. I looked out for him, I could not see him. I was going to call Grace to find out where he was when I went upstairs one last time – to look, to see better. And for no reason I looked the other way, I looked out to the Gun. And there he was!' A tremor passed through her then, she sucked in her cheeks. 'A long way off. Running. But I knew it was him. I knew! I could not understand it. I went out, I went to the Gun to find him. I saw water in the ditch. I could not think *why* there was so much water. Oh, but my eyes are no good any more! I couldn't see where the water was coming in. I couldn't see what Charlie was doing.'

She coughed lightly but painfully. Her brows creased, and when she went on again, it was at a more determined pace. 'I walk. I come to the sluice. I cannot believe the water is coming so fast. So much water! So fast! I start to guess. I start to understand something is very wrong. *Very* wrong. I walk faster. I see Charlie at the second sluice. Winding, winding. It's open. He has opened the sluice. I shout, "Charlie, what are you doing?" He throws the handle on the ground. He walks towards me, so *angry*. So *angry*. So wild in the eyes. *Wild!* I have never seen him like this. I walk with him. He will not speak. I am crying, I am weeping, I am begging him to speak. Nothing! Nothing!'

She was reliving each moment now, the helplessness and the bewilderment. 'We get back to the cottage. I take the other handle, but I know I am too weak, I cannot lower the gates. I am desperate for help. I am desperate to talk to Charlie. Charlie, he is in his room. He is on the bed, staring at the wall. I am going crazy. So I call Grace. I say, "What have you done to him? Why is he like this?" I tell her he's gone mad and opened the sluices. *I tell her!*'

The memory was still so raw that she grimaced, she groaned again at her own folly. 'His heart was broken, Alex. Broken. He had done everything to please her, to make her love him. This is the terrible thing about a cruel person, Alex. A cruel person makes a child desperate to win their love. A cruel person takes a good heart and breaks it, *crushes* it, and what does this good heart do? It cries out for this person's love! It is desperate for it. Why is this, tell me? Why should this be?' She lifted a despairing hand.

I said, 'Children are apt to blame themselves if their parents don't love them. It's a well-known thing. They tend to think it's their fault.'

'But, Alex, always she was so cruel to him, from the time he was a baby! Nothing he did was good enough. Nothing! A painting, a model – she would say, *what is that?*' She mimicked a caustic tone. '"*What do you call that?*" Always she would make him feel he was no good. Always she would make him feel he had failed. She would say, *"You're no good at anything, you're stupid, you'll never make anything of your life, you must go to this special school!"* Oh, he was so desperate to please her! But he could not go to this school. This was the one thing he could not do. All he wanted was to stay at home, to be on the farm with Will. No, in this one thing he could not give in to her. And she never forgave him – no! She was angry, and she wasn't going to let him escape. She was going to get her revenge!' She raised bent fingers, as if to forestall my protest. 'You think revenge is too big a word? You think I say this because I hated her? No, I tell you, Alex, revenge is not too big a word. She was planning it all, to get Charlie to this school, because she could not bear to be opposed. She could not bear for Charlie to have his own mind. No, he must bend to her. She was determined that he should be what she wanted him to be. No, I tell you, Grace had no heart – none at all. Grace was a bad person – there is no other way to say it, Alex. Grace was cruel, cruel and wicked.'

In the pause that followed, she shifted her head, she pulled a pillow behind her neck and lay back again. 'So . . . Grace comes over. Oh, she is angry! Such fury! Such rage! Vicious. Horrible. She is very nasty to me! Rude and nasty! She says *I* have let this happen! Says it's all my fault! But then, Alex, she calls Charlie names, she says terrible, *terrible* things to Charlie! She says he is the worst thing ever to happen to her, that she hates him, that she is never going to see or speak to him again. She grabs him by the neck, she pulls him downstairs, she yells at him – oh, she yells! She says he must go and close the sluices. She pulls him by the arm, he falls over, and *still* she pulls. She is like someone who is gone mad! Completely *mad*! She is in such a *rage*! I try to stop her, but she goes on pulling him, she does not stop! She gets him outside, and all the time Charlie is crying and screaming, he is trying to get free. And when he struggles, she hits him, Alex! *She hits him!*' Maggie grimaced with barely forgotten fury, her eyes filled with violent tears.

She glared at me as if to demand an explanation for such a monstrous and inexplicable act.

When she looked towards the light again, her expression grew cold and unyielding, her voice also. 'I grab her then, I pull her hair. *Hard*. She cries out. She yells. I don't care. I go on pulling until she lets go of Charlie. Then she hits me, oh so hard, Alex. My ear – I think it is broken, it bleeds. My head . . . She hits me three, four times.' She closed her eyes, she drew an anguished breath. 'I shout, I tell her we are going to close the sluices. Just her and me, the two of us – no one else. She starts to say things again. I tell her to shut up, that I am up to *here* with her.' She drew a clawed hand in a line across her eyes. 'She grabs the handle – angry, angry – she walks off towards the sluice. I want to go to Charlie, I want to see that he is all right, but I know that first we must close the sluices.'

Something beyond the window seemed to catch her eye, she stared for a moment before turning back. 'So I follow, and still she will not stop talking, saying bad things against Charlie. So I say to her, "You tell me why he is so upset, you tell me!" And she says there is no reason, none, but she is lying. I know she is lying! I tell her I am going to tell Will about this, that he will hear *everything*. And she says, "I don't care." She says, "I'm leaving anyway. I'm finished with him. I'm going tomorrow!" She laughs at the thought. She has an ugly face when she laughs. Then I understand. I remember the way she was when she arrived. Hair in a mess – and her hair was *never* in a mess. *Never*. And I say, "You were with someone. Charlie saw you with someone." And she does not deny it, she says, "Charlie shouldn't have come back when he did." She is cold, like ice. Then I say things, I speak my mind, I tell her what I think of her. I say many things – too many things – but I am so angry with her, Alex! Angry for what she has done to Charlie.' Her eyes blazed briefly, she clenched her lips together until the worst of her wrath had passed.

'Then she tells me, "Well, think what you like, but I've had enough, and I'm taking what I'm owed." "Owed!" I say. "What can *you* be owed?" "Money," she says. I cannot believe what I'm hearing. I cannot believe she can say such a thing! I just *stare* at her, Alex! I just *stare*! And then we come to the sluice. She says it's too hard for her to wind. We have to do it together. And then we can't finish it, it won't shut all the way.' She was racing on now, trying to get the story over as quickly as possible. 'There's something wrong, we cannot close it all the way, so we must leave it. So we go on to the next sluice. And Grace, she is angry again, saying bad things. She was like this, Alex, a very angry person. Deep down, underneath all this beauty, she was angry and heartless and cruel. You understand this? You—'

The telephone rang. We fell silent until it had stopped some time after the fifth ring. When Maggie resumed, it was in a quieter tone. 'I am thinking to myself, who is it that Grace is with? She is leaving tomorrow – who is she with? And why is she so angry about the sluice? She has never cared about the farm, she has never cared about the marsh. And then, of course, I see it, Alex! I see it! *Edward*. It must be Edward. And I think of what this will do to Will, to his pride.'

She chose her words with concentration, drawing deep on her memory. 'I said to her, "You don't get money if you cheat on your husband." And she laughed. She *laughed*, Alex. She said, "It's all different now. I get half the house, half the cash. I checked it out. I went to a lawyer." "But it will ruin Will," I said. But she didn't care, Alex. She didn't care. For her, this was a fine punishment to him for not giving her what she wanted. She was glad. I saw it in her face – she was *glad*. And then it comes to me – oh, it was like a knife in my heart, Alex – it comes to me: *Charlie*. "But not Charlie," I said. "After this, you will not take Charlie." She turned to me, and she said, very cool, "I will take Charlie. Of course I will take Charlie. He's mine."'

A car crawled along the quay, coming closer. Fearing the

Range Rover, I craned forward to look out of the window but it was a small black saloon, heading across the hard towards the edge of the creek.

'She was winding the sluice,' Maggie continued. 'All the time she was angry and full of hate. I watched her wind the sluice and I said, "But Will – he will fight you all the way. Each inch. He cannot be without Charlie." And she said' – Maggie bent her head towards me on the pillow, she reached out a hand as if to touch mine – 'she said, "But he is not Will's child in the first place!" I stared at her, I did not believe what I have heard. I thought she was just trying to say things, *anything*, to punish us all. But then she said, "Any test will prove it. He's not Will's, he is the child of my lover before Will." She said his name – some actor called Dan Elliott. She said the name proudly, she said he had loved her, that she could have married him, *should* have married him if she hadn't been crazy enough to marry Will. I stayed calm, I tried not to be angry. I said, "But Will – he loves Charlie so much, he cannot live without Charlie, you cannot take him away." "Why not?" she said. "Charlie's not his, I will tell him Charlie's not his."'

She was tiring now, her voice was raw, she ran her tongue over drying lips. 'Everything,' she breathed. 'Grace wanted to take everything from Will. For no good reason except that her soul was cold and unkind. She did not love Charlie, she had never loved Charlie. All she wanted was to *own* him, to destroy his soul, his—' She lost the word.

'Spirit?'

'*Spirit*,' she affirmed with passion. 'His spirit! If Charlie had gone with her, it would have broken Will's heart. And mine too – oh, Alex, it would have broken *my* heart too.' She had slowed up now, she spoke haltingly. 'I took hold of her arm. I said you will not do this thing. She tried to pull away, but I held on to her jacket. We pulled back and forth, her jacket tore. And still she tried to walk away. She tried to walk away! To go and do these terrible things she planned, but I kept hold of the jacket as though I was holding on to my *life*!

My *life*, Alex! Then she pulled her arms from the jacket, she pulled free, suddenly, with a – a *jerk*! She stumbled, she fell against the post. She was half over the gate. And then, Alex . . .'

Part of me wanted to stop her there; the other part waited silently to hear the end.

'I pushed her. I did not mean to push her . . . Well, I'm not sure what I meant to do. I was thinking of Will and Charlie, I was thinking that I loved them more than all the world. Perhaps I wanted her to have a shock – the water, the fall. I don't know, Alex! But I pushed her and she fell into the pool and she was still, no movement. She floated, face down. She must have hit her head – I don't know. I watched, I waited. I could not move. I did not want to move. I was a little mad, Alex! Crying, *crying* all the time. A little crazy! I kept thinking: This is God's will! This is God's justice! This is meant to be! And then, when the madness had gone from me, when I looked again, it was too late, Alex. Too late. She was dead, I knew she must be dead.'

Her voice had all but disappeared, she closed her eyes, her mouth fell open; except for the frown, she might have been asleep. When she began to whisper again, I had to strain to make out her words. 'The jacket . . . I knew I must hide it, it was so torn. The handbag, I thought if it was not found then they would think she had gone away.' She turned her head towards me and made a face of disgust at her own stupidity.

In the silence that followed, a faint breeze wafted in through the open window and stirred the dull still air.

When I looked back at Maggie her eyes were sharp again, almost sparkling. She laid her cool dry hand on my arm and rasped in her failing voice, 'But, Alex, I tell you something. I do not regret this. In the end I cannot.'

The heat of the midsummer Sunday had brought out dozens of walkers and holiday-makers. The marsh paths were sprinkled with families and dogs, and away on the shimmering dunes bright dots of colour moved ant-fashion along the ridges. Three strange cars were parked on the grass to one side of Reed Cottage while, on the path beyond, a family group stood idly watching while their children repeatedly climbed the bank and rolled down again.

Beside the outhouse, the clematis grew thickly up the wall, virtually overwhelming the rose, whose spindly stems and rust-spotted leaves were almost lost in its dense foliage. The earth around the foot of the rose looked dry and lumpy, and when I pushed at it with my foot, it felt hard as rock.

The spade was in its place inside the door of the outhouse. I noticed a pick as well, should I need to break up the crusty soil.

There were no clouds in the sky and no sign of a change: the marsh would be busy until nightfall. I spent the morning helping to clear up at Wickham Lodge, then slept for an hour or so on the swing seat under the mulberry tree. I ate an early supper from the leftovers, and drank a glass of last night's wine. Finally at nine thirty I set out for Reed Cottage again, dressed for the night, in dark T-shirt and jeans.

The unknown cars had gone, most of the people too. I heard a shout of laughter some distance away and saw a small group strolling along the Gun Marsh embankment. I waited a while, but no one came and, though the twilight was clear and the darkness still some way off, I fetched the spade and thrust it into the ground. The crust shifted easily, but the soil beneath was made of firmer stuff. I had to drive the spade in hard and step it down with all my weight before I could raise much earth. Six inches down and I had to chop through the roots of the rose. When the hole was a foot deep I paused to wonder just how far down Maggie had gone. Another six inches and I began to wonder if she was suffering some sort of delirium or memory loss.

The sweat hot on my brow, I shifted my efforts towards the clematis. A few minutes later, with night falling fast, the spade struck something dense but soft. Feeling my way with the edge of the spade, I aimed to one side of the object, and, driving the spade deep, stepping on it hard, I levered the handle down and loosened the object from the soil. Dropping on to my knees, I dug with my hands and felt first cloth, then leather.

My nerves were so taut, my mind so completely absorbed, that the voice close above me might have been a gunshot. I started with such violence that my body jerked back, my arms flew up, I let out a sharp cry and toppled over sideways before scrabbling desperately to my feet.

In such a moment of shock and adjustment, realization comes in stages. The first thing I registered was Will's dark figure looming close above me. A moment later, I took in what he had said: 'Why don't you let me do that?' In a final surge of awareness, I heard his tone, I saw in the dim dusk his expression, and both were full of concern, neither in the least hostile.

Panting hard, my heart still throwing itself against my ribs, I stuttered feebly, 'I think I can manage,' and immediately wished I had said something less abrupt.

'But let me, Ali.' I stood back while Will dropped to one knee and reached forward into the hole to clear away more earth. He pulled out the jacket and examined it solemnly before rolling it into a bundle and laying it carefully on the ground. Leaning forward again, he scooped away more earth and, with a small wrench, pulled the handbag free.

Getting to his feet, he picked up the handbag and rolled it inside the jacket, and tucked them both under one arm. It was so dark now that I could barely see his face. 'What's the safest thing to do?' he asked.

I thought of the petty criminals I had defended, of the evidence they had tried to hide or destroy, throwing weapons into canals or dousing clothing in petrol and setting fire to it; I remembered how often these things were found with damning forensic evidence still intact. 'Ordinary domestic rubbish is the safest,' I said. 'Well-wrapped in a plastic sack. But the purse should be emptied first, the credit cards destroyed, anything with a name on it. And, safer still, it should all be taken to somewhere far away and put in a stranger's bin. I could take them back to London, stop somewhere in a neighbouring borough.'

'I couldn't ask you to do that.'

Trying not to recall the stern view the law took of such activities – perverting the course of justice – I said, 'But I'd be glad to.'

'Thank you, Ali, but it's something I must do myself. I'll go to Cromer or King's Lynn, somewhere like that.' He dropped his head for a moment. Then, as if aware of the need for haste, he held out the bundle for me to hold while he began to fill in the hole.

'How did you know I was here?' I asked.

'Oh ... Maggie. She was rambling a bit – she does nowadays. Talking about you, about being able to rely on you. She wouldn't say more, but she'd been fretting about getting back here for something. I had a feeling – I walked over, I saw your car, I heard you digging.'

He trod the earth down a little before returning the spade to the outhouse.

Taking the bundle again, he led the way into Reed Cottage and switched on some lights. On the way to the kitchen, he paused suddenly and looked back at me. 'Maggie was right.'

'What about?'

He smiled faintly. 'About being able to rely on you.'

We drew the curtains and spread newspaper on the kitchen table before unwrapping the bundle. The pockets of the jacket were empty, but we cut out the label just to be on the safe side and put it on one side for separate disposal. We spread out the contents of the handbag. After some discussion, we decided to crush the mobile phone with a hammer and put it back into the handbag. We cut each credit card into about twenty pieces and, mixing the shards up, put half in the pile with the handbag, and half in the pile for separate disposal. The cash went into Will's pocket, the cheque book was cut up and put in the second pile. The empty purse, cosmetics, pens, pencils and sunglasses went back into the handbag.

Once the decisions were taken, we worked in silence, avoiding each other's eye, getting on with the task in hand, needing no reminder of the enormity of what we were doing.

When everything had been dealt with, we put the two piles into their separate bin liners, along with the newspaper, and sealed them tight.

Finally we sat back and looked at each other.

Will reached out as if to grip my hand. 'I'm sorry I was so angry with you, Ali. I was so desperate to protect Charlie. I wasn't thinking. I'm sorry.'

I realized I had no idea if he knew the truth about Maggie or whether he believed she had been covering for Charlie. 'The jacket was badly torn,' I said in a rush.

For an instant he looked at me blankly, then understanding stole over his face. 'Oh, I guessed most of it on the night of the storm. Well, I guessed quite a lot *before* that. I realized that both sluices had been opened, it was obvious from the flooding. And the one that was only half closed – it wasn't broken, just stiff. I knew from the state that Charlie was in that something appalling had happened. And from Maggie, too. With her I put it down to the flooding, to whatever was wrong with Charlie, but later . . . *Well*. And Grace's car. I thought I'd glimpsed it that night when I drove past the cottage. And then it wasn't there. I didn't say anything to you because Maggie was so adamant. And then, on the day of the storm, when I heard that Grace had been seen coming back – I knew where to look then. I *knew*.'

There was a pause. He took my hand solemnly between both of his and said, 'I should have told you. I thought . . . well, I thought that you wouldn't take us on. I thought at one point that Charlie might even have been there, seen her die, that for some reason he hadn't been able to help her. I thought that it would crucify him if he had to tell a court. I panicked. I took it out on Maggie, I blamed her for making such a mess of her statement, for making the police suspicious. And then, when I guessed the truth, when I realized about Maggie – well, that was no better. Whatever'd happened, I couldn't let her go through the hell of it all either.'

'In the end, you probably did the right thing. With someone like me, the truth isn't necessarily the best place to start.'

He smiled. 'Ali. Always so practical.'

'You make it sound like a failing.' And I smiled back because this time it was the best compliment in the world.

He released my hand and stood up suddenly. 'I'd better go and get rid of these things.'

'I'll go and check on Maggie, shall I? And Charlie.'

He said, 'You'll be there when I get back?' He added quickly, 'You'll stay?'

I remembered Jason coming up at Clerkenwell in the morning. 'I wish I could. But . . .'

He leant forward and kissed me gently on the mouth. 'It would be so good if you could stay, Ali.'

'I suppose . . . I could stay till four,' I said.

'Well, it's a start,' he said.

I drove him to Marsh House to pick up his car and stood at the gate in the soft summer night to wave him off.